"*Uptown and Down* is a passionate and intelligent novel about marriage, friendship, success, and the fragility of all our dreams and alliances. Dahlberg's characters are vulnerable and real, good and flawed, stretched by the dangerous allure of New York City glamour and conflicted about what it means to be Black and wealthy in today's world. *Uptown and Down* is a must read—sensual, satisfying, and thoughtful."

—Valerie Ann Leff, author of *Better Homes and Husbands*

"A wellspring of joy, *Uptown and Down* skillfully weaves a beautiful love story, rich friendships, and the fast-paced world of fashion and entertainment into a tale of redemption. The story will reverberate long after the last page is turned." —Persia Walker, author of *Harlem Redux*

"Jennifer Anglade Dahlberg's flair for words is so delicious, she had me holding on tight to each and every one of them until the very end. Richly drawn characters and vivid descriptions were authentic and enticing enough to keep me turning pages faster than the speed of light, anxious to see what waited for me next in the sordid and fascinating world of New York City's young, restless, and chic."

—J. D. Mason, author of *Confessions of the Other Woman*

UPTOWN AND DOWN

Jennifer Anglade Dahlberg

 NEW AMERICAN LIBRARY

New American Library
Published by New American Library, a division of
Penguin Group (USA) Inc., 375 Hudson Street,
New York, New York 10014, USA
Penguin Group (Canada), 90 Eglinton Avenue East, Suite 700, Toronto,
Ontario M4P 2Y3, Canada (a division of Pearson Penguin Canada Inc.)
Penguin Books Ltd., 80 Strand, London WC2R 0RL, England
Penguin Ireland, 25 St. Stephen's Green, Dublin 2,
Ireland (a division of Penguin Books Ltd.)
Penguin Group (Australia), 250 Camberwell Road, Camberwell, Victoria 3124,
Australia (a division of Pearson Australia Group Pty. Ltd.)
Penguin Books India Pvt. Ltd., 11 Community Centre, Panchsheel Park,
New Delhi - 110 017, India
Penguin Group (NZ), cnr Airborne and Rosedale Roads, Albany,
Auckland 1310, New Zealand (a division of Pearson New Zealand Ltd.)
Penguin Books (South Africa) (Pty.) Ltd., 24 Sturdee Avenue,
Rosebank, Johannesburg 2196, South Africa

Penguin Books Ltd., Registered Offices:
80 Strand, London WC2R 0RL, England

First published by New American Library,
a division of Penguin Group (USA) Inc.

First Printing, October 2005
10 9 8 7 6 5 4 3 2 1

NEW AMERICAN LIBRARY and logo are trademarks of Penguin Group (USA) Inc.

LIBRARY OF CONGRESS CATALOGING-IN-PUBLICATION DATA:
Dahlberg, Jennifer Anglade, 1971–
  Uptown & down / by Jennifer Anglade Dahlberg.
    p. cm.
  ISBN 0-451-21656-3
  1. Married people—Fiction. 2. Sound recording executives and producers—Fiction. 3. New York (N.Y.)—
Fiction. 4. Women editors—Fiction. 5. Adultery—Fiction. 6. Revenge—Fiction. I. Title: Uptown and down.
II. Title.
  PS3604.A34U68 2005
  813'.6—dc22   2005009004

Set in Adobe Garamond
Designed by Ginger Legato

Printed in the United States of America

PUBLISHER'S NOTE
This is a work of fiction. Names, characters, places, and incidents either are the product of the author's imagination or are used fictitiously, and any resemblance to actual persons, living or dead, business establishments,
events, or locales is entirely coincidental.
  The publisher does not have any control over and does not assume any responsibility for author or third-
party Web sites or their content.

For Mommy, my angel,

and

Christian, min prins

ACKNOWLEDGMENTS

I am grateful to so many people who generously provided their support, advice and encouragement throughout the evolution of this book.

Without my agent, Sara Camilli, there would be no *Uptown and Down*. Your kindness, concern and tenacity exceeded my expectations. Thank you for finding such a great home for my novel.

A heartfelt thanks to Serena Jones, my editor at New American Library. Thank you for "getting it" and for making me feel so comfortable from the outset. Your unwavering enthusiasm for the manuscript and your insight during the editorial process made the book come alive for me in so many new ways.

I am blessed with a nurturing family that has showered me with an unlimited supply of love and encouragement.

My sister, Dominique Anglade Neblung, is my best friend, alter ego and the sharpest reader I could have ever had. You have been on this journey since the beginning and gave me feedback on everything from title changes to grammar to trends. Above all, you were sympathetic when this book seemed to languish. Thank you for everything. I don't know what I would do without you. My brother-in-law, Eric Neblung, is a soothing influence on us all and a great human being. To my darling niece, Astrid, don't ever lose your love of reading—it is the basis for everything. And to my baby nephew, Sebastian, your cries will become words and I know they will be eloquent.

My wonderful Daddy has always been so proud of my accomplishments. Thank you for driving me around, for the pep talks and the laughter. You have always believed in me and I am so happy that an ocean no longer separates us.

I am grateful for all my lovely "Taties": Nicole Thermilus, Laura Ogé Moore, Edline Garland, Marie-Yolaine Mathelier and Jacqueline

Heaps. Thank you for sharing in my joys and for comforting me in my time of sorrow. I thank my cousin Christian Borges and his wife, Lavine, for their insights and encouragement. Thank you to my cousin, Claudia Simon Calavalle, for not laughing during your read-through and to the family matriarch, Loulouse Anglade Taluy, for believing that I had the talent to become an *écrivain*.

My brother-in-law, Johan Hallström, always sympathized with the ups and downs of the creative process. Thank you for understanding. Seeing you perform onstage always energized me. I would like to thank my late mother-in-law, Malou Hallström, for never batting an eyelash when I mentioned that I was writing a book. Your passion for the arts and culture enabled you to take my endeavors seriously. My father-in-law, Ove Dahlberg, deserves many thanks for his big heart.

My fabulous girlfriends have been steadfast and encouraging. You all inspire me so much. Diana McClure, Evonne Gallardo and I have had countless good times and the most stimulating conversations about art and happiness. Keep the faith and thank you for your love. Ania Siwek and Sachiko Takahashi Soong never let me forget S.V. and I love you for that. If I were more myself with you guys, I would be fourteen years old again. Laurey Lebenson, you are a dear friend and have truly become "Auntie Leb" to me and my family. Thank you for being a caring teacher and great cheerleader.

This book was written while I lived in Stockholm, Sweden, and I am indebted to so many terrific people who gave me their friendship and support. Fia Håkansson, Amelie Söderberg and Boel Mörner, thank you for making me feel at home. To all those who treated me like a writer before I actually had a book deal: Carola Faulkner; Magdalena Bonde and Niklas Sundberg; Denise Rudberg; Lotta and Ola Romney and Louise Sandå. Nina Hahn, you are the entrepreneur extraordinaire and what you taught me about starting your own business goes beyond what I could have ever imagined. My wonderful American girlfriends in Stockholm always provided good laughs and great company: Kim Andersson, Elise Alpen, Angelique Vega-Olsson, Alexia Jaldung, Oona Lagercrantz, Gina Wide and Leslie Maunsbach.

There were many people who provided their expertise and graciously opened their network of contacts to me. Thank you to my dear friend,

Laura Pontin, and her father, Ken Novack, Björn Nilsson and Evan Haymes. Thank you to Isolde Brielmeier for being a modern-day renaissance woman and to Herby Raynaud for making me laugh. Chinyere Sims Hubbard, your enthusiasm is contagious—thank you for offering to throw me a party. I am grateful to Laura and Jim Cooperman for providing me with helpful legal advice. "Lucky" Juste shed valuable light on record company deals. Many thanks to Vera Tertiropoulos and Ingrid Fridman, city friends who made the nineties memorable by showing me the best clubs and sharing shopping tips. Just look at us now! Erica Kennedy, you broke new ground and thank you for sharing your experiences with me. Thank you to Scott Renschler for understanding the novel's themes and characters so well and for challenging me to be more direct in my writing.

Many thanks to Tom "T.J." Johnson for being a special source of inspiration.

A huge thank you to Bojana Radak for taking such great care of my little ones while I worked on the book and for listening to me vent. You're a wonderful fit with our family.

To my lovely daughter, Yasmine, thank you for having the cutest voice, the most carefree laugh and for understanding when I couldn't play. Story time will always be our time. Sweet Baby James, I thank you for your smile, your hugs and for reminding me of my blessings.

I have my beloved late mother, Fredline Anglade, to thank for the person I am today. Your compassion, beauty, grace and courage have taught me strength and humility. Thank you for transmitting your love of books to me and for encouraging me to write. Although you didn't get a chance to see this novel published, I believe that you are blessing me from above. You are in my heart and I will always hear your voice. I love you.

My husband, Christian Dahlberg, supported this project from Day One. You gave me the freedom to pursue a dream. I had many moments of self-doubt, but you always believed in me. You, Yasmine and James put everything into perspective. I am eternally grateful and love you more than words can say.

CHAPTER 1

The raindrops landed on Nora Deschamps Montgomery's head like a faucet turned on full blast. It was one of those sudden, unrelenting Manhattan rainstorms that seemed to drown the city. Since Manhattan functioned only moderately well when the sun was shining, this downpour sent seasoned New Yorkers into unfamiliar patterns of activity. Midtown professionals looked like birds let loose, flapping their arms and scampering wildly, clamoring to evade this latest installment of urban chaos. Nora would have found it all hysterical *if* she hadn't just driven her foot into a greasy puddle *and* if her two-dollar umbrella hadn't been blown inside out. She shielded herself with a tattered and now soaked copy of the *New York Times* and desperately tried to hail a cab, holding up her right arm and slightly extending her index finger in that casual way she had perfected years ago when she first moved to the city. Naturally there were no cabs available. They were all either full or in a state that defied common sense: off duty.

Nora walked a couple of blocks, stopping every so often to wave, praying her distress signals would attract a sympathetic cabbie. She jumped over a puddle and sighed in exasperation. The October day had started out unseasonably warm and her light jacket was drenched. At least a dozen people on both sides of Madison Avenue were ready to pay double for an available taxi. Nora abandoned the *Times* covering her head and racewalked to Sixty-fourth and Third. Her building, the Piedmont, stood on a block filled with antique shops, and Luis, the doorman, always looked crisp and cheerful, regardless of the weather.

"Thank you, Luis," Nora said gratefully as he quickly opened the glass door. She tried to shake off the rain. "I feel like I've been on a sinking ship!"

"Seeing how warm it was this morning, I knew it was too good to be true," he replied.

"Well, I'm definitely not setting foot out of the apartment for the rest of the night!"

"You have a good evening, Mrs. Montgomery."

"Thanks, you too." Nora heard him humming as she checked her mailbox and walked to the elevator bank. The doors slid open and she stared right into the fading blue eyes and wrinkled skin of Mrs. Connors, who lived on the fifth floor. Nora stepped inside and ignored her. On at least three instances, Mrs. Connors had mistaken Nora for a maid, calling her "girl" and asking how much she charged for a day's work. At first, Mrs. Connors's remarks had brought Nora to tears. Why couldn't the old lady conceive broader roles for people of color? Had the Cosbys, Colin Powell and Mayor Dinkins completely passed her by? But later, Nora realized that she was more upset because she had always believed that her appearance and manners distinctly conveyed her education and social status. It was a harsh reminder that too much pride led to a distorted sense of self-worth.

Nora got out on the tenth floor and turned left towards her apartment door. She longed to take off her wet clothes and have a cup of black currant tea. Her husband, Jeff, wouldn't be home for a few hours and she wanted to dry off and unwind. She and Jeff usually worked until seven or eight in the evening and attended business engagements at least twice a week. Nights at home were often spent reading material, poring over documents or writing memos. The two of them would share their long living room couch, talking and laughing, exchanging ideas as well as kisses. Today, however, the torrential rain had been Nora's excuse to leave at the lazy hour of five. She loved being part of a highly motivated couple, but sometimes the pace wore her down.

Nora kicked off her soggy suede ballerina flats and changed into an old terry cloth robe. She purposely avoided looking at her reflection in the mirror. She knew that her shoulder-length hair, which was now matted to her scalp, would inevitably dry into a voluminous heap. She hastily pulled it up in a clip and hoped for the best. Once the tea was ready, she took the steaming cup into the living room, headed for her favorite armchair and turned the television to the news channel. Nora had always been obsessed with the news. Even as a young girl, she needed to know what was going on in the world around her. She would sit in front of the television set or behind a newspaper, dreaming of distant places and smarting from the painful pictures she couldn't understand but knew were unjust. News junkies grew up to be contestants on *Jeopardy!* or journalists. Nora had endured ten months of academic torment at Columbia's J-School—along with a debt of thirty thousand dollars—for the privilege of calling herself a journalist. Yet the hardnews reporting that she had been trained for was a far cry from the fashion and lifestyle articles she produced as editor-at-large of *Muse,* an upscale monthly dedicated to covering whatever was hot, new and alluring. Nora had been wooed to *Muse* from a competitor a few years before, after the editor in chief had been impressed by her journalistic merits as well as her innate sense of style. *Muse* had given her a unique platform and she served as a sort of roving reporter, keeping her eyes open and writing about anything from politics to popular culture. She was also committed to infusing the magazine's tone and content with a multicultural perspective. The rise in circulation seemed to indicate that the approach was working. Nora had been promoted to editor-at-large one year ago and never once regretted redirecting her career ambition.

She turned to the stack of mail she had carelessly tossed on the coffee table. Bills, bank statements and an invitation vied for her attention with the latest copy of *New York* magazine, Gotham's information and entertainment bible. A cover story entitled CHELSEA IS THE NEW SOHO would have to wait. Her eyes were drawn to the copy above the masthead that promised to introduce readers to THE 25 MOST EXCITING COUPLES IN NEW YORK UNDER 40.

Oh, no. She had deliberately blocked out her own involvement in that story.

When the magazine had called two months earlier to announce that she and Jeff would be featured on the list, Nora had been polite, but firm. "Of course my husband and I are flattered," she had told them, "but we really don't want that kind of attention." The editor airily informed her that their consent was not necessary for inclusion. She and Jeff had the option of posing for a studio picture, or the magazine would comb its archives and find one of them together. Nora was in the business; she knew it was better to have some kind of control over the piece's outcome rather than none at all. Otherwise an out-of-date "What was I thinking?" party picture would be splattered across four hundred thousand issues of *New York*. Surprisingly, Jeff had been really positive about the idea. He thought it would be fun to "model" with Nora. He was also proud to be recognized as a couple. The piece would be a sort of testament to the personal history they were forging together.

Nora turned to the appropriate pages and was amazed to see a full-page black-and-white photo with an attendant paragraph. She'd worn a black, strapless, knee-length dress that showed just the right amount of skin without being overtly sexy. Jeff, handsome in black trousers and an open-necked shirt, stood behind her in the photo. His head rested on her left shoulder, and his arms encircled her waist confidently. Jeff's curly black hair was short and neatly framed his face. His dark eyes, which had always entranced her, suggested mystery and intensity, and his cappuccino skin appeared even and smooth. He smiled without re-vealing any teeth, while she was caught in a wide grin reflected in the brightness of her eyes. The photographer had managed to capture a completely spontaneous and tender moment.

Nora had to admit that she liked the picture. Chuckling softly to herself, she focused on the text:

> With their good looks, brains and casual sophistica-
> tion, it's no wonder that Jeff Montgomery, thirty-five,
> and his wife, Nora Deschamps, thirty-two, are one of
> New York's rising entertainment and media couples.
> Jeff is a hip-hop entrepreneur and cofounder of five-
> year-old Rum Records, the innovative and successful
> independent record label. Nora reigns as editor-at-
> large for trendy *Muse* magazine. From their individual
> berths, they are perfectly positioned to influence the
> city's musical and style tastes. Although they are fre-
> quently spotted at fashionable parties and restau-
> rants, this down-to-earth, dynamic pair also supports
> a number of philanthropic and social causes. Jeff and

Nora have accomplished a lot in a short period of time
and should continue to be a formidable couple to
watch.

Nora exhaled, realizing that she had been holding her breath. She
thought that the sentences sounded somewhat shallow and presumptu-
ous. People who read it would probably think that she and Jeff were running their own PR campaign. Isn't that what she thought when she read
such glossy blurbs? At least the paragraph mentioned that they were involved with service activities. Although lately their participation had been
reduced to attending benefits or lending their names rather than volunteering. There simply weren't enough hours to do everything. Marriage,
work, her parents, friends, moments for herself . . . the commitments and
obligations went on and on. Nora's life had become a treadmill, constantly accelerating in speed, but also strangely exhilarating.

Nora was a first-generation American, a fact that she had considered
a major inconvenience while growing up. Her parents, Pierre and
Valérie Deschamps, had been members of a crop of young intellectuals
that emigrated from Haiti to the United States in the late 1960s. They
had been well-known agitators who fervently opposed the political and
economic repression of François "Papa Doc" Duvalier's regime. As such,
they were also targets of his brutal secret police and were forced to leave
everything behind, fleeing Haiti on an Air Canada cargo plane in the
middle of the night.

Pierre and Valérie first settled in uptown Manhattan with other ex-
patriates. Lively political discussions took place over cups of strong
black coffee or bottles of Barbancourt rum as these exiles discussed ways
to overthrow Papa Doc's government. They really believed that they
could amass an opposition force from a twenty-by-forty kitchen. Nora
was christened Eléonore after her paternal grandmother, but Valérie decided it was a mouthful for a baby and shortened it to Nora. At first
Nora didn't realize that her family was different. The tempo of her parents' lives was as comforting to her as the beloved crocheted blanket
she'd received for her first birthday. Valérie and Pierre took her everywhere with them—parties, baptisms, restaurants. She sat on cushiony
laps and the sight of people milling about only reaffirmed that she was

part of a larger family. Friendly faces smothered her with kisses and affectionate names. Everyone she knew spoke with their whole body, not just their vocal cords, as they recounted stories until dawn.

When Nora was three and her brother, Albert, was born, her family moved to Cambria Heights in Queens, a less hectic borough than Manhattan and the next step in the demographic shift of Haitian immigrants from the inner city to the surrounding suburbs. Pierre completed pharmaceutical school and worked steadily and saved for three more years until he was able to buy a house in the suburban haven of Westbury, Long Island. It was a perfect starter home for an émigré and his young family, but the world as Nora knew it turned on its head. She had been sheltered. Her parents had created a parallel world for themselves in America and she was now stuck trying to decipher the rites and rituals of an authentic American childhood. The comfortable fabric of her life had disappeared, only to be replaced by new faces and new rules. Her parents had always told her that their Haitianness made them special. Her father's ancestors were French Huguenots who had come to the island in the 1700s. Valérie was a direct descendant of a general who had fought in the battle for independence in 1804. Their family symbolized pride, ideals, culture and tenacity. But no one cared at St. Boniface, the Catholic school where Nora's parents had enrolled her, because *(a)* most of the other kids had never heard of Haiti and *(b)* those who had knew it was the poorest country in the Western hemisphere and thus associated Haitians with boat people. Her school uniform was an ugly navy-blue-and-green plaid meant to help her blend in with the other Irish- and Italian-American kids, but there was no use. They teased her about her braided hair, her parents' accents, the brown ceramic doll from her grandmother that she brought to school for show-and-tell. Nora realized early on that acceptance came from being like everyone else. And if you didn't look the part, you had to act the part. Pierre and Valérie downplayed Nora's misery and complaints. "Work hard and be yourself," they told her. They were steadfastly self-assured and automatically assumed that Nora had inherited this trait, but she usually felt awkward and out of place. Much, much later she would laugh at her lack of valentines and the lonely recess periods, but, oh, how those moments had ached!

Unlike Albert, who won respect and friendship through sports, Nora preferred to escape and bury her nose in a book. She discovered Judy Blume (at least someone understood her!) and Margaret, Iggie and Blubber became her best friends. Even if she wasn't really reading, no one disturbed her as long as the book lay open on a table or balanced on her lap. She daydreamed, listened, observed. It was amazing what she picked up when everyone thought she wasn't paying attention—information, gossip, nuances in tone and body language. She trained herself to be inconspicuous, to keep a distance.

Nora's passion for books made studying easier and she was always one of the two or three Black kids in the honors classes. She wasn't aggressive and spoke up only when she was absolutely sure about the correctness of her answer. She also enjoyed the look of stupefaction on her more assertive classmates' faces when she scored higher on exams than they did. She had always been lanky, but by high school, her long arms and legs stopped rebelling from the rest of her body and formed an elegant symmetry. Her slim neck had prompted more than one person to ask if she was a dancer. Nevertheless, Nora considered her looks a liability. They were the sophisticated kind that her parents' friends or strange older men with leering eyes and wayward fantasies found appealing. They certainly didn't go with the petite cuteness of Westbury, nor did they help her get a prom date senior year. She had some loyal friends, but they were very much like her. They wanted to break out, sensed that life offered something more exciting on the other side, but lacked the self-confidence or boldness to step out into the world and claim it as their own.

She often joked that she gave her parents the ultimate immigrant's dream by getting into an "Ivy." She considered Columbia her ticket to freedom. Not freedom from her parents and their values, but freedom to truly experience the promise and sweet independence they had sacrificed so much for. Her wealth of choices was their reward. It had less to do with Columbia's academic reputation than with the realization that it was perfectly acceptable to be different in New York City. In fact, it was encouraged. On her first day, she walked over one hundred blocks from Morningside Heights to Washington Square Park. As she passed the different neighborhoods, she observed the people and imagined what their stories might be. She absorbed the vitality of the city, entirely comfortable amid the noise, traffic and crowds. She wanted so much to belong to this place, but also felt truly free for the first time in her life.

She lived in Carman Hall, the chaotic freshman dorm, her first year. The cellblock rooms weren't much to look at, but with pictures and just the right lighting, they became less severe. Everyone was unusually nice, desperate to make a connection and not exclude anyone who could become a potential friend. Many secrets were shared and people peeled back the layers of their past lives in an astonishingly open way. Nora realized that they had fought many of the same battles with insecurity and identity that she had.

She joined the campus newspaper, the *Spectator*, and became a familiar face at university events. She met two other girls, Erica Daniels and Dahlia Robinson, while waiting for the downtown 9 train on her way to see Sade at the Blue Note. Nora heard them talking about the show on the subway platform and casually mentioned that she was going too. Erica and Dahlia were going for fun; Nora had to write a review for the *Spec*. By the time the 9 pulled into Christopher Street, Nora discovered that they shared a love of art history, thought Homer was dull and wanted to experience a side of the city that wasn't exactly mentioned in the student guidebook. Erica and Dahlia seemed fearless. Erica had spent the summer teaching in Panama and Dahlia had practically raised her two younger brothers after their mother died of breast cancer. They didn't care what other people thought of them, didn't feel obligated to conform to a code of behavior. Nora had spent her whole life being nice, polite and correct. She had been the self-conscious "immigrants' daughter" who didn't dare do wrong for too long. The time had come to *loosen up*.

She would study until eleven on Friday and Saturday nights, then change into a tiny top with a tight skirt or her leather jeans, and hit the city's best clubs with Erica and Dahlia. They believed that whatever was worth happening happened only at night and preferably downtown. The club scene was fierce and democracy nonexistent. Getting chosen to step behind the velvet ropes became their mission, and once inside, they danced all night. The first time Nora got drunk she hated the loss of control, but the first time she spent the night with a man emboldened her. She had walked along the city blocks the next morning still dressed in the previous night's clothes—the infamous walk of shame—but she felt sexy and liberated.

New York City had been her initiation. Jeff had appeared in her life when she least expected it and the attraction had been instant. But it had taken some time before Nora let him in. At first the expanse of her love and desire had filled her with fear. She sometimes believed that such contentment could only lead to disappointment. With Jeff, she had discovered that she deserved happiness, deserved to be loved and, most incredible of all, to return those feelings unreservedly.

Nora stirred when Jeff stroked her check. He kissed her lightly on the lips and she opened her eyes.

"You're finally home," she said groggily, sitting up. "What time is it?"

"A little after nine. How are you?" he asked, settling next to her on the couch.

"Fine, a little tired, though," she answered, smelling the rain on his skin as she kissed his neck. "And I wanted to fix dinner, but it's too late now."

"No problem. We'll do our special," he said easily.

"Let me guess—"

"Ordering in. So what'll it be? Chinese? Thai? Mexican? Burgers?"

"Mmmm. Thai sounds good," Nora replied. They'd lately become obsessed with Thai cuisine, reasoning that since it felt so healthy going down, it couldn't possibly be fattening.

During the spicy, satisfying meal, Nora told Jeff about the *New York* magazine piece.

"Sweetie, you'll die when you see it. The picture's OK, but what they wrote about us was a little embarrassing."

"Really?" Jeff asked. "Let me see it."

Nora got the magazine from the coffee table and waited for his reaction.

"I don't think it's so bad," he said, studying the photo. "The picture is nice. I think you look terrific. Look at those long legs!"

She laughed. "Oh, stop it. What will people think when they read it?

They'll probably say 'Who do these people think they are?' or 'Why are they on this list? I don't think they're so special.' "

"First of all, who gives a damn what other people think? Second, the magazine decided—we didn't ask to be on the list. And finally, why are you so hard on yourself? Most people in this city would pay to have their name and face in a magazine."

"I just don't see us the way we're described in that piece."

"Well, at least they got the facts right. We had to come across as a little more glamorous. Otherwise we wouldn't be worthy of this 'twenty-five most exciting couples under forty' business." He winked. "Could you pick up an extra copy for my parents?"

"Sure—I'll do it while I'm picking up the extra copy for mine."

They laughed and Jeff poured more mineral water into their glasses. "Just enjoy it, honey."

"I'll try." She and Jeff had married two years ago, after a three-year courtship. They had toiled for five years to achieve their individual dreams, but their passion, their curiosity for life and each other, had not disappeared. "In a way, being singled out like this will make it harder to fail." She unclasped the clip that held her hair in place. Her ends were still wet. She cursed the rain and sighed. "I guess I'm in an overanalytical mood tonight."

"There's nothing wrong with that. Sometimes we have to check ourselves. We might be in for some changes anyway," Jeff added mysteriously.

"Like what?"

"I'll know more tomorrow. Hilton and I have an important meeting planned."

"You know I can't stand the suspense! At least give me a hint."

Jeff laughed. "Baby, I honestly don't have anything more to tell. You'll get the full story tomorrow."

"How am I going to sleep tonight with these questions in my head?"

"I can think of a few suggestions."

CHAPTER 2

H ilton Frears waited for Jeff in the lobby of one of the most impressive skyscrapers in New York City. Jeff was running a few minutes late, but Hilton had wisely suggested they meet up half an hour before their appointment with Lawrence Stark. He watched the business executives and messengers who passed through the wide revolving doors. *The power and money housed in this building,* he thought. Dressed in a conservative two-button suit, Hilton could easily have passed for a young lawyer or investment banker. But, upon further inspection, the irreverent tilt of his head and the gleam in his eyes would have indicated that he was a man who enjoyed playing life by his own rules. Hilton was boyishly handsome. He still had dimples in his cheeks and the liveliness of his youth was evident in his booming laugh and quick steps. His thick black hair was wavy, a legacy of his mother's Native American ancestors. At five feet ten, he was well built and worked out at least three times a week. He had recently grown a trim mustache and it gave his face an added earnestness. Today he wore small round wire-rimmed glasses instead of his usual contact lenses. He wanted to look more businesslike and serious. Hilton had realized long ago that people were never quite sure what to make of him. His jocular nature was deceiving, causing others to underestimate him. Most of the time he found this amusing, but other times it proved to be a useful business tool.

Hilton spotted Jeff in blue pinstripes walking through the main door and rushed over to him. They'd been best friends for two decades, ever since meeting at prep school.

Jeff was out of breath. "I'm sorry I'm late, but the crosstown traffic was no joke."

"It's OK. We still have fifteen minutes to spare. Is there anything you think we should go over?" Hilton asked.

"Nah, I don't think so. I think our strategy is to just be natural, not overzealous. The facts speak for themselves. I got the impression that this is going to be more of an information-gathering session anyway."

"It might well be," Hilton said, "but you're definitely right about being cool. We have to remember that Stark is the one who called *us* to arrange this meeting."

"We have nothing to lose by giving him an hour of our time."

They rode the elevator to the forty-fifth floor and a sleek logo signaled that they had reached NRG Music Group, the jewel in the crown of one of the world's largest entertainment and media conglomerates, NRG, Incorporated. NRG, Inc., had interests in movies, television production and broadcasting, music, cable, magazines, electronic media and book publishing. It was a towering organization with the ability to influence popular culture through its latest best seller or prime-time sitcom.

After announcing their arrival to the receptionist, Hilton expected to sit and wait, but Lawrence Stark, chairman and CEO of NRG Music, appeared at eleven on the dot. He definitely looked corporate in an understated charcoal gray suit, but his tone-on-tone blue shirt and tie were a bit more stylish than Hilton had expected. A generous amount of gel kept Stark's brown hair firmly in place and off of his tanned face. His hazel eyes were friendly, but razor-sharp. They took in everything and Stark had a reputation for processing new information at lightning speed.

Stark gave Hilton an enthusiastic handshake and said, "Hilton, good to see you. So glad you could make it. It's been a while."

"Thanks for having us," Hilton answered. "I think the last time we bumped into each other was at the NARIP conference in Miami."

Stark rolled his eyes. "Those industry things make me feel more and more like an old-timer." He extended his hand to Jeff and said, "Jeff, how are you?"

"Fine, thanks."

"I've really been looking forward to this meeting," Stark added.

"So have we," Jeff replied.

"I really admire what you've both done with Rum Records."

Stark's mixture of humility and praise had the desired effect. Hilton relaxed and he and Jeff thanked him again.

Stark ushered them into his executive suite and the three men sat around a small conference table. In an absurd space-to-furniture ratio favored by many entertainment execs, Stark's oversized office had only the table, four chairs, a cedar desk and built-in cabinets that surely hid all of his paperwork. Two drawings by Picasso and a Japanese calligraphy panel graced the walls. Here, Stark seemed more Zen master than music mogul.

Stark had grown up at NRG, honing his skills in a variety of their divisions. He had been appointed chairman of the music group five years ago and it had enjoyed unprecedented growth under his leadership. Stark was forty-nine and rumored to be the first choice to run the multibillion-dollar group of companies when the current chairman and CEO retired.

Stark touched his chin. "I'd like to tell you a little bit about NRG Music. We've been having an incredible year with a nice roster of established stars and new artists, seven number one hits and ten Grammy Awards. We've got about a fifteen point two U.S. market position, and the music division has revenues of two point nine billion dollars." He paused and tapped his fingers on the table. "It's a solid record, but we don't want to rest on our laurels. Tell me, how have you managed to build a company from scratch to one that had sales of—oh, I'd be guessing—but around forty million dollars last year?"

Hilton had to exercise a great deal of self-control to hide his surprise. Rum was a private company and Stark's guess was frighteningly close.

"I think it has to do with a variety of factors, not least of which is our ability to spot new talent," Jeff said. "That's Hilton's forte. He's really attuned to what our core audience wants. In many cases, he's even anticipated what their tastes will be."

"You've got some really talented artists in your roster. Take that R & B crooner, Livingston. Market data claims that the audience for soulful love songs has shrunk, but his album will probably go double platinum by year-end," Stark observed.

Hilton was impressed. Stark had definitely done his homework. "Livingston's success is proof that you can't rely too heavily on market research. You also have to rely on your gut and when we heard Livingston, we knew he would be a refreshing alternative to the overproduced tracks crowding the scene today. Sure—people like to hear hip-hop or a funky dance jam while they're working or at a party, but at night, during those romantic times, they want to hear something sexy, cool and smooth. I call it subliminal soul. We want to give them music that caters to all their moods."

"What are your criteria for signing an act?" Stark inquired.

"Again, it's all about my instincts. The artists should be inherently talented and have something special to offer. I'm not interested in carbon copies of existing performers or riding the wave of a popular trend. Rum Records would rather create a trend," Hilton said.

Stark leaned back in his chair and Hilton's eyes flicked to the tall glass window behind him. These ten-foot windows covered most of the room, giving Stark panoramic views of the city. The jagged skyline was just as much a part of the decor as the minimal interior.

"How have you handled the administrative and financial end of the business?" Stark asked.

"Fairly well, I hope," Jeff replied, "since that's primarily my area of responsibility. We've got a fluid staff, a mixture of full-time and part-time employees. We try to keep production and marketing costs on budget and we don't have multimillion-dollar artists' contracts. Hilton and I have a policy of reinvesting the majority of the profits back into the company. As a result, we've been able to expand. We recently moved into a larger office space downtown and we've been working on a few Rum-related enterprises."

"Can you talk about these enterprises more specifically?" Stark prodded.

Hilton glanced at Jeff. His partner shrugged casually, giving him the go-ahead to continue.

"A lot of the plans are in their final stages. We've got the Rum clothing line, which is a collection of hip street wear—jeans, T-shirts, baseball caps, jackets. They're sold in specialty shops and the stuff is flying off the racks! We're in the process of renovating a retail space in NoHo and hope to have a freestanding store within the next six months. We're also scouting locations for a bar/lounge/restaurant," Hilton said.

Stark nodded in approval. "Sounds like empire building to me."

Jeff chuckled. "Hardly. But we do realize that we have a very marketable brand on our hands, the Rum label. By expanding into other areas, we can increase our visibility as well as solidify our identity."

Hilton realized he'd have to gamble in order to find out why Stark had called this meeting. He cleared his throat and said, "Larry, Jeff and I have a vision for Rum Records. We believe that it could be the foundation for a multimedia entertainment group. Music will always be our base, but we're interested in producing films, television shows, concerts—you name it. We want to bring the Rum flavor to a variety of media."

"What exactly is the 'Rum flavor'?" asked Stark.

"It's urban, bold, streetwise, in-your-face without being obnoxious—"

"We also have the potential to reach an even larger audience," added Jeff, catching on to Hilton's strategy. "Look, Livingston didn't sell a million eight albums by appealing only to a narrow segment of the Black listening audience. There's a strong market that's looking for more sophisticated, subtle diversions. Our demographics have been trending older, they have more discretionary income, and they want to see more representations of themselves."

"And we have the access to the artists, writers and performers who would be the nucleus of any project," Hilton finished.

"How would you finance your expansion plans?" Stark asked.

"We'd have to start slowly, of course, but we could raise the money through a number of sources—" Jeff began.

"Or you could get involved in a strategic relationship," Stark interjected. "A larger entity with greater financial resources and distribution channels could better support your projects."

Hilton pursed his lips and Jeff raised one eyebrow noncommittally.

"Jeff, Hilton, I've been watching Rum Records closely, particularly during the last year. Your results in the marketplace have been outstanding for such a young company. After listening to your plans, I don't think that it would be premature for me to tell you that NRG Music is very interested in forming an alliance with Rum. I don't have specifics yet. But why don't I look at the numbers and we can see if it makes sense to carry this conversation further? How does that sound?" he asked.

"That sounds fine," Jeff replied neutrally.

"Yes. Very interesting," Hilton agreed.

Stark pushed back his chair and stood up. He walked Hilton and Jeff to the door and the hand shaking began all over again. "We'll be in touch," he promised.

Hilton and Jeff said nothing to each other in the elevator or when they were outside, waiting for a cab to pull up. It wasn't until they were inside, inching their way to Rum's offices downtown, that Hilton broke the silence.

"Damn! That was some meeting. I'm not even sure what happened in there. How did we get to what I think Stark is suggesting?"

"Tell me about it," Jeff said. "That man sure is an operator. He didn't get to where he is today without perfecting the art of the deal."

"What do you think he meant, if we read between the lines?"

Jeff shrugged. "Who knows? Anything from a small investment to taking a major stake in Rum."

Hilton considered this. "I wouldn't want to lose too much control. Maybe I got a little carried away. Do you think we said too much?"

"No. I bet Stark knew most of what we told him already. He was playin' us, but in a very gentlemanly way."

"So, how would you feel about partnering with NRG?" Hilton asked pointedly.

"I honestly don't know. Depends on the deal. I'd have to get a little more comfortable with them first. We're coming from completely different business cultures."

"Not to mention social and racial," Hilton said half jokingly.

Jeff smiled. "I think we should just keep an open mind. We always have the right of refusal."

"But it sounded good, didn't it?" Hilton asked.

"What did?"

"Our plans for Rum. I could see it right in front of me, exploding into movies and television. I really believe in our potential." Hilton looked out the window.

"So do I, buddy," Jeff answered wistfully. "So do I."

Hilton stayed quiet for the remainder of the cab ride. Deep in thought, he contemplated the future with anticipation, impatience and a bit of apprehension.

CHAPTER 3

Nora stood in her kitchen, arranging rosemary sprigs on a platter of chicken breasts and russet potatoes. She and Jeff were having another evening at home and she had put a temporary ban on takeout. She was longing for a home-cooked meal, and the fact that Jeff also loved good food made cooking even more pleasurable. He had been her guinea pig for countless culinary efforts, the proven recipes as well as her invented concoctions. The sluggishness that had weighed her down yesterday had passed and she spent a productive day at the office. The finished proofs for next month's issue had gone to the printers and she was looking forward to tackling several new feature ideas. She put on a jazzy, chill-out CD, set the mahogany dining table and lit two white tapered candles. As she watered her potted orchid, she heard the familiar turn of Jeff's key at the door.

He walked into the kitchen. "What's cooking? Something smells good."

"It's just about ready and then you can taste for yourself."

They hugged and kissed in greeting as they always did. It was a meaningful ritual for them, reaffirming that they were still happy to see each other at the end of the day, that the other's presence was special and not to be taken for granted.

"So, how did your secret meeting go today?" asked Nora as she opened a bottle of Sancerre.

"Fine, actually." He took off his jacket and sat down at the table. "In many respects, it went much better than I thought it would."

"Who was it with?"

"Lawrence Stark," he replied, and noticed the blank look on Nora's face. "The head of NRG Music Group."

"Oh," Nora said, surprised, "*that* Lawrence Stark. What did he have to say?"

Jeff replayed his meeting for Nora. She listened carefully, watching him and sipping her wine.

When he finished, she said, astonishment in her voice, "But you and Hilton always talked about remaining independent. You guys always made a point of saying that you were"—she deepened her voice— " 'lean, but hungry, and would never sell out to those cash-rich but creatively weak labels.' "

"Were those our exact words?"

"More or less."

"When did we say them?"

"Three, four years ago."

Jeff smiled sheepishly. "A lot has happened since then that would allow for a change in policy."

"Such as?"

"For one thing, Hilton and I are sitting on something that has the potential to be *large*," he said. "We're interested in dabbling in all areas of the entertainment world. The time is right. There's a market for what we want to do. We should strike while the iron is hot."

Nora was always suspicious when Jeff used clichés. "You also run the risk of spreading yourselves too thin, doing all sorts of new things, but spending less time on what you do best—making music. The last thing in the world I would want is for you to get involved with NRG and then fail. I've seen it happen in the fashion industry. Young designers who get eagerly snatched up by a bigger house and then are never heard from again."

Jeff circled a potato wedge on his plate with a fork. "Don't you believe that we have the talent and skills to make something like that work?"

"Of course I do. There's a lot of mediocrity out there that's managed to break through and they don't have half of Rum's originality. Being 'large' changes people. It changes your philosophy of life, how you treat others. Everything becomes warped and reality is like a music video."

"That would never happen to me," Jeff assured her.

Nora took in his solemn expression. "Maybe not," she said finally, "but can you be so sure about Hilton?"

Jeff furrowed his brows. "Hilton? He's just as skeptical about this as I am."

She reached for Jeff's hand across the table. "Honey, there's no reason why you shouldn't just wait and see what happens. I'm sure whatever you decide will be the best thing for the company. NRG is well respected. You and Hilton would be foolish not to at least consider what they have to say."

"That's what we figure," Jeff replied. He seemed relieved that Nora sounded more enthusiastic. "There's something else I want to talk to you about," he said cheerily, changing the subject.

Nora smiled. "Like what?"

"The lease on our apartment is up in four months and I spoke to Mike Miller today." Mike Miller owned their apartment, which they subleased. "He wanted to know if we'd be interested in buying this apartment."

Although their apartment was located in a desirable part of the city, it was only a medium-sized two-bedroom, for which they paid a small fortune in monthly rent. They both knew that the apartment would be inadequate for their future needs, but had procrastinated looking for something larger.

"How much is he asking for it?" Nora asked.

"Much more than I think it's worth. But then again, the real estate market in the city right now is overheated."

"What are we going to do? Where are we going to live? Should we stay in the city? Maybe we'll get more for our money in the suburbs." Nora did not look forward to the nightmare they would soon face. Looking for a new place to live was undoubtedly one of the worst experiences for a New Yorker.

"I was thinking that we should buy a town house," Jeff began.

Nora nodded approvingly. "Brilliant idea."

"In Harlem," he finished.

Nora sank back in her chair. "In Harlem? Why?"

"Why not?"

She shrugged. "When I was at Columbia, I never went further than 125th Street," she answered, referring to Harlem's most famous cross street and major artery.

"Do you have anything against the area?"

"No, but I never considered it as a place to settle down and eventually raise a family. Maybe I'm not the Harlem type," she admitted.

"Meaning?" Jeff probed.

"I like being able to walk to work every day. I like the conveniences of having a supermarket, dry cleaner and stores nearby. And I'm also concerned for safety. I'm probably too uptight."

"Fair enough. But what if I told you that I found a wonderful town house in a historic section of Harlem?"

"Strivers' Row?" she asked. Strivers' Row had long been considered one of Harlem's most architecturally superb and genteel enclaves. Affluent Blacks had settled there since the 1920s.

"No," Jeff answered. "Hamilton Heights."

Nora thought for a second. "Where's that?"

"Around 140th to 145th Street, between St. Nicholas and Amsterdam Avenues. It's close to City College."

"Ha! You've been researching places without me! How'd you find it?"

"I stumbled upon it while Hilton and I were scouting locations for Rum's new offices."

"Then why didn't you take it?" Nora challenged.

"I knew you were going to ask that," Jeff laughed. "It just looked more residential. I pictured a family living there more than a company. It's a beautiful structure with a lot of traditional elements that you just don't find today anymore. Since we're not planning on staying here once the lease expires, I contacted the real estate broker again this afternoon and she told me that the house is still on the market. She offered to show us the place tomorrow at six o'clock. What do you say?"

Nora chewed on her last bite of chicken, mulling over Jeff's idea. "Sure. Why not?"

Patricia Wallace, the real estate broker, waited for Jeff and Nora on the steps of a Beaux Arts limestone town house.

"Hello," she squealed in delight, shaking Jeff's and Nora's hands vigorously. Well endowed with bright makeup, her active eyes quickly regarded the couple. "It's a pleasure to meet you, Nora. I was so glad when Jeff called again yesterday."

"Thanks for seeing us on such short notice," Jeff said.

"Luckily the town house was still on tap. You know, we've had tremendous interest in this area over the last year and people are just grabbing whatever is available. This house, however, is one of the best properties in the Hamilton Heights area," she enthused.

"Oh, then I'm surprised you haven't had an anxious buyer yet," Nora could not help saying sweetly.

"We've had several offers, which the owner, unfortunately, was compelled to turn down. He's pretty adamant about the value of the property," answered Pat firmly.

"I see," replied Nora.

Inside, Pat turned on the hallway lights. As she walked, her high heels clicked against the hardwood floor. "This building was built in 1902 by Henri Foucheau, a very well regarded architect of that era. It only had one owner until the Great Depression. At that time, many of Harlem's brownstones and town houses were converted into rooming houses, but this one managed to avoid that. So a lot of the original detailing is still in place. The seller's father bought the building for a great price in 1932 and the property has remained in his family ever since. Now he's elderly and doesn't want the responsibility of the building anymore. His children encouraged him to put it up for sale, seeing how strong the market is now. But he can afford to wait until the right buyer comes along," she stressed.

As Nora absorbed the house's history, she could not help thinking of the people and events that had traveled through its stately portal. This edifice was a living entity, so different from her and Jeff's sterile East Side apartment.

Pat stepped into the first room to the right of the foyer. "This was traditionally the parlor, but maybe that sounds a little too old-fashioned for today. Nevertheless, it could be transformed into a library or media room," she suggested.

Pat walked them through the spacious, newly renovated kitchen. The Sub-Zero fridge, Viking range and stainless steel drawers and fixtures were an amateur chef's dream. A sliding door led to the dining room. The ceiling was at least twelve feet high and the off-white walls were bordered by a series of ornate moldings. The room could easily seat fourteen around a large dining room table. The original chandelier still hung from the ceiling and its crystal teardrops glistened like prisms. The living room also boasted grand proportions and architectural embellishments. A built-in mahogany bookcase occupied an entire wall and an intricate frieze ornamented the fireplace. Large glass doors led to an enclosed outside garden. There, among the plants and small flowers, the harshness of the city vanished. They walked up the staircase, touching its rich maple banister, to the second floor. The master bedroom suite had an additional fireplace.

"The master bedroom gets excellent sunlight in the morning and you have great views through the windows," Pat continued. "This floor has been the 'family wing,' with three other rooms that could function beautifully as children's bedrooms, home office or guest suite. There's also another full bath."

As Nora visited the second-floor rooms, she was blown away by the expansiveness. The rooms weren't intimidating, but they presented a wealth of possibilities that she never expected to be in a position to consider in Manhattan. A series of studio apartments and small two-bedrooms had distorted her sense of space.

Pat led them to the top floor and explained, "There are three rooms on this level that'd be perfect for a home gym, au pair's quarters and play-room. However, the bathroom is smaller and only has a shower cabin."

Jeff pretended to be shocked. "Then that's it. Forget it," he joked.

Pat laughed. "You never know."

Jeff entered the first room on the left and walked towards the window. "Nora, look. You can see the Throgs Neck Bridge from here."

Nora joined him by the window, but remained quiet. In the night, the illuminated bridge was indeed beautiful, but she didn't want to seem overly enthusiastic. After they had visited the remaining rooms and made their way back to the ground floor, Pat summarized the tour.

"This house is an architectural statement. In spite of the formal elements, it still offers a lot of freedom. The seller has invested handsomely on renovations and it's rare to find a place like this in move-in condition. The rooms are generous *and* you have a garage. Where else in the city could you find that?" she asked, smiling.

Jeff nodded, but Nora worried that everything sounded too good to be true. "Pat, could you tell us a little bit more about the neighborhood? What are the people like?"

Pat crossed her arms around her chest. "The neighborhood is predominantly Black and has been growing increasingly diverse." Her tone had become less saleslike and more candid. "The exorbitant Manhattan real estate market has made people—Upper West Side lawyers and families with three kids who looked at Brooklyn Heights and Park Slope ten years ago—interested in Harlem. As you know, Hamilton Heights has been designated a historic district, so the residents take enormous pride in their neighborhood. They're solid people, ranging from middle-class on up. They have families and a real sense of community. I've lived not too far from here on Convent Avenue for sixteen years and I can tell you one thing: You really feel like you're part of a neighborhood here. Most people are friendly and look out for one another. You don't usually get that feeling in a place like New York."

"Is there a lot of crime?"

"In terms of crime, you know how it is in this city. It varies from block to block and Harlem is no different. Some areas are more volatile than others, but you just have to be aware of them. Drug dealing is a major concern for the residents here and they've made their voices heard at the local precinct."

"And the schools?"

"Most of the kids here go to public schools, which, as you know, have problems throughout the city, not just in Harlem. When the time comes, you'll have to decide if you want to take the public- or private-school route," said Pat.

"What about stores and other creature comforts?"

"The neighborhood has become more gentrified. Some of the newer residents are trying to bring in more amenities, like cute coffee shops and cafés. We even have regular 'town house meetings.' Harlem, in general, is experiencing a shift. With the Empowerment Zone on 125th Street, tax credits and renewed private investment, Harlem is going through a kind of renaissance again. It's nice to be a part of it."

"Pat, refresh my memory. What's the asking price for the town house?" asked Jeff.

"One point five million dollars," said Pat. "The price naturally factors in all the renovations, saving a lot of time and money for the new owners. A comparable property on the Upper West or Upper East Side would cost at least six or seven times more money."

"Oh, we're well aware of that," responded Jeff.

"I don't expect you to make a decision on the spot," conceded Pat. "The two of you should talk it over some more and really feel, in your hearts, that this is where you want to build a future."

Pat sounded almost maternal and Nora felt a rush of gratitude towards her.

"I think that's what we'll have to do. The town house is beautiful, but this is such a big step," Nora said.

Pat nodded sympathetically. "Buying a first home always is."

Jeff and Nora left Pat with the promise to touch base within two weeks. The drive home began smoothly, free of stop-and-go traffic and filled with the mellow bass of the Livingston CD. Nora rolled down her window to let in the cool evening air and found herself mentally decorating the rooms. The house was indeed extraordinary. She pictured warm cozy fires on cold winter nights, and light summer dinners in the garden.

Jeff turned onto Sixty-sixth Street, preparing to go through Central Park and across to the East Side. Traffic was stalled. He turned to Nora and said teasingly, "You're thinking about the town house, right? I can tell by the look in your eyes. You've probably decorated half the rooms by now."

Nora couldn't contain herself any longer and gushed, "It was spectacular, wasn't it? But I still didn't get a feeling for the neighborhood as a whole. What did you think?"

"Well, I've benefited from having seen it twice. And I like it even more now than I did the first time."

"Would you want to live there?"

"Absolutely. I can see us there. I like the vibe of the place and what Pat said about being part of a community really touched a nerve. I think it's time we laid down some real roots. It would also be nice to live in an area where I wasn't stared at and made to feel like a trespasser."

"You're saying the East Side feels that way?"

"Well, some people act like they've never seen a Black man before. I rode the elevator with this lady once and she looked like she was going to faint and held on to her handbag for dear life. The East Side is also materialistic and conformist. For my tastes, the area lacks character. That's what the house we just saw has: character."

Nora thought of Mrs. Connors. "But wouldn't we be giving in to their prejudices and bad manners by moving out? Wouldn't it be like running away?"

"Not at all. We'd be choosing to live in a more inclusive, healthy environment. I'd have no problems with that," Jeff answered. "We'd also be getting our money's worth. That town house would always be a good investment."

"So living in a Black neighborhood is really important to you?"

He grinned. "I guess I've always had a thing about the Harlem of folklore and legend. And—I don't know—maybe once some of us 'make it' we have a responsibility not to ignore historically black neighborhoods. Maybe our physical presence can make a difference."

"Why is that suddenly important now? You've spent your whole life weaving in and out of both worlds."

Jeff fiddled with the controls on the stereo and lowered the volume. "Sure, I managed, but it hasn't been without effort. Now the company is in good shape, I have you, and I've reached a point where my definition of quality of life has changed. It's not just about the latest car or the safe, socially acceptable address. It's also about what feeds my soul. I connected with Hamilton Heights."

"Jeff, you know how I am. It takes me a long time to make a decision. I can't go on a gut feeling like you. I have to think about this from all angles."

"Take your time. There's no pressure," he reassured her.

"Would you be upset if I said no?"

"Not upset, but maybe a little disappointed. But we could never be happy in that house unless you wanted to live there too. We'd just have to start looking for our dream house from scratch."

CHAPTER 4

It was Hilton's thirty-fifth birthday and he was eager to celebrate in style. He still felt young enough and sufficiently imbued with a party spirit to plan a gathering for 350 of his closest friends. Indochine, a chic downtown eatery that had smoothly survived the ebb and flow of Manhattan's quixotic restaurant scene, had been remade into Hilton's private lounge. Since he was hosting his much-talked-about celebration there, it was *the* place to be. Velvet couches, chairs and ottomans were artfully arranged around the main room. Framed black-and-white photographs of Hilton together with friends and artists decorated the walls. Rows of votive candles adorned the dining tables, and bamboo stalks rose from clear glass vases, honoring the French-Vietnamese cuisine that Indochine was famous for. The flickering candlelight bathed the room in a sensuous glow. Caressing, hypnotic rhythms of R & B transported the guests to an ethereal paradise. The A-list crowd flirted and drank champagne nonchalantly.

Nora and Jeff arrived an hour late and attempted to make their way through the tightly packed bodies along the bar. Jeff stopped every few seconds and greeted friends and acquaintances. Nora didn't recognize many of their faces, but she smiled and exchanged pleasantries. This was Jeff and Hilton's world and she had perfected the stance of the polite, supportive wife long ago. The knotted fur stole over her Chloé dress made her feel very glamorous, and strappy Christian Louboutin heels elevated her to over six feet tall. The Montgomerys finally reached Hilton's table of honor. He was sitting next to his date, the model Stephanie Thomas, surrounded by an assortment of friends.

"Hey," Hilton called as he caught sight of Nora and Jeff, "you guys finally made it."

"Happy birthday, buddy," Jeff congratulated Hilton, giving him a bear hug.

Nora stepped towards Hilton and kissed his cheek, flashing him an affectionate smile. "Happy birthday. This looks like a great party," she said.

"Well . . . you know . . . I try. I just wanted to throw a little get-together for my friends," Hilton attempted humbly, shrugging his shoulders.

Nora anticipated the night's festivities. Hilton approached organizing a party with the same zeal with which he managed an artist. Free-flowing food, spirits and music were a proven formula, but only *entry-level* party planning, according to Hilton. He modified the guest list regularly to reflect whoever was of the moment, choreographed the evening to the hour and sent everyone home with generous goody bags.

"I think you've succeeded," Nora laughed.

"Can I get you any champagne?" Hilton offered. They nodded and he signaled to the voluptuous waitress in a short black skirt. "Another bottle of Krug, please." His gaze lingered on her legs and he grinned at Jeff and Nora. "They have the best-looking staff in the city here. I'm convinced they have to include head shots with their job applications."

"So, what's the word, Hilton? What have you got planned for us tonight?" Jeff asked.

"A funk and soul band, an open mike downstairs, a little dancing," he answered, and paused. "I also invited Larry Stark. I called him up yesterday and told him to drop by if he had the time. He's here and I think we should go over there and chat him up a bit."

Jeff groaned. "It seems like I'm always on call. Love, I'll be just a few minutes." He squeezed Nora's hand before disappearing into the crowd.

Nora slid into the spot on the banquette that Hilton had vacated. She and Stephanie Thomas kissed on both cheeks and exchanged some idle fashion chitchat—who was in, who was on the way out, the shows Stephanie had done in Europe. The two women had met several times and Stephanie had appeared on a recent *Muse* cover. Hilton had been squiring Stephanie around town for a few months now. She was stunning, sweet and at least twelve years younger. Nora had almost exhausted her supply of gossip when an ethnically ambiguous man in rose-tinted shades interrupted their conversation and greeted Stephanie, alleging they had met before in Saint-Tropez.

Nora sipped her bubbly and tried not to feel abandoned. Whenever Jeff said "a few minutes" it could be an hour before he returned. Jeff and Hilton's professional and social lives were often indistinguishable. There were always people to meet, new acts to hear, artists to sign, egos to stroke. The nature of their business required that they be out and about, pursuing new opportunities or just making face time. It was all designed to demonstrate that Rum Records was still relevant, that Jeff and Hilton were still players in the game. Hilton was clearly the showman and relished his role as the flamboyant component of Rum Records. His exterior persona was fevered, spry and approachable, but he was no fool. He possessed a penetrating drive to succeed. Jeff was equally passionate, but provided the analytical, stabilizing force. He kept Hilton focused. Their respective roles had been carved out since the beginning and each man knew that he could not succeed without the other.

Jeff had altered the pattern of his life once he married Nora. They still enjoyed going to parties, restaurants and openings together, but realized the importance of creating a separate world of their own. Hilton often appeared in the city's gossip pages, usually in the company of a model at a trendy gathering.

Nora surveyed the crowd. Success had given Jeff and Hilton attention and access to the overlapping subsets of New York's social and professional environments. Celebrities, demicelebs and their trusty hangers-on blissfully inhabited the festive landscape that Hilton had created. Nora spotted Hilton and Jeff's friends from Harvard, Rum's best-selling acts along with up-and-coming performers, a few Knicks, models, flashy business personalities, actors and a photographer from the *Post*'s "Page Six." Some buttoned-up suits, probably lawyers and bankers, were trying to hit on the models. The crowd was very mixed— Black, White, Hispanic, Asian—Hilton's personal rainbow country.

Nora reflected on how closely intertwined she, Jeff and Hilton were. When she had first met Jeff, she understood implicitly that her ability to get along with Hilton would be a factor in their relationship. Luckily she and Hilton had been friendly from the outset. Nora loved him, much like a favorite cousin, and respected what he and Jeff had accomplished. She also felt protective of Hilton and was inclined to defend him against his critics, though few of Hilton's detractors would dare say anything to her. She was, after all, married to his best friend. But she had picked up on some jealousy, some bitterness about the way Hilton wore his ambition on his sleeve. She wondered how much success had changed Hilton and Jeff. Jeff seemed more stressed lately. The pressures of maintaining the integrity of an expanding business and Stark's impending offer weighed heavily on his mind. Hilton, on the other hand, was the consummate entertainment minimogul and harbored lofty aspirations for the future. Nora suspected that bigger would definitely be better for Hilton.

"You're so good. I don't know how you do it," Stephanie Thomas was saying, pulling Nora away from her thoughts.

Nora returned to reality in just enough time to see Stephanie's new friend amble off dejectedly. Stephanie must have set him straight, and quite possibly spoiled his evening.

"Hilton and Jeff are always networking. Hilton's never around when we go out together. Sometimes I think he just forgets about me, but you seem to handle it really well with Jeff," Stephanie continued.

"They're working, you know. It's all a part of what they have to do. It's not like a nine-to-five job. I've gotten used to it over the years," Nora replied. She wondered whom she was trying to convince more, herself or Stephanie.

"I guess, but sometimes it's too much. I'm getting really fed up and I'm going to say something to Hilton," Stephanie complained. "Just look at them over there. Do you think they're getting up anytime soon?"

Nora glanced towards the corner booth occupied by a man in a houndstooth blazer and polo-necked sweater. His brown hair was slicked back from his face and he drank from a glass tumbler. He was wedged in between two muscular men who looked more like bodyguards than business associates. Nora assumed that this was Lawrence Stark. Jeff and Hilton sat in chairs across the table from him. They were deep in conversation and nodded their heads from time to time.

Nora poured herself a second glass of champagne and selected a spring roll from a plate on the table. She munched and drank, filling her stomach while the bubbly swiftly went to her head.

"And all the girls that are always around him," said Stephanie. "There's always a bunch of groupies with Hilton. They see him as some kind of glamorous meal ticket. I can't compete with all of that female attention."

"Stephanie, you're a beautiful girl," Nora consoled, "and you have nothing to worry about. Remember, Hilton wanted you with him here tonight, not somebody else."

"It's me now, but it might be someone else next month," she whined. Stephanie had obviously drunk a little too much and was in a self-effacing mood.

"No, don't say that," Nora said. She, Stephanie and the bottle of Krug were a dangerous combination. Desperate for Jeff and Hilton's attention, they had turned into a couple of lushes.

"I love Hilton. There's a good heart beneath the surface."

"Yeah. He's a great guy," Nora agreed.

"Don't you ever get worried about Jeff?" Stephanie asked.

Nora hoped no one else at the table had heard Stephanie. The light-headed champagne buzz was hovering above her, floating determinedly, ready to make its final descent onto her consciousness. She selected her words carefully. "I'm confident that Jeff loves me and I feel secure in our relationship. Anyway, as a woman, it's important to have your own thing going on. Focus on your career and interests so you're not sitting at home wondering about your man all the time."

This seemed to perk Stephanie up a bit. "That's true. Did I tell you about the new tampon commercial I'm going to be in?"

Stephanie was thankfully moving on to less taxing subjects. Nora only half listened and redirected her attention to Jeff and Hilton. They were good-looking, educated, exciting men in an enviable position. Stephanie was young. Nora could understand her insecurity. She nursed her third glass of champagne and began to feel increasingly woozy as the thick, sweet smell of marijuana permeated the room. How had someone managed to light up a joint with the city's ban on smoking in restaurants? She never touched the stuff, but had always been susceptible to contact highs. Mentally, she was slowly going to a different place, to the time five years ago when she and Jeff had started dating. She had been living in Washington, D.C., then, working for a newspaper. Jeff lived in New York and set his sights on establishing Rum Records. The memories appeared at first like still frames, but slowly flowed into a coherent sequence.

During those first few months of Nora and Jeff's long-distance relationship they alternated cities. In the beginning, Jeff drove to D.C. on weekends to visit Nora, but she preferred to visit him in New York. She missed the vibrancy of the city, felt overworked and wanted to escape. She would take the inexpensive five-hour bus ride and stay with Jeff in the loft apartment that he shared with Hilton in the meatpacking district. Their place had been a mess—not dirty, but cluttered. Every corner was piled high with milk crates storing vinyl, tapes and CDs. Hilton's suitcases lined the hallway and Nora tripped over them almost every time. Jeff had a habit of spreading his papers out on the floor in different little stacks and the slightest sudden movement would send them flying. It was impossible to walk normally in that loft; they all had to tiptoe to maintain the chaotic balance. Only their fridge was startlingly bare, since Jeff and Hilton always ate out or ordered in. It couldn't have been easy having an extra body around those weekends, but Hilton was always a good sport.

Nora had arrived around ten one Friday night, weary and grubby from the journey. Jeff had been on her mind all week. She just wanted to take a shower and share those romantic moments with him that had become so essential to her sanity. Maybe tomorrow they could go to a museum or take a drive along the Hudson Valley. She rang the downstairs bell.

"Nora, is that you?" said a muffled voice.

"Yes, it's me," she answered, feeling instantly better once she heard Jeff's voice. He buzzed her in and she rode the elevator to the fourth floor. The apartment door was ajar and she walked in, setting her bag down and deliberately avoiding Hilton's brown suitcases.

She expected a warm welcome or a tender hug that would reassure her that all this back-and-forth was worth it. Instead she found Hilton in the kitchen, putting a slice of pizza in the microwave.

"Hi, Hilton. Where's Jeff? He just let me in."

Hilton smiled, scrunching up his face in an apologetic way. "That was me on the buzzer. Everyone sounds the same on those things. It's great to see you, but I have bad news." He saw her expression change to worry and quickly corrected himself. "It's not Jeff, but it's his grandfather. He had a heart attack and Jeff had to go to Boston to be with his family."

"How awful for them! How serious is it?"

"Pretty much touch and go. It's his mother's father and she's about ready to lose it, I hear. He's eighty-six. They're not optimistic."

"I should call him," Nora said.

Hilton checked the time. "He's still on the plane now. He wanted to call you, but everything was so rushed. You were already on your way here. . . ."

"Sure. I understand." She sighed. "I guess I made this trip in vain. I could probably catch a midnight bus back to D.C."

"You've got to be kidding. You're not going back to Port Authority at this time of night. I told Jeff I'd take care of you. Spend the night in his room and you can take an early bus back tomorrow."

Nora bit her lip. "The thought of getting back on that bus right now is definitely not appealing. But are you sure it's OK?"

"Positive."

"I don't want to mess up your plans. Do whatever you were going to do before. Don't worry about me."

Hilton took the finished pizza out of the microwave and set it on a plate. "Do you want this?" he offered Nora.

The pizza was probably a day old, but she was starving. "Thanks," she said, and smiled before nibbling into the crust.

He returned her smile. "I was just planning to go to a housewarming party. A friend of ours from college made a killing on Wall Street and just moved into a warehouse space in Tribeca. You're welcome to come along if you like."

"I'm a little tired and, well, I'd feel kind of guilty going out while Jeff's going through a rough time."

He nodded. "I know. But he knows there's nothing we can do from here. He told me to make sure you had fun."

Hilton was about Nora's height and her eyes were level with his. They were almost black with a mischievous glint. He smiled that infectious smile of his and she found herself saying yes.

Newly scrubbed and changed into jeans and high-heeled boots, Nora walked with Hilton from the far lower West Side even farther south to Tribeca. She always loved the pulse of the city on a Friday night. No one in Hilton's neighborhood seemed to notice the stench from the slaughterhouses or the trucks loading packaged meat for delivery. The bars and clubs were overflowing and dressed-up groups laughed and shouted. Cabs whizzed by. Dance music traveled from open windows. The atmosphere had a distinct I-can-sleep-in-tomorrow exuberance. Her mood had lightened considerably and she was glad she hadn't stayed secluded in the apartment.

During the walk, she and Hilton talked about the progress of the record company that he and Jeff had started. He spoke in the same enthusiastic tones as Jeff and entertained her with stories of wannabe artists. Nora realized that she had never been in a one-on-one situation with Hilton before. She really didn't know him that well, just that he was Jeff's sociable best friend. She was probably too love struck around Jeff to have noticed the potent charisma that Hilton radiated. A fact she was sure other women hadn't missed.

The party was in full gear once they arrived. The space was huge and industrial, but Hilton's friend had enriched it with hardwood floors and clean white walls to display a collection of bold contemporary art, the likes of which Nora had seen only in galleries or art history books. A Barbara Kruger, in particular, caught Nora's attention. Blocks of bold-faced type were superimposed on a photograph of an anguished woman: "PROTECT ME FROM WHAT I WANT," she begged.

Hilton introduced Nora to everyone as Jeff's girlfriend, which she didn't mind. He was attentive the whole evening, refilling her drink and making sure she didn't feel lost among the crowd. "Are you OK?" he'd ask her every half hour. She saw him work the room, laughing with guys, whispering in women's ears. She wondered inwardly what he said to these pretty young things, and rationalized her interest as rabid curiosity.

She told Hilton that he didn't have to babysit her all night and made conversation with a small group by the window. A friendly investment banker cornered her and steered their discussion to the stock market, of all things. Nora thought it a waste to be so serious in the middle of such a marvelous environment. The art was magnificent—Schnabels, a Basquiat, the Barbara Kruger that peered down and seemed to challenge her. The dense hot air had transformed the atmosphere. She noticed a man and woman caressing each other and saw another couple disappear into a room. An inexplicable sexual energy had been released and it was disorienting. At that second, she wanted to be the object of a careless flirtation. She wanted lightness and innuendo, the teasing glances and double-talk that others luxuriated in.

She heard the investment banker say her name. He had asked her a question.

What exactly had he said? She racked her brain for a standard response. "Well, as long as you can afford to sit on a stock for a while, then the market fluctuations aren't really that bad—" She didn't know what the hell she was saying and unexpectedly, Hilton appeared and seized her by the hand.

"Sorry, John. Nora has to come with me for a second!" he called out, and led her out to the dance floor.

John fired off such a look of annoyance and hostility at Hilton that they burst out laughing. Tears filled the corners of Nora's eyes. "What was that all about?"

"I thought I'd save you from that suspender-wearing, Gordon Gekko—"

"C'mon, he was nice," she protested. "Totally harmless."

"That's what you think. He was trying to lure you in with his knowledge. I know John—his game is totally off."

She gave him one of her big smiles. "I didn't think you were paying attention." *Now, why did I say that?*

They were dancing, a distance of no more than a foot between them. Hilton gazed at her intently. It was only for a few seconds, but made her feel very exposed.

"You know I was," Nora thought she heard him say, but she was too afraid to ask him to repeat it.

They stayed on the dance floor for quite a while, feeling the music change from bouncing beats to cozy grooves that seduced the senses. They swayed dangerously close to one another and when Hilton's hands closed around her waist and she felt his fingertip on the base of her spinal cord, a charge coursed through her body. The alcohol had made her deliciously confused. Could he see how tense she felt? Did he know that she didn't mind being this close to him? She followed his lead, patterned her body after his until they finally moved in unison. She experienced the pleasant stirrings that she reserved only for Jeff, and a very small voice inside her head told her to pull away. It was wrong to feel these physical emotions with another man, least of all Hilton. But the room was dark and smoky and she willed reason away. *We're just dancing,* Nora repeated to herself, but knew it was one of the most sensual experiences she'd ever had.

They were very loud and talkative during the cab ride back to the apartment. Nora knew it was an attempt to bring the evening back to its original course, cleansed of the forbidden sexual tension at the party. They staggered through the door laughing and Nora raided the kitchen cabinets and fridge, searching for a snack.

"You guys never have any food here," she complained. "I'm starving. I won't be able to sleep."

"I'll go and get something at the twenty-four-hour deli," Hilton said, and disappeared out the door.

She walked slowly to the living room couch, sank down and closed her eyes. She felt the room spinning through the darkness. She knew she was too giddy and had to calm herself. She'd been crafty in sending Hilton out again. She needed to regain her control and hoped the food he bought would sober her up.

He came back with slices of cantaloupe, a Sara Lee pound cake, a pint of vanilla Häagen-Dazs and two bottles of water. He arranged everything on the coffee table and sat down at the other end of the couch.

Nora bit ravenously into the cantaloupe and pretended to be too hungry to talk. Then she attacked the pound cake and washed it down with huge gulps of water. Hilton said nothing. He poked a spoon into the ice cream, eating it directly from the carton.

The silence suddenly made her very self-conscious. "Hilton," she said delicately, "thank you so much for looking after me tonight."

He turned to her, eyes strangely aware, reflecting a bewilderment that she recognized all too well. "My pleasure. I'm glad you had a nice time." After several seconds he added in a gentle voice, "You really can move."

Nora laughed nervously and answered, "So can you."

She had then looked directly into his eyes and couldn't exactly remember what happened next. Was it her face or Hilton's that leaned forward? It had been like a physical force, the simultaneous, instinctual tremor of desire drawing them to each other. They began kissing—not slow, tentative kisses, but greedy, lustful explorations. Mouths joined—his was cold and sweet—they feasted on each other, touching furiously, searching for the buttons and zippers that would free them from their clothes. Somehow they made it to Hilton's bed. Then collapsing onto the sheets, he kissed and kneaded her breasts, magically working his way down her body. She moaned and, in her haze, thought not of Jeff, only of her immense, wicked pleasure. When she finally opened herself to him, she cried out and completely surrendered, granting him permission to discover her again and again that night.

When Nora awoke the next morning, she knew immediately that something was terribly wrong. She looked at Hilton lying naked next to her in the depths of sleep, and panicked. What had she done? She extricated herself from the bed, hastily threw on her clothes, grabbed her bag and fled. At Port Authority, she paid for her fare back to D.C. with shaking hands. She settled into a window seat near the back of the bus, wanting to hide, fearing that what she had done was written all over her face. She shivered when she replayed her actions of the night before. What had she been thinking? With her boyfriend's best friend? It was too mortifying and vulgar for words. She wasn't someone who could behave like that without guilt. She knew that she had ruined her prospects with Jeff for good. Jeff could be the love of her life—trusting, decent, optimistic Jeff. How had she let it go so far with Hilton? Where had her unexpected attraction to Hilton come from? And his to her? Had it always been there below the surface, biding time, patiently waiting for the opportunity to come out? Most disturbing of all, Nora knew that she had enjoyed last night—all of it.

Hilton called her a few hours after she arrived in D.C.

"Hi," he said, his voice hoarse. "You left so quickly, I just wanted to make sure you got home OK."

"I got home fine," Nora told him, hoping her voice sounded normal. An uncomfortable silence followed.

"Look," they both started to say at the same time.

"Listen to me," Nora said firmly. "What happened last night was a mistake. It was all the alcohol and came completely out of nowhere. I'm not the kind of girl who . . . who . . . falls into bed with men so easily!"

"I know. I know. I'm the one who should be apologizing to you. We just got carried away, I guess." He paused and said, "Nora, I have to ask you something."

"Yes?" she whispered.

"How do you feel about Jeff? How do you see the two of you together?"

Nora sighed and dared to confess what she had been feeling for weeks, in spite of the messy last twenty-four hours. "I think I'm falling in love with him," she murmured, ashamed that she could love Jeff and still be so dangerously tempted by Hilton.

After what seemed like an eternity, but was probably no more than ten seconds, he spoke. "I think he feels the same way about you. There's no reason to ruin what the two of you have. Forget about last night. You can be sure that I'll never tell Jeff—for my sake and yours."

Relief swept over Nora. She had desperately wanted to hear those words. "Thank you," she choked out. "That would mean so much to me."

She didn't visit Jeff in New York for months after that. She knew that she couldn't be in the same room as Hilton, breathing the same air, laughing at his jokes, without thinking about their surreal night of passion. For a very long time, she looked at Jeff and saw only her deception with Hilton. Sometimes when Jeff touched her, she remembered that Hilton knew her the same way. And when she was alone and aroused, she wasn't always sure which man she wanted to soothe her loneliness away. Maybe she would have exorcised her guilt quicker if Hilton hadn't been such a big part of their lives.

Only when she and Jeff were married could Nora unburden her conscience and accept that her dirty secret was part of the past. Only then did she feel safe.

* * *

"I'm feeling dizzy," Nora announced to Stephanie as she took off her stole. "I need to move around and get my blood flowing." She walked to the entranceway, made a sharp turn at the door and went down the stairs. The restaurant had opened its lower level especially for Hilton. When she was in college it had been a club called Undochine. She remembered a stuffy atmosphere with a thumping bass and unexpected visits from the New York City Fire Department.

The lower level was hot, noisy and packed. The crowd was younger; students, artists and Rum interns congregated in front of the stage where a young MC was giving shout-outs to his crew, his baby's mama and anyone else he had met along the way. It wasn't about business down here; it was about having a good time. Nora wiped the tiny beads of sweat that had begun to form around her face. She eased her way to a spot against the wall. The DJ resumed spinning and after two tracks, an energetic reveler bounced his way in her direction.

"You're Mrs. Montgomery, right?" he screamed.

"What?" Nora shouted. She shrugged and pointed to her ears. "I can't hear you."

He yelled louder. "You're Jeff's wife. I recognize your picture from the one he keeps in his office. I'm Brian Harris. I work as an intern for Rum," he said, extending his hand.

"Nice to meet you, Brian." Nora smiled and returned his handshake. "Are you having a good time tonight?"

"This party is da-bomb!" he exclaimed. "Those guys always do it right. I love working for Jeff."

"I'll tell him. I'm sure he'll be happy to hear that."

"I'm learning a lot and soon—the sky's the limit." He offered her his hand again. "You shouldn't be standing by yourself. C'mon, let's dance."

Nora followed Brian's lead, an amused smile on her face. He couldn't have been older than nineteen. He was tall and thin and dressed in the requisite baggies and retro Air Jordans that she hadn't seen since junior high. His young face had an endearing quality and Nora liked the bold way he had introduced himself to his boss's wife. Brian executed a series of dance steps that didn't require the assistance of a partner. He jumped and spun around, taking over the dance floor without a second thought. Nora tried hard not to laugh at her own efforts to keep up.

After a long set of classic Prince, Brian checked his watch and stopped abruptly. "We gotta go."

"Why?" Nora asked breathlessly.

"It's almost midnight and they're going to be cutting Hilton's cake soon. We gotta leave now if we want to get a good spot," he explained.

"Oh. Of course, let's go."

They reached the stairs just as a five-layer chocolate cake was being wheeled out on a trolley. The crowd fell into enthusiastic applause and Stevie Wonder's "Happy Birthday to You" pumped from the loudspeakers.

Hilton, clearly in his element, took to the stage and picked up the microphone. "This has undoubtedly been my best birthday ever. I want to thank all of you for coming and helping me celebrate. I love you all—the Rum crew; my friends; my partner, Jeff; his terrific wife, Nora; and my girl, Stephanie. There's still a lot more fun to be had this evening. Enjoy the cake and champagne and let's *get it on*!"

Everyone cheered. Nora saw Stephanie beaming and knew that the pretty model would go home a happy woman tonight. A line formed around the cake, but Nora stood at the tail end. She soon felt familiar arms around her waist.

"There you are. Where have you been? I've been looking all over for you," Jeff murmured in her ear.

Nora resisted the urge to remind him that he had disappeared with Larry Stark for over an hour. "I'm here, honey. How's it going?" she asked.

"Great," he said, turning Nora around so that they faced each other. His voice was husky and his dark eyes heavy. "I'm here with my favorite person. I love you so much. You understand me. In the middle of this crazy crowd, I love knowing that I have you to come back to." His eyes searched hers. "Right?"

Those words gave her such a sense of completeness and Nora was overcome with love for the man in front of her.

"Always," she responded, giving Jeff a long kiss and tight embrace. This was something that Stephanie Thomas would hopefully understand one day. *They do need us.*

* * *

The following morning, Nora awoke to the sensation of cymbals clanging in her head. She shifted her position, threw the pillow over her face and pulled up the comforter, but it was useless. Nothing could make her champagne headache go away. Jeff, on the other hand, was in an impenetrable sleep. His bare torso was only half covered and she impulsively tickled his chest. No response. She glanced at the digital clock. One p.m. Feeling queasy, she got out of bed. She took two aspirin and ordered brunch for them both from the diner on Second Avenue. An omelet, fries and a chocolate milk shake should rejuvenate her. A hangover obliterated any thoughts of a sensible diet.

She ate, but couldn't shake the restlessness that tugged at her. She sifted through the bulging *Times,* straightened up the apartment and made a to-do list for the coming week. However, she kept getting distracted by the bright sunlight that streamed into the living room, and finally stuck her arm outside the window. It was her favorite type of fall day, mild and fresh, reminiscent of the first day of school and Halloween.

She left a note for Jeff on her pillow.

I've gone for a walk and will be back in a couple of hours. There's food from the diner in the fridge. N.

The streets were alive with families and couples enjoying the weather. The neighborhood Italian restaurant had set up tables outside and provided their patrons with wool blankets. A line had already formed around the movie theater on Sixty-fourth Street. Shielded behind her sunglasses, Nora shook her head in amazement. Everyone looked like they had been up since nine in the morning. She walked across Seventy-second Street to Madison Avenue. Always chic and opulent, Madison had replaced Fifth Avenue as the mecca for exclusive, expensive shopping. High-end designer shops, specialty boutiques and cafés covered the blocks. Nora walked at a steady pace, stopping once in a while to admire a window display. She kept an interested eye on the individual styles of the people walking up and down the blocks. They were always her best source of inspiration for *Muse.*

Nora started to feel tired at Eighty-sixth Street, but didn't want to go home just yet. She saw the northbound M4 bus approaching and decided to hop on. As a student, she had loved riding the bus. Not pressed for time, her face glued to the window, she had watched the city's cornucopia of images float by. It was a remnant of her shy youth, the way she didn't mind being by herself, observing the world from her private perch. Jeff could never understand how she could walk for blocks around the city without a specific purpose. The few times she had included him on one of these excursions, he had tried unsuccessfully to mask his impatience. Nora had reasoned that maybe you couldn't share everything in a marriage.

The bus continued on past Ninety-sixth Street, the unofficial line of demarcation. The contours of the city changed abruptly. Buildings were more worn, accents more mixed, skin tones darker. Here were two layers of the city that lived side by side but rarely ever met. The condition of the northern parts of the city was a complicated story of economic hardship, social neglect and racial misunderstanding. To Nora, it looked as though the city had simply turned its bureaucratic head away and chosen to ignore the situation.

The bus turned left on 110th Street. She remembered that the M4 didn't go up Madison Avenue, but instead completed its voyage on the West Side, on Broadway. She could get off near Columbia and transfer. Or she could stay until 145th Street and walk the short distance to the town house. She was suddenly filled with a need to see it again, to understand why Jeff was so taken by it.

The bus stopped near Amsterdam Avenue, a wide boulevard dotted with bodegas, storefront law offices, variety shops and video stores. Restaurants and beauty salons catered to almost every ethnic group. Voices called out to each other above the beats of merengue music and the shrill of honking horns.

As Nora walked, she heard a sidewalk preacher proselytizing through a megaphone. "Come to Jesus," he cried out. "Come to Jesus. Be careful crossing the street. I don't want you to get hit by a car without making a decision."

She continued to Convent Avenue, with its picturesque town houses and tree-shaded entranceways. The street was quiet and neat. She saw well-dressed men, women and children who she guessed were returning home from Sunday services. Several of them nodded politely in her direction. She noticed a yellow house, its Federal style seemingly out of place with the neighborhood's overall design. Nora read the sign in front. It was Hamilton Grange, which had been the summer home of American revolutionary and politician Alexander Hamilton from 1802 to 1804. She concluded that this was how the section came to be called Hamilton Heights.

Nora made her way to Hamilton Terrace, reflecting on the feelings that being in Harlem gave her. She was walking through history—the history of America, the ascent of New York and, closest to her, the struggle and progress of Blacks.

Night had already fallen when Jeff had taken her to Hamilton Terrace that first time, so she had never seen the neighborhood. In the daylight, she felt as though she had stepped back in time. A succession of dignified town houses lined the path, and the circular street pattern made it a protected enclave. Nora searched for number 35. Against the shadow of the setting sun, the town house stood graceful and inviting. Its imposing limestone facade exuded security and tradition. Wide windows led to the light-filled rooms where Nora imagined families had once sat down for dinner and children played. The town house undoubtedly held many stories, but as Nora considered its empty shell, she knew that she and Jeff could create new memories. He was right. They did need to establish a foothold, to find an anchor in a city that seemed like a blur most of the time. They could be happy here.

It was early evening when Nora returned home. The apartment was dark except for the light of the television set. Jeff was sprawled out on the couch, watching a football game.

"Hi. I'd ask you how you are, but your expression says it all," Nora teased good-naturedly. She hung her leather jacket in the closet and walked to the living room.

"I guess I wasn't such good company today," Jeff said. "I must be getting old. It'll probably be Tuesday before I feel better. Where have you been?"

"Oh, just walking around a bit. I actually went to our house again."

Jeff looked puzzled. "Our house?"

"The town house, silly. I don't know about your short-term memory these days. . . ."

"I'm having delayed reactions. So? What do you think?"

"I think," Nora began, "that we should go for it! It pulled me in when I saw it today. I remembered what you said about picturing us living in it. I did too. And Hamilton Terrace is lovely. I can't believe such old-fashioned charm exists in the city."

Jeff jumped from the couch and hugged her. "I'm so glad! I've been hoping you'd feel this way. You won't regret it. I promise."

"Neither will you. We'll fill the house with kids and good food. We'll get old there and sit on the steps reminiscing about the good ol' days. We'll . . ." Her voice trailed as Jeff put a finger to her lips.

"Did I tell you how much I love you today?" he asked.

"No. Too hungover."

"Well, I do and can't wait for the future."

CHAPTER 5

S purred on by their enthusiasm for the town house, Jeff and Nora organized the closing and move within six weeks. She now stood in her empty East Side living room and watched the crew from the moving company pack up and carry out the last of their possessions. Jeff had gone ahead to open up the town house and she thought of how the last ten years of her life had been compressed into those cardboard boxes: Haitian and African masks; a collection of black-and-white photographs; a treasured first edition of *Invisible Man;* an antique Louis Vuitton trunk she had bought at a Paris flea market. Every one of those objects held so much significance, but once they were packed away she began to feel less attached to them.

Although Nora was exhausted from all the cleaning and packing, she was incredibly excited about what awaited them on Hamilton Terrace. After she had shown her old college roommates, Erica and Dahlia, the town house, they had spent a hectic weekend scouring many of the city's antique shops and flea markets in search of the eclectic pieces that would give the house the modern and traditional mix Nora was aiming for. They had gone particularly crazy at the Twenty-sixth Street Flea Market.

"Contrary to our college days, now you're moving uptown in style," Erica had joked as she stopped at a table filled with ceramic animals, snow globes and other kitschy knickknacks.

"Depends if your definition of stylish is that glazed Buddha over there," Dahlia interjected, pointing.

"Hey, if Jeff convinced me to keep those futuristic leather cubes, I can take the Buddha home. Maybe it'll bring me luck," Nora said. "You guys should move uptown too. Then it would be just like old times."

"I'm lovin' Brooklyn, but will gladly come and visit," said Dahlia.

She and Erica had been roommates on and off for several years after college, but she had bought her own apartment in Clinton Hill last year and it was her pride and joy. She was still single and a successful advertising account executive.

"I guess this means that I'm the only renter in the bunch," lamented Erica. Her studio on Mott Street could barely contain her growing art collection, but luckily her job as an appraiser for a top auction house in the city often kept her on the road.

"You can take my mortgage payments if that'll make you feel better," offered Dahlia.

Erica and Dahlia had helped Nora weed through the enormous array of objects for sale and among her best finds was a gently scuffed Mies van der Rohe Barcelona chair. She also couldn't resist the bronze Buddha. As she bade her girlfriends good-bye, Erica hugged her tightly and said, "I really have a good feeling about your new place. Just don't build an ivory tower around yourselves. Go out there and get involved."

Those words had stuck. Erica saw their move as a statement, a declaration that she and Jeff were investing in their own future as well as Harlem's. Nora had been amazed by the variety of unsolicited opinions she'd received when she'd announced that she and Jeff were moving to Harlem. Julian Cortès, *Muse*'s creative director and Nora's dearest friend at work, had naturally seen the emergence of a new trend and wanted to do a layout on Hamilton Terrace. Nora stopped him from getting carried away, as she imagined the displeasure on her new neighbors' faces if they saw photographers and models parading around the block. Her parents, on the other hand, had expressed surprise. "We left uptown thirty years ago," her mother had said. "It seems strange that you would want to move back there. Especially since you could get a great house in Westbury for your money." Nora had laughed because they would have had to take her back to the suburbs kicking and screaming.

Once the moving crew finished up, Nora took one more look around the apartment and then closed the door for the last time. She gave back the key to her favorite doorman, Luis, along with a thank-you note and a sizable tip for all his help throughout the years. She would miss his kind ways, but was otherwise leaving the Piedmont with no regrets.

A little bit of her excitement wore off after the boxes and furniture had been delivered to Hamilton Terrace. She lifted a box labeled "Kitchen Plates" and groaned.

"I'm not looking forward to this. I don't know which is worse—packing or unpacking."

"Oh, we can wait a little longer," Jeff coaxed. "Let's go and explore our new house."

"Are you procrastinating again?" she teased. "We went through everything during the walk-through."

"But now it's really ours. C'mon. We can take a little break."

Nora didn't need further convincing and followed Jeff to the kitchen.

He opened the faucet taps and said, "Water looks good. It's the right shade of *clear*."

She giggled and he slid open the door that led to the dining room.

"Our table's a little small, but"—he pulled her to him and started to dance—"maybe we can turn this room into a ballroom instead."

When they entered the garden, Nora grabbed a handful of newly fallen leaves, pressed them to her face and inhaled the rich earthy scent. *Life,* she thought, *they smell of life.* They moved on to the second floor and at the top of the stairs, Jeff suddenly grabbed Nora and scooped her into his arms. His grip was tight and she wrapped her arms around his neck, fascinated that their bodies were a perfect fit and that his strength never made her feel too heavy.

"What are you doing?" she asked.

"I'm carrying you over to our new bedroom," he said, stepping dramatically over the threshold.

He deposited her gently on her feet and Nora caught her breath. Jeff had lit pillar candles and placed them along the window ledges. A quilted down comforter, blankets and several oversized pillows were arranged in front of the fireplace, where a fire burned. Their empty bedroom shimmered with light and warmth, suffused in romance and otherworldliness.

"You're so sweet," Nora whispered, her eyes welling up. "How did you do this?"

"I got one of the movers on my side," answered Jeff mischievously.

She sniffled. "It's beautiful."

"This is a happy moment. I didn't mean for you to start crying."

"I know. This is just a bit emotional for me. The past, present and future all rolled into one."

Jeff nodded understandingly. "I have something else that'll cheer you up." He reached for a basket behind the door. "Pat Wallace sent this ahead as a housewarming gift."

"How nice of her!" exclaimed Nora as she untied the bow on the transparent paper covering rich cheeses, water wafers, olives, white pears, and a bottle of Veuve Clicquot. "I think Pat is a woman after my own heart."

They christened their new house with the champagne and sampled the cheeses and fruit until they couldn't tuck into one more bite. Content, Nora smiled languorously and lightly caressed Jeff's arm, her fingers trailing down to the inside of his wrist. It was her favorite spot; his skin was so soft and she could make out the faint outline of his veins. He glided his free hand through her hair, lightly massaging her head— provoking utter relaxation, allowing her to focus only on his touch and how he could isolate the most sensual parts of her body. She moaned softly, and still holding on to the back of her head, he brought his face down to meet her lips. They kissed endlessly, each drowning in the power of their mouths, at once innocent and erotic.

Jeff shifted position and turned Nora around so that she lay beneath him. He unbuttoned her shirt and skillfully undid the front clasp of her bra. While he was still kissing her, his hand probed the soft flesh of her breasts, squeezing and tracing her nipples until they were firm and she burned. He moved his mouth to her right breast, nibbling wildly at the small hard peak, and she shivered. He palmed her stomach and traveled lower, stopped briefly at the elastic of her panties and pulled them down with her leggings. He caressed her mound of dark hair, rubbing continuously, teasing her, waiting until she writhed with anticipation, then inserted his fingers to meet her supple moistness. She placed her hand on top of his, guiding him deeper, fuller. She was intoxicated, thinking of nothing and feeling everything.

She wanted only the merest distance to separate them and slipped her hands underneath his sweater, dragging it up his body and over his head. She groped for the buttons on his jeans, pushed them down his legs and felt his stiffness against her thigh. The intensity of his erection excited her and she touched him, rhythmically moving up and down while he swelled in her hands. He buried his face in her neck, stifling a cry. She parted her legs and guided him inside, experiencing an extraordinary shot of pleasure as she stretched to fit him. He stirred inside her, pushing forward—slowly at first—then with greater insistence. She stroked the back of his neck, his shoulders, his hips—anywhere her hands could reach. She wanted to mold his body to hers. She squeezed his behind and his breathing became uneven. He pressed a nipple with his fingers, knowing she was sensitive there, knowing it would make her hot. She moaned, arched her back and moved her hips with his. Eyes closed, Nora felt possessed, thought the release would overpower her, and saw only a brilliant explosion when the spasms finally rocked her body. After a final thrust, Jeff stayed frozen inside her womb, gasping as his body trembled from spent emotion.

They uncoupled reluctantly when he softened, but wrapped the blankets around their sticky bodies and fell asleep.

A surprise awaited Nora the next morning, a Saturday, as she carried a trash bag filled with Bubble Wrap out her front door. A white box and card sat on her doorstep. Curious, she put down the garbage and picked it up. The attached card read in nice, even script:

Welcome to the neighborhood. We look forward to meeting you.
Sincerely, Anna and Webster Parekh, 33 Hamilton Terrace.

Nora opened the box and was touched to find a cake covered with creamy white frosting. Impulsively, she walked next door to number 33 and knocked on the Parekhs' door. An impish woman with a sunny smile in purple corduroy jeans and clogs answered. Her hair was a halo of frizzy curls tamed in the front by a pair of small pink rhinestone barrettes.

Nora returned her friendly expression. "Hello. I'm Nora Montgomery. Thank you so much for the cake. That was so nice of you."

"My pleasure. I only hope you like carrot cake," she said.

"It's actually my favorite," Nora told her warmly.

"Please come in. I'd like to introduce you to my husband. Webster," she called out to a figure sitting behind a desk in their study, "this is Nora Montgomery. She and her husband just moved into the old Booth house next door."

"Hello, hello," greeted a bespectacled middle-aged man, and he stood up. His hair was completely gray and he resembled a laid-back academic in khakis with a tiny silver hoop earring in his left ear. "It's about time that house was sold. It's too beautiful to stand empty. The owner was so picky."

Nora laughed. "Yes, he was quite a character when we met him at the closing." She paused. "I'd like to invite the both of you over for coffee and some of the cake. Do you have time this morning?"

"I'd love to," Anna answered quickly.

Webster declined. "Unfortunately, I have to finish grading some papers. But trust me," he assured Nora, "you'll love Anna's cake. I keep telling her she should go into business for herself, sort of like a Mrs. Fields."

Once outside, Nora said to Anna, "We're in a similar situation. My husband, Jeff, also went into the office to work this morning."

Anna chuckled sympathetically. "I thought college professors were supposed to have a better schedule. Although sometimes I think that Webster uses his job as an excuse not to do some of the real work around the house—like changing the bathroom sink or waxing the floors."

"Does Webster teach at City College?"

Anna nodded. "Political science. We met at school."

"Are you a professor as well?"

"No. I was actually one of his grad students."

"Oh, my!" Nora exclaimed.

Anna smiled conspiratorially. "We've lived here for about five years. Let me tell you, it's an interesting neighborhood. Full of vivid personalities."

Nora warmed up to the subject. "Sounds fascinating. You'll have to tell me more."

"Why don't we sit out on your doorstep and have the coffee and cake there?" Anna suggested. "Then I can fill you in on our wonderful cast of characters."

The air was cold, but it was a clear day. Nora took a thermos of Arabian Mocha Java and two mugs down to her stoop. Anna had an unassuming air, they were about the same age, and Nora found her very easy to talk to. Anna was originally from Rhode Island, and after stints with a political consulting firm ("I had to dish out so much BS!"), retail ("I hated working weekends") and running her own mail-order business ("The less said about that, the better!"), she had finally found her niche as a freelance travel photographer ("There *are* still some unspoiled places left in the world").

"Oh, look—that's Grace Wheeler," Anna said, pointing to the old woman who had opened her front door to retrieve the mail. "She's about seventy years old and has lived here forever. She considers herself the 'grande dame' of the block. She's always investigating people who try to move in, making sure the neighborhood stays to her liking. She's extremely nosy."

Nora wrapped her hands around the steaming cup of coffee and furrowed her brows. "Really? I wonder if she said anything about us."

"She probably gave old man Booth an earful! She sure wasn't happy when Webster and I moved in, given the age difference between us." Anna laughed. "I think it's fun to shock her! The funny thing, though, is that while she's passing judgment on everybody else, she's not taking care of her own business. Her youngest son, Carl, was in the army and fought in the Gulf. He can disappear for days at a time and then just come back as though nothing happened. I think he suffers from post-traumatic stress disorder, but Mrs. Wheeler's too proud—or too ashamed—to get him any help."

"How sad," said Nora. She squinted and motioned to the blond woman herding two caramel-colored kids into a station wagon. "Who's that?"

"That's Ursula Jones, one-half of the block's interracial couple. She's from Germany and came to Harlem on a walking tour. She fell in love with the place, rented an apartment here when she moved to New York and married the neighborhood doctor."

"Mmmm . . . interesting."

"Sometimes I think she's blacker than you or me!"

Nora grinned. "I know the type."

The two women continued talking for another two hours and nearly polished off the cake. When Nora returned to her unpacking, she felt that maybe she had made a new friend.

CHAPTER 6

Hilton held the phone to his ear and stretched out his legs on the glass coffee table in his apartment.

"Listen, don't worry about it. The video is great. I only think that we need to make a couple of changes. . . . Yes, your cousins can still be in the video, but they need to do something. They can't just stand there and stare into the camera. . . . I loved what you wore, but maybe there was just a tad too much leather. I'll have Vanessa, the stylist, work on a new look with you." He listened patiently to the concerns of Rum's newest artist, one-half of a rap duo tagged Nickel 'n' Dime, who wanted to make considerably more than that in the music game. "The important thing here is that the song is great. Everything else will fall into place. I promise."

Hilton hung up and moved his neck in a circular motion to get rid of the tight knots. It took so much patience and willpower for him to keep it all together. He had to soothe the temperamental or shy artists who needed constant attention. Not to mention the arrogant stars who felt that one hit gave them the right to bark their way around town. It was all such a delicate balancing act, but he still loved it, now more than ever. Maybe they were on the cusp of something big with NRG, but one thing troubled him. He still hadn't heard from Larry Stark since his birthday party over a month ago. He assumed Stark was interested, but his inaction made Hilton nervous. Since their last conversation, Hilton had grown receptive to the idea of joining up with NRG. He saw it as his best chance to finally emerge as a real player in the high-stakes entertainment world. That he could even contemplate such a possibility gave him an incredible rush. He had come up against many brick walls, but nothing had stopped him.

* * *

Hilton couldn't live without music. It framed his whole existence, filling in when he was lonely, inarticulate, festive or romantic. His earliest memories were of his mother playing Motown tunes when he was a child growing up in Long Beach, California. Sally Frears had colored his life with love and music to compensate for the abandonment of his father. When Hilton was ten, Sally explained in full the circumstances of his birth. Hilton's father, Jacob—a man she called only by his first name—had been a first-shift supervisor at the aerospace factory where she worked as a receptionist. Sally and Jacob had dated and when she became pregnant, he urged her to terminate the pregnancy. When Sally refused, Jacob angrily stated that he would not play a role in raising the child. She broke off their relationship, quit her job and moved in with her mother, Henrietta. She never contacted Jacob again. She wanted nothing to do with a man who didn't want their baby.

When Hilton was born, Henrietta cared for him while Sally worked at her new job as an office assistant for a consumer products company. Her days were long, but she rushed home to bathe Hilton, read him stories and sing songs by the Supremes or the Four Tops until he fell asleep. As Hilton learned to walk, he was also instinctively able to move his small hips to the music. Sunday night dinners were more entertaining with little Hilton sashaying and bobbing up and down the linoleum floor. Sally and Grandma Henrietta laughed and clapped until their sides hurt.

Hilton would say that he wanted to be exactly like Stevie Wonder or the Jackson 5, but Sally told him that the surest avenue to success was a good education. Hilton was born with a quick mind and a sharp wit. He attended public schools and tested in the top fifth percentile, proving to Sally that he was gifted and could go far with the proper guidance. But Hilton enjoyed being in the center of a group more than in a classroom. He was popular on the playground and made others laugh whenever he told a story, spicing his tales with vivid language and human sound effects.

"I have to push him," Hilton overheard Sally say to Henrietta one evening. "Otherwise he'd do only the bare minimum and nothing more. He reminds me of his father sometimes—that same lazy grin and he gets his way. Hilton can't get through life on charm alone."

Sally's demands for good grades prevented Hilton from becoming the carefree class clown. She checked his homework every night and helped him study before an exam. They'd sit at the kitchen table doing long division and spelling words. When he did well, she rewarded him with a new record or a piece of stereo equipment. By the time he was thirteen years old, Hilton began to feel constrained by the academic stress his mother forced upon him.

"Mom, you're working me too hard!" he complained. "Can't I hang out with Kyle and Eddie from the neighborhood?"

"Just saying their names is enough to keep you locked up in the house! Those boys are up to no good. I see trouble in their eyes," said Sally.

Hilton was exhausted when he ran into Eddie and Kyle that morning. He'd been up late completing an assignment about volcanoes and dragged his way to school, carrying the cardboard project in his hands and a knapsack full of books on his back. Eddie and Kyle waited by the corner store, chewing gum and throwing pebbles.

"What'cha got there?" Eddie asked.

The coarse high-pitched voice broke into Hilton's daze, but he didn't reply quickly enough before Eddie and Kyle started badgering him.

"You're such a good boy, Hilton," Kyle taunted. "Always doin' what your mama tells you."

"You guys don't know jack about that," Hilton retorted, in a tone he hoped was tough and dismissive. He didn't have the energy for a fight.

Eddie and Kyle stared at him for a moment, not sure whether to continue their bullying or to leave him alone. Finally, it was Kyle who decided.

"I bet you don't have the balls to skip school today and hang out with us. You ain't smooth enough to just go with the flow," Kyle said.

"Fuck school," Eddie dared. "We could give you a real education out here!"

This was the episode that Hilton had always feared—his coolness being called into question. One thing was for certain: He didn't feel cool at that moment. The rules at home and the weight of his mother's expectations were turning him into a sucker. He desperately wanted to prove to Eddie and Kyle that he was just "one of the boys." His heart pounded and his stomach fluttered with nervousness. It was an easy choice, really. Somewhere in his subconscious he had been waiting for an excuse to do the wrong thing.

"Yo, I can hang with y'all. What'cha got in mind?" Hilton smiled as he spoke the words.

Eddie and Kyle looked at each other, grinned and patted Hilton energetically on his shoulders.

"First thing you gotta do," Kyle instructed, "is dump that project."

Hilton threw the amateurish volcano he'd been up half the night finishing into the nearest trash can.

The day started out well for Hilton. They played basketball with some guys who were friends with Kyle's older brother. Basketball was something Hilton was allowed to do only on weekends, and dribbling and passing in the middle of the morning on a school day filled him with strength and abandon. The older guys gave him pointers on blocking and it never occurred to Hilton to wonder why these able-bodied men weren't working or studying. He was enjoying his freedom and didn't feel much guilt. He wasn't thinking about tomorrow, what he would say to his teachers or how he would evade his mother's questions.

Eddie and Kyle didn't have fathers either, but each had a couple of half-siblings, and their mothers seemed to have new boyfriends all the time. Hilton had never seen Sally bring a man home. He couldn't even visualize her with a boyfriend.

"What do you do for fun besides study all the time?" asked Eddie.

"I listen to music," answered Hilton, and he told them about the new speakers his mother had gotten him for his birthday. Eddie and Kyle were impressed and Hilton felt that he had gained some street cred. His mother was wrong. Eddie and Kyle were no different from him.

Eddie grew fidgety and suggested they grab some food from the corner store. The boys walked, following the path of unkempt, deserted bungalows. For fun, they looked in through the windows and saw dilapidated walls and rotting floors. The second-to-last house they approached matched the others, but inside was a small white refrigerator, a television set, a lumpy plaid couch and a green Formica coffee table that had definitely seen better days.

"Look in here," Kyle said. "There's a TV and refrigerator. Nobody's here but us. I say we go in and investigate."

Eddie agreed immediately. Hilton was hesitant, but decided that the chances of getting caught out in a vacant lot in a bungalow that nobody cared about were very slim. The boys climbed through the window, all feeling the headiness of a forbidden adventure.

Eddie walked around the small room as though he had the right to be there. He opened the refrigerator—it reeked of garlic and one of the shelves had caved in—and reached for a bottle standing on the side shelf.

"Check it out," he said, waving the forty-ounce bottle of Colt 45 in front of Kyle and Hilton. "There's even some brew. Fellas, I think we can make ourselves pret-ty com-fort-able here!" He unscrewed the cap with the small can opener he kept on his key chain, took a sip and passed the bottle around to Kyle and Hilton. Hilton thought that the beer smelled like diesel fuel and tasted just as bad.

"Have some more," Eddie urged.

Hilton took another sip, the beer went down his throat and then up again, and he burped. Eddie and Kyle started cracking up and the three of them passed the beer around until the bottle was empty. Hilton was feeling nauseated and worry began to set in. He cupped his hands and blew into them. His breath stank! How could he hide that from his mother? Eddie was hyper, exploring the room and jumping on the dirty couch. Kyle turned on the TV set and fumbled with the antennae in search of a clear picture. Hilton stood in a corner. He just wanted to get out of there. The novelty of being bad had worn off.

He was figuring out what he would say to Kyle and Eddie when he saw a man standing outside in front of the window, his beady eyes fixated on the scene inside the bungalow. "Yo!" Hilton shouted. "Someone's coming!"

The only escape routes were out the door or through the window. The man guarded the door and could easily grab them. They wouldn't have time to make a run for it. They were cornered.

Suddenly, the door swung open and a deep voice bellowed, "What the hell are you kids doing in my house?" The man was huge, like an ex–football player, with a thick neck and a high uneven Afro. His brown velour warm-up jacket strained to meet the demands of his massive bulk. With one swoop of his large hands, he threw Eddie off the couch. Kyle and Hilton stared at him in terrified silence.

"Hey, man," Eddie told him as he caught his breath. "We ain't done nothin'. It look like nobody was livin' up in here."

"I think that when y'all saw my brew and workin' television, was obvious somebody was livin' up in here! Y'all are trespassin' on private property. *My* property. I'm callin' the cops." He reached for the rotary phone that sat on the Formica table.

"Sir—wait!" Hilton pleaded. "We're sorry if we've caused any damage, but *please* let us go. We didn't mean any harm. We were just fooling around. We'll just leave and you won't have to call the cops."

The man stared witheringly at Hilton. "Y'all think it's that easy, huh? You gotta learn your lesson. Sit your asses down until the cops come. Y'all ain't gettin' away with this."

Hilton, Eddie and Kyle sat and waited. They began to sweat. Hilton thought he heard silent cries coming from Eddie. Hilton didn't know what frightened him more—the cops or what his mother would say. Two cops came, looked at all three of them on the sofa and shook their heads.

"They just keep getting younger and younger," one of them said, and Hilton wanted to crawl into a hole. The police transported the boys to the station in a patrol car. In television shows, the patrol cars looked so cool and intimidating. Hilton had always wondered what it would be like to ride in one, but now, sitting behind the metal grille on the criminal's side, he felt pathetic. At the station, the boys were asked to provide the telephone numbers of their adult guardians. For a minute, Hilton considered giving the policemen his grandmother's number, weighing the severity of her reaction against his mother's. But there was no way he could hide this from Sally. He wrote down Sally's work number and the cop broke the news to her that Hilton had been arrested for trespassing.

Hilton could surmise Sally's reaction from the police officer's responses.

"Yes, I'm sure it's Hilton Frears," the cop said. "His date of birth is ten seventeen seventy." Pause. "Well, he definitely wasn't in school."

Pause. "Does your son know Eddie Russell and Kyle Torrell?" Pause. "Hello? Mrs. Frears, are you still there?" Pause. "He's at the station house. You can come down here and see him." Click.

Sally arrived at the station frantic and furious. The man with the high Afro wanted to charge the boys with breaking and entering. They were charged as juveniles but, if sentenced, would have to spend time in a detention center. Sally looked sick. Hilton was released into her custody and the silence between them as they rode home was more agonizing than anything he could ever have envisioned. He wanted to hug her, to hear her voice nag him about school. *Anything* to cut through the deep stillness.

"Why?" Sally asked Hilton when they got home. His grandmother sat in the kitchen, sadness and worry on her face. "Why did you feel the need to do this? You should have gone to school like I expected you to. I told you not to hang out with Eddie and Kyle. They're nothing but trouble! Do you understand how this will ruin your future? Your life is over before it ever really began."

Would his mother understand his intense need to be part of the crowd? To break away from the bounds of always following her rules? He decided to give it a try.

"They were teasing me," he began, "calling me a 'mama's boy.' I wanted to be like them for a while. Free and tough without worrying about what you would say or what I was supposed to do."

Sally's face contorted and she let out a sharp laugh. "Do you hear that, Mama?" she asked Henrietta. "Hilton wanted to be just as shiftless as Kyle and Eddie, instead of following the rules of this house. The rules here are nothing compared to what you'll find at the detention center. There you'll be begging for your mama." She turned around and started speaking again, more to herself than to the others. "All your life I've fought to give you the best I could. It wasn't easy, but I was proud of what I'd done and where you were headed. Is this the thanks I get? I struggled to give birth to you, sacrificed to give you the best I could, and you rejected everything I've ever taught you in a second. I don't know if I can take this. This is worse than when your father denied you!"

Hilton was scared and the torrent of tears he had been suppressing finally gushed out. He went over to Sally, hugged her and tried to reassure her. "Mama, I'll still make you proud. Please don't be sad. I am so sorry about this. I was stupid. I don't know what I was thinking. I love you! I love you!" he cried again and again.

Henrietta, who had been watching the two of them, put her arms around Hilton and said in a calm tone of voice, "OK. I know this is difficult, but we have to figure out what we need to do. We should hire a good lawyer and try to get the charge reduced. Those guys always know how to work the system. You're a good boy, Hilton. We'll just have to prove that to the police."

Sally and Henrietta pooled their modest savings together and hired a lawyer who specialized in juvenile offenses. He built his case around Hilton's exemplary past history, which included good grades and no previous encounters with the law. The charge was reduced to illegal trespassing with a punishment of 250 hours of community service. Upon completion of the community service, Hilton's record would be expunged. Hilton was lucky and he knew it. Since Eddie and Kyle each had a previous shoplifting charge, they were condemned to six months in a juvenile detention center.

Hilton noticed how this ordeal had drained Sally. She had lost some of her enthusiasm, and worry lines began to etch her face. "I feel like I'm up against the world trying to raise you right. It makes me wish we had a man around to keep you straight. How can I be sure that you've learned your lesson? This neighborhood is changing—how can I protect you from the evil and temptation of the streets?" she asked.

Sally found a plan to save him. While researching some corporate-donation information for her boss, she learned of A Better Chance. ABC was a program started by prep schools across the country to provide educational scholarships to talented students of color. The academic requirements were rigorous, but students would find an environment committed to excellence and it would prepare them for future success. When she discussed ABC with Hilton, he didn't oppose the idea. His 250 hours of community service had exposed him to the painful side of life in Long Beach, bringing him too close to the weak and despairing and reminding him of his own frailty. He made the beds at an elderly rest home and the smell sickened him. It was a musty stale odor, as though all the reasons for living had just been extinguished and only a dull shell remained. He also swept floors at a detox center and had accidentally witnessed a heroin addict go through withdrawal. All the vomiting, writhing and moaning in agony had left Hilton shaken. He promised himself that he would never be in a position of dependence or mired in hopelessness. He completed his application and received word that he had been accepted as a freshman to Phillips Academy in Andover, Massachusetts. In September 1984, Hilton hugged Sally and Henrietta good-bye and left for the Northeast. Of course, he took his stereo and extensive record collection with him.

A steady downpour welcomed Hilton when he arrived at Andover. It drenched the oxford shirt his mother had bought him and made him slip on the pavement as he carried his bags from the taxi. He saw the library, a wet cold manor house with white pillars, lording over him like a stern headmaster and was instantly intimidated. His whole world had been a five-mile stretch of Long Beach and he was suddenly surrounded by a five-hundred-acre hilltop campus. The school even had two museums! An assistant dean waited for Hilton at the entranceway of his new residence hall. He asked Hilton about the flight, remarked that the cool weather would be a stark contrast from sunny California, and was generally overnice. Hilton felt like a valuable specimen, an experiment Andover didn't want to bungle.

He navigated his way clumsily around campus and it took him over a week to find his dorm, the dining hall and his classes without getting lost. He shared a room with a first-generation Korean-American who was focused more on studying than socializing. Hilton saw a few other Black and Hispanic faces that he assumed belonged to scholarship students like himself. But the majority was clean-cut, well-scrubbed White boys and girls. They all possessed the cool self-assurance and resoluteness that came from never having to question their place in society. And they were all so preppy! Thank goodness his mother had gotten him a new conservative wardrobe. The right clothes—wool sweaters, polo shirts, striped ties and chinos—had a leveling effect. She also told him that he had no reason to feel inferior. Being Black was not a curse. His family wasn't rich, but they had solid values and ambitions. Hilton silently repeated those words over and over again, embedding them into his mind.

He eventually adjusted to the grind of classes, study sessions and activities at Andover. A D on his first writing assignment had been a wake-up call. There was no way he would leave Andover with mediocre grades, the ABC kid who couldn't make the cut. He missed home but was determined to take advantage of his new circumstances. He mingled with children who measured success according to family wealth, Ivy League degrees, vacation homes in Nantucket and gap years in Europe. He watched what he said, never wanting to sound too rough or unsophisticated. Although he loved basketball, he didn't want to be ghettoized and joined the lacrosse team instead. He tentatively began to make friends, but the spontaneous, unguarded part of his personality lay dormant. At least he had his music to keep him company.

One day in November, after Hilton returned a book he had borrowed from a classmate who lived in another residence hall, he was drawn to the sounds of funky, syncopated beats coming from a room down the corridor. The rhythms touched the natural impulses in his body and he found himself walking towards the source of these vibrations. He didn't quite know what to expect, but when his knock was answered by a tall, brown-skinned boy in a soccer jersey and sweatpants, he was relieved.

"Hey, I was just walking down the hall and heard those dope sounds coming from your room. I just wanted to check it out and see what you were playing," he explained.

The tall boy smiled and opened the door wider. "Sure, come in. Nobody here gets this kind of music. I'm glad at least someone got the vibe. I'm Jeff Montgomery."

"Hilton Frears," Hilton said, and they shook hands.

Jeff's room was about the same size as Hilton's, but seemed smaller because one wall was covered by a huge poster of Bob Marley. Expensive stereo equipment and crates stacked with records and cassettes took up an entire corner of the room. Books and a typewriter sat neatly on the desk. The closet door was open and revealed an interior filled with khaki pants, dark blazers and real Ralph Lauren shirts, not the knock-offs his mother had bought him in Long Beach. Sweaters, sweatshirts, shoes and sneakers competed for space on the closet shelf and floor. Jeff had a relaxed manner, friendly and not stuck-up. He had invited Hilton into his room on sight, without Hilton's having to prove that he was good enough to be there. Jeff spoke with a distinctively unaccented voice, a clear delivery that didn't sound Black or White. It was the kind of voice that couldn't be neatly categorized. A quick appraisal of Jeff and the room told Hilton that he probably wasn't a scholarship student.

Hilton spent hours hanging out with Jeff that day. It was like a dim lightbulb had been rekindled in his head. He'd been hiding a piece of his soul to the world and meeting Jeff, another Black kid who had the audacity to boom rap music from his room at Andover, made him feel less alone, less like a fraud.

They became best friends at Andover. Jeff's easygoing nature rubbed off on Hilton. He recaptured his spontaneity and ability to crack a joke, toning down his obsession about the "right" thing to say or having the "correct" background. Jeff's ease and confidence with all types of people mirrored what Hilton's mother had told him about not having to apologize for who he was.

Hilton's admission to Harvard marked him as the first person in his family to go to college. But he wouldn't be blinded by Harvard's reputation for producing senators and Fortune 500 CEOs. Those goals didn't apply to his life or his history. He knew from the beginning that he wanted a career in the music business. He couldn't sing or play an instrument but had an ear for what sounded fresh and entertaining. He was also a keen promoter, an old-school high roller who could speak passionately and convincingly about whatever he was endorsing. After graduation, he contacted Warner Music Group in Los Angeles and fast-talked his way into a job as an assistant in the Artists and Repertoire Department. He steadily moved through the ranks and became an A and R director for Urban Music. Hip-hop was reaching a wider audience and Hilton thrived on discovering new talent, cultivating acts and shaping artists' images. He spent his nights in clubs, watching acts vocalize and gyrate through red, green and white lights, music thundering in his ears. He learned to spot a winner in five minutes. Artists begged Hilton to give them a chance and he held their dreams in his hands. With the right coaching and packaging, he could transform humble singers into high-voltage stars. He ate, slept and breathed his job. It became his second skin. That skin toughened him, inspired trust in others and gave him the opportunity to capture the popular imagination.

Some years later Hilton heard that Eddie had been killed in a drive-by and Kyle was locked up for life. That mistake in the dingy bungalow had made everything possible for him. Hilton couldn't bring himself to question why he'd been spared and they hadn't.

Hilton hailed a cab on Sixth Avenue. He was meeting Jeff and Nora uptown for dinner. They wanted to explore the nightlife in their new neighborhood and Hilton had heard of a couple of spots worth checking out. He climbed into the taxi and told the driver his destination. The drive would take at least twenty minutes and Hilton's mind returned to NRG. He and Jeff seemed to have entered into a silent pact and deliberately avoided discussing it. If they pretended that they didn't care one way or another, maybe they would be better prepared for possible disappointment.

The cab let him off right at the corner of Strivers' Row. He entered the Sugar Shack and saw Jeff and Nora sitting at the bar. They were sipping daiquiris and Jeff whispered something in Nora's ear. She threw back her head and laughed and if Hilton hadn't known otherwise, he would have thought the two of them had just met and were enjoying the opening notes of a heavy flirtation. After they swapped hellos and hugs, the hostess led them to their table.

"How's the new place?" asked Hilton.

"Great," said Nora. "We love it."

Jeff chuckled and said, "She's not mentioning what happened last night."

"This sounds good," said Hilton. "Do tell."

Jeff began to describe Nora's reaction to a car backfiring and her thinking it was gunfire. By the end of the story, even she was laughing.

"I really thought it was something dangerous!" she cried.

"Nora, you wouldn't have lasted an hour where I'm from in Long Beach," Hilton joked.

"Well, everything is fine now." She looked around the earth-toned brick and wood room. "I like this place."

Harlem's economic boom had reinvigorated nightlife and every one of the Sugar Shack's tables was full. Laid-back neighborhood regulars teased the waitresses, while the Saturday night crowd, dressed in everything from three-piece suits and fedoras to tight jeans and stilettos, primped and postured. The house band had gathered onstage and was tuning up to play some jazzy funk.

"Anything happen while you were at the office today?" asked Hilton.

"I was just working on some of the clearances. I think there should be at least a twenty-year waiting period before you can sample from somebody else's music. You'd be shocked if you knew what some of our 'talented' artists have in mind," said Jeff.

"I know." Hilton nodded in agreement. "I've got to talk to a couple of them about that. I don't want to get too much in the way of their artistic freedom, but . . ."

"Let's face it," added Nora. "Some of those songs weren't even good the first time around."

"It's all remakes. Maybe it's true what they say. . . . Hip-hop is a young man's sport," said Jeff.

"Nah. Don't say that," Hilton admonished. "We've still got many more good years left in us."

They ordered dinner and discussed old friends. One of their college buddies was on the mayor's staff and they debated the upcoming mayoral race.

Hilton supported the incumbent. "He's whipped this city into shape. Show me another mayor who's reduced crime as much as he has."

" 'Whipped' being the operative word," said Nora.

"He doesn't care about minorities," remarked Jeff. "Our votes don't matter to him."

"If you try to clean up a city like New York, you're always going to have enemies. Besides, Jay says the mayor comes across as much more obnoxious than he actually is. You guys being able to feel safe moving into Harlem is a direct result of his policies."

Nora shivered dramatically. "I'd hate to think we owe him anything."

After dessert, they decided to go to the Lenox Lounge for a nightcap. This legendary Art Deco club had been a favorite of Billie Holiday's and Malcolm pre-X's, and stepping into the Zebra Room, with its murky lighting and black-and-white fake-fur chairs, was like entering a time machine. Nora went to the ladies' room and Hilton took the opportunity to bring up NRG with Jeff.

"Aren't you a little curious as to why we haven't heard back from Stark?"

"Yeah," Jeff admitted. "The thought's crossed my mind."

Hilton rotated a glass of Sambuca in his palms. "So what do you think the deal is with him? He seemed very enthusiastic that night at Indochine."

"You know how it is with those guys. They say one thing, but do another."

"I know. I spent six years working with that breed. But Stark is different. He doesn't seem like a bullshitter. In fact, I tested him that night, just to see if he would show up at my party. If he wasn't serious, he wouldn't have bothered."

"Hmmmm . . . good point." Jeff moved his chair closer to Hilton's. "This is what I think: All of this is like a mating game, a courtship. They make the first move. We respond. They back off a bit, just to whet our appetites further. Even though they approached us first, they still want to make it seem like we're the ones who want to get into bed with them."

"So what do you think we should do next?"

Jeff pondered this for a while. "I think we should do nothing. Just lie low until they come to the table with something."

"But what if they're waiting for further signs of interest on our part?"

"We'll never be able to know what they expect from us or what the 'right' next move should be. But I can tell you one thing. It's also a matter of pride for me and I don't want to feel like I kissed NRG's ass in order to get a deal."

"I haven't gotten where I am today without being aggressive. I don't know if I agree with that strategy," Hilton argued.

"Hilton, NRG Music is a three-billion-dollar company. I'm sure they have other things on their minds besides us. I always defer to you on the artistic side. Give me some credit on this call."

Hilton sighed and nodded. "You're right. I don't know. This whole thing has gotten me so wound up." He paused. "I'm almost embarrassed to admit it, but I think that I really want this. This could mean so much. My head's been filling with all kinds of ideas and projects."

"But you chose to leave that whole corporate world behind you when we started Rum. You hated it. Why are you so willing to consider going back?"

"Because I'm finally being recognized for what *I've* done, what *we've* built up. I'll no longer feel like an errand boy, but as a man with power in my right," he explained.

"But you have that power at Rum," Jeff reminded him. "Why would it be better with NRG in the equation?"

Hilton saw Nora striding back to their table from the ladies' room. "Jeff, there's power within our own closed circle and then there's power at large. A deal with NRG would send a signal, would announce that we had risen above the ranks of an underground record company. We would be perceived differently."

"Maybe," said Jeff. "I think we have to be really careful about this. Think about what we'd be giving up in order to get that power or respect. Remember, it's 'our own closed circle' that made it possible for NRG to even give us a glance." He raised his own glass in salute. "Don't worry about Stark. I'm sure we'll hear something from him soon."

CHAPTER 7

J eff's words turned out to be prophetic. Three weeks later—and five days before Christmas—a messenger appeared at Rum's office to deliver a "highly confidential" (as he put it) document from NRG, Inc. Fortunately, Jeff happened to be in the reception area at the same time and intercepted the package without provoking too much suspicion from Rum's staff. Safely ensconced in his office, he locked the door and lowered the shades. He wanted complete privacy. He stopped himself for a moment, aware that he was acting as though he had something to hide. If truth be told, none of the staff knew of NRG's overtures. He stroked his chin and tried to shake off the nagging doubt he felt about the envelope that lay before him. Should he open it now? Hilton was in the studio and wouldn't be back in the office for several hours, if at all. It was difficult to set a fixed schedule when an artist was recording. Maybe he should wait for him and they could go over it together. But Jeff was almost certain that Hilton would want him to read the document first, make some sense out of the legalese and get down to the nitty-gritty.

Jeff's right hand shook slightly as he worked his letter opener across the envelope that had been addressed to Messrs. Frears and Montgomery. He recognized NRG's familiar logo on the letterhead and began reading what was probably the most important document of his life.

Jeff read it twice, just to imprint the particulars in his mind and to make sure that his eyes were not deceiving him. He let out a nervous laugh. It all seemed like a joke. A big, obscene joke. It couldn't possibly be based in reality. But the facts were staring him in the face. NRG, Inc., was prepared to pay fifty million dollars for a fifty percent stake in Rum Records. *Fifty million dollars!* His and Hilton's baby, their creation, was worth fifty million dollars to them! It was mind-boggling. NRG was also presenting Rum with a multimedia production deal to develop projects for film and television. NRG's production, distribution and promotion resources would be made available and the revenues that resulted from music, film and television would be divided evenly.

Jeff's initial reaction and the myriad of emotions he was feeling were all new sensations for him. He considered himself a passionate person, especially regarding Nora and his work, but he always felt that he was in control. He felt there were no surprises he could not handle. Still, Jeff considered the seductive power of the zeros in the dollar amount. All his life, he had taken a casual attitude towards money. He didn't believe in wasting it, but it had been a constant in his life. He had always possessed a cushion of financial security and was grateful for it. But fifty million dollars was in a completely different league for Jeff. Since he and Hilton were Rum's sole investors, they stood to make twenty-five million dollars each. It still had not completely sunk in.

He had to talk to Hilton. Jeff dialed Hilton's cell phone number, but his voice mail came on immediately. Annoyed, Jeff wanted to hang up. Where was Hilton at this most crucial moment?

He decided to leave him a cryptic message. "Hilton, it's Jeff. I've got an early Christmas present here that I'm sure you'd be interested in. We should meet tonight and I'll fill you in. Later."

He knew that he wouldn't be able to concentrate for the rest of the day, and working was out of the question. He would just have to sit and wait.

Jefferson Clifford Montgomery's favorite grandmother, Grandma Lila, lovingly called him her "golden brown boy," implying that he was unique, that somehow he had been chosen to do great things.

"How is my golden brown boy?" she would ask, sitting in her favorite chair on the wraparound porch of her house in Oak Bluffs, Martha's Vineyard. Lila Jefferson's family proudly traced their lineage to Boston's earliest Free People. Her husband, Angus, was a successful general practitioner, serving not only Boston's Black elite but a number of liberal upstanding Whites as well. Lila performed the duties of a physician's wife gracefully and diligently, entertaining and serving on the clubs and committees that catered to Black women of her standing. Once she reached her sixties, she said that the sea air was kinder to her health and retreated to Oak Bluffs on an almost full-time basis. Angus joined her there on the weekends.

Jeff's mother, Angela, had first laid eyes on Taylor Montgomery, the son of a prominent Black family from New Rochelle, New York, at her debutante cotillion and married him five years later, directly after he graduated law school. The men in Taylor's family had been influential New Rochelle clergymen, lawyers and politicians, actively taking part in the Civil Rights movement and helping preserve the dignity of their race. Taylor went on to build a successful law practice and then wisely invested in a number of profitable business ventures. The Montgomerys were wealthy and did not hesitate to spend that money on Jeff, their only child. Jack & Jill membership, tennis lessons, soccer camp, expensive clothes and a private day school education were bestowed on Jeff to ensure that he would perpetuate the status and success of the Jefferson and Montgomery clans.

Summers in Oak Bluffs were just another component in the carefully programmed march of Jeff's life. He was expected to socialize with other children of the Black elite, to reinforce his positive self-image and to start building a network that would last him for the rest of his life. He was one of seven grandchildren who stormed into Grandma Lila's house and ran wild for eight weeks. Jeff romped around with the best of them—playing tennis, clamming, catching fireflies—but also made time for Lila. He sat and watched her preparing crepes in the kitchen and sometimes after a particularly action-packed day, he would just collapse on the porch by the legs of her wicker chair as Lila gently hummed him to sleep.

"Jeff," said Lila in the summer of his tenth year, "I have something very important to show you. I'd like it if you didn't go to the beach with the others this morning and stayed with me."

Jeff looked at Grandma Lila. Her white linen dress showed off her suntanned skin and she'd worn the same shade of coral lipstick since he was old enough to remember. She had just curled her silver hair and would be hosting a barbecue for his grandfather that night. But her hands trembled whenever she picked something up or held a pencil to do her daily crossword. The change disturbed Jeff. The beach would be there tomorrow, but he couldn't imagine what he would do if his grandmother was gone.

She took him to the parlor and closed the door. Jeff and the cousins were expressly forbidden to enter the parlor. The room was very old-fashioned with lace curtains and dainty doilies underneath crystal bowls and small statues. It also housed many of the family's treasured heirlooms. Two gleaming silver candelabras had a high monetary value, but freedom papers, marriage licenses and birth certificates carried immeasurable ancestral worth. Photographs of Lila's and Angus's solemn-faced forebears lined the walls.

Jeff lifted his chin and stared. "Grandma, how come none of those people smiled?" he asked.

"Jeff, darling, you really shouldn't say such things," she scolded, but there was laughter in her eyes. "Those pictures are from the 1890s. Our family had it better than most, but it was still tough. There wasn't always that much to smile about. And if we smiled too much, then we didn't know our place."

She took Jeff's hand in her own and led him through the photo gallery. "That's Grandpa Angus's grandfather in the 1920s," she said, pointing to the man in front of a Ford Model T. "He was so proud of that car. He was the first one in his neighborhood to get one."

She moved on to the portrait of an exquisite woman bedecked in a feather headpiece and starburst diamanté ear clips. "That's my mother photographed by Van Der Zee." She sighed. "What a beauty. She attended Cornell when there were only a handful of Black students. Your mother—my Angela—looks very much like her."

Lila continued her photographic tour, remembering so much and reliving the stories that her parents and Angus's parents had told her. She told Jeff about the distant cousin in uniform who had fought in the trenches during the First World War. She related the tale of a desperate great-great-aunt who had decided to pass for White and disavowed her Black roots. She stopped in front of a color image of a toddler dressed in a blue sweater with sailboats woven through the fabric.

"Do you know who that is?" she asked.

Jeff grinned. "How could I forget that sweater? That's me."

She stepped back and admired the photo. "You were a lovely baby. Do you have any idea why I told you all of this today?"

He shook his head.

Lila sat down on the piano bench and signaled for Jeff to join her. "Jefferson, you come from a line of very accomplished people. Our families—mine, Angus's and now your father's—have set an example for generations. Much is expected of you." She noticed Jeff squirming lightly in his seat. "Don't be embarrassed and don't be scared. You were given something special—a gift, a lucky star, a guardian angel—whatever you want to call it. Do something with it. The next generation is always our best hope, but out of all my grandchildren, you are the one who will go the farthest."

"How can you already tell?" he asked softly.

"Oh, I just can. I've lived long enough. I've seen what's needed to succeed and you have it."

"But what if I mess up?" He sensed a huge weight falling on his growing shoulders.

She kissed him on the forehead and hugged his skinny frame to her ample bosom. "You won't mess up. We won't let you."

Grandma Lila died of a massive stroke six months later and Jeff grew disenchanted with summers in Oak Bluffs. His mother or one of his aunts supervised the kids and Jeff watched the atmosphere grow more and more competitive.

"Did I tell you that Jeff won the junior varsity tennis championship at the club in Westchester?" Angela, fanning herself on a sun chair, would brag to her older sister Rosalyn.

"Oh, Preston gave up tennis ages ago," countered Roz, adjusting her straw hat. "He's moved on to golf and already has a fourteen handicap."

It was a miracle all the cousins weren't going at one another's throats. Jeff loved his mother but sensed her obsession with material possessions and maintaining her social position. His father was often preoccupied, but Jeff admired his work ethic and commitment to his family. He learned to develop a secret distance between his parents' beliefs and what he truly thought and wanted. His parents and their circle of Black bourgeois friends had a sense of noblesse oblige towards the less fortunate members of their race. Jeff thought that they often sounded arrogant, basking in their own success and shamelessly adopting snobbish styles and opinions. It was an exclusive Black world and Jeff found it increasingly confining.

Perhaps it was a reaction to his parents' generation. Or maybe Jeff wanted to hear something other than the formulaic disco that dominated the radio waves. Either way, he was attracted to the deejaying, cuttin' and scratchin', emceeing, break dancing and graffiti art that originated in New York City in the mid-1970s. By the time he was thirteen, Jeff would secretly take the Metro-North train to the South Bronx to hear the latest rhyming to the beat of music. The acrobatic dance style and big, bold art that invaded the storefronts and concrete surfaces symbolized defiance, creativity and originality for Jeff, raw forms of expression. He never break-danced or sprayed a can of paint on a wall. All of the regulars knew that Jeff was just a kid, hungry to observe this new art form in all of its manifestations. The rhyming became rapping and the elements of this street culture became hip-hop. Young Jeff had been an early witness to what would later become a cultural revolution.

Jeff's mother shuddered whenever she heard the scratchin' that came from his records and tapes. She often asked him to shut off the "junk." Jeff knew she couldn't understand and his father had the sense to tell Angela to let him be. At fourteen, he left for Andover with an attitude of breezy acceptance. He was following in the footsteps of numerous cousins who had made boarding school sound like their divine right, a necessary pit stop for chocolate preppies. His mother wept as they left him in his dorm room, and his father struggled to be stoic. Alone in their sprawling, empty house, Jeff was sure his parents would have given anything to hear one of his scratchy albums.

Andover was teeming with other overindulged overachievers, and not surprisingly, Jeff fit in very well. He realized that the transition would have been more difficult if his background had not been a privileged one, but his parents had prepared him for this environment. He supposed, ironically, that he should be grateful for that. His roommate listened only to Pink Floyd and Queen and they fought over who would get stereo rights every night. Meeting Hilton at Andover was like being introduced to his long-lost brother. They had so much in common—no siblings, demanding mothers and a love of rap music. He and Hilton talked the same language, developed a shorthand that didn't require superfluous explanation.

At Harvard, Jeff encountered an atmosphere that was academically competitive and socially complicated. The campus was divided into factions. Even the Black students were separated. Radicals, bohemians, bourgies, jocks and Afrocentrists sought to convey a "genuine" Black identity. He sympathized with these individual desires for meaning and self, but glided in and out of various groups, stopping short of being labeled. By his sophomore year, he and Hilton spent Friday and Saturday nights partying at clubs in Boston. Sometimes they would go to New York City to hear the latest rappers and check out the newest styles. The vibe off campus was definitely more loose and casual.

Jeff's rebellious streak lasted only until the second semester of his senior year. Unsure exactly about what he wanted to do with his future, he opted for law school and embarrassingly acknowledged that it was a completely traditional and secure route. Needless to say, Taylor Montgomery was pleased with his son's decision. Jeff stayed on at Harvard for law school and did well but never got the fire in his belly that he saw in his classmates. They didn't merely discuss law; they *plunged* into it, rushing from moot courts and clerkships with the eagerness of ants at a picnic. He disappointed his father when he decided to pursue a career in the fiercely competitive and, in Taylor's opinion, relatively crude world of entertainment law.

Jeff was hired by Davis & Thatcher, one of New York's top law firms, which had a comprehensive entertainment, media and intellectual-property practice. He spent long hours poring over contracts, negotiations, trademarks and copyright clearances. He also assisted a senior partner within the sophisticated and rapidly developing world of new technology. He had landed among the ranks of New York's young professionals. They worked fifteen-hour days, partied like hell from Thursday to Saturday and then returned to the office on Sunday to prepare for the coming week. Jeff knew that he was in danger of burning out. It was all too true that at New York's investment banks and law firms only the strongest survived. And for the first time in his life, he questioned his energy and desire to be in the game.

Jeff was well regarded at Davis & Thatcher. He got along with his colleagues and could play a decent game of golf, but he also experienced the pressure of having to prove himself over and over again. He had to establish a comfort level with his senior partners, case team members and clients all the time. They had to feel certain, in that implicit unspoken way, that this Black guy was not going to *fuck up*. In the beginning this pressure kept Jeff from becoming complacent, but it steadily became exhausting. He could withstand it for a few more years, but he feared becoming one of those overworked, uninspired legal drones. Or worse yet, an embittered Black man who felt shafted by corporate America. In his heart, Jeff knew that he wasn't satisfied. It was all interesting, but not compelling. He was hungry and ambitious, but longed to feel passionate about whatever he was doing. At the end of the day, he always asked himself, *Is this really me?*

As a fourth-year associate, Jeff's schedule became a little easier. He worked until nine rather than midnight. As he packed up a set of documents in his briefcase one evening, he received a phone call from Hilton. The two men had remained best friends over the years and spoke to each other several times a week. Their improved financial situations also allowed them to visit each other in Los Angeles and New York. Hilton's world was far more glamorous than Jeff's, and Jeff thoroughly enjoyed attending music industry parties and Laker games with Hilton. He had also cultivated some entertainment contacts that could prove valuable to his legal career.

"What are you still doing at the office, buddy?" Hilton greeted Jeff. "It's almost nine thirty. Time to go have a drink and chill out."

"That may be how you do business in LA, but here we have to work for our money," Jeff joked. "So what's up?"

"Well . . . ," Hilton began dramatically, and paused, "I've quit my job at Warner Music."

"You did what?" exclaimed Jeff, shocked. "Did you get a better offer?" Hilton had been advancing impressively at Warner. Why would he quit now when he was on the fast track?

"No. I'm sure I could get a job at one of our rivals, but I've gotten pretty sick and tired of all the bureaucracy and politics at these big media companies. Especially around here. My boss has taken credit for what I've done too many times. It's crazy. He says that he discovered

Honorary Sons. He knows damn well that I scouted and developed them." Honorary Sons was the hot rap duo of the moment. Holding the number one spot on both the pop and album charts, they were a certified crossover hit and further evidence of hip-hop's growing appeal from urban areas to Middle America.

"I hear you. I know how you get fired up about these things. But maybe you should think about it a little more and have a backup plan."

"Believe me, I have. I have a backup plan," Hilton responded confidently. "I also have a proposition for you."

Jeff hesitated for a moment. "What do you have in mind?" he asked as he settled himself more comfortably in his chair. This might be a long conversation.

"I want to start my own record company and I want you to be my partner," Hilton announced simply.

Jeff was totally caught off guard. "What? Now I know you've lost your mind! We don't have the experience to go out on our own."

"Oh, but we do. That's the whole point. We're young and in tune with what's going on out there and what the tastes and styles are. We see them in our friends and we see them out on the street. Most fat record execs don't have that perspective. We feel the pulse because we're looking for it. We need it to feel alive. You couldn't work in that office eighteen hours a day if you couldn't go home or go to a club, listen to some music and hang out with the brothers and sisters. The time is right for us now. There's a lot of interest in hip-hop culture and we've been with it right from the beginning. Music, film, television—this is the moment for Black creativity and business. We know who's real and who's only going along for the ride."

In spite of himself, Jeff was intrigued by Hilton's proposal. He could be pretty persuasive. No wonder he had succeeded in the hustling world of entertainment.

"Go on. I'm listening."

Hilton laughed. "I knew I'd get your attention. Think about it. Our partnership would make perfect sense from a personal and business standpoint. First of all, we're like brothers and can trust each other completely. There'd be none of the bullshit and backstabbing that's par for the course here. This is the best time of our lives to take this kind of risk. We have no families or mortgages to think about. Finally, our skill sets completely complement each other. I would focus on the A and R piece, scouting talent, building up our roster. You would handle the legal and business end. And of course, you would give your opinion on any acts or potential deals. Everything would be divided equally and all decisions would be made together. We would be like copresidents."

It sounded good so far, but Jeff decided to add a dose of reality. "How would we accomplish this? Where are we going to get the financing? Where will we be based? You're in LA. I'm in New York. And we can't have a record company without any records. Where are we going to find talent? What's going to make them sign up with an unknown label?"

"That's why I need you on my side—you're always thinking of stuff like that. But in this case, I've got it all covered. This isn't some random idea that I've just thought up. This has been a dream of mine for some time. I've got about forty thousand dollars saved up from past bonuses, which I would put towards the new company. I also plan to move to New York. I want our label to have an East Coast flavor. I won't need my car anymore, so I could sell it and get about another ten grand. You could invest about the same amount. I've also found our first act to sign up and promote, a rapper. His rhymes are quick, but also deep. He's not about the superficial, simple stuff that's becoming so popular."

"I do have some savings and stocks that I could sell. But if he's so good, why isn't he signed by Warner?"

"I tried, but my boss thinks he's too edgy and won't have mass appeal. I fought for him, but Warner doesn't want to touch him."

"Is he a gangsta rapper?"

"No. He's not talking about killing the police. But he's rapping about some serious stuff—his neighborhood, miseducation, feeling hopeless. I really think he could connect to how a lot of young people feel right now. At least listen to him," Hilton pleaded. "Listen to him and then make your decision."

"OK. Send me his demo and then I'll let you know if I'm in," Jeff said. He hung up and thought, *What am I getting myself into?* But he was strangely excited, more than he had been in a long time. They *were* young. Why did he put so much pressure on himself to be respectable and cautious? He had never wanted a conventional lifestyle, but was inexplicably slipping into one. He thought of his Grandmother Lila's prediction. Well, greatness came in many different forms.

Jeff received Hilton's tape on a Friday and listened to it throughout the weekend. The rapper went by the name Sherpa. His style was unprocessed and poetic. The tracks were a mixture of fast and mellow beats and he used innovative samples. Sherpa was musically gifted and definitely had potential. With Hilton's confidence and marketing savvy, maybe it could work after all. Jeff's mind was brimming with ideas about the new company. In his heart, he knew that this was the opportunity that he had been waiting for. He would finally be able to work with something he loved.

Jeff called Hilton on Sunday night. "So what are we going to call our new record company?"

"Rum Records, of course," Hilton answered.

Jeff chuckled. "Rum" conjured up old memories of Jamaican spring breaks soaked in reggae, women and a bottle of Appleton White. He resigned from Davis & Thatcher the following Monday.

Within a couple of weeks, Hilton moved to New York. Jeff's loft apartment was transformed into narrow living quarters for Hilton as well as a makeshift office for Rum Records. They purchased a fax machine and computer and installed another phone line. They lived a frugal existence, channeling all their energy and resources into the new company, and spent a chunk of their investment to buy studio time for Sherpa. Fortunately, Hilton had extensive radio-station contacts and was able to get some playing time for one of his tracks. Slowly, a buzz started to form around Sherpa. The song gained urban credibility and could be heard coming from cars, radios and clubs. Hilton and Jeff sprang for an inexpensive video by using the unmined talents of an NYU film student. Video exposure widened Sherpa's reach. After several months, the single rose to number one on the R & B charts and number three on the pop charts. Everyone wanted to know about this unknown talent and the upstart record label that had ventured to bet on him. When Sherpa's full-length album was released, it debuted at number one.

Jeff was awed by the success and relieved that their risk had paid off.

He and Hilton treated some friends to a celebration weekend in Vegas but were determined that Rum Records would not be a one-act wonder. They never wanted to hear, "Whatever happened to *those* two guys who started *that* record company?" They followed up with a piano-playing hip-hop/soul diva whose raw sultry voice redefined the R & B experience for the new millennium.

Originality, authenticity and independence. This was the credo that separated Rum Records from all others.

Now Jeff wondered exactly how much farther he wanted to go.

Hilton met Jeff downtown at Balthazar for a late dinner. It was a quiet night, a Tuesday, and the only other diners were a few neighborhood regulars. Jeff ordered a hamburger and a Coke. Hilton chose the chicken club and mineral water.

"So what's up, man?" Hilton asked. "Your message sounded mysterious."

"Good. I wanted to get your attention," Jeff replied.

Hilton sipped his water. "I'm on sensory overload right now. It'll be so good to get away." First he planned to celebrate Christmas with his mother in California. Then he had booked a trip to the Caribbean playground of St. Barth through the New Year. Much of the entertainment and media elite decamped to St. Barth over the holidays and the tiny, exclusive island became a virtual pleasure den of private parties and power sunbathing. It would be Hilton's third season there.

"Are you taking Stephanie with you?"

"She kind of assumed she was joining me. I don't want to disappoint her."

"C'mon, man. Why can't you just admit that you wouldn't mind having her there with you? There's no harm in that. In fact, I think it would be good for you."

Hilton's face broke into a wide grin. "What the hell? It'll be fun."

Jeff leaned forward and said sedately, "We've got some important things to discuss. I got a package via messenger from Stark's office today."

Hilton had just picked up the sandwich the waitress had placed before him. He held it in midair. "And?" he questioned anxiously.

"NRG wants to buy a fifty percent stake in Rum for fifty million dollars," Jeff whispered.

Hilton dropped the sandwich back on the plate. "Ge-ge-get out of here," he stammered. "Get the fuck out of here!"

"I'm dead serious. I've got a copy of the letter here with me."

"Incredible. In-fucking-credible," he repeated in disbelief.

Jeff laughed. "It's real, man. I felt the same way. I didn't expect them to be so generous. But we're living in strange times. They must really believe that we would be a good investment to shell out that kind of money."

"What exactly does the offer say?" Hilton asked excitedly. "Break it down for me."

"Well, it's basically a joint-venture arrangement whereby NRG Music would own fifty percent of Rum Records. They'll give us fifty million dollars up front to buy out half the company and we'll just continue doing our thing: recording albums. We'll sign artists, pay them, take care of marketing and promotions. But with NRG's resources we'll be able to grow the company faster and be more profitable. We'll be able to attract and keep good talent. Future profits would be shared fifty-fifty."

"And we get to keep this fifty million dollars?" Hilton asked.

Jeff smiled. "Yeah. Twenty-five million for me and twenty-five million for you."

"I can't believe it. . . ."

"But remember, we'd be signing away half our company to them. NRG will be on our board and expects to be involved in our decision making. Each party will have to work on building consensus. Otherwise we hurt Rum Records and we all lose. It's going to be a different set of rules."

"Fifty mil is no small change! Look at me: I always had to struggle. The first time I made a hundred thousand dollars, it felt like a million bucks. When you grow up having no chips, you dream about becoming rich. But they're kids' dreams. They almost never come true. I didn't expect this much, this soon," he confessed.

For Hilton, every success, every penny earned, signified his triumph over the hardships of his youth and the abandonment of his father. He had once wondered to Jeff about his father. Did Jacob know who he was today? Could he see what he had become from the magazine articles and profiles? If his father was alive, why didn't he try to contact him? Gradually, Hilton's sentimentality turned bitter and he had damned his faceless father to oblivion.

"You deserve this, Hilton. You had the guts to go out on your own, to chase a dream. I've always admired that. And you brought me in. If it weren't for you, I'd still be cranking away at Davis & Thatcher wondering about why I hadn't made partner yet. This NRG thing seems like icing on the cake, but even without that, we've come a long way. Don't ever forget that."

Hilton rubbed his eyes. He looked a little flushed. "But now the real pressure begins. They want us as a platform to tap into the urban audience. We have to make sure we produce so they get a return on their investment."

"Don't sell us short. This can't be any harder than when we started out in my loft apartment. That's why NRG wants to pull fifty percent of Rum into their fold. They're confident that we can deliver."

"We had nothing to lose then. The stakes are higher now."

"In a way, the uncertainty has always been part of the fun. Are the records going to sell? Can we afford to sign a new artist? We can't lose our identity, the essence that drives our company."

"From what I'm hearing, you think we should do it. Are you in favor of their offer?" Hilton asked.

"There are a couple of terms in the agreement that I have issues with. But if we can get those sorted out, then I think the deal can work," Jeff explained.

"What are some of those issues?"

"Ownership of the retail store and restaurant, budget approval, production approval, NRG's input on the artists we sign . . . standard contractual stuff. I'm actually going to call an old colleague of mine at Davis & Thatcher and ask him to represent us."

"You're not planning on doing the legal work on this?" Hilton asked.

"I'll provide my input, but I think we'd be in a stronger bargaining position with a third party in the picture. I think they'll take us more seriously."

"Damn. This is real. Lawyers, contracts, money. I feel like a kid. This is the big time. Well, I'm in, man. I'm definitely in. Maybe we should have a drink after all," he suggested, and ordered two snifters of Hennessy. He tasted the cognac, and warmth spread over him as the spicy full-bodied liquid eased down his throat. He was in a reflective mood.

"Jeff, remember those parties we used to throw at Harvard? We must have been crazy." He made a fist, brought it to his mouth and said in an announcer's baritone, "Rum Productions welcomes you to a Hip-Hop Jam."

"The way we begged the Student Activities Office for a space, I was so nervous that party was going to flop or get wild. If we'd gotten busted, I don't know what I would've done. *Black students cause mayhem on campus!*"

"But everyone had a great time. Those parties became legendary."

"And then we started throwing them in our apartment."

"The floor tiles broke—everyone was dancing so much!"

"Those parties added a lot to the Harvard days."

"Hell, yes. We made some money too," Hilton said, remembering the five-dollar admission fee and dollar cans of beer they sold.

"And we got a name for the company."

Hilton, smiling at the thought of the NRG deal, added, "Jamaican rum punch never tasted so good."

CHAPTER 8

Jeff contemplated Nora's potential reaction as he drove uptown. She could be surprising. Whereas some women might consider only the money, what it represented and what it could obtain, Nora was more complicated. He knew this about her and it was one of the main reasons why he loved her. She liked comfort, had a weakness—*terrible* weakness—for nice clothes and shoes, but had always been an independent woman. She never expected nor took it for granted that a man would provide these things for her. In fact, when he had first given her an expensive gift, she seemed almost embarrassed by his largesse. She accepted presents more easily over the years, but she wasn't a slave to material goods and never let them define who she was.

It was past eleven o'clock when he entered the house, but Nora was still up trimming the Christmas tree. They had found a glorious full spruce and its rich pine scent floated across the living room. Both sets of parents were coming over for Christmas dinner and she had told Jeff that she wanted everything to be perfect.

"So many of these ornaments broke during the move. I don't have enough to fill the tree," she complained.

"You still have time to pick up some new ones," Jeff said.

She wrinkled her nose. "Yes, but I wanted to finish this tonight. Oh, well." She plopped down on the couch and smiled. "What's new with you?"

"We got an offer today from NRG. Are you ready for it?" Jeff paused theatrically. "Fifty million dollars for fifty percent of the company."

Nora's eyes and mouth opened wide in amazement.

"Did you hear what I said?" Jeff asked.

"I heard, but I'm not quite believing. I'm flabbergasted . . . so much money." But then she jumped up and threw her arms around Jeff's neck, excitement in her brown eyes. "Oh, honey. I'm so happy for you—and proud of you! This is what you wanted, right?"

Jeff laughed tentatively and shrugged. "I guess so. I don't know. I didn't really know what I wanted until I had the papers in front of me. Now I think of it as fate. Maybe this is the next step for Rum. It's beginning to feel more right as the day goes on."

"Of course it's all a little confusing and overwhelming. People don't get offers like this every day. But I assume NRG will want to be involved in a lot of the decisions that Rum makes. Are you prepared for that?"

"I'm sure it'll be an adjustment in the beginning, since Hilton and I have only had each other to answer to. But the benefits might outweigh that. We'd be going into some new territory, movies and TV, so NRG's guidance would actually be helpful."

"It's exciting, though. You're going to have a real creative think tank going."

"How do you feel about the money?" he asked candidly.

"Well, it's a lot," she joked.

Jeff looked straight into her eyes. "Seriously. All jokes aside."

"I have to admit it: It's thrilling. Enticing. I've never *ever* imagined that I'd be near that kind of money. I'm a first-generation American. This is the kind of stuff my parents read about. But—"

"There's always a but."

Nora sighed. "*But* we've already been given a lot. Good jobs, doing what we love. Thankfully not having to worry about the bare essentials, being able to indulge in the extras. I hope it's not going to change our lives *too* much. I don't want to lose our grounding. But who am I to say that you and Hilton shouldn't get as much as you can? That's the American way, right? And as sick as it sounds, fifty million is probably a drop in the bucket for NRG. They probably write off more money than that every year."

Jeff hugged her. "Good. I wasn't sure what you would think. But our lives *will* change. There'll be more attention, more pressure. Some people will act differently towards us. It'll take several more months before this is finalized, but you have to be prepared for the changes ahead."

"Don't worry," Nora assured him. "I can handle it."

*   *   *

Nora woke up early on Christmas morning. Jeff had accompanied her to midnight mass at St. Ignatius Loyola, even though he was Episcopalian and rarely attended church throughout the year, but she didn't want to lose the spiritual significance of the holiday and he had gone without complaint. After several mild winters, it had finally snowed on Christmas Day. Nora glanced outside their bedroom window and marveled at how Hamilton Terrace looked like a postcard. The street was quiet and the newly fallen snow was still untouched. Snowflakes rested on the trees, and several town house facades were decorated with wreaths and lights.

Their parents were expected at three o'clock and there was still much for Nora to do. She was disappointed that her brother, Albert, couldn't join them, but he was completing his residency in a Chicago hospital and would be working almost nonstop until after the holidays. She and Anna Parekh had spent hours at the Fairway supermarket on 133rd Street. It had been difficult to choose among the endless rows of food and ingredients, but Nora had finally settled on a Christmas menu of smoked salmon, fennel and goat cheese on toast; filet mignon roast in a mushroom-sherry sauce; potatoes au gratin; fresh vegetables; and crème brûlée for dessert. The crème brûlée would probably be her downfall, but she had made the custard cups the night before and hoped for the best. Thankfully, the house had been cleaned from top to bottom. Their parents had been so skeptical about the move and she and Jeff wanted to impress them.

The Montgomerys and Deschamps arrived shortly after three. Nora was still in the kitchen when Jeff welcomed them at the front door. This was only the third time both families were gathered together in a social setting. The first time had been two years ago at Nora and Jeff's engagement party, and the second at their wedding. The two families thought themselves to be quite different from each other. The Deschamps never felt like they had been embraced by their Black American brethren. Valérie and Pierre remarked that competition for limited opportunities and resentment of the perceived advantages given West Indians soured relations and prevented both cultures from banding together. On the other side, Nora had once heard Angela Montgomery complain about West Indians who waxed poetic about the mother country, "If things were as great as they say, they would have never come here to begin with."

However, they were more similar than they thought. Both families were extremely proud and confident. Both came from commendable backgrounds—the Deschamps in Haiti and the Montgomerys in the United States. They were also fierce champions for their children. When Nora came to hug and kiss her parents and the Montgomerys, she glowed with pride the minute she saw them. Valérie was wearing wide-legged black velvet pants and a brocade blazer. Angela was impeccably turned out in a red suit with gold buttons. The gray hair that edged Pierre's temples gave him a distinguished air and Taylor's distinctive salt-and-pepper beard was, as always, immaculately groomed.

"I'm so glad you're here," Nora exclaimed. "I hope there wasn't too much trouble with the snow."

"No, no. They plowed the roads early this morning," Pierre answered. His voice still carried traces of his accent and "they" came out like "zay."

"You two look wonderful. You lead such busy lives, but it obviously agrees with you," said Valérie in an accent that was less pronounced than Pierre's. Everyone told Nora that she looked like her mother. They shared the same almond-shaped eyes and well-defined cheekbones, but Valérie had a spunkiness that Nora, as a child, had often felt was lacking in her own personality. To this day, she could still hesitate before telling the dry cleaner that a dress had come back with the stain still on it, but Valérie wouldn't mince words. Nora guessed allowances were made for Valérie's directness because it was usually accompanied with a smile and the graceful rhythm of her accented voice.

"Son, this is a nice piece of property you've got here," Taylor complimented. "I remember my father telling me about a cousin of his who lived on Sugar Hill. It's like you've entered a different place in time, the era of high Negro style."

"I know," Jeff agreed. "That's why we love it here."

"You'll have to give us a tour of the house, Nora," added Angela.

"Of course. I'll lead the way." Nora took them to every room, making sure to point out the special elements of each space. Valérie commended Nora's decorating choices, admiring her juxtaposition of antique and contemporary pieces.

"Nora, I've got a fantastic interior designer that I could introduce you to. He's got a great reputation and did a number of houses in Westchester," Angela offered.

Nora wasn't sure if Angela was trying to tell her that her own efforts were a disaster and she needed professional advice. Nonetheless she answered diplomatically, "Why not? That sounds good. I'll get the number from you later."

Valérie and Nora looked at each other and exchanged secret smiles. Angela was a piece of work, a luxurious cat that purred and clawed capriciously.

Angela thought she downplayed her superior airs, but they came out at almost every opportunity. In Nora's opinion, Angela had never really gotten over the fact that her beloved only son had married the daughter of Haitian immigrants. Nora knew Angela had expected Jeff to choose a wife with a "proper" African-American pedigree and had made several attempts to match him up with the daughters of friends from the Vineyard and her social club, but to no avail. Jeff had told her bluntly that he was looking for a soul mate, not a match. Nora finally met the indomitable Angela Montgomery at a family dinner and was grilled on everything short of her parents' income tax statements during the four-hour meal. In the end, Angela pronounced through tight lips that she was so happy Jeff had found someone with "enough poise to carry the Montgomery name." Nora came to gradually understand that Angela considered her competition. Any displays of affection from Jeff or attention from Taylor made Nora uncomfortable, since she was never sure how Angela would take it. And when Angela deigned to issue a compliment, it was usually followed by an account of her own glory. Nora was always gracious and treated Angela with respect, but she sensed that Angela would have much preferred that Nora try desperately to win favor with her. Nora knew her armor of self-possession unnerved her mother-in-law.

Conversation flowed smoothly during the first course. Nora had been so nervous about the mood of the evening that she was surprised to find her father and Taylor chatting away about politics, sports and the economy. When the discussion inevitably turned to the latest Washington scandal, she excused herself to go check on the filet. Nora heard them debating the topic for ten minutes before the table fell silent. She needed to cut the filet and bring out the red wine and wondered why Jeff wasn't doing a better job of initiating conversation.

"That's a lovely bouquet," Nora heard Valérie say, most likely referring to the low floral centerpiece on the table.

"Yes, it is," agreed Angela. "Smells good too. I wonder what it's made of." Pause. "I think that's holly."

Valérie joined in again: "I think there's some gooseberry too."

"That scent has got to be cedar," added Pierre.

"Those red roses are magnificent," piped Taylor.

Help! thought Nora. She searched for the special bottles of Bordeaux—which she should have already uncorked in order to let them breathe—in the wine rack, but they were missing. She threw her arms up in the air and surveyed her "professional" kitchen, her laboratory for culinary delights. It was more like a disaster area. Just as Taylor asked Valérie about the alarming rate of violence in schools, Nora realized what she had done with the wine.

The door slid open and she turned her attention from the sink and the wine bottles she was dunking in hot water.

"Is everything OK?" Jeff asked.

She pulled up her rubber gloves. "Everything is not OK. I chilled the red wine by mistake. The bottles were so dark, I couldn't tell if they were red or white. I didn't read the labels, and just threw six bottles in the fridge. I'm trying to heat them up now, the filet is probably drying up as we speak, and you left our parents alone in the dining room."

"Is that it?" he laughed. "You're never going to heat them up like that. You might as well put those bottles in the microwave."

"You think that would work?"

"I'm kidding. Just give me the wine. They probably won't even notice."

"My parents may not say anything, but your mother will."

"You think so? Well, we must have some more red wine."

"I bought this vintage especially for our Christmas dinner. The only other red in the house is some cheap table wine we have with pasta."

Jeff bent down in front of the wine rack and started sliding out bottles. He examined the label on a bottle of Chianti. "Is this it?"

She peered at it and sighed. "Yes. I hope it doesn't turn anyone's teeth purple."

Jeff carved the filet and they returned to the dining room with it on a serving platter. Nora sat down all smiles and hoped that nothing else would go wrong. The crème brûlée didn't disappoint and over coffee and brandy, Taylor asked Jeff about Rum Records.

"We've actually been approached to enter into a joint venture with NRG, Inc.," said Jeff.

Taylor nodded thoughtfully. "Good company. Gerald Higgenbotham is a member of the board of directors there." For the sake of Nora and her parents he added, "He's a former secretary of labor and a good friend of the family."

"Really? I didn't know he was on the board," Jeff replied. "NRG is interested in buying fifty percent of Rum."

"Interesting. How much are they offering?" Taylor probed.

Jeff looked uncomfortable and sipped his brandy. "Fifty million dollars," he said finally.

"What?" Valérie and Angela cried in unison.

Pierre let out a long whistle. "Only in America."

Taylor appeared unruffled, but a smile had started to form around his lips. "Very good. Very, very good," he repeated. "Your childhood hobby has ended up capturing the interest of one of the country's biggest media companies."

"There's still a lot to go over," Jeff added quickly. "We haven't even begun formal negotiations with them."

"Well, if you need a sounding board, you know I'm here. Although I suspect you won't be needing much of my help. You did this all on your own. You could probably teach me a thing or two," Taylor praised.

Nora knew that Jeff's decision to leave a promising law career and start a hip-hop record label had been nothing short of *scandalous,* but Taylor had come to respect the hard work that Jeff put into the company. Taylor was also a man of the times. He knew that the climate had changed. In his day, Blacks had gained respectability in the traditional professions of law, medicine, teaching and the clergy. Now high technology, entertainment and media were the engines that drove the economy and a new Afristocracy was emerging from these industries. Jeff had been daring enough to get in the game early and NRG's offer completely legitimized Rum Records.

Jeff smiled at him and said, "Thanks, Pop."

"I only wish I were young again," Taylor added.

"What are you going to do with all that money, Nora?" Angela's voice emerged from the silence, breaking the tenderness of the moment.

"Me?" Nora looked up, stunned. "It's not my money. Ask Jeff. I'm perfectly happy with things as they are."

"It's a little too soon to be making plans for the money, Angela. I've always told my kids, Don't count on what's not in your pocket," Valérie said. She took a small bite of Godiva chocolate and added, "Besides, money doesn't make a marriage."

Angela let out a barely audible "Humph" and finished off the rest of her Chianti. Nora could have been hallucinating, but she swore Angela's lips had changed to a bizarre shade of plum since the main course. She changed the subject. "Why don't we go into the living room and open the Christmas presents? I don't know about you all, but I can't wait."

"Good idea," Valérie echoed, and later whispered to Nora out of Angela's earshot, "You're a saint, to put up with her the way you do. She really tests my patience."

"Mom, please don't say anything. You promised. I can manage."

"Mothers and sons . . . I hope I don't act this way with your brother's wife one day."

Nora crooked her arm with Valérie's. "He's got to find a wife first. Then you can start misbehaving."

Nora stood by the fireplace mantel and began distributing the stocking stuffers, an assortment of books and spa gift certificates, and then moved on to the primary presents. She loved giving gifts and soon heard a chorus of oohs and aahs around the room.

"Darling, this scarf is beautiful!" Valérie exclaimed, touching the fine Hermès silk. "I love the colors and it'll go perfectly with a suit I have. Thank you. Thank you both." She gave Jeff and Nora each a kiss on the cheek.

"Ooh! You know exactly what I like! How did you ever find it? Thank you," Angela cooed over the limited-edition bottle of Joy, her favorite perfume. Nora wanted to tell her she had hunted through the streets of Paris on a business trip in the middle of a strike but refrained. Angela would never doubt she was worth the trouble.

Pierre and Taylor had been more difficult to choose for, and defeated after a whole afternoon of shopping, Nora and Jeff bought them each cashmere sweaters. Taylor's was a genteel camel crewneck, Pierre's a very professorial black turtleneck, and both seemed pleased. Since Nora and Jeff had recently moved into a new home, they received housewarming gifts; a sterling silver monogrammed box from the Montgomerys and a small abstract sculpture by a young Haitian artist from the Deschamps.

"What about you two?" Valérie asked.

"We opened our presents this morning," Nora answered.

"What did you get Jeff?" Angela inquired.

"I got him a plasma screen TV," Nora responded.

"A TV set seems kind of boring," said Angela.

Jeff shot Angela a sharp glance.

"Well, your son sure loves his TV! He's crazy about new gadgets and high-tech stuff," said Nora more pleasantly than she felt.

"I think it was very clever," cut in Taylor. "And what did Jeff get you, my dear?"

Nora looked down shyly and raised her right arm. "This," she said, pointing to the gold bangle that moved on her wrist.

They all admired it.

"It's beautiful. You've got great taste, Jeff," said Valérie.

Angela put on her reading glasses and leaned in closer. "Isn't that a Cartier Love Bracelet?"

"Actually, it is."

"Well, Taylor gave me the same bracelet for our tenth anniversary," Angela said smugly.

"That's why Jeff wanted to give one to me. He knew how much you loved it," Nora said evenly. *This woman is insufferable. She can never say a simple sentence that isn't laced with sarcasm or snootiness.*

Jeff suggested that they try to watch the last half of the football game.

Nora groaned. "I don't think so, honey."

"Do you mind if I watch it?" Pierre asked. "Is it on the flat screen?"

Jeff laughed. "No. It's not hooked up yet."

"Oh, Pierre," Valérie scolded, "all you ever think about is sports." She turned to the others. "You'd think he was born in this country. He loves it all—hockey, baseball, basketball."

"Why don't we leave the ladies in here and go watch the game in the den?" Taylor suggested.

It was a losing battle. Nora shooed Jeff, her father and Taylor away and continued speaking to her mother and Angela.

"So, Nora, when are you going to bless this house with children? We're all getting a little impatient to become grandparents. Isn't that true, Valérie?" Angela asked coyly.

"They'll have children when the time is right, Angela. But it would be nice if it were sooner rather than later," Valérie admitted.

"What's taking you so long?" Angela interrogated, as though Nora bore sole responsibility for becoming pregnant.

"Oh, you know. Our careers, our schedules, all the responsibility it would entail. I guess Jeff and I aren't ready yet," Nora answered truthfully.

"But Jeff loves kids. He told me that he can't wait to become a father," Angela said.

Nora raised an eyebrow suspiciously. She wasn't sure if Angela was being completely honest or just playing games.

"Nora, having children is far less complicated than you think. They bring so much happiness to your life. When you and your brother were born, it sure wasn't easy for me or your father. But I wouldn't trade those times for anything in the world," Valérie recalled.

"Your generation just plans too much. You consult your calendars before you even take a small step. Be careful you don't wake up one day and find that it's too late," Angela counseled.

"I do want children, at least two. And it's been on my mind much more lately. I guess you could say I've been having these maternal urges. But I have to move from *thinking* about it to actually *doing* something about it."

"That part, my dear, is entirely up to you and Jeff," Angela joked, and they all laughed. She had adopted a softer tone and Nora felt momentarily guilty for having thought ill of her.

Their visit continued until ten o'clock and waving good-bye to her parents from the window, Nora could not help thinking that Christmas next year could be even more special with a baby. She broached the subject with Jeff as they prepared to go to sleep.

"My mother said what?" he exclaimed. "She's such a busybody. I have to say something to her."

"No. Please. It's fine. In fact, it's the only thing she said all evening that I agreed with."

Jeff sighed resignedly. "I know she's a handful. And you're so patient with her. Don't think I don't notice it."

"So what *is* stopping us from becoming parents?" Nora prodded.

He considered that for a minute. "Nothing, I guess. We're always talking about a right time, but maybe there never really is a 'right time.' We love each other and having a baby would be a beautiful thing."

"Yes," Nora agreed softly.

"And I think we should work very hard on it in the coming months," he quipped.

"Oh, goody. I can't wait to chuck the rest of my birth control pills. I've been waiting"—she started counting—"thirteen years to do that!"

"Thirteen years? You've been sexually active for thirteen years? I thought I was your first lover," he needled, feigning shock.

Nora threw her pillow and it hit him across the forehead. "You weren't my first. But you're definitely the last."

CHAPTER 9

The merriment of December faded into memory and the January blues descended over the city. Streets were quieter with the retreat of holiday tourists, and the stinging cold kept people home. Department stores and restaurants were less crowded, patiently waiting out the doldrums until New Yorkers sprang back to life.

Jeff was largely unaware of all of this since Rum Records was entering one of its busiest periods. Several award ceremonies were planned and they were zealously priming and promoting their top artists. A long-awaited album release was also scheduled. And the NRG deal was naturally never far from his mind. He and Hilton had retained a lawyer who communicated directly with NRG's attorneys. Rum had outlined its concerns and was hopeful that NRG would be willing to negotiate the new terms. Jeff fully expected the deal to go through in the next couple of months.

It had been another late night at the office and Jeff sat in the car with Brian Harris, Rum's young intern. Brian lived uptown on Lenox Avenue and Jeff often drove him home. Brian was street-smart, high-voltage and honest. Jeff considered him his window into the youth market. He buried himself in Jeff's training and advice and never once complained about any of the tasks to which he was assigned. Brian was itching to work for Rum full-time, but Jeff urged him to finish his studies at City College first. As long as Brian wanted it, there would always be a place for him at Rum Records.

"SuperNatural's new album is tight!" Brian was saying with characteristic aplomb.

Jeff chuckled. "You think so? It's kind of tough sometimes with a sophomore effort."

"But that's the beauty of it, man. He waited two years before dropping his second album, gave his fans some time to miss him and then bang! Radios all over are gonna be pumpin' the tracks," he predicted.

"I hope so. We've got a lot riding on this album. The marketing budget alone—" Jeff's words were cut short as he saw a dim figure in the middle of the street frantically waving his arms back and forth. Jeff pushed on the brakes and the SUV stopped only a few inches in front of a teenager in a pouffy black jacket.

Jeff rolled down the window and shrieked, "Are you crazy? What are you doing standing in the middle of the road? I could have hit you!"

The kid panted and tried to catch his breath. He was perspiring through the cold and terror was spread across his face. He walked to the driver's side and swallowed hard before speaking. "You've got to help me. My friend's hurt. We have to get him to the hospital. I've been waving for the past ten minutes trying to get help. You're the only car that's stopped. Please help me."

Brian regarded him suspiciously. "Call 911," he suggested coldly.

"Please!" the boy begged. "We don't have time to wait for them to get up here. He might die! Can't you even help a brother?"

That last sentence stung. "OK. Calm down. We'll get your friend to the hospital. Where is he now?" Jeff asked.

"He's lying down in the doorway of that building," he said, pointing to a weathered brownstone. "He has to be carried over here. You'll have to help me."

"We'll help you bring him to the car. Stay calm for your friend," advised Jeff.

He turned into 136th Street and parked in front of the building. He and Brian bolted out of the car and ran up the steps. The front door was ajar and they entered easily. A weak lamp shone from the ceiling, spotlighting a contorted figure in the corner. It was an eerie scene, still and noiseless, and Jeff was unprepared for the sight of a young man propped up against the wall. Eyes closed, his head was tilted backward and he labored to breathe through his mouth. He covered his chest with one hand to stop the gushing blood, but it was seeping between his fingers and had stained his jeans and the hallway floor.

Jeff struggled to think decisively. "We have to be careful how we move him." He bent down and gently straightened the boy's legs.

"Brian, you and I will hold him on each side. We'll put one of his arms around our shoulders and then carry his legs." He turned to the bleeding boy's friend. "Keep the door open for us so we can get him to the car quickly."

As they raised the boy's body, he wailed and continued to trickle blood. His sturdy weight seemed to increase with each effort, but they managed to make it down the brownstone steps.

"Open the back door of the car," said Jeff, and they carefully laid the limp body across the backseat. Jeff took off his own jacket and gave it to the boy who had flagged them down. "Keep this on your friend. We've got to stop the bleeding."

They jumped in the car and sped towards Columbia-Presbyterian Hospital on 168th Street. Jeff parked behind a row of ambulances near the emergency wing. The swirling red lights pierced his vision and he winced. He opened the back door of the SUV and drew the bleeding boy towards him. Taking a deep breath, Jeff hoisted him from the seat and cradled the giant rag doll of a body in his arms. The boy's limbs dangled loosely, swinging back and forth as Jeff rushed through the maze of ambulances. At the entranceway, the automatic glass doors slid open and Jeff searched for an empty hospital cot.

A nurse hurriedly wheeling a gurney surfaced and helped Jeff position the boy on the mattress. She cut open his sweatshirt and examined the bleeding gash on his chest.

"What's the nature of his injuries?" she asked.

"I don't know. I think it's a stab wound. I found him like this," answered Jeff.

"Are you related to him? Friend of the family?"

Jeff shook his head.

"Do you know his name?"

Jeff turned around and looked for the boy's friend, who stood in the corridor, staring into space. He walked over and asked, "What's your friend's name?"

"Huh?" he answered weakly, his voice thick and stuffed up from crying.

Jeff repeated the question.

"André. André Wilson." With those words, his eyes moistened again.

Jeff filled in the admittance forms with the little information he had available while the hospital staff prepared to move André into emergency surgery. Jeff stood by his cot until the nurse secured an operating room. André was quiet, but still breathing. Jeff wondered if he was aware of the needles and tubes that had been inserted into his body. "We'll be moving him into surgery now," the nurse informed Jeff. "I think you should call his family."

Jeff nodded and leaned towards André. "Hang in there, André. You'll get through this. Stay strong."

At the sound of his name, André's eyes flung open. He reached for Jeff's arm. "I don't want to die," he uttered shakily. "I don't want to die. Please don't let me die."

"You won't die," Jeff promised. "They're going to take good care of you."

The nurse looked into Jeff's eyes, gently squeezed his arm in sympathy and led the gurney away.

Jeff walked listlessly to the waiting area, his legs dragging from fatigue and worry. He sat down, closed his eyes and said a silent prayer, ashamed that he called on a Higher Power only in times of need. But he wasn't praying for himself, but for André, whom he didn't know, but badly wanted to survive. Surely that was a valid prayer?

He fished in his pocket for his BlackBerry. It had been on all day and the battery signal was dead. Wearily, he turned to André's friend, whose name, he found out, was Khareem Thurman. "Khareem, we have to get in touch with André's family. What's their phone number?"

Jeff scribbled the number on the cover of a frayed magazine he found on the table. He went to a pay phone and dialed the digits, but an operator's voice told him the number was out of service. Thinking he misdialed, Jeff tried again, but received the same message. Frustrated, he slammed down the receiver.

He sat back down in his chair and asked Khareem, "Are you sure this is the right number? The operator says it's out of service."

"Yeah, that's the number. The phone's probably disconnected," said Khareem.

"So how are we supposed to tell André's parents about his condition? Don't you think they're worried that it's"—Jeff glanced at his watch—"two a.m. and their son still hasn't come home yet?"

Khareem looked blankly at Jeff, but didn't respond.

Jeff hunched down so that their eyes were level. "Khareem, what went on tonight? How did André get stabbed?"

Khareem remained quiet and rubbed his eyes.

"Answer me!" Jeff shouted, startling Khareem and the other half-asleep people in the waiting room.

"André's a runner," Khareem whispered, avoiding Jeff's gaze.

Jeff was taken aback. "As in—"

Khareem nodded. "He delivers drugs for one of the local dealers. I'm not 'officially' a runner, but André's my best friend. I sometimes help him and he gives me money."

"Were you guys doing a deal tonight?"

"Not exactly. André met the dealer in the building where you found him. He told me to hide in the stairwell, since the dealer didn't know about me. He was supposed to give the dealer money from customers and get more stash."

Khareem talked about it all like it was another day at the office.

"When did things go bad?" asked Jeff.

Khareem sighed. "Well, the dealer accused André of stealing money from him. André denied it, but the dealer could tell he was lying and threatened André with a knife. André got so scared, he finally admitted to taking the money. He promised to give it back. The dealer said OK, he'd forgive André this one time, but he wanted his money."

"So what happened next?"

"The dealer started to walk away and André lost control. He started screaming, cursing him out. I guess he got really angry about getting busted and being threatened. The dealer came back and asked André what the fuck was he saying, did he know who he was talking to. I remember this so well—he called André 'a sorry piece of punk shit.' There was some noise, feet moving, and the next thing I heard was André screaming. I was so scared. I just stayed in that stairwell until I was sure the dealer was gone. As soon as I saw André, I ran outside trying to get help." Khareem buried his face in his hands, breaking down at the memory.

Jeff stared at Khareem, shaken by the false bravado that had caused such a useless tragedy. He also felt a surge of pity for the kid. "Khareem, how old are you?"

Khareem moved his hands to his lap and picked at a piece of loose skin on his thumb. "Fourteen."

"André?"

"Sixteen."

Khareem looked like so many of the other young men Jeff saw uptown with their cocksure swagger and designer logos, but winding tears streaked his face and a gob of snot threatened to run down his nose. They were boy men and couldn't escape their own vulnerability. Jeff pulled out a wad of tissues from a box on the table. Khareem took it and blew his nose.

The anger Jeff had been trying to control erupted. "What the hell do you guys think you're doing? Do you think you're living in a movie? Do you think this is *Scarface*?"

"I know. I know, but we had done it so many times before. It wasn't supposed to be a big deal. . . ." Khareem's voice trailed.

"You guys had no business getting involved in this drug nonsense. You risk your lives every time you make a drop or meet with the dealer. Your best friend is lying in this hospital fighting for his life!"

"We needed the money. . . . It wasn't supposed to happen like this!" Khareem sobbed again.

"For what? Was it worth it? Look what you're doing to yourselves and your community!"

Khareem's sobs intensified and Jeff patted him gently on the back. "Look, maybe this isn't the right time," he apologized. "I didn't mean to get preachy."

"It's OK."

"Have you considered going to the police?"

"No! I can't. He'll come after me!" Khareem cried.

"Listen to me. He'll keep coming after people until someone stops him. He just left André to die tonight."

Khareem just kept shaking his head and Jeff reluctantly let the matter drop. His eyes traveled around the room. Faces were anxious and tired. Waiting like this had to be the worst. Jeff had almost forgotten about Brian, but the intern sat near the vending machine, his head slowly bobbing back and forth as he nodded off. Jeff woke him, thanked him for his help and gave him cab fare to go home. He'd wait until André was out of surgery.

The doctor appeared about an hour later. "Who's here with André Wilson?" he asked.

Jeff stood up and walked over to him. "I am."

The doctor looked at Jeff just long enough for Jeff to catch the sorrowful expression that passed through his eyes. It vanished and the doctor became businesslike again. "We did everything we could, but André passed away a short time ago. He suffered a serious stab wound to his right lung. It severed an artery and he lost a lot of blood, causing him to go into shock. I'm sorry."

There it was. André's plea to live had not been granted. Jeff's prayer had not been answered. Or was it more simple? A sixteen-year-old had been playing a dangerous game and got caught. But did he deserve to die?

"Can you notify his family, so that the proper arrangements can be made to release the body?"

The doctor's voice broke into Jeff's thoughts. *Release the body.*

"Yes," Jeff managed.

He led Khareem to a private corner of the room and told him the news. Khareem was oddly calm—no tears, no screams—just a sniffle and a nod. Jeff suspected he was still in shock.

Since there had been no way to reach André's parents, Jeff was left with the grim task of telling them in person. Khareem gave him directions to the Wilsons' apartment in a zombielike voice. During the ride, Jeff tried to rehearse what he would say. How much would he tell them? He didn't know their son. He couldn't lessen the blow with a tribute. He was merely a messenger.

The Wilsons lived in a walk-up on Lenox Avenue. It had seen better days, but was in decent condition and didn't explain why André had turned to dealing drugs. Jeff followed Khareem up the stairs to the third floor. When they reached the door, Jeff hesitated. Summoning all his courage, he knocked, softly at first and then with greater insistence.

"I'm coming. I'm coming," a woman called out after a short while. "Is that you, André?" Her voice bore a ring of hope.

"No," replied Jeff gingerly, "but this is about André."

She opened the door in a pink velour bathrobe. She looked at Jeff nervously. "Yes?"

"I'm Jeff Mont— Well, I found—I met your son tonight. He was badly hurt and Khareem—you know Khareem, right? Khareem and I took him to the hospital."

She tightened the bathrobe around her chest with clenched fingers. Her tone strained to remain normal. "How is he? Which hospital? Let me get dressed. Come in. It'll just take me a few minutes."

She turned her back and Jeff walked only a few steps before he called out to her, "Ma'am"—he stopped, holding back his sadness—"André didn't make it. We lost him."

She gasped. "No, no, no, no. Please tell me it's not my son! Not my son!"

"I wish with every part of me that it wasn't."

"Not my son," she repeated. "Not André!" Jeff steadied her to a chair. She put her head in her hands and rocked from side to side.

André's father appeared, sleepy-eyed and bewildered. Sitting with these strangers in their blue velvet living room, Jeff had to explain the grisly details. He told them as much as he could about André's last night, but dropped the criminal element. He didn't think it was the right time to give them that secondary shock, but maybe they had already guessed.

Jeff would never forget the anguished wails of André's mother, her denials and, finally, her resigned acceptance. Dawn was breaking when Jeff left them and instead of bringing the promise of light and a new day, the sky made him think only of death.

Nora sat in an armchair in the living room. She was on her fourth cup of tea and her taste buds had become numb. Jeff had called her at ten before he left the office, but eight hours later he still wasn't home. She'd been unfazed at first. Things come up; he would be home soon. By midnight, she began to worry and tried to call him on his cell. No service. Nora grew hysterical, pacing her bedroom until she couldn't take it anymore. She always assumed the worst. It was a bit of neurosis she tried to hide beneath her smiles and calm demeanor. She was close to calling all of Jeff's friends when the creak of the door opening jolted her. She jumped from the chair and ran towards the foyer. She saw only Jeff's face and threw herself on him, clinging to his chest.

"Thank God! Where have you been? I've been out of my mind! I thought something terrible happened to you!"

She released him from her grip and looked at him again, but this time from head to toe. "What have you been doing?" she asked, fear on her face. She inspected the amber spots on his jacket and jeans. "This is blood! Have you been in a fight? Are you all right?"

He dropped his keys on the console table. "I haven't been fighting. It's been a rough night. My cell wasn't working and I didn't think to call you." Jeff's voice wavered. "I tried to save a man's life . . . but he died."

Nora was confused. "What are you saying? What are you talking about?"

"*Tonight,* when I was driving Brian home from work," he tried to explain, "we were stopped by this kid in the middle of the street . . . and a sixteen-year-old kid was stabbed to death. . . ." He collapsed on a chair and had difficulty continuing.

"Come on, honey. I'll help you up," Nora said, reaching for him. "You won't be comfortable here. Can you make it up the stairs?"

He nodded.

"I'll get you cleaned up and make you breakfast. You can tell me what happened after."

She ran a hot bath and sat next to the tub, using a washcloth to rub the blood from Jeff's skin. He almost fell asleep, but she lightly sprinkled water on his face. She made him a bowl of oatmeal—comfort food always did the trick—and he dozed after his last spoonful. She called Jeff's office and told them that he was taking a sick day and informed *Muse* that she'd be working from home. Outside, the morning rush of wheezing garbage trucks and sputtering subways was well under way. Nora stayed in the bedroom, trying to conjure up a story idea, but her laptop screen remained empty. She stole glances at Jeff, thinking that men always looked like babies when they were sleeping. Feeling drowsy herself, she leaned back on her pillow and slept.

When Nora's eyes opened four hours later, Jeff was throwing logs and crushed newspapers into the fireplace. She jerked up. "What are you doing on your feet? You need to rest!"

He smiled vaguely at her. "I can't sleep anymore. I can't shake what happened last night. It's better for me to keep busy."

She had never seen him with such a weakened spirit. "I'm so sorry, Jeff. I wish there was something I could do."

"You've done so much already."

"I was really worried. I'm just glad you came home in one piece." She didn't really know what to say next and turned towards the window. A plastic bag had been carried by the wind and was caught on a branch. Finally, she asked, "Do you want to talk about it?"

Jeff lit a spark and climbed back into bed. "There's so much to say. I think it was one of those moments when your path crosses with someone else's, but you don't really understand why."

He described what happened. Nora listened without interrupting, but she felt a peculiar sense of doom about how life could be snatched away so quickly.

"Can you imagine," he demanded at the end, "having to tell a mother that her son died? It was the most difficult thing I've ever had to do in my life. And Brian and I didn't even want to get involved. We were suspicious, thought that maybe it was some kind of scam." Jeff shook his head in shame. "André would have died like an animal in that abandoned building. My problem is that I think I'm so down, that I know what's going on with young people. We sell records to them every day, right? But I haven't got a clue."

"Jeff, you know it's complicated. Their situation—"

"Nora, please don't give me that intellectual bullshit. I've heard it so many times, but it still doesn't change the fact that there are kids messing with their lives every day. There must be something we can do."

"Jeff, your heart has always been in the right place. You're still upset about last night, but you did everything you could. It was out of your hands. Please don't blame yourself."

He turned to her. "Nora, don't you see? I can't forget about it. I can't go back to my life as though nothing happened. I have to do more. I *want* to do more. I hope you understand what I'm talking about."

Her soothing words sounded hollow, even to herself, so she fluffed up his pillows and told him she was going downstairs to make a pot of tea. She found half a bagel in a brown bag on the counter and dipped the crusty dough in her mug. She didn't know anyone who had died a violent death. Cancer, heart attacks, old age—never murder. New York could make you immune to such tragedies too. You learned to block it out or you'd worry that sudden death awaited you at every corner. She doubted the press would report on André's killing. To them, he was just another statistic. His poor mother. Rather than hugging or nagging her son, she had to select a coffin, a suit, flowers.

Nora rinsed her mug and stuck it in the dishwasher. She should really straighten up the kitchen. At least a week's worth of newspapers was strewed on the table, and forgotten dry cleaning hung on the doorknob. She sighed. What was the point? A piece of Jeff's innocence, a piece of himself that he may not have even known existed, had also died with André last night.

Jeff and Nora attended André's funeral later in the week. Family, friends from school and neighbors made up the crowd that sat straight-backed in the pews, staring at a gray box, listening to a pastor tell them not to question God's divine plan. Jeff passed the open casket. The interior was white satin, the delicate folds and lace too childlike for the brawny young man André had been. But maybe that's how his parents still saw him, as their innocent child. They were burying him in a black suit and maroon tie, but a faded red baseball cap with the letters XL rested on his folded hands. The floral arrangement Jeff and Nora had sent stood off to the side on a pedestal.

He and Nora waited to pay their respects to Mrs. Wilson. A protective group huddled around her, but she broke away from them to embrace Jeff.

"I didn't thank you properly the last time," Mrs. Wilson said.

Jeff shook his head. "Under the circumstances—"

"Please," she insisted. "Thank you for all you did, for telling me about André's death." She clutched the gold cross on the chain around her neck. "And for leaving out what I didn't want to hear."

Jeff bowed his head. What could he say?

Mrs. Wilson looked at Nora. A small veil attached to Mrs. Wilson's black hat shielded her eyes, hiding the sorrow and dashed dreams of every mother in her face. "Do you have children?"

"Not yet."

"When you do, please hold on to them. Hold on to them for as long as you can."

Jeff went back to work and on the surface, everything continued as before. He held meetings, did the budget and released SuperNatural's album. He also called Khareem Thurman. No matter how hard Jeff pleaded, the kid wouldn't go to the police about the drug dealer who had killed André. Jeff called Khareem every day for a week, feeling like a pest, but Khareem never told him to go to hell or to stop bothering him. He seemed to like the calls and talked to Jeff about sports, school, how he wanted to move to North Carolina with his uncle. Jeff realized that Khareem was lonely. The boy's mother worked two jobs and his best friend had just died. The situation was so sad it made Jeff furious.

"I'll go with you to the police and personally help you file the report about André's death," Jeff finally told him.

Khareem said nothing and Jeff heard a radio in the background. Jeff let the silence linger. He wasn't going to nudge Khareem this time—the boy had to decide what kind of closure he wanted.

"All right," said Khareem in a subdued voice, "but you gotta have my back. I can't do this on my own. Promise?"

"You've got my word," assured Jeff.

At the police station, Khareem, who had only seen the dealer around the neighborhood from a distance, flipped through binder after binder of mug shots—fronts, profiles, hundreds of vacant faces—until he was able to identify him. The police guaranteed Khareem anonymity until the case went to trial.

Afterward Jeff asked, "How do you feel about what you've just done?"

"Better," Khareem replied. "I hope I'm doing the right thing."

"You are. You're looking out for all the other Andrés out there."

For the first time, Jeff saw Khareem smile and felt that all was not lost.

Yet Jeff had no intention of abandoning the pledge he had discussed with Nora. He researched ways in which he could "make a difference." He knew it was an overused expression, but he genuinely wanted to do his share, to touch lives for the better. He first thought of establishing a foundation but rejected the idea. It was too staid and distant. He wanted to get directly involved, not merely supervise. Gradually a plan began to materialize. It was a variation on a program that was under way in many parts of the country, but had not yet been tried in their neighborhood. It spoke to the interests of young people, but also provided them with guidance and support.

"Have you ever heard of Midnight Basketball?" Jeff asked Nora after their Sunday morning run in the park. It was a peaceful time, with only joggers and dog walkers for company, and the chilly air unburdened his mind.

Nora's eyes lit up. "I've heard of those midnight basketball games. In some places, they've had really positive results."

"Exactly. By providing alternate late-night activities in a safe environment, these kids can meet up, shoot some hoops and talk about what's on their minds."

"What's your plan?"

"I'm thinking education as well as recreation and not at midnight. But a basketball game combined with a tutoring session one or two evenings a week, from seven to eleven. There'd be a place for kids to go for a couple of hours to study and play ball."

"I could help too. I wouldn't mind tutoring. Have you found courts or a venue?"

"I want to talk to the administration at the Mahalia Jackson School. Maybe they'd let me use the gym if they think it's for a good cause." Jeff shrugged. "Who knows if this'll work? But at least it's an idea. It's a start."

"Absolutely," Nora agreed.

"They're allowing us to use the gym on Wednesday nights," Jeff announced triumphantly two days later. "The janitors and a security guard will still be on duty, but we have to make sure we clean up after each session. We can start in two weeks."

Jeff and Nora approached the Parekhs with their idea and both Anna and Webster signed on without reservation. Webster wasn't athletic, but he would be a perfect tutor. Jeff and Nora would buy the juice, soda, chips and sandwiches, considering it a minor but worthwhile expense. She also suggested contacting Columbia and City College for student volunteers. They taped flyers to phone booths, storefronts and subway stations around Hamilton Heights, St. Nicholas Park and Lenox Avenue to spread the word. They also met with pastors from neighborhood churches, who all promised to mention the program in their Sunday services.

The first Wednesday in February, the group assembled in the Mahalia Jackson gym: Nora, Jeff, Anna, Webster, Brian Harris and three student volunteers. New basketballs were lined up in a neat row, ready for action. Pencils, pads and basic schoolbooks rested on one folding table. The other was laid out with food and refreshments.

At a quarter to seven, Jeff cleared his throat and spoke. "I want to thank all of you for volunteering your time and skills tonight. We want to help an important part of the community here—young people. This is a small step, but my feeling is that every little bit counts. I don't have any prior experience with something like this, but my guess is we should just do what feels natural. If some kids seem shy or embarrassed, reach out to them. They may not be sure what to expect." He took a deep breath and smiled. "We may even have fun in the process."

They sat in the chairs, engaging in small talk as they waited. The student volunteers, two from Columbia and one from City College, looked fresh-faced, sincere and determined. Khareem came in at seven thirty with two of his younger cousins. The youngsters sat down with Webster and emptied their backpacks on the table, leafing through workbooks until they found their assignments. Brian organized basketball teams, three against three until more people arrived.

At nine o'clock, Anna said to Nora, "You know how it is, 'colored people's time,' " she joked. "I'm sure more people will come soon."

Nora wasn't entirely convinced, but she smiled and nodded anyway. By ten, Khareem and his cousins left. One student volunteer read from her philosophy book and the other two played cards. Brian shot baskets by himself. Nora, Jeff, Webster and Anna sat and said nothing.

Finally, Jeff remarked, "I know it's been slow tonight, but I think we should stay until eleven as planned. A couple more people might come through, thinking we'll be here until then."

They all stayed, but the hands on the gym clock shifted to eleven and no one else had come. They gathered the basketballs, food and books and left.

Later, as Nora stored the bottles of soda in the pantry, she said to Jeff encouragingly, "It's freezing outside, below zero. I bet that's what kept people from coming. They're probably apprehensive about trying something they've never heard of before. We'll just have to get the word out more."

"Who are we kidding, Nora?" Jeff asked wearily. "Tonight was a disaster. Look at me." He tugged her arm. "I thought I had it all figured out with my big ideas and plan of action. Maybe nobody gives a shit. Maybe I should just forget about it."

"I don't want to hear you talk like that," she retorted sharply. "We care. Everyone who came tonight cares. You can't give up after only one try. Maybe you were being idealistic. Maybe you are an 'outsider' trying to move mountains, but they didn't build the pyramids in a day. Don't let your ego get bruised by this."

He sighed and said, "It's Rome."

"What's Rome?"

"The expression 'Rome wasn't built in a day.' "

"Whatever. Who cares. You get my point?"

"Yes, ma'am, I get your point."

"Good. Because I think we should really see this thing through. You're doing something good."

Jeff kissed her nose. "Thank you. I can't see tonight as a failure, just a minor setback."

"Exactly," Nora answered, and crossed her fingers for good luck.

CHAPTER 10

H ilton sipped his second cup of morning coffee. He'd been out late the night before at a movie premiere, but always made a point of coming into the office no later than eight. He also lived a few blocks away, which made rolling out of bed that much easier. Spread out before him were the latest issues of *Billboard, The Source, Vibe, Variety, Vanity Fair, Entertainment Weekly* and the *Wall Street Journal.* He wanted to be well versed in all aspects of the music and entertainment business. He browsed through the "Markets" section of the *Journal* and grinned. Tech stocks were up. But scanning farther down the page, he grimaced. Entertainment stocks were down. Well, he couldn't win them all. He gazed at the plaque facing him on the wall. It was a reproduction of the front-page story the *Journal* had run about him and Jeff two years ago. He always laughed when he considered the pencil rendition the *Journal's* artist had done of their faces. She hadn't *quite* captured their features accurately.

He turned back to the front page and recognized the facial sketch underneath the headline on the upper right-hand side. The slicked-back hair and expression were incredibly familiar. His eyes traveled upward to the headline:

IN A SURPRISE MOVE, STARK NAMED
CHAIRMAN AND CEO OF NRG, INC.

Hilton had a sense of foreboding as he read the article. "Damn," he exclaimed when he finished. "Damn, damn, damn!"

He shoved back his chair and marched to Jeff's office. He arrived just as Jeff was hanging up his coat.

"Have you read the *Journal* this morning?" demanded Hilton.

Jeff creased his brows together and gave Hilton a strange look. "Good morning to you too. No, I haven't looked at the papers yet."

"Check this out," said Hilton, throwing the *Journal* on Jeff's desk.

Jeff picked it up, sighed and sat down. "Shoot. Read the article to me."

Hilton folded the paper in quarters and began:

> IN A MOVE THAT CAUGHT many in the entertainment industry by surprise, Lawrence W. Stark was named chairman and chief executive officer of NRG, Inc., the country's fourth largest entertainment and media conglomerate. Industry analysts have long known that Stark was being groomed to assume the top position when Michael Sandell retired, but were shocked by the timing. Sandell's contract would have expired in two years, but he opted for an early retirement, saying he wanted to spend more time with his family. Sandell also reiterated his confidence in Stark. "I feel very comfortable about the health of the company. Larry has proven himself time and again within the music group and I'm confident that he'll successfully steer NRG in this complex marketplace." Stark is largely regarded as an astute businessman as well as a successful schmoozer of the stars. He began his career with NRG in 1975. . . .

Hilton perused the text. "Blah, blah, blah. They're just rehashing his career history. But here. This is important. 'Stark distinguished himself at NRG by his creative business alliances and willingness to take risks. Stark's successor has not yet been announced and NRG is characteristically silent about who the potential candidates are. Many industry experts are already wondering about the fate of the projects initiated by Stark. "I don't intend to micromanage my successor," Stark stated. A leading industry analyst commented, "Given that Stark's imprint has always been so strong in the music division, he'll definitely be a tough act to follow." ' "

Hilton regarded Jeff expectantly. "Do you know what this means?"

Jeff rubbed his temples. "Why don't you break it down for me?"

Hilton was impatient. "Our deal, man. What's going to happen with NRG's proposal? Stark was the driving force behind it. It may end up in limbo now. We don't know anything about who will take over Stark's position. This person might have a totally different vision for the company. We could end up being seriously screwed."

"Hilton, what can I say? We're at the mercy of NRG. I guess we'll have to wait until they get their act together."

"Jeff, I can't believe your defeatist attitude."

"That's because everything seems to be coming apart at the same time! Attendance at my Wednesday night basketball games still hasn't improved after three weeks. One student volunteer told me last night that she wouldn't be coming back and I can't blame her. The possibility of our NRG deal falling through is only the latest bad news," said Jeff.

"That's why we need to fight back. We have to stay confident on all fronts. We need to remind NRG about the deal and their commitment. I'm not going to let this collapse." Hilton looked squarely at Jeff. "And I'm going to be persistent about it."

"Meaning?"

"Meaning I don't want to skirt around the issues." He paused. "Let me do it my way, Jeff."

"Do it," Jeff said after some time. "Just keep me posted."

Hilton ran back to his office and wondered if it was too early to call Stark's office. Would he seem nervous, desperate? In the early days, his brashness had sprouted from his own ignorance. He had never feared rejection because it was a small price to pay in order to achieve his goals. Today, he had his image and reputation to consider. Every move was calculated. Everyone was playing a role. He was relieved Jeff hadn't objected to his strategy. They were too close now. The NRG deal had been brewing in his mind for so long that it had become an indelible part of his consciousness. He had constructed his future around the money, status and opportunities associated with the alliance. He refused to allow a change in leadership to thwart his plans.

Hilton turned his options over in his mind. *I'll call Stark up and congratulate him. Then the conversation will naturally move onto our deal.* Pleased with that tactic, he picked up the phone.

"Mr. Stark's office," answered Jeannie, Stark's no-nonsense executive assistant, after the second ring.

"Good morning, Jeannie. It's Hilton Frears. How are you on this lovely day?" said Hilton in his best velvety voice.

"Fine, thank you, Mr. Frears."

"Will you be joining Mr. Stark in his new position?"

"He's asked me, but I would have to move to Los Angeles. I'm not sure about that yet."

Hilton laughed. "LA's not as bad as people think." He paused. "Is Mr. Stark available?"

"Unfortunately not. He took the jet to LA this morning. He has a meeting with the board of directors."

"Of course."

"But I'll definitely tell him you called. I'm sure he'll get back to you as soon as he can," Jeannie assured him.

"Thank you, Jeannie. I'd really appreciate that."

Disappointed, Hilton drained the last of his tepid coffee. Maybe Jeff was right. They were at the mercy of NRG.

Fashion editors are a funny bunch, thought Nora as she waited for *Muse*'s staff meeting to begin. They had access to the world's most wonderful clothes and accessories, collaborated with some of the most ingenious personalities in the business and could don a trend before it hit the mainstream. But ironically, they seemed antifashion. The untrained eye would be unimpressed. Only the real fashionistas would discern the tailored cut in a pair of plain black pants or that a simple pullover was, in fact, twenty-four-gauge cashmere. The fashion editor intimated, *I really don't take any of this very seriously. I am above disposable styles.* Clothes had to be worn with effortlessness and ease, a studied insouciance that implied, *This Gucci suit? I found it at the bottom of my closet!*

Nora thought back to when she had made her first foray into the magazine world. She had been terrified to work as one of three assistants to Jim Kay, a hardworking editorial director with oversight for five magazines and a serious addiction to Diet Coke. He didn't believe there was such a thing as being "unavailable" and didn't hesitate to leave messages in the middle of the night, fully expecting his staff to have sorted out the matter by morning. He kept Nora on pins and needles but also advised her to keep the journalistic bar high, regardless of the subject matter. Famine or cosmetics, he would say, she had a responsibility to produce good informed writing. By year's end, she was the only one of the three editorial assistants left and Jim became her mentor. He pushed and critiqued her, but she learned to manage his neuroses after realizing their root cause was his fear, as a man in his fifties, of being labeled "out of touch."

After a few years of nice promotions, Nora confronted Jim about her future prospects. She had pushed him into a corner, challenging him to be direct, and he was uneasy. But he reluctantly spelled out what she had already suspected. The insular company wouldn't have the courage to appoint a Black editor in chief for one of its established magazines. They still associated skin color with sensibility and didn't want to stray too far from the mainstream. Anything that couldn't be backed up by numbers was considered a risk. Nora could settle for a senior position, but never the top position. "And would that be so bad after all?" Jim had asked. "You still have incredible opportunities here. Everybody likes you. Your work is excellent. You'd still be among a select group. Isn't that good enough?"

No, it wasn't good enough and Nora let him know it by resigning three months later to join *Muse*. She didn't want to settle for well regarded and loyal, while being passed over for the more visible, sexy jobs. Jim had also made it clear that he wouldn't be prepared to fight for her, which hurt most of all. She had always identified with the underdog. It reminded her to take nothing for granted. She had learned from her early disappointments and, of course, from Jeff and Hilton.

All the fidgeting and chatter stopped once *Muse*'s editor in chief entered the conference room. Candida Blakely was British, cool, and always wore her blond hair in a tight bun. She had worked at all of the important fashion books, but had jumped at the chance to edit an upstart magazine. She was tough and intimidating, but valued teamwork and pushing the envelope. She also surrounded herself with people who shared the same view. Candida had scoffed when market research reported that putting a Black model on *Muse*'s debut issue would be unwise. It had become one of their bestselling issues.

Candida sat upright in her chair and folded her hands on the table. It was the stance indicating that the meeting had begun.

"This meeting will be about business," she declared, "the dirty word around here. I know we all love to pretend that we're doing this simply for the love of style, but our publisher reminds me every so often that it's also about *money*."

"I only do it for art's sake!" quipped Julian Cortès, *Muse*'s creative director, from his chair near the window.

Nora and the others laughed at Julian's comment. Only he could get away with teasing Candida in public. Nora and Julian had a terrific relationship, both inside and outside the office. He was a considerate friend, funny and tremendously creative. Julian was dark-haired with a strong nose. His eyes were an extraordinary green, flecked with bits of blue and gold on the edges of the irises. Depending on the light and his mood, different shades were in ascendance and the total effect resembled a peacock's feather. He'd been her Secret Santa her first Christmas at *Muse* and gave her a CD of remixed house music and opera—Soul II Soul meets *Madame Butterfly*. Nora had loved it and the polite nods they'd shared in the hallway turned to shopping expeditions and shared confidences.

Candida smiled. "Seriously now, we have to think about advertising and generating more ad revenues. The numbers are pretty good this year, but there are some key advertisers we still don't have. When we started the magazine three years ago, they gave us the usual song and dance: We were too young, untested. With their limited dollars they preferred to go with a sure thing."

Candida's assistant came in with a platter of fruit and sparkling water. There would never be any syrupy pastries or soft drinks for this calorie-conscious group. A newcomer in circulation services piled her plate high with strawberries and melon. Candida glared at her and the nervous girl shrank back in her seat.

The scurry of picking fruit and pouring beverages died down and Candida continued. "I think we've proven ourselves and that argument just doesn't fly anymore. I have an advertising goal for this year. I want us to focus on snatching one key account and milking it for all it's worth. And doing so will be a total team effort." Her incisive eyes registered the eager faces in the room. "I want no less than the Giacotti account. For those of you who have been living under a *rock,* the Giacotti Group is one of the most important fashion and luxury goods houses in the world. Couture, ready-to-wear, perfume, leather goods, wine—they've got their fingers in everything."

"Wouldn't I love to be Signora Giacotti?" mumbled Kate Cook, the director of Special Events.

Candida stood up and smoothed down the creases of her trouser suit—the latest Prada, of course. "We have to put together a multi-pronged campaign to woo them. And I'm going to need everyone's help. All departments—promotions, sales, editorial—will have to work together in order to prove to Giacotti that he can't afford *not* to advertise with us." She snapped her fingers playfully. "You've had a minute to think about this. What have you guys got for me?"

"How about throwing a party in his honor?" proposed Kate Cook.

Candida shook her head. "No. I want something more substantive."

"Kate never met a problem that couldn't be solved with a party," remarked Julian.

"It's never failed me in the past," Kate shot back.

More suggestions flew around the room.

"We could cohost an event with Giacotti on behalf of his favorite charity."

"Mmmm . . . ," answered Candida.

"Wine and dine his advertising director."

"Hire his daughter at the magazine."

Everyone giggled.

Nora listened to her colleagues and an idea slowly started to develop in her mind. This call to action was exactly what she needed. She had been so self-involved with the new house and Jeff lately that she had taken a routine attitude towards her work. She realized just how much she needed a professional challenge to feel revived. "How about coming up with an advertising campaign for him?" she offered.

Candida petted her blond bun protectively. It was her calling card, rumored to be set by a stylist from Frédéric Fekkai every morning. "Now, that's an interesting idea, Nora. Do you have anything specific in mind?"

Nora smiled. "Not yet. But I will."

* * *

Hilton answered his phone on the first ring. "Hilton Frears."

"Hilton, it's Larry Stark. I'm . . ." Stark's voice faded out.

Static.

Hilton bit his lip. "Hello? Hello?" he called out hopefully.

More static.

"Sorry about that, Hilton," came Stark's booming voice again. "I'm somewhere over the Grand Canyon now and the phone on my jet is not exactly cooperating."

"Thank you so much for getting back to me, but it wasn't urgent," Hilton lied. "I just wanted to congratulate you on your new appointment. The *Journal* piece didn't do you enough justice."

Stark laughed, clearly pleased. "It was all a bit sudden, but this is what I've been waiting for my whole professional life. I've got a board meeting as soon as I touch ground in LA. I'm going to be swamped."

"Of course. You're going to be an even more important figure in the industry now." Once the words were out of his mouth, Hilton wondered if he was being too obsequious with his praise.

"Yes," agreed Stark, without missing a beat, "but I don't want that to change what we have in the pipeline with Rum. I'm still committed to the partnership and my successor will be too. You have nothing to worry about."

"Oh, I wasn't at all worried," Hilton fibbed, "but thank you for reaffirming that."

"Hilton, you'll . . ." The words fought through the static.

"Yes?"

"You'll be hearing from us soon!" The connection was cut abruptly and Stark's voice echoed.

"Famous last words," Hilton grumbled, and hung up.

That evening Nora sat in the kitchen expectantly, watching Jeff prepare crepes for dinner. He was the crepe expert in his family, having learned the recipe from his grandmother Lila. It was the only thing he knew how to cook, so he did it with a flourish, packing them with fruit, jam or chocolate spread. Tonight, however, his movements were mechanical and the aroma wafted dispiritedly around the room.

Jeff had summed up the events of the day for Nora.

"It's all a bit exciting, in its own way," she observed as Jeff set down her plate. "Sort of like a corporate drama. We all want to know what the next move will be."

Jeff looked at her curiously. "I don't think it's so fascinating. I find this all very stressful. Hilton and I need to be sure that this thing is going to move forward."

"What's the rush?" Nora asked between mouthfuls. "You're letting Hilton's mad ambition stress you out."

"I don't think there's anything mad about it. We're just protecting our interests."

In spite of Jeff's moodiness, Nora was in good humor. He could be so intense and she was used to his occasional brooding.

She cast him what she hoped was a flirtatious look. "C'mon, honey. All work and no play. How much fun can that be?"

Jeff stared at her and started laughing. "Is that supposed to be a sexy look?"

Nora nodded.

"With jam dripping down your mouth?"

She dabbed her lips and cracked up. "I have no shame. At least I got you laughing."

Just then the doorbell rang.

"I'll get that," Nora announced, still smiling as she opened the front door. A thirtyish woman and her young daughter waited patiently on the doorstep. Nora recognized both from Hamilton Terrace but had never exchanged words with them before.

"Good evening," said the woman, meeting Nora's eyes. "I'm Olivia Sampson. This is my daughter, Kiara. We live in the apartment building across the street. I heard that you and your husband sponsor a Wednesday night community evening. I wanted to learn more about it and see if I might be able to help."

Nora realized that she had been locked in place, her mouth half open. She felt awkward and to make up for it, she became overfriendly.

"Hi. I'm Nora. It's so nice of you to stop by," she babbled. "Please come in. My husband and I were just having a bite to eat."

"We can come back another time," said Olivia.

"Oh, that won't be necessary. Let me take your coats." Nora bent down to retrieve Kiara's down jacket. The little girl smiled shyly and surveyed Nora closely.

"You're pretty," Kiara finally concluded.

Nora took in Kiara's creamy skin and puffy cheeks. Her brown eyes were wide and curious and her single braid moved in concert with each turn of her small head. *Too cute.* "And so are you." Nora smiled.

Jeff had heard their voices and came out to inspect. After the initial introductions were made, he suggested that they talk in the living room. He and Nora shared one of their twin sofas and Olivia and Kiara sat opposite them. They all faced each other, unsure about what to say next.

"I wanted to come by sooner," Olivia explained apologetically, "but I'm in the last year of my doctoral degree and with Kiara—time just escapes me." For the first time, she smiled and displayed a row of even white teeth.

"Believe me, we understand. I think it's great that you want to get involved. We can use all the helping hands we can get," Jeff said.

"Well, maybe my background could be of some use. I have a master's in social work and have worked for several nonprofit agencies and community centers. I'm actually a bit ashamed. I wish that I had taken the initiative and organized something like this myself. You know how it is. You get so caught up in your own stuff. . . ." Olivia's voice tapered off.

Jeff and Nora nodded knowingly.

"Maybe you could tell me a bit about your program and its goals. How has it been doing so far?" Olivia inquired.

Jeff and Nora looked at each other quickly.

Jeff leaned forward and began to speak. "We're still in the beginning stages, and have had, to be honest, mixed results. . . ."

Nora listened to Jeff explain their Wednesday night trials. She nodded occasionally, but basically gave him the floor. Olivia listened intently and made comments drawn from her own personal experience. *Sharp woman,* thought Nora as she evaluated Olivia. With her average height, bone-colored complexion and fluffy hair, which she kept in a short natural, she was the physical opposite of Nora. She wore small silver earrings and two thick silver bands on each middle finger. Olivia looked fit, even though her figure was hidden under layers of clothing. She reminded Nora of those collected but impassioned bohemians from her college days. Sanctimonious, they had shunned meat, dressed only in natural fibers and never read fiction. They had been so sure of themselves and worn their ideals like armor.

She noticed Kiara fidgeting on the couch, her small frame steadily sinking into the oversized cushions.

"Excuse me," Nora interrupted. "Would anybody like something to drink? Maybe Kiara would like a glass of juice?"

"I'm fine, thank you," answered Olivia. She looked at Kiara, who nodded. "Kiara, you can only have juice if it's natural. Otherwise, please give her water, Nora."

Hiding her smile, Nora tendered her hand to Kiara and the little girl's fingers linked easily with hers. In the kitchen, Nora removed the dinner plates and Kiara sat down. Her small legs didn't touch the floor and she swung them back and forth in the air. The cranberry juice in their fridge had last been used to make a Sea Breeze and was definitely not all-natural. Nora settled on seltzer and grabbed a small glass. As she poured the seltzer, Kiara asked if Nora had any rice cakes.

Nora peeked in one of the cabinets. "As a matter of fact, I do." She gave Kiara two and remarked, "You sure are a healthy eater."

"I try to be. Mommy says I have to start early. But I have a terrible sweet tooth," she admitted.

"All kids do."

"I'm not that young."

"How old are you?"

"Seven."

Nora thought for a second. "So you must be in second grade."

Kiara shook her head and munched on a rice cake. "I'm in third grade. I skipped a class."

Nora was impressed. "That's wonderful! Do you like school?"

"I love it!" Kiara squealed.

"What do you like about it?" Nora asked.

"I get to see my friends and my teacher, Mrs. Bridges. I get to read and draw. I have a part in the spring play . . . ," Kiara continued, and she and Nora bantered back and forth. Nora deliberately avoided the singsong some adults affected and spoke to Kiara in her natural voice.

I can do this, Nora thought. *Motherhood would be fun.* Since Christmas, she and Jeff had been trying to get pregnant, albeit without attempting a scientific approach. Checking the calendar, measuring body temperature—those were for obsessive couples. They made love two or three times a week and hoped the natural powers would take control.

Jeff and Olivia appeared in the kitchen doorway.

"We're going now, sweetie," Olivia told Kiara.

Kiara wrinkled her nose and lifted herself from the chair.

Jeff and Nora walked them to the door.

"Thank you again for coming by. We'll see you next Wednesday," said Jeff.

"Yes. It was really a pleasure meeting the both of you," added Nora.

Olivia and Kiara grabbed their coats and, chanting good-bye, walked out the door.

"Hmmm," commented Nora, "that was an interesting visit."

Jeff nodded. "Unexpected. But I think Olivia could be a lot of help. She made some really good suggestions."

They went back to the kitchen and their cold crepes.

"What does she do for a living?" asked Nora.

"Who?"

Nora rolled her eyes. "Olivia."

"Didn't she say she was completing her doctorate?" responded Jeff.

"Is she doing that full-time? How does she support herself?"

"She told me that she has a fellowship. It must be enough for her and Kiara to get by."

"I wonder if she's married."

"Nora, you are so nosy."

"I'm a journalist," she retorted. "I'm supposed to be nosy." After a few seconds, she continued, "I don't think she is. I didn't see a wedding band and Kiara didn't mention a father."

Jeff flashed Nora a stern look. "Nora, what difference does it make? We don't need to know their personal business."

Nora raised her hands in front of her chest in surrender. "You're right. You're right. Olivia just seems like an interesting person. That's why I'm wondering what her story is."

"Maybe Olivia will tell you herself one day," said Jeff, effectively closing the subject.

Later, in bed with the lights off and the moonglow seeping through the windows, Nora kissed Jeff. She showered his eyes, nose, lips and neck with her mouth. He murmured lightly and she raised her camisole over her head. She peeled off his tee and her insides felt dewy as she interlaced her body with his. Skin to skin, her breasts tingled as they touched his warm chest. Just as her hands wandered down his body, Jeff caught them.

Nora stiffened. "What's the matter?" she whispered.

He spoke in a raspy voice, his eyes half closed. "Mmmm . . . this feels terrific, but I'm a little tired."

"Uh-huh . . . ," Nora managed, confused and a little embarrassed. She cringed at this type of rejection. Maybe "rejection" was too drastic a word?

"But I still want to be close. Couldn't we just lie next to each other and cuddle?" he suggested sweetly.

Nora gave Jeff a peck on the cheek and moved her nude body into a fetal position. He'd had a rough day at the office. Lovemaking could be exhausting. "Sure."

Jeff curled himself behind her. He smoothed back her hair and cupped one hand around her breast. Nora heard him breathe regularly almost immediately. It took her a longer time to brush off her mixed-up emotions.

CHAPTER 11

"Bob Butler wants to meet with us to discuss our deal," Hilton told Jeff a month later. Bob Butler held the momentous honor of being Larry Stark's handpicked successor at NRG. Many people had been taken by surprise when the diminutive chief operating officer was given the top job over the charismatic executive vice president of Artist and Label Development—who subsequently resigned in a flurry of disbelief and anger. "Lunch at the Four Seasons tomorrow. Twelve thirty."

"The Four Seasons?" asked Jeff, bewildered. "That's a bit of a public place to go over the particulars."

"It was his call. I told him we'd be there."

"Fine."

The *Journal* had recently done an extensive profile on the five-foot-four-inch Butler, and Jeff had come to this conclusion: Whatever Butler lacked in physical stature, he substituted with ruthless business acumen. Whereas Stark was polished, Butler was gruff and direct. He nurtured his reputation as a tough, abrasive business manager and earned the nickname "Pit Bull." When NRG was forced to make staff cuts a couple of years ago, Butler took the blame as the hatchet man. Butler acknowledged that he was too much of a realist to relate fully to the mercurial qualities of making music. He was an operations guy by training and instinct. Let other people coddle the artists; his main concern was the bottom line.

Butler was in his early forties, with a balding pate and a lingering New York accent. The *Journal* reporter had almost mockingly described Butler's Italian suit, handmade shoes and Vertu cell phone. Recently divorced from his high school sweetheart, he had married the breakout star from a hit reality show that NRG produced. He was enjoying the honeymoon period of his new position and had already fielded requests to join the board at some of the city's most venerable charities.

Jeff and Hilton dusted off their conservative corporate attire for the lunch meeting. Butler was already strategically placed at a power table in the Four Seasons' famous Grill Room. Key players from finance, politics and media filled the walnut-paneled chamber. Jeff and Hilton provoked curious stares as they sat down with Butler. The new head of NRG Music had a satisfied smile on his face as he shook hands with them.

After the requisite chitchat, they ordered lunch.

Butler folded his hands on the table. "You were very fortunate to capture Larry's attention. The deal we've proposed is *very* generous," he reiterated, suggesting that Jeff and Hilton should feel lucky. "But I understand there are some sticking points?"

"There are a couple of issues we want to clarify in terms of management control and Rum's independence," responded Jeff. He wanted to go over his concerns point by point with Butler.

"The transition from an independent label to being part of a multi-billion-dollar music group will be a challenge," Butler stated, "but you can't expect us to be out of the loop. NRG's a public company. We have stockholders, have to keep an eye on our share price. We have to have controls in place with anything we do."

"We're very well aware of that. But take, for example, your stipulation that NRG gets a first look at all projects. That's fine. But if you turn down a project, why should the whole idea die? Rum wants the power to go to other parties for funding too. We're willing to commit to NRG, but we also don't want our hands tied," said Jeff.

Butler considered that for a moment. "It would look very bad for NRG if we rejected something that went on to become a hit for one of our competitors."

Jeff shrugged. "Well, that would be unfortunate. But if NRG doesn't recognize the value of a property from the beginning, then that wouldn't be our fault."

"We have terrific development staff—in all of our divisions. We've had hit after hit with our music and movies. Last year was our best year on record," replied Butler curtly.

Jeff thought of the assault of action movies that NRG Studios had released the previous summer. Despite their simple plots, each had grossed over one hundred million dollars. NRG Music's current chart-buster was a five-member pop group—and they were more a production act than singers. NRG's philosophy focused on the mainstream, the masses. Jeff wanted to raise the taste level. He wanted to blend humor, sophistication and intelligence. He was convinced audiences would respond.

Hilton cut in. "And we'd like to contribute to that, but in case of differences of opinion, we'd like options. We only want to cover ourselves," he finished tactfully.

Butler pursed his lips. "What else?" he asked.

"The contract states that NRG wants to cap any movie budgets at ten million dollars." Jeff laughed sardonically. "I find that a little unrealistic considering the average movie budget is thirty to forty million dollars. We want more leeway. That's the only way we'd be able to attract the right people to a project."

"The cost of making a movie has gotten way out of hand. That's a big concern of ours right now," explained Butler.

"There's a lot of waste, for sure. But that hasn't stopped your studio head from making hundred-million-dollar movies or paying fifteen million for a big-name star. What we're aiming for is definitely on a smaller scale, so you wouldn't have to worry about that. We just want a fair and realistic cap," asserted Jeff.

Their lunches arrived. Butler picked up his knife and fork and stabbed his steak. "You guys have a good business as well as music sense," he remarked stiffly. "Most people get bogged down by the details."

What did he expect? thought Jeff. *That we would have come to the meeting unprepared?* "Well, I practiced entertainment law before we started this company," he answered.

Butler rolled his eyes. "Lawyers—I only use them because I have to."

"Really?" said Jeff superciliously. "And what did you study in college?"

"Uh . . . communications," answered Butler vaguely. His eyes scanned the Grill Room as he ate. "Oh, there's Richard Graham," he observed to no one in particular, waving to the aforementioned figure.

Two suits approached their table. One of them grabbed Butler good-naturedly by the shoulders and said, "Bob, nice to see you again. Don't eat too much—it might mess up your golf game on Saturday."

"I'm light on my feet, remember?" Butler quipped back.

The suits looked at Jeff and Hilton with interest. An uncomfortable silence followed. When it became clear that Butler was not about to make introductions, they murmured farewell and walked away.

"We belong to the same country club," Butler explained. "In fact, I think"—he looked pensive—"that our kids went to summer camp together too." He then proceeded to rattle off about other unrelated topics.

Hilton was doing an admirable job of faking interest, but Jeff was seething. He didn't care about Butler's rudeness, but the man wanted to reaffirm his big-shot status and was deliberately avoiding the purpose of the meeting. By the time coffee arrived, Jeff tried to steer the conversation back to its original course.

"Bob, we've almost finished up here and there's another thing we'd like to discuss. It's probably the most important point. We'd like to retain the right to control the creative content of recordings. We don't want it to be a joint effort or decided by a committee."

Butler grunted and widened his eyes. "Surely NRG should have the right not to distribute any material it deems objectionable or too controversial," he said in a superior tone. "We are entitled to a voice. It'll be our money and reputation on the line too."

"We've been doing this for five years now and we haven't had any controversy so far. And we intend to keep it that way. But Rum's a place that encourages creativity. We make suggestions, but we also respect the artists' freedom. That's why they sign with us," said Jeff.

"We don't need any bad press," snorted Butler. "At the end of the day, I have to take the heat for it."

"Bob, trust us. The gratuitous stuff—sex, violence—it doesn't sell anymore," Hilton interjected, trying to settle Butler's doubts. "We were never in that business. You'll have nothing to worry about."

"If NRG insists on having a say on creative content," added Jeff, "I want a clause stating that if you turn a song down, then Rum retains the right to distribute it ourselves or through a third party."

"I'll have to think about that," Butler said, and reached in his jacket pocket for a pack of Nicorette gum. He popped a piece in his mouth and chewed very slowly, his mouth rotating like a cow's. "I have to release the nicotine," he explained to Jeff's and Hilton's stricken faces.

Hilton recovered and asked politely, "Does that stuff work?"

"It's not bad, especially since you can't have a decent smoke anywhere in this city anymore." He wiped his hands and signaled for the check. "I think you have a damn good deal on the table already. I think you could live with most of it. You'll just have to get used to having a partner, that's all."

"NRG will get more out of Rum, talent- and revenuewise, if you let us maintain the character of our company. Or else our core market will notice a difference," warned Jeff.

Butler signed the bill and tossed his napkin on the table. "By the way, I run a really tight ship—cost savings, rationalizing staff and expenses, that sort of thing. We will, of course, have to audit your company beforehand." He grinned. "Thank you for your time."

Outside on Fifty-second Street, Jeff couldn't contain his anger.

"Butler is an asshole," he growled. "He's a pompous, rude jerk. I can't believe we'd have to report to him."

"Let's walk and talk for a little while. It'll calm you down," Hilton suggested. "I agree—Butler's no Larry Stark. But he's a nuisance, an annoying fly. We put up with his attitude in order to cinch the deal." Hilton laughed to himself. "It must be tough for the guy. I think he's really insecure about his height."

"That must explain his Napoleon complex. And what the hell was he doing with that gum?"

"But, Jeff, you were a little feisty in there. I saw the muscles twitching in your jaw. You have to treat some of these suits with kid gloves," Hilton reproved mildly.

They walked eastward to Lexington Avenue. Spring was in the air. But the calm breeze and pastel candy colors in the shop windows belied the tight circulation and noxious fumes on the street. Jeff recognized the vendor in front of Bloomingdale's. Chip-toothed, he'd been around for years, selling clothing hangers imprinted with Chanel or Armani logos, mysteriously procured from these chic boutiques. Africans in dashikis peddled fake designer pocketbooks. Their straight faces and fervent claims of authenticity lured status-conscious women every time. This colorful bazaar annoyed Jeff today. Foot traffic was hampered and the heavy lunch lodged in his stomach like a bowling ball.

"Oh? So I should have just sat there while he went off on tangents?" he snapped. "Listen, we're in a good bargaining position. SuperNatural's album is number one. Except for that bubblegum pop group, NRG has an aging roster of acts. That's why they want us—for new blood. If I were as accommodating as you, we'd never get down to business. Believe me, I'm happy about the NRG offer. But do I feel grateful? No. I'm looking out for us—our company, artists, employees—when I'm being the tough ass. We have to show them from the start that we're not a bunch of stupid Black men they can take advantage of. Otherwise they'll never take us seriously. Do you really think Butler would make it so easy for us to become millionaires? He's showing us no respect. I wonder if he would act the same way if we were a pop or hard-rock label."

"C'mon, Jeff. Let's not get into that. I think we've proven to them what we're capable of."

"You think so? Don't get soft on me. It's a never-ending cycle of proving and asserting ourselves. We both know it."

"Why are you turning this into a racial thing? I don't think it's about that."

They had stopped midstep on Sixty-first Street. People walked around them, but Jeff ignored the irritated stares as they continued their heated discussion.

"Let me ask you something," Jeff began. "Doesn't it annoy you that someone who obviously lacks any musical sense, social skills or hipness like Bob Butler got the top job at NRG Music? Why isn't someone like you, who's lived for music his whole life, is intelligent and cool, in that job? Ask yourself that question. You might not like the answer."

Hilton let out a deep breath. "Of course I've asked myself that question. That's the whole point, Jeff. But I finally understand how the game is played now. Damn, I could outplay all of them. It means nothing to me to put up with Butler's bullshit to get what I want. I may not respect him, but I know how he operates. I'll be more demanding after we've signed the papers."

"Will you, Hilton? Will you be willing to stand up for the artists and the people working for us? You heard Butler. He's thinking staff cuts. I know it. Or will you be blinded by the money and prestige? You make excuses now, you've reasoned it all to yourself, but life isn't all about expediency."

"Jeff, please. You're looking too deeply into this. I won't let you or the company down. I'm doing this for Rum's future as much as for myself. Don't worry." He held out his hand. "Let's shake on it."

"Please," said Jeff. "That's not necessary."

"No. I want to."

Jeff saw that the twinkle was back in Hilton's eyes. He wanted to be the best friend again, not the combative business partner. Jeff took him on his word and shook on it.

On Wednesday night, Jeff and his loyal band of volunteers were setting up in the Mahalia Jackson gym. The longer daylight and pleasant weather had brought a moderate increase in attendance, and the new influx of young faces had strengthened everyone's sense of purpose. Tonight, however, the gym started filling up early and the crowd was also a bit older, with many more teenagers decked out in an alphabet soup of designer logos. They strutted inside and sat in small groups around the bleachers.

Jeff mentioned this to Brian Harris, who was standing next to him. "Something's up. We usually don't get this many teenagers. Don't get me wrong—I'm glad. But I wonder why."

Brian looked at Jeff sheepishly. "It's because of me," he said meekly.

"What did you do?"

Brian turned down the corners of his lip, shamefaced. "I spread the word that SuperNatural would be here tonight."

"You did *what*? How?"

"I scribbled it on a lot of the flyers we have hanging around the neighborhood and I told a couple of friends, who told a couple of friends. . . ."

"Brian, I think I understand what you're trying to do," Jeff said slowly, "but you promised something we can't deliver."

Brian smiled secretively. "Yes, we can. I talked to SuperNatural and he was more than willing to come here tonight."

Jeff scratched the back of his neck in thought. No wonder the kids were whispering and stirring excitedly in the bleachers. "Brian, we shouldn't be asking one of our artists for a personal favor like that. It's a conflict of interest," he said at last. "Every one of SuperNatural's appearances is tightly scheduled."

"I know, but he wanted to do it. He's from uptown. He knows the vibe here. He wants to do something for the neighborhood. Touch his fans. Keep it real. I think we can pull this off. Besides, this is how you gotta get kids interested. You gotta give them something they want. It's a little shady, but that's the way it is," explained Brian.

Jeff regarded Brian's innocent face and laughed. The kid was perceptive. "Brian, you'll go far one day."

Brian laughed along with him. "You're taking this a lot better than I thought you would."

From the table where she was helping nine-year-old Talita with reading, Nora watched with fascination as the arrival of the rap star of the moment was met with wild cheers, stomping feet and deafening applause. For these uptown kids, SuperNatural was one of their own who had made good. They were falling over each other to get close to the superstar, flooding him with pats on the back, elaborate handshakes and words of praise. SuperNatural symbolized celebrity, success and hope. Maybe his special mystique would rub off on them too.

Once the clamor had subsided, Jeff organized basketball teams. Nora could tell he was pumped by the fortunate way in which his work and program had come together. He observed from the sidelines and animatedly called out instructions like a proud father at his child's first game.

Nora refocused her attention on Talita. "Now, that word is 'augment,' then we have 'de-scent,' and next is 'pre-vent,' " she repeated the syllables with the little girl. Nora enjoyed tutoring and had even found it necessary to brush up on some of the subjects. The kids were fantastic and she loved the light on their faces when they finally solved a problem. Jeff's program lent a satisfying balance to her life. At the office, everyone got excited over rising or falling hemlines, as though the fate of the world depended on them. This program reminded Nora otherwise.

Olivia sat across the table from Nora, helping a young girl with social studies. Olivia turned out to be very committed to Jeff's program and had not missed a session since she and Kiara had first come knocking on their door. Olivia never talked down to the kids and had a unique ability to coax the answers out of them. Nora had invited Olivia over for coffee once, but she had declined. Olivia hadn't given an explanation either, but had merely said, "Thank you, but unfortunately I can't." Something final in her tone kept Nora from asking again. Nora sensed that Olivia was circumspect and kept her own counsel, so she never pried. Unlike Anna Parekh, whom Nora felt she had known for years, Olivia didn't open the doors to her inner self very easily. And Nora didn't push it, for she suspected that she and Olivia probably had very little in common.

"You have a great way with the kids," said Nora when Olivia finished working. "Jeff and I really appreciate your help."

Olivia turned to her, surprised. "Thank you. I've had plenty of practice with Kiara. I've learned what works and doesn't through her."

"Oh, she seems so harmonious. I can't imagine she'd be much trouble," replied Nora, thinking of Kiara's ease with adults and the way in which she had befriended Nora. Olivia always took Kiara with her on Wednesday nights and during downtime, Kiara would seek out Nora for a game of Uno or to show her a new picture she had drawn.

"I didn't say she was 'much trouble,' " countered Olivia.

Nora was taken aback and wondered how she had gone from complimenting Olivia to being put on the defensive. Flustered, she replied, "Right—that's not what I was implying. Anyway, look. There's Super-Natural."

Nora stood up and clapped her hands, blocking out Olivia's attitude. She felt as though she were back in high school being snubbed by the cool kids. *I'm guilty of trying too hard.* But Olivia was proving to be a big help to Jeff's program. It wasn't so simple for Nora to dismiss her. Furthermore, Nora had a real affinity for Kiara and did not want any tension.

A boom box bellowed out an instrumental version of SuperNatural's hit single. He clutched a microphone and once the first lines of the song escaped his lips, everyone erupted in riotous energy, waving their arms in the air, rapping in tune with him. SuperNatural inserted new lines to his hit song. "Stay in school!" he chanted. "Follow the rules!"

After signing autographs and receiving heartfelt thanks from Jeff, the rap star was gone. The gym emptied out and Nora rushed over to her husband to congratulate him.

CHAPTER 12

I t was the Friday before Memorial Day and Nora and Jeff languished in stalled traffic on the Long Island Expressway, bumper-to-bumper with the rest of the Manhattan mob fleeing the city for the Hamptons. Every weekend, from now until Labor Day, these pilgrims would converge to enjoy the Hamptons' beautiful beaches, fine restaurants and distinctive pastoral charm. The two-and-a-half-hour drive—on a good day—from Manhattan seemed a small price to pay in order to relax and enjoy life at a slower pace. Once a haven for discreet Establishment families and quirky artists and writers, the Hamptons had skyrocketed in extravagance and social competition. Wall Street, Hollywood and IT cash had irrevocably altered the landscape. The price of a three-month rental had reached the stratosphere, traffic jams threatened to engulf small main streets, and invitations to the season's parties and events were highly sought after. And one never really got away from it all. The same disagreeable faces one wanted to avoid in the city turned up in the Hamptons. Not to mention the fact that everyone always complained that the Hamptons were really losing their appeal and *simply* not as good as before.

Nora had resisted the pull of the Hamptons for a long time. She had convinced herself that she could really take advantage of the city when it was less crowded. Plus, weekend trips to different inns and seaside towns along the East Coast were much more pleasant and original. She finally gave in to the hype when the sweltering humid New York heat forced her to stay indoors for fear of fainting on the sidewalk. And anyway, she always waited until the last minute before planning those "unique" excursions. Jeff begged her to reconsider and she finally admitted that having fixed weekend plans for the whole summer might actually be a good thing.

They reached the classic shingled house in Bridgehampton at nine in the evening. It was designed in haute rustic style and had five bedrooms, four baths, a pool, a French country kitchen and state-of-the-art audio and video systems. They were renting with Hilton; James Parsons, a bond trader; Edwin Collins, a pediatrician, and his consultant wife, Sheila; Gordon Williams, an Internet guru; and Raymond Emmanuel, a vice president at Rum Records.

"Are we the last ones here?" Jeff asked as he carried their weekend bags into the airy living room.

"No. Edwin had an emergency tonight, so he and Sheila are coming tomorrow afternoon," Hilton answered.

"Great. That means there's still a good bedroom left," said Jeff.

"We've already staked out our beds, so you guys will have to fight over the double beds with Edwin and Sheila," laughed Hilton.

Jeff disappeared upstairs to investigate the remaining bedrooms. "Nora," he yelled. "We're taking the master suite with a bathroom."

She giggled and shrugged, "First come, first serve, I guess. How'd you get here so fast, Hilton?"

"I took a helicopter. It's really easy, right on Thirty-fifth Street. I got here in less than half an hour," he replied.

"You're kidding me!" exclaimed Jeff, hopping down the stairs. "Leave it to you to figure that one out."

Nora shook her head.

Hilton noticed and commented, "I knew you wouldn't go for it so I didn't even mention it to Jeff."

"It's just that helicopters freak me out," she said quickly. "Is that going to be your mode of transportation for the whole summer? It'll get awfully expensive."

"It'll be worth it. I can keep my car out here and start my weekend early. You guys should reconsider," said Hilton.

"Maybe we will," replied Jeff.

"Well," Nora sighed, "I'm ready to go to sleep. I'll see you guys in the morning."

"So soon? Ray, Gordon, James and I are going to Nick and Toni's for dinner and then we're going to check out the new club. I was hoping you guys would join us," said Hilton.

"I'll have to pass, but thanks anyway," answered Nora.

"What about you, Jeff?" asked Hilton.

Jeff considered it for a moment and turned to Nora. "Would you mind if I went with them? It sounds like fun."

"I thought you were tired," Nora sniffed.

"I'll sleep tomorrow. That's what weekends are for. I won't be home too late," he promised.

"Fine. Have fun," Nora mumbled.

She always felt like the evil stepmother at times like this. She knew that she couldn't prevent Jeff from doing something that he really wanted. She couldn't strap him to the bed and demand that he keep her company. But as unreasonable as it seemed, it was exactly what she wished for. The differences in their personalities had become more apparent lately. Jeff seemed to function in extremes, moments of pure happiness or sulking disappointment. He threw himself into everything—work, fun, her. They all fought for a piece of him and when Nora couldn't have it all, she suffered in silence. She felt strangely pathetic when she went to bed.

The temperature had already reached an unusual eighty degrees when Nora awoke at noon Saturday. She attributed her long slumber to the quiet of the country. The piercing horns and sirens of city life always kept her on the periphery of sleep. She shook off the sheets, but Jeff's back was to her and it didn't rouse him one bit. The guys had bounded in the house well after five in the morning—so much for Jeff's promise that he wouldn't be home late. Nora assumed she should be relieved they had all come home in one piece.

She felt rejuvenated and, after a quick bath, changed into her bikini. The kitchen was well stocked and she ate toast and orange juice for breakfast. No one else was up yet, so she leafed through *HAMPTONS* magazine. Pages of tanned smiling faces in summer whites at Bridgehampton Polo Club and in crazy hats at a benefit for Southampton Hospital stared back at her. Ads urged frantic weekenders to book tables *now,* lest they should find themselves turned away from this season's swankiest restaurants on a Saturday night. Many popular restaurants and clubs from the city had opened outposts in the Hamptons. People loved referring to the Hamptons as the "country." How could that be, when every conceivable amenity from the city and other far-flung corners of the globe had been transplanted here?

She walked towards the deck and slid open the glass door that led outside. It was humid, intensifying the lush scent of honeysuckle that perfumed the air. Bumblebees fluttered giddily around the climbing vines before diving like missiles into the red flowers. A squirrel leaped lithely from branch to branch on an apple tree, shaking leaves and nibbling furiously on tiny green fruit. The well-manicured lawn didn't have a stalk of grass out of place and the smooth turf neatly boxed in the pool.

In spite of her brown skin, Nora thought her face looked a bit washed-out. She wanted that sun-kissed glow. She padded down the steps and positioned a lounge chair by the pool for sunbathing. So engrossed in that simple task, she didn't notice an outstretched female form reclining lazily on the other side of the pool until she was finished. Who was she? Nora was sure she had been the only woman in the house last night. She walked barefoot to the other side and peered down at the long-legged figure, scantily clad in men's boxer shorts and tank top. Nora stared at her for several minutes, willing her to wake up, and the stranger eventually opened her eyes.

"And you are?" Nora asked curtly. She didn't like how this girl had made herself so comfortable, with no introductions or explanations as to why she was there. Nora found her presence instantly annoying.

She giggled. "A friend of Hilton's. I was left stranded at the club last night and couldn't remember my way home. Hilton said I could spend the night here and then call my friends."

"How nice of him," answered Nora sarcastically.

"I thought so," she purred, turning her back to Nora.

That girl has no intention of going home anytime soon. She went back to her chair and closed her eyes, trying not to think about the haughty girl who had invaded her solitude. After an hour, she was baking under the sunlight and had already turned a shade darker. Nora rubbed her stomach, prizing the deep brown hue. She swam twenty laps up and down the pool. As she dried off, she saw Hilton making a cup of coffee in the kitchen. Wrapping the towel around her waist sarong-style, she joined him.

"Hilton, what's up with Miss Thing over by the pool?" she asked.

Hilton looked confused and then, gradually, a look of recognition appeared on his face. "That's Belinda. No. Melinda. I think her name is Melinda."

Nora sighed heavily, obviously piqued. "How could you bring a strange girl you barely know to our house?"

"She had no way of getting home. What was I supposed to do?"

"That is the biggest line I've ever heard. She knows exactly what she's up to. Well, you better take care of her. I'm not babysitting her," Nora remarked tautly.

"Ouch, Nora. The claws are coming out."

"You know I'm not like that. I just don't get you sometimes. Whatever happened to Stephanie?"

"Same old story. She wanted to get more serious. It's not a good time for me right now," he explained matter-of-factly, pouring milk into his coffee.

"So, you think it'll be better with a stranger who's more than willing to be taken advantage of? Not cool, Hilton."

"Nora, stop being my conscience. I promise to behave."

"I'm watching you," she shot back half jokingly.

Hilton went outside, coffee cup in hand, and sat down near the edge of the pool. He dangled his feet by the shallow end. With his sunglasses, well-developed torso and athletic looking swim trunks, he was the picture of fitness and masculinity. He stared straight ahead. *What goes on in that mind of his?* Nora wondered, not for the first time, as she spied on him from the window. She had visions of wheels constantly in motion.

Melinda shifted position in her lounge chair. Upon noticing Hilton, she got up and stretched. She dived into the pool and swam to the shallow end, where the water was only waist-deep. She stood and slithered towards him. Melinda's white cotton tank top was wet and transparent, outlining her heavy breasts. Hilton gave her an indulgent smile as she flirted with him. Nora watched the prelude to the seduction and couldn't stop the longing she felt in her own body. She turned away abruptly, hoping to erase the sensation.

Edwin and Sheila arrived soon after and Nora was grateful for their company.

"Hi, sweetie," Sheila sang in her melodic Southern drawl as they hugged. She had been in New York for years, but her accent had never changed. Jeff and Hilton had been friends with Edwin since their undergraduate days. They badgered Edwin for disappearing once he'd married Sheila, and inviting him to share the house for the summer had been a way to bring him back into the fold. Nora liked Sheila and found it refreshing that she was on a completely different wavelength that didn't revolve around music or fashion.

Nora led them outside to the pool, where the rest of the group had assembled. Jeff, Raymond, Gordon and James were fixing the goal nets for water polo. Melinda was rubbing sunscreen on Hilton's back.

Nora gave Jeff a peck on the cheek. "So how was last night?"

Jeff looked at Raymond. "Should we tell her, Ray?"

"I don't know . . . ," said Ray. "She might not like it."

"I think we should leave out the after-party on the beach."

Nora punched Jeff in the arm. "That's not funny!"

"Who says we're joking?" taunted Ray.

Edwin was already perspiring and held his polo shirt away from his chest. "I love this house!" he exclaimed. "I think it's going to be scorching hot this summer. This was definitely a good move."

"That's not what the neighbors thought when the broker took us out here," said Gordon facetiously.

"They just got nervous when they heard that most of us were in the music business," laughed Jeff.

"Afraid that we'd travel in packs. Truckloads of people coming down for the weekend, blasting hip-hop from the windows, ruining the neighborhood!" Hilton added.

They all roared with laughter and made plans for the carefree weekends ahead.

Later that afternoon, Nora sat on the bed and watched as Sheila unpacked her and Edwin's things.

"I can't, for the life of me, understand how we can pack so many clothes for one weekend," Sheila said.

Nora nodded. "But you want to have choices and who knows when the weather will suddenly change?"

"What are you wearing for the party tomorrow?"

The group had planned a garden party on Sunday to inaugurate the start of summer. Between the eight of them, they had invited one hundred people, mostly weekend Hamptonites like themselves.

"It's either a Missoni or a Matthew Williamson dress. What about you?"

"I don't know. Nothing fits me anymore." Sheila refolded a cotton sweater and stuck it in a drawer. "Nora, do I look different at all?" she asked.

Nora leaned back and scrutinized Sheila. "Physically, I can't really tell. You just seem really happy."

Sheila grinned broadly and sat down next to Nora. "I can't help being happy." She paused. "I'm four months pregnant!"

Nora caught her breath and exclaimed, "Oh, Sheila! That's wonderful! I'm so happy for you and for Edwin. I didn't even know that you were trying."

"I got pregnant six weeks after stopping the Pill. Isn't that amazing?"

"My goodness. Bet you never knew you were that fertile."

Sheila laughed. "Edwin is so happy and proud. He can't wait. And the best part is that I know he'll be a good father. I see him with his patients. We only wish that we didn't have to wait until November."

"So you'll have a baby just in time for the holidays," Nora said. *Exactly what I wanted.*

"He'll be the best present ever."

"You already know the sex?"

"Edwin and I didn't have the willpower to wait until the end to find out whether it would be a boy or a girl. We did an ultrasound after fourteen weeks and you couldn't miss his little . . . *thing.*"

"Sheila, I'm so happy for you. You'll be a terrific mother." She peeked down at the slight swell of Sheila's stomach, which now seemed so obvious. "Of course Auntie Nora will help."

"I plan on leaving the firm once the baby is born. I don't want to work those crazy hours anymore. And all the traveling. I'm on the road every day except Mondays and Fridays." Sheila shook her head. "I've had enough. I've done the career thing. I know I'm good at it. Time for the next stage of my life."

"Do whatever you feel is best for you and the baby," said Nora.

The two women held hands. "It would be so nice if we could have kids around the same time," Sheila said.

Nora held back the lump in her throat and forced a smile. "I know."

She excused herself to take a nap, but she really wanted to think. The air conditioner was turned up high in her bedroom and she crawled underneath the covers and closed her eyes. She was sincerely happy for Sheila and Edwin. She remembered how Edwin had put a protective arm around Sheila's waist as they walked down the stairs, and sensed the strengthened bond between them. What could be better than expecting a child together? She knew that she shouldn't compare herself with them. But in a matter of months, she had transformed from a focused career woman, who was content to smile and wave vaguely at children, into a fawning baby lover. She practically tripped over strollers in the city and questioned new mothers doggedly. They always responded patiently, secure in the fact that they had successfully given birth and in their duty to impart that knowledge to other wistful women. Once, Nora had even followed a chic mother and her equally adorable kids down several city blocks, just to get a better look at them.

Her mother also nagged her about it during their phone calls. Valérie's normally relaxed attitude had disappeared with the thought of a bouncing grandchild on her lap.

"How's it going?" Valérie would ask tentatively.

"Hmmm . . . it's going. Nothing so far," Nora would respond.

"I think you should gain some weight. You're too skinny," Valérie had proclaimed during their last conversation. "You have to have some meat on you in order to conceive."

"I'm big-boned enough as it is. Is that an old Haitian wives' tale?" Nora had asked.

"I know what I'm talking about. Listen to me. . . ."

And on and on it went. Each conversation left Nora feeling more depressed than the last.

She put some of the blame on Jeff. He didn't seem to place a conscious priority on getting pregnant. His attentions were focused on his company and his Wednesday night community program. He was also considering an additional basketball evening once school closed for the summer. She would see even less of him then. Maybe she should start penciling in a time for sex in her diary. Somewhere between her boxing class and a manicure, perhaps?

Something wasn't sitting well with her. Ever since Jeff had declined her advances that night, she had turned inward. She knew that it was imperceptible to him. She was a master at masking her true feelings. She had resolved not to make the first move anymore. If he wanted it, let him come to her. Except she was painfully aware that it was less frequent than before.

On Sunday, Nora stood in front of her bedroom closet, ruminating over what to wear. The balmy weather called for something light and she wanted to look sexy. The ivory Matthew Williamson dress had delicate layers of silk chiffon and she hoped the flashes of pink and gold would add luster to her dull mood. She sprayed her summer fragrance—a citrusy combination so bewitching it was almost edible— on her chest, back, stomach and arms. She applied light makeup and lipstick, brushed her hair into a side part and tucked her long bangs behind her ears. She looked cheery again, her usual composed self. She took a deep breath and smiled in front of the mirror. She had to banish her insecure thoughts. *My problem is I think too much. Marriages go through hot and cold phases. A sexual dry spell doesn't necessarily symbolize disaster.*

She heard a soft knock. "Who is it?"

It was Melinda, Hilton's unexpected houseguest.

"Hi," Melinda said humbly after Nora let her in. "Am I disturbing you?"

"No," Nora answered, noting the girl's reformed attitude.

"What's this barbecue going to be like?" Melinda asked.

"Just some friends. It's not a big deal."

"But everyone will be dressed up, right?"

"It'll just be casual summer chic. These people usually look pretty well put together," said Nora, stepping into a pair of gold sandals.

Melinda looked sullen. "I have nothing to wear except my outfit from Friday night. And I don't think it'll be right for an afternoon party."

Oh, no. Here it comes. You should have thought of that before you threw yourself on Hilton and this house.

"I was wondering if I could borrow something of yours. We're about the same size," Melinda continued hopefully.

Nora wavered. "I don't know. . . ."

"Please," Melinda begged.

Didn't Melinda realize the questionable situation she had placed herself in? She was neither Hilton's girlfriend nor friend, merely a weekend fling. Maybe she wanted to shield that with new clothes. Suddenly, Nora felt sorry for Melinda and her good nature gave in.

She went through her dresses and pulled out a bias-cut multigraphic print.

"There," she decided. "This one will look good on you."

Melinda hugged the dress to her chest. "Thank you so much. I really appreciate this."

"But be careful," Nora added. "It's a Pucci."

Once Melinda had left to change, Nora went outside to admire the light, summery environment the event planner had arranged. Stark white chairs and tables trimmed with linen, and tin cachepots of electric blue cornflowers and yellow yarrow, were scattered elegantly around the back lawn. A buffet of summer vegetables, salads and berries would be served with marinated chicken, steak and shrimp scampi right off the grill. A DJ, waiters and two bartenders had been hired for the day to attend to the guests.

Jeff strolled over and gave her a glass of rosé. He burrowed his face in her neck. "You smell so nice." He ran his hand over Nora's bare arm. "So soft and beautiful," he whispered.

Jeff could take her anywhere with words like that. Her anxieties were probably unwarranted.

The invited guests filtered in around two, gradually dotting the back lawn until the cacophony of easy laughter and clinking glass became its own melody. Nora saw Erica and Dahlia climb out of a red Mustang convertible—top down, scarves wrapped around their heads, sunglasses perched on their noses. It was all very *Thelma and Louise*.

Nora met them on the gravel driveway and exclaimed, "Great car!"

Erica untied the long scarf from her head and threw it casually around her neck. "The best Avis had to offer," she boasted.

"Cha-ching!" screeched Dahlia, and all three of them burst out laughing.

Dahlia was petite and Erica more curvaceous, but with their tawny complexions and shoulder-length dark curly hair, the two were often mistaken for sisters.

"So, who's coming today?" asked Erica.

"You know—the usual suspects," said Nora. Most of the guests were connected to each other through school, work, family or mutual friends.

"What we really what to know is, are there any hotties?" plugged Dahlia.

Nora grinned. "Plenty."

Erica and Dahlia went inside to freshen up and Nora walked on, mingling and catching snatches of conversation.

"Which is better—a house in Tuscany or Provence?"

"If you go to Bali, you have to stay at Amankila. . . ."

"There's a three-year waiting list for a Gulfstream IV. . . ."

Nora stopped and spoke to William Hightower, a dapper writer who was a contemporary of Taylor Montgomery's. William was an eighth-generation resident of Sag Harbor. His forebears, attracted to the opportunities in the whaling industry, had moved to the community in the 1840s and William had written a critically acclaimed account of those early days. He kept a quaint cottage in the Ninevah section, a historically Black enclave in the village. He belonged to a different time, with a fondness for bow ties and pipe smoking, but he was a witty and insightful observer of the world. She preferred to talk to him rather than engage in the bragging and gamesmanship that often afflicted their group of friends.

"Quite a group you've assembled here today," said William, puffing on the pipe.

She liked the smell of pipe tobacco and didn't turn away when curls of smoke flitted up her nose. "I remember you distinctly saying that you enjoy"—she made quotation brackets with her fingers—"young people."

"Indeed. They keep me on my toes much more than my generation." He hooked his thumb on the first belt loop of his seersucker trousers.

"Taylor tells me that you and Jeff have been really busy." He winked. "That there's a big project you're working on."

"You mean the NRG deal?"

William looked baffled. "No. Baby making."

If it were possible, Nora knew, she would have turned red. "I'm so embarrassed!"

"Don't be. Taylor and I go back a long way. He's started thinking about progeny, carrying on the family name and all that."

William possessed an air of amused detachment that made Nora believe she could be frank with him. "All of that talk is starting to give me stress."

He patted her arm affectionately. "Don't let them put pressure on you. You have time. Now, what was that you said about NRG? Should I be calling my broker?"

She did a zipping motion across her mouth. "My lips are sealed."

Nora made her rounds, but socializing seemed to require a larger effort than usual today. She felt disassociated from herself, as though she were watching her behavior from across the lawn. *I feel so phony. Can anyone else tell that I'm trying too hard? That I'm having one of those "alone in a crowd" experiences?* She heard James shout "Gotcha!" as he and Hilton played dominoes for a small audience of onlookers. Even Erica and Dahlia were preoccupied. Nora had hoped that they could sneak away and she could confide her worries to them, but her friends drifted from group to group, laughing and flirting. And Nora couldn't fault them. She had invited them over for a good time, not a session on the couch. She looked past the apple tree and saw Melinda sitting with one of Edwin's friends. The Pucci dress gave Melinda a more refined look and she sat with her legs crossed demurely. At that, Nora couldn't help chuckling. If Melinda couldn't land Hilton, she would have no problem bagging someone else.

Most of the guests left by sundown. Nora had held out a little hope that Erica and Dahlia would stay longer, but they had befriended two guys who were in from LA, and went back to the city with them.

The more things changed, the more they stayed the same.

About a third of the guests, mainly single men and women, lingered. They were the true revelers and knew that the real partying would now begin. Sensuous gusts of music—what did Hilton call them? corny, horny songs?—pierced the afternoon's poised behavior, replacing it with loose conversation and flirtatious gestures. Nora began to relax. The evening air had turned cool and misty and she didn't feel as much pressure to be "on." The pool shone from underwater lights and glittered beneath the purple raven sky. She began to lose herself in the moment, but shouts and the commotion of car engines interrupted her tranquillity. She ran with a few others to check and was shocked by the sight before her.

Two black Escalades, filled to the seams with bodies, unloaded. Judging from their loud voices and laughter, this wasn't their first stop. Nora was about to ask who they were when she saw Hilton and Ray welcome them enthusiastically. At least twelve people headed for the backyard. The young women sat down at a table and began retouching their hair and makeup. Several of the men made for the bar. A posse of roughnecks had invaded their party!

Nora took Jeff aside and hissed, "Who are these people?"

"Some other music industry types who heard we were throwing something here today," he replied easily.

"But this wasn't an open party," she reminded him. "These people look rowdy."

"I know. But we can't just throw them out. It doesn't work that way. Besides, we have plenty of food and drink left over."

"Remember, we'll be the ones responsible when they mess up the house," Nora muttered, stomping off.

Someone raised the music volume yet again and the loud beats vibrated in Nora's chest. Raucous jibes flew back and forth. A steady stream of new faces sailed in until rows of cars haphazardly lined their neighborhood. Their house had become the impromptu party of the night. She recognized the flamboyant billionaire who never met a model he didn't like; the rap star arrested for soliciting a prostitute; the socialite who had made headlines when her fiancé jilted her at the altar; the songstress who was ridiculed for lip-synching during a live telecast. They were all there—Noah's ark of the rich and infamous. Hip-hop royalty cavorted with high society and other boldfaced names. The Establishment wanted to be down and the 'hood wanted respectability. It was a confusing, bizarre moment, sort of like the Black Panthers' being feted on Park Avenue.

Nora was fully in favor of intermingling but a persistent unsettling element marred the spectacle in front of her. They were at the crossroads of a new social order, a blend of celebrity and society where the racial and class lines were blurred. Money was still a badge of entry, but hype, perceived power and notoriety had become equally important. Park Avenue princesses and real estate tycoons could go back to their rarefied circles and crow about how MC XYZ had them shaking and grinding in their Belgian shoes. This month it was cool to hang out with hip-hoppers. Next month it would be something else—purple camels, jugglers, whatever. What mattered now was being at the right place at the right time. Jeff and Hilton may not have courted such attention, but it had fallen in their laps. What would happen to them and the soul of hip-hop afterward?

With so much excess, Nora knew things were likely to get out of hand. It took only one act to alter the course of the whole party. Melinda had progressed from toying with Edwin's friend to flirting with a movie producer. She had probably overreached herself. After some horsing around and false alarms, he pushed her fully clothed into the pool. Melinda landed with a loud splash, showering all within range. Nora stared in horror as her Pucci dress soaked up water and chlorine. A cluster of the jeunesse dorée thought that a spontaneous dip seemed like a great idea and jumped in too. They screamed and frolicked—their wet shoes, handbags and jewelry be damned. Not to be outdone, a pouty redhead unzipped her dress and plunged in nude.

Nora recoiled. She had seen enough. She needed an ally and searched the crowd for Sheila. Sheila was squeezed around a table with the balding billionaire, a gold-toothed rapper-cum-actor and their entourage. She looked stone sober, but her conversation was animated, no doubt brought about by her current proximity to celebrity. Nora went inside the house. It was teeming with people and she found Gordon leaning against a wall, nursing a can of Red Bull.

"You know with the music and crowd, the neighbors might call the police," she shrilled.

Gordon shrugged. "Only the police could break up this party. Just pray no one calls them. Or else we're all in trouble."

She'd forgotten how laid-back he was.

"Fuck tha police!" screamed a blond homeboy in a furry red Kangol who'd been eavesdropping.

Feeling very alone, Nora moved through the hallway, tripping over legs and bumping elbows. A strong hand grabbed her arm.

"Hey, Slim," said the gruff voice attached to it. "Can I talk to you?"

Nora tried to wriggle his hand off. His touch repulsed her. "Who the hell are you?" she scowled. "What are you doing in my house?"

"Hey, be nice."

"Don't fucking touch me," Nora warned.

He pulled her closer. His eyeballs were yellow and he was completely loaded. His breath was rancid and she fought with her natural need to inhale. She stared back defiantly and he finally let her go.

She massaged her stinging arm. She had to go to the bathroom. She cut through the living room and noticed an open plastic bag filled with dried greenish brown leaves on the coffee table. She bent over and picked up a glass, sliding the bag towards her as she did so. She squeezed the bag into a ball and rushed to the bathroom. She locked the door and leaned against it. She saw her reflection in the mirror. Her makeup had disappeared and her eyes were bloodshot. The bathroom was littered with forgotten drink glasses. A roll of toilet paper had fallen on the wet soiled floor. She took several deep breaths, dumped the weed down the toilet and flushed twice.

"What's going on in there? Other people have to go too, you know!" a voice shouted, banging roughly on the bathroom door.

Will this night ever end?

Nora didn't remember exactly when she had gone to bed. The last of the interlopers had left at sunlight. She stumbled into the living room, her clumsy steps a sign of her overwrought fatigue. It was worse than she thought. A storm had ripped through the room, leaving stains, spills and trash in its wake. Hilton, James and Raymond were already up. Or maybe they had never gone to sleep.

"This room looks and smells like shit," were the first words she uttered. She inspected a foul-looking brown circle on the white slipcovered couch. "I think someone threw up there."

The guys looked at each other and laughed.

"I fail to see the humor," Nora remarked testily. "We've got to straighten this place up."

"Don't worry about it. The housekeeper and lawn doctor will come tomorrow and everything will be back to normal," Hilton said.

"I would be embarrassed to leave the house in this condition for someone else to clean. Let's at least pick up the dirty cups and plates," she proposed.

They all protested, citing headaches, dizziness and hunger.

"Fine. I'll do it myself." She took a giant garbage bag and went systematically around the house, throwing cigarette butts, crunched glass, even a cell phone, away. She found her Pucci dress on a deck chair, twisted stiff and carelessly forgotten. After she finished, she trotted back to her bedroom and shook Jeff uncontrollably.

She ignored his cries for mercy and snapped, "Wake up. We're leaving. We're going home now."

"Why?" he asked. The rumpled pillowcase had left diagonals on his cheek, and his eyelids drooped stubbornly. "We have the whole day left."

How could he be so blind? "I don't want to stay in this filthy house anymore. And we can beat the heavy traffic back into the city."

"Nora, I'm too tired to drive."

"Don't worry. I will." She yanked the covers off him. "Go shower and get dressed. I'll pack our stuff." She didn't care if she was being unnecessarily mean. Her mind was made up.

They hardly spoke to each other during the ride home. Jeff was slumped in the passenger seat, dead to the world. Nora concentrated on the traffic around her. There were always crazy drivers on the road during a holiday weekend. She crossed the Queensborough Bridge into the city and took the West Side Highway northward. When Hamilton Heights finally came into view, she relaxed. Home at last. Inside, Jeff went to lie down and Nora sought refuge in their garden. She loved the garden. She had painstakingly repainted old wrought-iron furniture and planted hydrangeas, peonies, daffodils and lilies in the flower beds.

The garden had become her personal retreat—a place to read, think or just be. She desperately needed the peace and quiet right now. Communing with nature usually made her feel more centered. She took the trowel from her garden bag and began digging out weeds.

She did that for two hours before Jeff appeared.

"Hey," he said softly. "How're you doing? You're out here all by yourself."

"I needed some space after this weekend," she answered.

"I know. Things got a little out of control." He caressed Nora's cheek, but she sat still, unresponsive. "What's the matter?" he asked. "You don't seem yourself."

"And what is myself?" she demanded. "Smiling? Agreeable? Is that what you want? Do I always have to be happy when it suits you?"

He looked puzzled. "I'm only asking how you feel. You're obviously upset about something. What's wrong?"

Nora hesitated, but carried on. "I saw a side of everyone this weekend that I'm not sure I like. I suddenly don't feel very comfortable in our world."

"After one crazy weekend?"

"I see a pattern. Take Hilton," she pointed out. "His values are completely distorted. All he cares about are pleasure, women and money. I almost don't recognize him anymore. And he's dragging all of you down with him. I think I've outgrown this whole scene—the fast life, fake people. I can't act like it's nothing when someone vomits or smokes weed in our living room. It's not me. I don't think it ever really was. We're not kids anymore! We should all know better."

"But it's not me either," Jeff protested.

"You can't help being a part of it. You teeter between two worlds—the righteous side and the glamorous, privileged side. You've been doing that your whole life. You like the attention, the people, the parties."

"Nora, honey, that's the music business. You know that. I can't help all that stuff."

"I know, but it's taking its toll on me. I need my weekends to relax and have fun. I don't want the Hamptons house to become party central."

"I promise you it won't be."

"And we need to spend more time together. *Quality* time."

Jeff took her dirt-stained hand in his. "We're together all the time."

Nora pulled back. "You really don't understand. I'm talking about time alone, without people all around us. Or when we're alone, you're always tired. How do you think I feel when I see you carrying on all weekend, full of energy? With me, you're too tired, have a lot on your mind. And I just have to sit there and understand. God, we can't even make love unless you say so!" she blurted.

"What did you say?" he asked, startled.

"You heard me."

"Is that what's bothering you?" he cried. "That one time and you've been holding it against me!"

"No! Yes! Of course I felt rejected! I can't take everything like a saint!"

"I was tired that night!"

"And since then? We haven't made love in a month."

"Nora, I can't believe you're keeping track. This conversation is making me feel very inadequate."

"Good. That's exactly how I've been feeling!"

Nora blinked and tears flooded her cheeks, a ruptured hose that she couldn't seal shut. She hated this—crying was a sign of weakness. She wasn't going to take back her words or sugarcoat them to make him feel better. She just sat and forced her blurry eyes to focus on a mass of pink peonies.

"Listen, I love you so much," he said at last. "I guess I've been acting selfishly lately. You *are* always understanding. Maybe I take it for granted that you'll always be there to support me."

Nora sniffled. "I have my issues like everybody else. I just can't keep them all locked up anymore."

Jeff pulled her close again. She didn't resist and he whispered, "You don't have to. You don't have to."

CHAPTER 13

"So I hardly talked to anyone the whole weekend," Julian was saying on the Tuesday directly after Memorial Day. "This is the last summer I'll take a time-share in a house where I only know one person."

"You sound like your weekend was just as bad as mine," Nora sympathized.

"The worst part is that I'm back at the office feeling totally exhausted. The Hamptons are *not* vacation. Next summer, I'm renting in Connecticut," he declared.

Nora laughed. "I may join you."

She and Julian were bent over the storyboards they had collaborated on for the Giacotti pitch. Nora had conceived the idea and Julian had done an ingenious job executing her mental images. They had created a look book similar to the ones fashion designers put together to display their latest collections. It was entitled "Amuse Me" and carried stylish black-and-white photographs of a thoroughly modern, fashionable woman in a variety of smart and seductive settings—boardroom, restaurant, hotel lobby, ballroom, bedroom. Nora had styled her in clothing and products from the diverse Giacotti lines. Each picture was accompanied by a witticism like "Amuse me with your mind, not your wallet" or "Amuse me with your dreams—I promise not to laugh." Their muse was self-confident, inquisitive and provocative. Well-traveled and well-read, she was always moving forward—an iconic ideal meant to convince Emilio Giacotti that *Muse* was the place to be.

The magazine's presentation to Giacotti was scheduled for next week and Candida was driving them all ragged with her demands. She had finally approved the shots, text and graphics for the look book and it would soon go to the printers. Nora was pleased with the product, but would her point of view, her vision of what *Muse* represented, capture Giacotti's imagination?

"Julian, I'll lose my mind if I have to look at these pages again!" she cried, scraping back her chair and stretching.

"That's usually a good sign that we shouldn't play with this anymore," he agreed, shuffling the storyboards together in a neat stack.

"The proofs have to come back from the printer no later than Friday. If there are any mistakes, we could fix them up by the time Giacotti comes next Wednesday," Nora instructed.

Julian yawned. "That man's invisible presence has been in the office too long. I think we'll all be glad when it's over."

"I've kind of enjoyed this whole thing. It's given me a chance to stretch creatively. I needed that."

"Is everything all right?" he asked gently.

Nora smiled. "Everything's fine," she reassured him. "You know how it is sometimes—how you can just feel kind of blah."

Julian regarded her skeptically.

"I'm serious," Nora laughed.

"If you say so."

The subway ride home that evening was noisy and crowded. For a brief moment, Nora missed the ease of walking home from work. While her commute allowed her to catch up on her reading, she usually ended up watching the other riders. Her subway line was a veritable microcosm of the city. Young and old, every ethnicity imaginable, students, professionals, artists, laborers—all of them forced to coexist for the length of the subway ride. Her eyes focused on an elderly woman who sat primly with her purse on her lap and a shopping bag between her legs. From her lined face and soft skin emanated a certain peace and wisdom. Nora wondered if that calm came only with age.

After confessing her anxieties to Jeff, Nora had begun to feel that she had made too much of recent events. She was supposed to be bigger, tougher, stronger. After all, she worked in the media and fashion industries and had seen her share of decadence. But it had never infiltrated her private life or the people she cared about. That's why she found it all so disturbing.

The subway doors slid open at her stop and she mounted the steps from the caged heat of the station to the relative coolness of the street. She passed St. Nicholas Park as it rustled with twilight activity. A dozen or so men played their nightly games of chess to the beat of loud music blaring from radios. Kids jumped rope, dribbled basketballs, wheeled around in bikes and hopscotched without a care in the world. It was a pure neighborhood collage, a dose of reality and normalcy that Nora cherished. She walked up the steep hill to Hamilton Terrace. Blooming buds of red, yellow and purple peeked out like butterflies from flower boxes on window ledges.

She was surprised to find Jeff home.

"Remember those lists we wrote about the places we'd like to travel?" he asked.

She nodded. One afternoon during their honeymoon in Venice, feeling wonderfully light-headed from Bellinis and lazily watching gondolas pass through the canals, they'd written separate lists on paper napkins of the ten places around the world they wanted to visit most. The places they both had in common would be the ones they visited first. Capetown, Hong Kong, Kathmandu, Costa Rica—they had promised to take at least one of these trips a year. Two years later, work and everyday life had encroached on those dreams. The napkins were frayed and folded in a keepsake box in Nora's closet with the pledge of *someday*.

"Well, I think it's finally time we took one of those vacations," he said, waving two plane tickets in the air.

"Really?" said Nora, excitement building in her stomach. "Where to?"

"Guess."

"I can't guess. Just show me the tickets," she begged, and reached out for them with her hands.

Jeff hid them behind his back and laughed.

"You're really enjoying this, aren't you?" she said, and tickled his ribs until he clutched his stomach and the tickets fell from his grasp. They were faceup on the floor and she picked them up, eyes frozen on the destination.

"No!" she shrieked, and hugged him. "Marrakech!" Morocco had been on both of their lists. "This is fantastic!"

"We leave tomorrow night and come back on Sunday. Is that OK? Anna and Webster said they could cover for us at the tutoring session."

Tomorrow? Nora would have to get Candida's approval and thought of the proofs that were due to come back on Friday. Her oversight and input would be crucial before they did a final run. Jeff must think she had a really flexible schedule at *Muse*. But she knew he was trying, especially since he was willing to be away on a Wednesday night. She didn't want to dampen the lighthearted mood and explain her predicament. "Not at all," she finally answered. She'd figure it out later. "Nothing would please me more."

Candida gave her permission on two conditions: the first being a promise to scout Marrakech for future shoots and articles, the second an OK from Julian that he could polish up "Amuse Me" on his own. When she asked him, he pretended to strangle her, but assured her he could handle it and wished her bon voyage. Nora knew she owed him, big-time.

She and Jeff landed in Marrakech on Thursday morning. Nora had really begun to feel the thrill of the trip when the captain announced they were leaving Portugal and she saw the uneven coastline break into the fabulous green blue of the Mediterranean from her airplane window. And when she spotted the Rock of Gibraltar, a sense of history and adventure almost overtook her.

The airport at Marrakech was a kaleidoscope of exquisite colored tiles. Nora saw Berbers in traditional cloths lying on blankets on the floor of the transit lounge, modern-day nomads traveling by air instead of camels. Schedules of daily flights to Lisbon, Marseille and Toulouse only reinforced how linked this North African country was to Europe. French and Arabic echoed against the tiled walls. Armed guards wearing starched light blue shirts, navy trousers and trim mustaches patrolled the airport, keeping a stern eye on beggars. Nora and Jeff were picked up at the airport by a driver from the hotel, Sami, a friendly man in a lightweight white tunic and fez hat who spoke Arabic (of course), stilted English and rapid French.

Jeff squeezed Nora's hand and whispered, "You'll have to be our translator."

Nora's French was rusty, but the driver was enthusiastic when she started tying words and phrases together.

"*Nous habitons à* New York," she told him after he had asked where they were from.

"Ah, *j'ai un cousin qui habite à* Brooklyn," he said.

"*Mais oui?*" she answered, and then to Jeff, "He says he has a cousin who lives in Brooklyn."

Jeff laughed, "I caught that much."

The journey to their hotel, La Mamounia, was short but vivid enough to capture a tantalizing layer of this ancient city. Marrakech was a tableau washed in orange-red, from the desert to the tall city walls to the turreted rooftops. The dramatic scent of camels, incense and woodsmoke penetrated the open car windows like the lid had been lifted on a slow-simmering pot of stew. They saw camels and donkeys weighed down with goods reposing on patches of sand. Green palm groves and irregular tufts of vegetation sprouted from the parched earth. The majestic snowcapped Atlas Mountains guarded the horizon. Bicycles, carriages, mopeds, taxis, small cars and children riding piggyback swarmed through the bustling streets.

"La Koutoubia," said Sami, pointing to the minaret projecting from a gated park in the middle distance. It was the spiritual beacon of Marrakech, summoning Muslims to prayer every morning with the call of the muezzin, he explained.

Sami entered the curved courtyard of La Mamounia and deposited them in front of the grand doors. A porter dressed in baggy knee-length pants, complete with pointy slippers and a fez, removed their bags from the trunk.

"*Je reviendrai demain. Les souks. À quelle heure?*" asked Sami, clamping the trunk shut.

"*Onze heures,*" said Nora, waving good-bye. "We've got a date at the local markets tomorrow. Eleven o'clock in the morning."

They checked in and took the leisurely route to their room. La Mamounia was an illustrious oasis in the middle of the desert, an Art Deco world of Arabian Nights. Endless tiles, mirrors and doors painted in vibrant geometric patterns bombarded their vision. There were roses everywhere too. Redolent long stems jutted from elaborate bouquets.

Pink and red petals were sprinkled on tabletops and floated in fountains.

Their room had a cozy balcony that faced the pool. They unpacked quickly—the promised heat of Marrakech in June hadn't necessitated a lot of clothes—and went down for a swim. The immense pool was a cool blue sheet made more tempting by the dry terrain adjacent to the hotel's compound. Couples had claimed intimate pockets of water, whispering and holding each other below the surface. Jeff and Nora trod water until their skin was blissfully soft and puckered. Exhausted from the sun and jet-lagged, they got out and rested in deep lounge chairs underneath an umbrella.

Suddenly, Nora grabbed a magazine from her canvas tote and opened it to hide her face. "I know that guy over by the bar. The one kissing that woman. He's a photographer. I don't want him to see me."

"Why?" asked Jeff.

"He's scheming. He shouldn't be with that woman."

Jeff stared inconspicuously through his dark shades. "So he left his girlfriend back home and is having a little something on the side. Thought he'd be safe all the way out here in Morocco."

Nora disentangled herself from her own chaise and squeezed onto Jeff's. Half her body touched the cushion and the other half was on top of him. Her chin was on his chest and she felt his hand on her back. His fingers fondled the knot of her bikini top. The ceaseless heat and intermittent chanting that broke out beyond the pink walls of La Mamounia were dizzying, almost narcotic. The paradox of Marrakech—exoticism, solemnity and sensuousness—aroused her.

She set her cheek on his shoulder and closed her eyes. "It feels so good to be thousands of miles from home," she murmured.

"I know."

He played with a clump of her hair, which was drying like straw in the unforgiving warmth. She felt herself drifting off, escaping into a very serene abyss.

The pool was empty when they woke up a few hours later. Midday had turned into early evening and the sun was setting. Hot pink and orange streaked the sky as the sun disappeared behind the Atlas Mountains. They returned to their room, showered and changed for dinner.

Nora finished first and went down to the reception desk to convert their currency from dollars to dirhams. Afterward, she sat on a couch and waited for Jeff. She watched him walking from the elevators—the nice smile he gave the woman coming from the opposite direction, the way his light blue shirt complemented his toasted skin, the confident strides he took across the marble floor. If she were a stranger and not his wife, she would have wondered who he was, whom he loved, what made him laugh. What was it about him that gave her so much strength, yet made her feel insecure too? Jeff caught her eye and grinned, incapable of ever guessing the incongruous thoughts swimming in her head.

They ate at the hotel, devouring a meal of tajine, a lamb and vegetable stew cooked slowly in an earthenware dish over hot coals, and succulent clementines soaked in sugar with cinnamon and mint. After dinner, they strolled through the gardens. The sky was pitch-black with a luminous full moon. They passed the tennis courts and found a stone bench nestled between two trees. Jeff sat down, but Nora stood. She faced him, waiting for a clue that would erase the shy, careful emotions she struggled with lately when they were alone like this. He took her hand, bringing her forward to a spot between his legs. His head hugged her stomach and he touched the small of her back, snaking down, curving his fingers around her firm bottom. She sighed and gripped his shoulders. His hands moved up and down and she felt the increased pressure through the clingy jersey of her new dress. She knew what he was thinking. The fabric sculpted her body and discouraged panty lines, thong or otherwise. She had never gone out without underwear before, and in a Muslim country where some women still covered their heads, arms and legs, she felt deliciously blasphemous and wanton.

Jeff's hands were underneath her dress now, inching up her thighs and pausing at the opening of her sheath. He thumbed the sensitive fold of her skin and she felt the warm wetness flow out of her body. When had she become so excited? So utterly titillated and moist? He pushed the dress up her waist, loosened his trousers and pulled her towards him on the bench. Everything was in slow motion and darkness bathed their secret corner. She could make out only the shadow of his head and the dials of his watch glowing in the dark. But their bodies met, invisible signals communicating in the night. His rigid penis disappeared inside her and she straddled him, moving her hips, finding a tempo, bringing a moan to his lips as she contracted and relaxed her muscles. His hands squeezed her breasts and she trembled with pleasure. The dress, stretched out by Jeff's seeking hands, was bunched up by her ribs.

"Take it off," he told her. His voice was gasping, strained.

She lifted the dress over her head. She was naked and the cool night sent drafts of air on her bare skin. She heard conversation and laughter in the distance, the whistling of birds and insects around them. He sucked on her nipples and goose bumps surged across her body. She liked being taken like this. The urgency of his desire erased everything else. He carried her from the bench, her legs wrapped around his waist, and placed her softly on the grass. It was dewy and pricked her back like the hairs on a brush. He entered her again and she came at exactly the same time the call to prayer wailed out of the Koutoubia.

Sami was already waiting in the lobby the next morning. He was chatting with a porter and waved vigorously when he saw Nora and Jeff.

"We travel by foot. *Ça va?*" asked Sami. "That way I can show you all the special places."

"That sounds wonderful," said Nora.

They crossed the street onto the Avenue Mohamed V in the direction of the old city, the medina, of Marrakech. Sami described aspects of Moroccan history: how the country had been ruled by Berbers and then conquered by a succession of empires—the Phoenicians, the Romans, the Vandals and the Byzantines—and the introduction of Islam in the year 682.

"Islam keeps all the different people in the country together," he stated simply.

They reached the square, an eccentric palpitating market crowded with stalls, snake charmers, fortune-tellers, musicians and orange juice sellers. Nora checked her watch. It was only half past eleven, but a carnival-like atmosphere pervaded nonetheless. She doubted that much had changed over the centuries.

"Djemaa el-Fna," said Sami, pointing towards the ground. "*This* is the heart of Marrakech."

A skinny man in a turban caressed a snake wrapped around his shoulders. He grasped the snake's head and pointed it towards Jeff, just as the snake's quick tongue flicked out. Jeff staggered back and collided with a wood-carver. The snake charmer snickered and planted a kiss on his scaly companion. Sami glowered at him, mumbling something in Arabic, and the snake charmer scampered off.

Sami turned back to them, a reassuring smile on his face. "You have all kinds here in the square. I take you someplace nice where you can find beautiful objects. *Objets d'art.*"

He led them through a labyrinth of alleyways, telling them not to be fooled by the dusty doors and entranceways. Behind them were large and fine private homes.

"So much time is spent in the home," explained Sami. "Four or five families living under one roof."

"If Sami disappeared right now and we had to find our way back to the hotel, I would just call it a day," whispered Jeff.

"Don't even joke like that," she said. The alleys were never-ending, abruptly twisting into new passages like the branches of a tree. Squalid little workshops churned out leather goods, textiles and pottery. Merchants stopped Nora and Jeff every ten paces, begging them to come in and sample the wares. Little old ladies bent over like wilted flowers smiled toothless grins as they hurried past. Sami was on a mission and brushed all of them aside. He stepped through a low doorway and then another one, and Nora and Jeff entered a shabby garden with a tarnished sculpture of a horse in the center. Although the garden was weather-beaten, time and nature had given it a certain nobility. Sami shook hands with a mustached man in jeans and a T-shirt and escorted them into the house. Nora had never seen anything like it before—gorgeous cobalt blue tiles, vaulted ceilings, indoor fountains, a sauna, secret doors. She touched a mirror and the mustached man rushed up behind her.

"You want?" he asked.

Surprised, she answered, "It's very beautiful."

"I put it away for you," he said, and unhooked the mirror from the wall.

Anything she or Jeff showed the slightest interest in was promptly placed to the side on a coffee table. Nora was flustered at first but then realized that everything in the house was for sale. Their pile of goods grew and Jeff scrunched his eyebrows together. She knew that look meant that they had to cool it. There was no way they could carry everything home.

"You ready?" asked the mustached man.

They nodded.

"I'll get Boss," he said.

"What's going on here?" asked Jeff, an intrigued expression on his face.

"I have no idea," Nora answered. "But don't forget to haggle."

Sami had gone outside to smoke and they sat down around the carved wood coffee table. Boss came out. He was compact, balding and missing two front teeth. He shook hands with them, but Nora could tell by his guarded demeanor that he would be tough.

"You want mint tea?" offered the Mustache.

"Sure. Why not?" said Jeff. He smiled at her. She knew he was looking forward to the challenge of bargaining.

The objects on the table were moved to make room for a silver tray with beautiful multicolored tea glasses. Mint leaves floated like seaweeds in the steaming liquid. Nora and Jeff drank the tea and went through each item individually with Boss.

Boss held up an embroidered fabric. "This? It's an antique."

Jeff looked at Nora.

"I thought it was pretty," she said, "but we don't really need it."

Boss snapped his fingers and the Mustache briskly removed it from the table. After they had narrowed down their wish list, Boss took out a pad, tapped his lips with a pen and wrote something down. He turned the pad over, sliding it and the pen across the table to Jeff. Jeff inhaled and picked up the pad. Nora glanced at the sum, did a quick conversion to dollars and concluded that Boss was crazy. She whispered to Jeff and he scribbled in a new number, sliding the pad back to Boss in the same manner. Boss raised an eyebrow, looked at the pad and rose from his chair in a great huff.

"*This!*" he bellowed. "*This!* Is insulting! I have a family to feed!" He disappeared from the room, muttering in Arabic.

"Shit," mumbled Jeff. "What do we do now?"

"Everyone says you should go down to half the asking price," said Nora apologetically.

"Where's Sami? I don't know if we're welcome here anymore." Jeff got up to leave and Boss strutted back into the room.

"We start over," said Boss. The pad went back and forth; a few items were removed and then replaced again; more mint tea was poured. Boss loosened up, dropped an anecdote about Tom Cruise that was meant to impress them and finally agreed on a price—sixty percent of what he had originally asked for. Nora and Jeff now owned a Moroccan tea set; two dhurrie rugs; silver star lanterns; a fabulous mirror inlaid with coral, turquoise and camel bone; a small silver box used by Muslim women to carry the Koran; and beaded floor cushions. Nora had also fallen for a black-and-gold djellaba, knowing the caftan looked like something straight off the Paris runways. Boss was overly demonstrative as they paid, and even threw in free shipping.

When Sami resurfaced, Jeff and Nora were chorusing good-bye and thanking Boss for the mint tea. Boss said a few words to Sami in Arabic and patted him on the back. Nora and Jeff felt hot and surprisingly winded from all the haggling, so they told Sami that they wanted to go back to the hotel for lunch and a swim. In front of La Mamounia, Jeff paid Sami for his services as a guide.

Sami bowed slightly. "*Merci.* Next time you come to Marrakech just ask for me. They all know me here. *Au revoir.*"

Upstairs in the room, Jeff chuckled and said, "I bet you Sami gets a cut from Boss for every tourist he brings to the store."

"You're probably right. Well, at least we got some good deals—" Nora smacked her forehead with the palm of her hand. "Damn!"

Jeff was on his way to the bathroom but stopped in his tracks. "What's the matter?"

She began laughing hysterically. "I think we got taken for a ride!"

"Why?"

"Honey, Boss gave us free shipping. *Free* shipping from Marrakech to New York. That's not cheap. We think we haggled him down, but he must have made a bundle on us anyway. Otherwise he couldn't afford to be so generous."

Jeff considered that and peals of laughter shook his body. He threw himself on the bed and turned on the air conditioner. "Boss was definitely slick."

Nora kissed him on the cheek. "The slickest."

On their last night, they left La Mamounia and had dinner in the medina at a restaurant that had once been a private palace. Dinner was served in a majestically tiled dining room lit by candles and dazzling chandeliers. Rather than facing each other across the table, Nora and Jeff sat side by side on a faded crimson velvet couch, holding hands. Ever since that rendezvous in the garden, they'd more than made up for lost time. She also knew that she was ovulating, desperate to fulfill her new hunger for a baby. Had coming together in this mystic corner of the world created life? *Please. Oh, please.*

They had ordered an assortment of dishes—chicken with prunes, lamb with almonds, couscous, Moroccan *harira* soup, *bastilla* pie layered with chicken, nuts, onions and parsley—and sampled from each.

Nora munched on bell peppers and tomatoes seasoned with Moroccan spices. "Mmmm . . . cumin. I'm going to miss this food."

"Find the recipes and make them at home. You're the chef in the family," said Jeff.

"But it wouldn't be the same. Everything is more intense, more delicious, because we're here right now. It's the whole package—the smells, the noises, the dust, the colors, the people," she explained as musicians paraded through the dining room, rattling bells and banging on tambourines.

He gestured at the spectacle before them with his wineglass. "This has been a feast for the senses. It's incredible being able to lose yourself in a place."

"Or find yourself." Something had unfolded within her here in Marrakech. She'd been sleeping in a way, sliding into that New York nonchalance, forgetting all the simple discoveries that used to bring her so much happiness. She put down her fork and said to Jeff, "How did you know I needed this trip?"

He looked happy too; the crease between his brows had relaxed and he hadn't complained once about the stress ache in his shoulder that had bothered him for weeks. She'd gotten his undivided attention, had given him all of hers. Why couldn't it always be this way? But of course it couldn't. Marrakech was a marvelous dream, one that would end tomorrow. Why was she thinking about that now?

His hand stroked the nape of her neck. "I just knew."

The musicians had stopped twirling and gathered at one end of the dining room. The leader sat in the middle on a brocade cushion and blew on a thin, trumpetlike instrument. Next to him, an old man chanted, reeling everyone in with his hypnotic voice. The spell was broken when a belly dancer made her entrance, resplendent in green-and-gold chiffon; arms raised, her swinging hips seemed magically dislocated from her torso. The music escalated and she gyrated wildly, her face locked in ecstasy as she danced in front of the tables. A man and a small boy tucked money in the waistband of her harem pants. Two tables down, another man knelt in front of her in homage, while his bemused wife looked on. The belly dancer had everyone in her thrall. She oscillated her hips to the last beat of the drums and flew out of the room in a cloud of green chiffon. She received a standing ovation.

Jeff sat down and gulped his water. "Now, *that* was amazing."

Nora could still feel the belly dancer's kinetic energy crackling in the room. "There should be a warning on her: Don't try this at home."

"That little boy who put money in her pants was so cute."

She laughed. "I know. Start them out young, I guess. It's cool that his parents let him stay up so late."

"I think it's good for parents to take kids along with them when they do things. He'll probably remember this for the rest of his life. We can be so neurotic in the U.S. when it comes to raising kids."

"Are you referring to the playdate appointments, waiting lists and trilingual nannies?"

Jeff rolled his eyes. "God help us."

She wanted to tell him about the problem that had been blinking like fluorescent lights in her subconscious. "Don't you think it's strange that it's taking me so long to get pregnant? I've spent a good part of my life trying *not* to get pregnant and when I finally want to, it doesn't happen."

"Has it really been that long?"

"Six months."

"What did the doctor say?"

"That six months wasn't a cause for worry. If it takes more than a year, then he'll do some tests. On me *and* you."

Jeff shrugged and said straight-faced, "There can't possibly be anything wrong with me."

"Why do all men assume their sperm is sacred?"

He chuckled. "It's all about the timing. It'll happen when it's supposed to happen. Stressing about it just slows everything down. I'll do those tests if it's necessary."

She hoped they wouldn't be. But hadn't she read somewhere that one in ten couples had trouble conceiving? "Wouldn't you be happy if it happened here in Marrakech?"

"Definitely. I wonder when. . . . In the garden? The tub? The balcony?"

She felt those shivers again. "Stop."

"Am I embarrassing you?"

"No. The opposite."

"Oh. So I'm making you—"

"Don't say it."

A basket of fruit appeared on their table and Jeff ripped a blue black grape from its stem. He held it near her lips and put it in her mouth. "It's a good thing I know you're really not a prude."

Nora could scarcely believe that she was back in New York after the striking sights and intimacy of Marrakech. She had always believed that she needed order and structure, but could now understand how people gave that all up to travel around the world, relying only on their impulses and thirst for new experiences.

She put the notes on Marrakech she had hastily written down on the plane ride home in Candida's mailbox. Inside her own mailbox was a finished copy of "Amuse Me." Julian had done a fabulous job and Nora's mind instantly switched back to the present. The glossy book resembled art, not a flashy sales tool. Each department had done its share too. Sales figures, promotional material and *Muse*'s awards and honors had been researched, gathered and readied for presentation.

On Wednesday, Emilio Giacotti and his entourage entered *Muse*'s office and discovered a staff determined to impress them. Luxury encircled the fastidious Italian. He took fine things for granted, so Nora, Candida and Julian had bet on something else—attitude. Giacotti assumed his place at the head of the conference table and looked at the assembled group expectantly.

After welcoming Giacotti profusely, Candida began her pitch, describing *Muse*'s demographics and newsstand sales. Her voice, with its clipped British accent, was self-assured but not intimidating. Nora would speak next. She performed small breathing exercises to loosen the knots in her stomach.

"And now, I'd like to introduce *Muse*'s editor-at-large, Nora Deschamps Montgomery."

Candida's introduction broke into Nora's thoughts. She rose, straightened her shoulders and flashed the room her number one smile. "*Muse* celebrates the beauty, diversity and complexities of the modern woman . . . ," she began. Her nervousness abated and a building confidence inspired her delivery, bringing life to the magazine that she believed in and that had believed in her. Nora moved to a laptop computer and hit a few keys, bringing the PowerPoint presentation of "Amuse Me" to a wide screen on the wall. All eyes rested on the enlarged photographs and once Giacotti and his team laughed appreciatively at the unconventional captions, Nora knew she had them.

All too quickly it was over. The brainstorming, the months of creativity and preparation, climaxed in a ninety-minute meeting. The Giacotti people applauded graciously and were led to a private room where they met with Candida and the publisher. Julian and Nora hugged each other and exhaled exaggerated sighs of relief.

"We did it!" Nora exclaimed.

"You did, honey. I was just your humble servant, carrying out your wishes," Julian said with fake modesty.

"If he doesn't go with us, it won't be our fault. We gave all we have."

Nora went back to her desk and sorted through the pile of papers and messages that had backed up during the last few days. Filled with positive energy, she managed to reduce the mountain after two hours. But her uncertainty resurfaced when she was summoned to Candida's office.

"Nora, please sit down," Candida said kindly. "I really want to congratulate you and Julian on the terrific job you did putting together 'Amuse Me.' Giacotti loved it. He was crazy about how you presented his products. He's committed to advertising with us. This will mean significant money—and I do mean *a lot*—in ad revenues. If all goes according to plan, we're on track to exceed this year's profit projections."

"That's wonderful, Candida," said Nora. "That's what we all worked for."

"Giacotti wants us to release 'Amuse Me' as a supplement with the September issue." September, normally the thickest issue in the magazine world, was an influential harbinger of new trends. "Everybody will be talking about it. I guarantee you. We'll create a buzz around the whole thing," Candida continued.

"I don't know what to say," Nora managed, chiding herself for her dearth of words.

"Nora," Candida said firmly, "I know how much this magazine means to you, how hard you've worked to give it a singular identity in the marketplace. You've gone above and beyond my expectations. I accepted this job at *Muse* based on blind faith, but I've brought the magazine up to speed and put together a great group of talent. Management wants me to take on one of their other ailing books. I'm really going to need a right hand here during the transition. I would like you to be associate editor and then formally take over as editor in chief when I move on. You're a good journalist and you have perspective about this whole business. You never get fooled by the hype and I think that's probably the most important quality for an editor in chief."

Nora was too stunned to speak.

"The decision has already been approved. It's only up to you now to accept or decline."

Nora knew this was the crowning step of her career thus far and it didn't take her long to reach a decision. "Candida, I am so honored that you considered me for the position and I happily accept. Thank you!"

Candida smiled. "Good. We'll work closely for the next six months and then I'll hand over the reins to you. You'll be thirty-three and editing one of the hottest magazines in the country. Not bad. Not bad at all." She took the latest edition of *Women's Wear Daily* from her in-box.

"Oh, by the way. We have a closing dinner with Giacotti tonight. Seven thirty."

"I'll see you then."

Nora ended up running late for the Giacotti dinner. She had become absorbed with proofreading an article and lost all sense of time. She always kept emergency outfits in her office and hastily reached for a black wrap dress and slingbacks from her tiny closet.

"Nora, are you ready?" Julian asked, passing by. "The car's coming in five minutes."

"I'll be right there. I just need to freshen up."

The phone rang. Nora thought twice before answering, but her sense of duty prevailed. She tottered to the receiver, jamming her left foot into a high-heeled shoe.

"Hello," she said breathlessly.

"Nora, it's Jeff. Where are you?"

"What kind of question is that? I'm still at work."

"We're all waiting for you at the gym. It's Wednesday. Are you coming?" he asked.

"I can't come tonight," Nora explained. "We made our Giacotti pitch today and we're having a closing dinner. You've known all about this. I've been talking about it for weeks."

"The presentation, yes. But nothing about a dinner."

"Jeff, you know as well as I how these things are done."

"Can you get out of it?"

"I can't believe you're asking me that! I can't get out of it, nor do I want to. I worked my butt off for this thing and I want to see it to the very end."

"But we need you here tonight. We weren't here last week because of Marrakech. There are lots of kids. They have finals and need help studying."

"Jeff, I'm sorry. I really can't. Not tonight."

Julian reappeared in front of her door and pointed to his watch.

"Nora, I'm really disappointed. . . ."

Julian remained standing in front of her door, tapping his foot and reminding her that she was making them late.

Nora finally blew up from all the pressure. "Listen, I really can't talk now. I'm not like you. I don't have my own business and can't come and go as I please. I work for a company and they need me tonight. That's just the way it is. I'll see you when I get home," she snapped, and slammed down the phone.

Nora grabbed her purse and rushed out with Julian. Inside the car, as she tried to powder her face during the bumpy ride, she realized what she had done. *I just hung up on my husband! So be it,* she thought. *How dare he say that he was disappointed in me!* She had her own priorities and refused to feel bad.

She and Candida sat on either side of Emilio Giacotti during dinner at Daniel. The celebrated businessman had a humorous streak and he kept them well entertained. Candida had let her hair down—literally. Her standard bun had vanished and her loose, blond tresses softened her features. Nora thought that Candida was actually flirting with Giacotti, who was either married or between divorces. The sumptuous dinner and wine were liberally consumed and Nora guessed that *Muse* was already making a dent in the advertising dollars promised by Giacotti. Nora wanted to maintain a clear head, so she sipped her red wine slowly. She should have felt ecstatic. Today had been the pinnacle of her professional life, but conflicting thoughts began to creep in. *Damn Jeff. It's because of him.*

Nora declined her colleagues' invitation to continue the celebration at a downtown lounge and asked one of the waiting town cars to take her home. She and Jeff had reconnected in Marrakech and she didn't want to ruin their newfound peace. With her higher-profile job, situations like tonight were destined to come up again and again.

"Jeff? Jeff?" Nora called out as soon as she entered their house.

The rooms were dark, except in the kitchen. She followed the light and was prepared to make peace with Jeff. Instead, she found him sitting with Olivia, sharing coffee at the table. Nora tensed. It came upon her like a jolt. She resented seeing Olivia at the very moment when she needed desperately to be alone with her husband.

"Oh, hi," said Nora blandly.

Olivia looked up from the pad where she had been scribbling down notes. "Hi, Nora," she replied, taking notice of Nora's appearance from head to toe. "We missed you tonight."

"Unfortunately it couldn't be helped," answered Nora crisply.

Jeff pushed back his chair. "Thanks for the brilliant idea. We'll have to talk about it some more, but I'm excited. It sounds really interesting."

"What was that all about? Her 'brilliant idea'?" Nora inquired once Olivia left.

"There's a building over on Amsterdam Avenue that's for sale. Olivia suggested applying for a government grant and buying it, with the thought of eventually turning it into a community center. It would be a way of expanding what we're doing now," Jeff explained.

"I see."

"Don't you think it's a great idea?"

"Of course. Very charitable," she said with a hint of sarcasm.

"Maybe we should just go to bed," Jeff suggested wearily.

Nora changed into her pajamas and tried to read Jeff's disposition. He had obviously decided not to mention their peevish telephone conversation. He probably still expected her to explain herself—as she usually did—and which she had been prepared to do again until she saw Olivia. Worse still, he clearly didn't realize that he'd been inconsiderate towards her career obligations. He seemed to purposely not ask her about the dinner or her presentation. And just to punish him, she didn't mention that she'd been named editor in chief of *Muse*. She would keep that news to herself for now.

CHAPTER 14

I
t was only the end of June, but record temperatures indicated that this could be one of the hottest summers to hit New York in a long time. The heat gave Nora a headache and she longed for nightfall, when the sun finally went down. But she knew that her grumpiness had to do with a lot more than the weather. She hadn't forgotten Jeff's rebuke and then his deliberate indifference. Their uneasy truce at home rested on two pillars: He didn't ask her about *Muse* and she didn't ask him about his program. She came home from work one evening and found Kiara sitting in front of 35 Hamilton Terrace.

She reached the steps and hugged Kiara, lifting her from the ground.

"Hi, honey," she said. "It's so nice to see you, but it's getting late."

"I was waiting for you to come home," replied Kiara.

"You shouldn't just be sitting here by yourself. Something might happen."

"Nothing would happen. There are lots of people outside."

Nora looked around and saw neighbors talking to each other, fanning themselves and sipping cool drinks. Yes, people kept an eye out here.

"Do you want to come in and have some lemonade?" Nora offered.

Kiara nodded. She skipped to the kitchen and watched Nora mix the lemonade with rapt attention. Nora led Kiara to the garden and lit a scented candle.

"What have you been up to?" asked Nora.

"Summer camp. I take a bus to Westchester every day."

"That sounds like fun."

"It is, but too many bugs. I have so many mosquito bites. Do you want to see?"

Nora bent down and touched the pink scabs on Kiara's leg. "You shouldn't scratch them. They'll leave scars." Nora chuckled. "Kiara, I think you're a city girl. The country's dangerous to your health."

Kiara giggled. Her front teeth were growing in, the left one longer than the right. She brought the glass of lemonade to her lips and the tall glass almost obscured her small face. The candle had been burning for a few minutes, releasing a bouquet of freesia, and Nora and Kiara sat in a pleasant silence.

"I went to Girl Scout camp when I was your age," continued Nora. "I had to learn how to pitch a tent and took swimming lessons in this disgusting lake. It was filled with mud and weeds. . . . I hated it!"

"I've been taking swimming lessons too. The pool is freezing!"

"Nothing beats the ocean."

"I want to swim in the ocean."

Nora weighed an idea in her mind and decided to go for it. "Kiara, you know how Jeff and I have been going to a house near the beach on weekends?"

"Yes," Kiara answered.

"How would you like to come out there with us one weekend?" Nora asked. "Do you think your mother would let you?" And because she knew it was the right thing to do, added, "She could come too."

Kiara jumped from her chair. "Yes!" she exclaimed. "I'd love to! I'm sure Mommy would let me."

"Ask her tonight. We'd love to have you."

Kiara smiled and kissed Nora's cheek. Again, Nora marveled at how Olivia could have given birth to such a spontaneous and affectionate daughter. Olivia was raising Kiara to be self-sufficient, mature and independent. It was evident to all that Kiara flourished. She was smart, verbal, not unnecessarily silly. Kiara had all the ingredients to become an exceptional woman. Yet Nora supposed that she also longed to be treated like a child experiencing all the giddiness of growing up. She seemed to have discovered that freedom with Nora, who had readily opened her heart. And being with Kiara made Nora want a child of her own even more, especially tonight. Seeing Kiara waiting for her on the steps had made her forget the tension with Jeff. She was ready—no— wanted to give love, attention and care to a child, and not knowing when that day would come was beginning to consume her.

Kiara was so excited during the car ride the following weekend that it only reaffirmed Nora's decision to bring her and Olivia along. Kiara talked nonstop, so Nora didn't feel the strain of trying to make conversation with Olivia. Nora didn't really know what to expect from this weekend. She hoped that Hilton, James, Gordon and Raymond would be a little less spirited, if only for Kiara's sake. Edwin and Sheila were visiting Sheila's parents in Atlanta, so Olivia and Kiara would stay in their room. Weekends in Bridgehampton had calmed down, so to speak, and some ground rules had been established. Unexpected guests were no longer welcome, but the house was still a magnet for social gatherings. However, nothing had ever come close to that reckless first weekend.

Kiara's presence did have a calming effect and Nora could tell that the guys were on their best behavior. Nora invited another family over who had a daughter about the same age as Kiara and the two girls virtually lived in the pool, coming out only for lunch. As for Olivia, she seemed to have struck up a steady conversation with James. Nora kept spying on them talking. James looked particularly attentive. Olivia's black Lycra one-piece accentuated her petite curves and she had managed to get a tan. She was already attractive, but once she loosened up, she positively bloomed. *That woman needs to get out more,* Nora thought cheekily.

Nora, Olivia and Kiara spent Sunday at the beach. In spite of erosion and new construction, the Hamptons had preserved long stretches of unspoiled sandy shores, complemented by sun-splashed beach houses and dry reeds swaying in the breeze. The water never achieved a vibrant azure or turquoise blue, but the blue gray sea was mesmerizing in its subtlety. Kiara took her bucket and shovel and busied herself building a sand castle, frothy water pooling at her feet. Nora and Olivia sat on beach chairs and Nora decided to initiate conversation.

"What do you think of James? You've been talking to each other quite a bit this weekend."

Olivia spread sunscreen on her legs. "He's nice. Not my type, though. Could you imagine me with a bond trader?"

"Why not? Opposites attract."

"He's not—how could I put it?—intellectual enough for me. I like my men a little deeper."

"Well, in another lifetime, James was a Fulbright Scholar and spent a year in Senegal. I'm sure he still has some of that curiosity in him."

Olivia concentrated on smoothing the lotion on her arms. "Interesting. Truth of the matter is, I've never really been interested in these bourgeois types."

"What's Kiara's father like?" Nora dared to ask.

"Six feet tall, an IQ of one fifty-four. Brown hair, brown eyes, writes poetry."

Nora laughed. "Sounds perfect. But what's he *really* like?"

Olivia looked at her seriously. "That's all I know. Kiara was conceived with the help of a sperm bank."

Nora tried to hide her surprise.

"Shocked?" Olivia asked.

"A little, but more fascinated than anything else," replied Nora honestly. "What made you do it?"

"I was thirty, not in a relationship, and I knew that I wanted to have a child. I also wanted to get a Ph.D. I didn't want to leave everything up to chance," Olivia revealed. "She was the best thing I ever did."

Nora had to know more. "What did your family and friends say?"

"I'm from the Midwest and my parents are very involved with their church, so they didn't approve. But I'd sort of—I call it 'evolved'; they say 'disappointed'—a long time ago. I questioned too much, was more interested in the rational than the religious. They were too limited to know what to do with me. They see Kiara only once a year. My friends were divided. Half of them said 'Go on, girl' and the other half thought I was doing myself and Kiara a disservice."

Nora regarded her with new eyes. "You're so confident—and brave."

"Why shouldn't I be? There are enough people out there who try to hold you back. I never let them. I just do my thing and have never had any regrets," Olivia finished. "I would think that it would be the same for you and Jeff."

"Oh, I guess it is," Nora answered quickly. She wanted to change the subject. "I'm so glad Kiara is having a good time."

"She really is. I don't think I'll hear the end of it."

Nora laughed. "I love the city and can't imagine moving, but whenever I come out here, I get a *little* tempted. I guess it's ideal if you can have a taste of both."

"Well, you and your friends obviously can."

"Mmmm . . . maybe we'll be able to buy a place out here someday." Nora smiled and said, "If we do, Kiara is always welcome."

A cloud had eclipsed the sun and the air felt cool. Nora grabbed her long-sleeved T-shirt and pulled it over her head.

Olivia twisted the cap back on the bottle of sunscreen. "I don't think it's a good idea for us to come here again."

Nora did a double take. "Olivia. What are you talking about?"

Olivia let out a long, deep breath. "Listen, Nora, I appreciate what you've done by inviting us here this weekend," she conceded, "but this environment is not for us. It's make-believe."

"It's a weekend escape! It's supposed to be idyllic!"

"Everyone out here is basking in their success. Just look at Hilton's car. You could feed a village in Africa for a year with what he paid for that thing."

"Maybe he can be a little over-the-top," Nora admitted, "but he didn't have it so easy growing up."

"Neither did I, but I'm trying to help, not hoard!" Olivia exclaimed.

"Well, it takes some people a little longer to figure that out!" Nora shot back.

Olivia lowered her voice. "I just don't want Kiara getting used to this kind of lifestyle. I want her to live in the real world, with real people." She paused. "That's why I have so much respect for your husband. He's giving something back."

"We *both* want to give something back," Nora corrected her.

"Mommy! Nora!" Kiara cried out, running up the beach. "Come see my sand castle. It's finished."

Nora got up and brushed the sand from her legs. She was seething, but Kiara stepped in between them and held their hands. Together they all walked towards the sand castle.

"That was really nice of you to invite Olivia and Kiara out to Bridgehampton. Olivia told me that they had a really nice time," Jeff said late

Sunday night. They were back in the city and sat absentmindedly in front of the television.

"Oh, is that what she said to you? She expressed it a little differently to me."

"How?"

"She basically criticized our friends. Thought they were all too smug and shallow. What right does she have to say that? She doesn't even know them! *I* can criticize them—she can't!" Nora retorted.

Jeff leaned towards her. "What else did she say?"

"That the Hamptons were too showy, not exactly the kind of environment she wanted to expose Kiara to. It was so rude! After I went out of my way to invite them for the weekend! I thought it was really ungrateful. And Kiara had a wonderful time. She loved the beach, the open air. I just don't understand it." Nora shook her head. "Olivia seemed to be implying that our lifestyle was somehow unhealthy for children. The nerve."

"Well, I guess she was just being honest," Jeff reasoned. "She may have been put off."

"*Please.* She just thinks she's better than everybody else. I try to like her, to build some kind of friendship, but we are not compatible. She has this holier-than-thou attitude I can't stand. I've had it with her Earth Mother routine."

"Think about why Olivia may have said what she did."

Nora looked puzzled. "I told you why."

"But, honey, she may have said those things to you just as some sort of defense mechanism. Maybe she just isn't very comfortable in that kind of environment. She's not used to it, but she would never admit that. So she covers it up by pretending she's above it. Also, she's able to take good care of herself and Kiara, but she can't afford to take fancy trips or buy really expensive stuff. If Kiara spends too much time around things that Olivia isn't in a position to give her, then it might be damaging. She just doesn't want Kiara to become superficial. Olivia's a single mother, trying her best," he explained.

Nora considered Jeff's explanation carefully. "Why do you always have to make perfect sense?" She moved closer to him. She wanted him near, to forget their differences. "I can't help thinking, though, that she never would have said those things to you. For some reason she felt she could say them to me and I don't like it."

"That, I can't answer."

"Jeff, you can work with Olivia, she can help you apply for that grant, but please don't expect us to be friends. It just won't work," Nora insisted.

He kissed her forehead. "Don't worry about it."

CHAPTER 15

Jeff sensed that everyone in the office knew that something was going on. The way he and Hilton spent hours together in closed-door meetings couldn't have gone unnoticed. He had even heard some whispering—some of it hadn't been off the mark either—but no one had the nerve to question them.

The day of reckoning came when Bob Butler paid a visit to Rum's office. Butler had come by for his grand tour, the walk-through of Rum Records. He was on the lookout for the subtle intangibles that would not be reflected on balance sheets. Craig Turner, the studious CPA from NRG who would coordinate the due diligence process, loyally followed three paces behind Butler.

The visit started off badly.

"Your receptionist ignored me when I came in the lobby!" stormed Butler.

Jeff winced. "Maybe she didn't see you," he ventured.

"She saw me all right, but her *personal* phone call was obviously more important. I had to knock on the counter to get her attention."

"I'm sorry, Bob. I guarantee it won't happen again," said Hilton.

"What's her name?" asked Butler.

"Bianca Curry," answered Hilton.

Butler turned to Craig Turner. "Remember that."

After that rocky start, Butler began his walk-through. He and Turner marched down the hallway like foreigners invading sacred territory. Jeff sensed the shock waves reverberating around the office.

Jeff and Hilton had private rooms, but most of the office was separated into unrestricted working areas. Desks and bulletin boards were decorated with pictures and funny signs. People helped each other and shouted ideas across the room. The concept was free, hip and creative.

As long as the work got done—and it always did—there was no need for cumbersome rules.

"There are a lot of people here standing around talking. They don't look very busy to me. Why aren't they working? Isn't that what they're getting paid for?" Butler inquired.

"Bob, I think they're just naturally curious as to why you and Craig are here. We also have a very congenial working environment. Many of our employees socialize together. But the work is always top priority," explained Jeff.

"Let's all hope so," sniffed Butler.

They proceeded to the marketing department, which was undoubtedly the most dynamic spot in the office. Huge posters of the latest artists dominated the walls, the newest tracks boomed from the radio, and the staff sizzled with fresh ideas and plans.

"Bob, Craig, this is Raymond Emmanuel, our vice president of Marketing," said Hilton.

Raymond shook their hands and made professional small talk. But before they left, he passed Jeff a questioning look.

Jeff saw the confusion and disappointment on Raymond's face and mouthed the words, "We'll talk later."

In the hallway, Butler zeroed in on a young woman dressed in baggy cargo pants and a tight tank top that exposed her bare midriff. "Doesn't she get cold in that outfit?"

"We have creative office casual here," Jeff intoned.

"Not very professional, though, eh?" Butler pressed.

"Last I checked, we weren't performing brain surgery or moving markets. We're producing and distributing music. Giving people a little bit of pleasure. That's it," Jeff retorted.

Butler smirked and trained his eagle eyes on the next target.

They completed the tour and circled back to the conference room. An apprehensive silence ensued while Hilton and Jeff waited for Butler to speak. Butler sat down in a leather swivel chair and fished for his ubiquitous Nicorette gum in his breast pocket. He shook his head and let out a small laugh. "I have to say, my hat goes up to both of you. How this company has been able to function—and flourish—with the loose way you manage it is beyond me." He gnawed on two pieces of gum, his shoulders shaking from suppressed amusement.

Jeff stared at Butler and asked calmly, "What do you mean?"

Butler shrugged and raised his hands, as if the answer were painfully obvious. "You have no discipline here, no controls. People are coming and going as they please, dressing inappropriately, chatting away. Your receptionist out front doesn't even know how to address guests. There's no professionalism. And the head count is too high. You can't possibly need all these employees." Butler paused. "At NRG Music, we have trimmed the fat. I'm talking about decreasing expenditures." He pointed to Turner, who sat to his right, jotting notes on a legal pad. "Craig's job is to see where we could do that here. We should also fold some departments at Rum, like accounting and purchasing, into NRG. After you see how much more organized things can be, you'll be thanking me."

"With all due respect, Bob, we must be doing something right. Otherwise NRG wouldn't be interested in us. We've run this company with our vision and our own brand of professionalism. We may interpret that differently, but it works for us," said Jeff.

Butler rejoined, "You may think so. But may I also remind you that we're all here to maximize our profits."

"We understand that, Bob," interjected Hilton. "But you have to appreciate the differences in our business cultures. However, we'd be willing to consider cost-saving measures."

Those words placated Butler and he left the premises with his sneering mouth set in a straight line. Jeff stayed on in the conference room and studied the framed platinum album—Rum's first—hanging above the credenza and tried to stem the animosity fermenting in his blood. Twice now Butler had provoked these alien emotions in him. Butler's game seemed to involve breaking them down, belittling Rum's accomplishments and chalking it all up to "luck." Jeff refused to let Butler diminish them.

Hilton popped his head back in the room. "That wasn't so bad, considering."

"Considering what?"

"That Butler has no concept of what a hip-hop label's about and could have found fault with a lot more."

"Hilton, I think we should have an emergency meeting and finally tell our employees what's going on."

"Isn't it still too soon?" asked Hilton.

"When are we going to tell them? Once the ink's dried on the papers? No way. They know something's up. We're doing this today. Now."

"What do we tell them?"

"How about the truth?"

Hilton gave in. "OK. OK. I'm ready."

Forty-seven people filled the room within ten minutes of their request. Worried, bewildered expressions demanded an explanation.

Hilton spoke first. "As I'm sure many of you noticed we had a visitor today, Bob Butler, chairman and CEO of NRG Music Group. They've approached us with a multimedia offer for fifty percent of Rum Records. After we sign the agreement, Rum will be branching out into new areas—television, motion pictures, possibly publishing. It's a very exciting proposition, but some changes will be in store for us too. The demands will be greater, but we're being given the chance to expand the business. We'll all have to rise to the occasion."

The room froze for several seconds before the din of gasps and whispers tumbled out. A few reacted with muddled looks, not fully comprehending Hilton's announcement. Raymond Emmanuel's arms were crossed and he nodded, suggesting that he had long suspected such a deal was in the works. Jeff's hostility towards Butler was replaced by his sense of responsibility towards his employees. He had to make sure the NRG transition went smoothly, and decided to put a positive spin on the situation.

"Hilton's right. This will be a very exciting time. And we couldn't have gotten this far without your contribution. If this moves forward, there'll be many more opportunities, new areas of growth, for all of you. We just have to be a little patient in the meantime. If anyone has any questions or concerns, please let us know."

Raymond raised his hand and posed the burning question, "Why didn't you tell us about this before?"

Was it Jeff's imagination or were others looking at him and Hilton accusingly? "Raymond, I'll be honest with you. We have been talking to NRG for some time, but everything had to remain confidential. Nothing was finalized. It still isn't."

"Are there going to be layoffs?" asked Daniel, a project manager who had joined Rum a year ago. "I just got married. I need job security."

"And I just bought a car!"

"I just had a kid!"

Jeff figured this must be how Captain Queeg felt during *The Caine Mutiny*. Had he and Hilton shown faulty leadership by keeping the cards so close to their chests? The staff had already divided into two camps—those who saw the NRG alliance as a blessing and those who saw it as a threat. Jeff didn't know whether or not staff cuts would be necessary, but he didn't want to destabilize the company and ruin morale. So, before Hilton had a chance to respond to Daniel's question, he cut in, "No. There'll be no layoffs. We may need to reorganize some departments, but no one will be let go or demoted." *And I'll do everything I can to keep that promise.*

When the room had cleared out after the meeting, Hilton closed the door and cried, "Jeff, why do you keep saying 'if,' 'might,' 'maybe'? This thing is going through. The staff had better get used to the idea."

"And you would have preferred to just throw it in their faces, before they even had a chance to think about it! We owed them more than that. And I keep saying 'if' because we don't know what's going to happen. It all depends on the audit."

Hilton scoffed and paced the room. "You take care of all that stuff, so I'm sure it's all aboveboard."

"I don't like Butler's demands that we fix things. I don't think there's anything wrong with the way we've been managing the business."

Hilton snorted. "I agree with Butler. I'm sure there's room for improvement. Change is good. We started out as a garage record label; it's time we grew up."

"If that means letting some people go, I don't like it."

"Those same people would leave in a second if they thought something better came along! God, some of them would leave if they thought you looked at them the wrong way one morning. It's not about loyalty. It's about doing what's best for the company. Should we become stagnant instead? I don't think we can keep this company going for the next five years—at the level I'd like—unless we join up with NRG. Some people will have to go and others will have to be brought in for the new projects. That's the reality."

"The reality is that I still feel like a traitor."

"Get over it, Jeff. I did a long time ago."

"After the deal goes through, we'll have to give bonuses to the staff. Let them have a little bit of the fortune."

"What? You've got to be kidding!"

"Raymond will definitely have to get a nice bonus and some stock."

"Him, yes. But why should we include everyone else?"

"Everyone, Hilton. I mean everyone, right down to the guy in the mail room. We'll figure out some kind of fair formula. They deserve it. You'll hardly notice the difference in your bank account," remarked Jeff dryly.

"Nora, I got the OK to use the gym for two nights a week for the rest of the summer," Jeff told her several days later as he stacked the dishwasher after dinner.

Red pen in hand, Nora was marking up some copy from *Muse*'s beauty editor. "Good. That'll be a nice diversion for some of the kids. Especially now that the weather's so warm. Maybe you could play the basketball game on the outdoor court."

"I was thinking the same thing."

"What day have you decided on?" she asked.

"Thursday."

"Oh." She knew what was coming next.

"So mark Thursday nights on your calendar now."

Nora took a deep breath and deliberately didn't look up from her copy. "I'm sorry, but I can't."

"Why?" He had shut off the running water and stared at her. "I was counting on you to help out."

"Counting on me? Without even asking me?" She paused. "Well, Candida has made me her successor as editor in chief for *Muse*. I'm swamped with work and it's only going to get worse. I doubt I'll have the time. I don't want to promise you something that I may not be able to deliver." There. She had finally said it.

He was surprised. "This sounds very sudden. When did it come about?"

"A couple of weeks ago."

He closed the dishwasher door with a thud and Nora heard the utensils jingle. "A couple of weeks ago! Why didn't you tell me about it before?"

"Because you haven't particularly taken an interest in my career! You don't ask me about my work anymore." She put the copy away in a folder. There was no point pretending she was working.

He lowered his voice, but his eyes were cool. "You know I care about what you're doing. If something big happened, I figured you would just tell me about it."

"That's not how it used to be."

Jeff threw up his hands in exasperation. "Nora, there is so much I have to deal with right now. You wouldn't believe the shit going on at the office."

"I have my own share of shit to deal with too. You're doing it again— getting wrapped up in your own stuff. Lately I feel like the only thing I'm good for is a shoulder for you to lean on. I can't only be an appendage of Jeff Montgomery. I'm losing myself. I have the opportunity of a lifetime at *Muse* and I'm taking it."

"I come to you because you're my wife!" he exclaimed caustically. "But if that's how you feel, fine. Do it. Congratulations. I won't hold you back." And, almost as an afterthought, he added, "I just don't understand how you expect us to start a family under these conditions."

Nora pounded the table. "Don't throw that at me! I never once doubted you would be a good father when NRG came around, flashing all that money and opportunity in your face. I knew it would probably mean that I would see less of you, but I was sure we could work it out. Now that I'm going to be busier, you suddenly think about us having kids. What you can't handle is the fact that I won't be there *exactly* when you want!"

"That has nothing to do with it!"

"Yes, it does! Why can't you just be happy for me? Why do you have to spoil it for me?" she cried.

"You know that's the last thing I'd ever do!" He shouted. "Why are *you* blaming me for everything? No matter what I say or do, it isn't good enough!"

"Jeff, I can't take the arguments and tension anymore! What's happening to us?" They had always understood each other, communicated without ever having to say a word. She wanted him to go to her, to soothe away her fears, to tell her he loved her and that he was scared too.

"I don't know," he finally answered, and walked away.

Since things with Jeff had gone from bad to worse, Nora deliberately filled in every hour of her day, from early-morning workouts to evening editing sessions. She needed the distraction and willingly became Candida's alter ego. She was dragged along to every meeting with the publisher, advertisers, designers, department stores and other *Muse* contributors. Candida wanted Nora's face to be well-known around Seventh Avenue and the magazine community. She wanted to reassure them that her successor was up to the task. Nora would smile so hard that her mouth hurt. She had never much cared for the ass-kissing aspect of the fashion game, but was now living every minute of it. She sometimes longed to hide in her office, behind her computer, bringing life to the world of style that she loved more when she was a safe distance from it.

She had bought herself a black leather notebook, small enough to keep in her handbag or pocket, and kept it with her at all times, scribbling down ideas, words and themes for future *Muse* issues. Work was her source of comfort and she knew that her life revolved around it. It had become her center, in place of Jeff or her marriage. The old Nora would have set aside time for her personal life, fighting for those precious moments with her husband. So many times, she wanted to share her new experiences with Jeff or ask his opinion about some of her plans. But she didn't, or wouldn't let herself do it. She knew there was a huge block of ice between them. But as with ice, she hoped it would miraculously, effortlessly melt away.

Jeff also found his own escape, but work and his home life were equally to blame for his troubles. Rum Records had been turned upside down. Craig Turner and his team of auditors had virtually taken over the office. They scrutinized every document, down to the lunch receipts. They interviewed Jeff, Hilton and several other employees, and Turner's incisive presence totally transformed the vibe at the office. People became nervous, testy and indignant. Some surreptitiously conspired to foil Turner by hiding important papers, so he would have to delay a crucial part of his work until the documents inexplicably turned up hours—or days—later. Anyone who cooperated too easily with Turner was scorned. The instability threatened to destroy the creative sparkle of the company. *We've done this,* Jeff thought. *Hilton and I are allowing this to happen.*

Hilton himself had become unemotional. He told Jeff it was all business. Turner was a mere trifle until the deal was signed, sealed and delivered. Hilton preferred to visit the recording studio and held meetings with the key people he wanted to lure to the new, enlarged Rum Entertainment Group. His frequent absences upset the staff. They needed an advocate, to see both bosses sweating out Turner's drill with them. Jeff was left alone to pick up the pieces, grappling to give them leadership and encouragement.

He never denied to himself that he needed Nora, but he deliberately didn't turn to her. She didn't want to hear his dilemmas, his laments. She had made that perfectly clear. *Why should I burden her with my problems?* So Jeff turned to the one thing he had left, the one good thing that still gave him satisfaction: his community program. He threw himself into the semiweekly evenings. He played basketball until he was tired and drenched—hoping the physical activity would cleanse his psyche—and fell into bed as soon as he got home. He felt that he was making an impact. The kids recognized him around the neighborhood and they began confiding in him. And Jeff wanted to be their friend, a brother figure who cared and told them the truth. Those moments of kinship kept him going. Nora made up excuses and had stopped participating completely, so he and Olivia worked tirelessly on the proposal for the grant. Olivia's experience and commitment had turned out to be a godsend for his program. After the grant proposal had been sent out, they discussed the layout and structure of the community center—betting on the side of optimism that it would come to fruition. This hardly left any time to focus on his weakening relationship with Nora. The irony was not lost on him. He wanted to help others and change lives, but was too bullheaded to fix his own life.

It also helped that Jeff and Nora had fewer and fewer opportunities to be alone together. People always seemed to be around. In the city or Bridgehampton, they were the perfect couple and avoided situations where they would be forced to confront each other. When it was just the two of them, they purposely carried on as though nothing had happened. They lacked their tender intimacy but were extremely polite to each other, careful not to get in the other's way. It was a forced veil of politeness that underscored their unease. Jeff wanted to break through the dense wall, but not just then. Maybe after he signed the NRG deal, or when Nora returned from her trip to Europe, or when the summer was over and they had the weekends to themselves again. . . .

CHAPTER 16

Craig Turner had finally wrapped up his audit and Rum Records had been awarded a seal of approval. Hilton was back in the office on a regular basis and wanted to crystallize his plans for the new Rum divisions that would be forming. He had sent out several feelers and already had a drawerful of potential film and television ideas. The month of September had begun with a lot of promise and he and Jeff were scheduled to sign the papers for the NRG deal on the fifteenth. Hilton couldn't wait to finally put the business component to rest. His creative impulses had been obscured for the last few months and he was yearning to bring them back. He saw so much artistic potential before him—the synergies between music, film and new media. Hilton had had many sleepless nights while the negotiations with NRG shifted gears. It had been an arduous journey, but the prize was near. Of course the money would be nice, but he was too young, too ambitious, to sit complacently on a pile of cash. Hilton liked to describe himself as an old-school entrepreneur—striving, tenacious, enterprising. He wanted his name and his company to reach a broad consciousness. He wanted Rum to become an imaginative and well-known source of popular entertainment and artistic pursuits. That's what he had been fighting for, what had constantly sustained his focus during this time.

His vibrating cell phone tore him away from his daydream. It was Bob Butler.

"So is everything set for the fifteenth?" Hilton asked.

"Absolutely," Butler responded. "We'll be glad when we can finally seal this partnership."

"We feel the same way."

Hilton paused, waiting for Butler to get to the point of his call, but all he heard was the little man's breathing on the other end.

Butler continued. "Hilton, Rum coming on board will be the best news I've had in weeks. We've been having a bit of a situation here, you know."

"Are you talking about the trial? What a travesty," Hilton sympathized. "Anybody with half a brain would know that those guys are guilty. Music had nothing to do with it."

Hilton had been following the sensational reports about NRG's legal problems in the city's tabloids. It was a slow news week, so the media were having a field day with one of NRG's former artists, a controversial rapper called Loverdose. Hilton liked to think that Loverdose was the incarnation of what a mainstream (read "White") record label thought a hard-core rap star should look like—overgold, clothes so baggy they weighed him down and a bombastic attitude. All of this might have worked, if he'd had true talent. But his efforts were categorically rejected in the marketplace—bad beats, bad rhymes. No one paid attention to him until two years ago when he released a single entitled "Pink Bits," a scathing musical diatribe on sex and women. An association of African-American women was the first to protest the vulgarity and misogyny in his lyrics. They were a small force but had loud voices. Their condemnation reached a fever pitch and they succeeded in enlisting the support of other women's-rights and conservative groups. Media coverage escalated and in one of life's peculiar ironies, Loverdose, the dim, middling rapper, became a poster boy for freedom of speech, censorship, degeneration and other postmodern ills. Activists threatened to boycott NRG unless they took "Pink Bits" off the market. Protesters picketed NRG's headquarters and wrote impassioned letters to the board of directors. The company's stock price fell and it was besieged by a flurry of bad press. All of this happened on Larry Stark's watch. In public, he presented a strong front, defending artistic freedom. However, it was rumored that in private he wanted to make an example of whoever had produced the song. In the end, a couple of junior executives were fired and Stark issued a public statement that "in the best interests of all involved, NRG will recall the Loverdose single and release him from his contract."

But NRG's problems didn't end there. For a segment of the listening public, the fact that the Loverdose single provoked so much controversy made it all the more appealing. Bootleg copies of "Pink Bits" became a hot commodity and his insensitive lyrics incited a certain kind of sophomoric humor and freakish tendencies. The unfortunate victim was a college coed who was raped by three male students at a party. Though shattered, she pressed charges and went public with her story. The defendants, terrified of jail and punishment, blamed "Pink Bits." They had been listening to the song and, in their drunken stupor, committed the violent acts. They claimed to be well-behaved young men, driven to depravity by a raunchy rap song. As unbelievable as it sounded, they had a canny lawyer on a mission to shift the blame from them to Loverdose. Hilton couldn't even begin to predict the final outcome. He had seen stranger things happen in the American legal system.

"Yes, yes," Butler acknowledged, "but the publicity coming down on us is beginning to take its toll. You never know which way the tide will turn."

Hilton started to nod and then realized that Butler couldn't see him. "But, Bob, common sense is on your side," he reassured.

"Hilton, let me be honest with you. This trial is turning into a litmus test on my leadership. Do the press care that our profits have increased this quarter? No. Or that our back-catalog sales are up six percent? Of course not. All they care about is that ridiculous Loverdose creature. All I've gotten is hate mail and negative editorials." Butler sucked in his breath. "I've even started smoking again."

"Oh, no," said Hilton. There was no doubt: Butler was on the verge of losing it. It would have been funny if Hilton's future weren't so tied to Butler's.

"Maybe we can fight back a little by having some people close to the company plead our case. We really need to get some positive press right now," said Butler.

"I'd be willing to help in any way I can," Hilton volunteered. "You tell me what to do. Maybe I could do an interview about music and individual responsibility."

"That sounds interesting. I appreciate the thought, but I actually had something else in mind," Butler hinted.

"Such as?"

"Remember when you mentioned to me that Jeff was making plans to establish a neighborhood community center in Harlem?"

Hilton's beating heart became almost audible. He hadn't expected Butler to bring that up. "Yes."

"Well, this is what I was thinking. . . ."

Hilton appeared in Jeff's office about an hour after he hung up with Butler.

Jeff was tapping away on his laptop. "Welcome back, Hilton," he hailed. "So nice of you to grace us with your presence."

"I guess I deserved that."

"You sure did. The office didn't fall apart in your absence, but almost."

"I didn't mean to disappear, but Turner drove me crazy. And I did feel a little guilty about what we were dragging the staff through," Hilton admitted.

"They've come through it," Jeff said. "I think we'll all survive."

"The papers will be signed next week and we'll finally be able to get on with running and growing this company."

"Hmmm . . . ," Jeff answered vaguely.

"I'm sure you've heard about how much shit NRG has been getting in the press lately."

"How could I miss it? Stupid."

"The press?"

"No. NRG."

"Why?"

"That rapper Loverdose is horrible. A *joke*. We would have never signed him. I'm appalled that NRG did. And Butler kept pontificating about offensive lyrics." Jeff pursed his lips and mimicked Butler, " 'We don't want any controversy.' What a hypocrite. At least it's not our problem."

"Butler asked us to do him a favor," Hilton blurted out.

"What is it?" Jeff asked, annoyed. "I don't want to be used, Hilton."

"Just listen first. He knows about the community center you want to build uptown."

Jeff slammed the laptop shut. "How the hell does he know about that?"

"I told him one day."

"Why would you do that?" Jeff demanded.

"Butler once asked me what you were all about. I think it was a fair question, given the edginess whenever the two of you were in a room together. I told him about what makes you tick, some of the things you're involved with." Hilton saw Jeff's dumbfounded expression and added, "Don't worry. Everything I said was very positive."

"Oh, thanks," replied Jeff sarcastically.

"I have a proposition here from Butler that would solve all of your problems for setting up the community center."

"What?" asked Jeff resignedly.

"NRG would buy the building, provide money for renovations and assume the operating costs of the center. You wouldn't have to wait and see if the government grant goes through. You wouldn't have to deal with fund-raising. You would be assured a standing, functioning center," Hilton announced.

"Why would NRG want to do that? Why are they suddenly interested?"

"Butler wants to foster goodwill in the community. Wants to show that NRG Music cares about the inner city and its people."

Jeff grunted. "What's in it for him? There's no way in hell Butler would just do this for altruistic purposes."

"Favorable press. Good publicity," Hilton answered. "And the community center would be called the NRG Neighborhood Project."

"You're saying they would want to get credit for the whole thing?"

Hilton nodded.

"After I struggled and fought to get it off the ground? Where were they then? I could have used their money when I bought the basketballs and books out of my own pocket. Where were they then? Where were you, Hilton, for that matter?" Jeff insisted.

"You never asked for my help," Hilton responded.

"If I did, you would have done it as a favor to me, not because you really wanted to do it."

"Maybe that's true, but what difference does it make now? So what if NRG gets credit for the center, as long as the project's up and running. That's the main thing."

"The difference is that NRG couldn't be bothered with the plight of the inner city until their reputation and bottom line were at stake. I can't attach my project to that kind of hypocrisy."

"Jeff, be reasonable," Hilton implored.

"I am being reasonable. I won't do it."

"After all NRG has offered us? You won't even think it over?"

Jeff held his ground. "No."

"You know, Butler has been really patient with us. He's met almost all of our demands about creative freedom, potential film budgets. OK, he's been strict on the operations side, but he's got a business to run. Butler has made a lot of concessions. We should do him this favor."

"Is that how he spelled it out to you?" Jeff exclaimed. "It sounds like a veiled threat to me. Did Butler say that the deal would fall through if I didn't agree to his plan?"

"No. He did not say that, but I think it would be pretty awkward if you refused. It wouldn't be the best way to start a partnership. You'd be saying that you didn't trust him. Please, Jeff. Say you'll do it."

"No. It's my idea. My project. I'm doing it with no interference from NRG." He paused. "Something has been bothering me about the NRG deal since we began talking to Butler. They're like wolves, circling around, ready to swallow us. If they get their hands on every aspect of our business, *who we are,* then they've really got us. We'll be at their beck and call. They'll have really succeeded in swallowing my integrity for a few bucks. It's not worth it. I don't want anything to do with them anymore."

"What are you saying, Jeff?" Hilton asked, fear in his voice.

"The deal's off. I'm not signing the papers next week. We retain one hundred percent of our company and one hundred percent of our self-respect."

"You can't be serious," Hilton challenged. He wanted to sit down—his heart was vaulting out of his chest—but he felt stronger standing up, looking down at Jeff.

"But I am," Jeff repeated. "Hilton, look at what this deal has done to us. I guess it takes fifty million dollars to ruin a company and upset a friendship. I don't like what's happening to us, professionally or personally. Someone has to put a stop to this madness before it tears apart everything we care about."

"All I care about is my twenty-five million dollars and the chance

NRG is giving us!" Hilton shouted. "Are you losing your mind? You can't just throw this all away!"

Jeff cocked his head to one side. "It's always been about the money for you, hasn't it?"

"Yes! But don't give me that superior look. I just have the guts to admit it whereas you don't!"

"I'm prepared to walk away from Butler and NRG's money."

Hilton chortled. "Of course you would, but I don't come from a wealthy family like you. I don't have that security to lean back on. I have to take care of myself, make sure that everything's tight! I'm building a legacy here—for my future family and myself. You can't do this to me, Jeff," Hilton begged. "You know damn well that this deal can't go through unless we both sign off on it."

Jeff sighed and said, "Hilton, I'm saying this to you as your best friend: We don't need NRG. I'm doing this for us. I've never been surer about anything in my life. We already have a terrific company. We can grow it by ourselves."

"No!" Hilton cried. "That's not good enough for me anymore. I'm counting on this—the money, the stature, the exposure. I want it all. Money is power! And you're not going to get in the way of this. What gives you the right to decide what's best for the company? You promised me that you would sign this deal. I'll do whatever I have to, but it's going through!"

"My God—I feel like I'm seeing you for the first time!" Jeff cried. "You'd be willing to go behind my back for this—after almost twenty years of friendship. You're willing to sell your soul for the best price. Don't you realize that without that, you're nothing? No amount of money or power could ever make up for that. Nora was right. You are out of control!"

Hilton looked at Jeff contemptuously. How dared they judge him! He was sick of Jeff's piety, Nora's subtle reproaches. They were supposed to be his best friends. Ha! They didn't know him at all.

"Your wife thinks I'm out of control," Hilton spit out. "The two of you have obviously been talking about me, dissecting my personality." Rage boiled inside him and spilled over. "Did your perfect wife also tell you that I fucked her?"

Jeff's eyes hardened and he stiffened in his seat. "What?" he shouted. "What the hell are you talking about?"

Hilton sneered. "You know damn well what I said. Go ask her about it."

"You sick bastard—" Jeff lunged towards Hilton, but he had already slipped out of the room.

Nora sat restlessly passing time in the British Airways lounge at Heathrow Airport. Her flight back to New York was boarding in fifteen minutes. She had arrived in London two days ago to attend a store opening and interview a designer and an artist. The store opening had been filled with British celebrities and socialites she didn't recognize, the designer who the fashion world hailed as the Second Coming was truculent, and the painter festooned his canvases with elephant dung. She would have to window-dress the articles, and studying her interview notes while she waited would make the minutes go by so much faster. But instead her thoughts returned to the morning of her departure. She had left the house so early and Jeff had hardly noticed. And she had boarded her flight with only a minute to spare and hadn't had a chance to call him, which was very unusual. She and Jeff had a little rule. Before either of them left on a business trip, they always wanted to say a loving good-bye to each other because one never knew if it would be the last. How many people had boarded flights thinking they would see their loved ones again but never did?

Nora didn't like what her marriage was becoming and intended to do something about it. Back and forth, passive/aggressive, fight/make up—these were the games that she and Jeff played. And they weren't people who played games either; the unnecessary theater went against every instinct in their personalities. They had always made fun of drama queens, or men who were pathologically jealous, or couples who argued as a form of foreplay. But their resentment had reduced them to clichés. Nora couldn't take it anymore. Between her stretched hours at the office and her hectic schedule, she had also found the time to look deep within herself. The truths weren't always kind, but they were certainly accurate. She now understood that she had been jealous that Jeff devoted so much time to his community program. He had become a crusader, passionate about helping underprivileged youths, and instead of being proud of him, she had pulled away. She had been afraid that he would one day look at her and realize that they no longer connected. He needed her support, but she had deliberately focused on her own life. And as much as she loved her job, needed her career to feel productive, it wasn't enough. Family and a healthy home life were more important. She and Jeff would have children and she would find a way to meld all the parts together. She felt more determined and confident now than she had in months.

A businessman in a chalk-stripe three-piece navy suit, red-and-white checked shirt and garish yellow tie lowered his portly frame into the chair next to Nora. He smiled and promptly shoveled nuts into his mouth from the bowl on the table. She smiled back. Only Englishmen could get away with conducting business in such clashing attire. Uptown he would have been mistaken for a pimp.

Yes, Jeff could be self-involved and intense and he was equally to blame for their problems. He could have easily put aside his hubris and reached out to her. But Nora knew that he was hurting inside too. His despair matched hers. She wanted to have an honest dialogue with him, one that didn't erupt in shouting, lonely tears or confusing signals. She was prepared to face him and whatever he had to say because in the end, she knew they would work it out. Their love was strong enough. She, not Jeff, was again the one taking that crucial first step, but at this point she was sick of keeping score—

An announcement filtered out of the PA system. "Due to an unidentified piece of luggage on the plane, boarding will be delayed for thirty minutes. We appreciate your patience."

"Bloody hell," muttered the Englishman beside her.

Nora sighed and took off her jacket. The lounge was stuffy and passengers began grumbling about the delay. She checked her watch. They were supposed to land at JFK at 5:55 P.M., but that was now unlikely. A lounge attendant circled the room with a tray of champagne and gin and tonics, magic potions meant to shut everyone up. Nora rummaged through the L.L. Bean tote bag she used as a carry-on for her interview notes. She dug farther in the bag for a pen and her fingers touched a flat etched surface. She pulled it out. It was the small silver box—no bigger than a pack of cigarettes—from Marrakech. What was it doing in her bag? She felt something moving inside. She opened the lid and found a small piece of white paper. She unfolded it and read: *Have a nice trip. I love you, Jeff.* Tears clogged Nora's eyes. Jeff had put it there. He remembered. And Nora wanted more than anything else to get on that plane and go home.

Jeff was slumped over in his chair, Hilton's venom ringing in his ears. The vehemence and ugliness of their argument stuck to him like a parasite. What had Hilton meant? He and Nora? It couldn't be. Jeff tried to steady himself and went over the last few months of their three, inextricably linked lives. Hilton had been the characteristic womanizer, but his biggest rush had come from dreaming about the NRG deal. Nora had been disgusted by Hilton's antics. Neither gave any indication of being attracted to each other. There were no mysterious glances or excuses to be alone together. Hilton was his best friend and Nora was his wife, for God's sake.

Yet there had been a peculiar undercurrent between him and Hilton. It had become apparent that they had conflicting goals and values. Jeff had always wanted to believe in Hilton, to trust him. Their once unflagging friendship had been tested numerous times in the last several months and Jeff had put faith in Hilton's reassurances. But Hilton had shown his true colors today. He was slippery, capable of betraying Jeff. He wasn't above going after the one person that meant everything to Jeff—Nora. And Nora. Jeff thought of how their sanguine life was on the precipice of deteriorating. Nora had told him how she felt suffocated by his needs. On top of that, their sexual relationship teetered like an unsteady roller coaster.

It became conceivable to Jeff that Hilton and Nora could turn to each other—Hilton in his egotism and resentment and Nora in her vulnerability—just to spite him. Hilton wouldn't have taken pleasure in delivering such spiteful news to Jeff unless it had really happened. How could they do this to him?

Jeff locked himself in his office for hours. He didn't answer the phone or the knocks on his door. Nora returned home from London today and he still didn't know what he would say to her. Hilton and

Nora—the two people who shared the most important parts of his life—had turned against him. Jeff finally picked himself up. His intuition told him that Hilton had fled. Refusing to take responsibility for the chaos he unleashed was only one of Hilton's newly acquired bad habits. Some staff members registered surprise when they saw Jeff, rumpled and forlorn, come out. He moved lifelessly until he was outside in his car. He turned the key in the ignition and only habit enabled him to drive through Manhattan in his confusion.

His BlackBerry went off and he read the message. It was an e-mail from Olivia asking him to stop by and pick up documents. Acting natural for Olivia's benefit was the last thing he wanted to do. How could he get out of it? But it was simple—go in, get the papers, leave. Maybe he could muster a phony demeanor for five minutes.

Olivia had the papers ready for him in a folder. Jeff took it from her and prepared to leave.

"Can you come in for a few minutes?" she requested. "I want to go over something with you."

"I'm actually sort of rushing—" Jeff said.

"Please, Jeff," she interrupted. "Kiara's playing with a friend down the hall. If we do this now, it'll save us a lot of time later."

Jeff suppressed his impatience. He knew that he should put aside his personal troubles for the good of the center he was fighting to build.

"OK," he answered.

He followed Olivia to the living room and she spread the documents out on the coffee table.

"Now, since the center will be a nonprofit organization, we'll have to apply for a 501(c)(3) status when filing taxes," she explained.

Jeff struggled to follow her. She rattled off numbers and tax codes and the information made no sense to him. Under normal circumstances, he would have had to pay full attention, but today he was entirely incapable. His mind and his heart just weren't there.

"Jeff! Jeff!" Olivia called. "Are you listening to me?"

"Yeah. Yes. I'm trying to," he said.

Olivia examined his face.

"You look weak. Are you hungry? Have you eaten today?"

"I really don't remember," Jeff replied. "I don't think so."

"That's what's affecting your concentration. Let me fix you something."

"No, thank you. You really don't have to. I should be going soon."

"At least have a cup of coffee. It'll perk you up."

Jeff reluctantly considered her suggestion. Small aches darted in the hollowness of his stomach.

"Sure. That'll be fine," he answered.

Olivia lived in an apartment that had once been two units in an old rooming house. Though relatively small in square footage, it had high ceilings and wide windows. Jeff noticed the stacks of books crammed on bookshelves, windowsills and the floor. Half-burned candles in holders with twirled melted wax rested arbitrarily on tables and ledges. The atmosphere evoked meditation. Only bright prints and Kiara's playthings, strewed behind an armchair, made it less ascetic.

Olivia set down a tray with two coffee cups and a sandwich for Jeff.

Jeff lifted his cup. It was steaming hot and he blew on it. "Thank you, Olivia. You didn't have to go to all this trouble."

"Oh, it was no trouble at all."

Jeff wanted to seem less preoccupied and searched for a conversation topic. "How's your dissertation coming along? You've been spending so much time helping me. I hope this project is not keeping you from your work."

"It's"—Olivia paused and laughed—"getting there. It feels like an endless process sometimes, but I hope to finish it by this time next year."

"Getting a Ph.D. makes law school sound like a breeze."

Olivia smiled. "How's Nora doing? I haven't seen her in a while."

A cloud shrouded Jeff's face. He cleared his throat. "She's fine. Was in London. Working a lot," he answered uncomfortably.

"How do you two manage? You hardly get to see each other," Olivia remarked.

"Well . . ." He couldn't think of an adequate response and his hand shook as he put the cup down. A wave of hot coffee brimmed over and scalded his skin.

"Oh, no! You've burned yourself!"

"I'm fine. It's nothing." Jeff started to wipe his hand on his shirt, but Olivia stopped him.

"Don't do that. You'll make it worse. I'll get a clean towel and ointment."

Olivia's comments had hit too close to home and Jeff paced the room while he waited for her to come back. She returned with a first aid kit and patted the couch for him to sit down. She held Jeff's fingers in the palm of her hand and gently rubbed medicine on the small wound. Jeff found her closeness disconcerting. He could smell her perfume too, a sweet and woody patchouli blend that blanketed her arms, shoulders and hair. He intentionally kept his back straight and concentrated on a smudge on the wall. Olivia unwrapped a Band-Aid and flattened it on top of the wrinkled, dark circle on his hand.

"That should be better," she said when finished.

Jeff awkwardly shifted position and smiled crookedly. "Thanks."

Jeff looked down and his eyes locked with Olivia's. Her face was up-turned, her lips parted in a hopeful oval. Jeff wanted to look away, but she beheld him. She leaned forward and stroked his cheek with her fingers. Jeff sat motionless, conscious of what she intimated, but unprepared to stop it. Her touch was warm, but not arousing, and Jeff knew that he could still put an end to it. He could lightly move her hand, mutter something so she wouldn't feel embarrassed, and go home. Jeff didn't want to cross that line, to descend into that wretched pit of disloyalty. He didn't want to emulate his wife.

He saw Nora's face just as Olivia pressed her lips against his. It was a short, seeking kiss. She pulled back and her eyes questioned him, almost giving him a chance to break the spell. Where was his voice? He opened his mouth, but sound baffled him. Olivia divined an answer from his expression and kissed him with more feeling. And to Jeff's utter, total shame, his body responded. His body detached from his rational mind and he returned her kiss. A strange physical urge dominated and he wondered if, subconsciously, he had been attracted to Olivia. He would never have acted on it, but something had snapped in him today, perverting his sanity. Had Nora experienced similar pangs of guilt and lust?

Olivia led Jeff to her bed. He kissed and touched her out of desperation, a need to purge his senses of Nora's betrayal. Olivia welcomed his rashness by biting and licking his neck, unfastening the buttons of her shirt, leading his mouth to graze her breasts. The agony of his anger and desire stunned him and he raised her skirt, tugged at her panties and plunged inside. Her back was against the headboard and after a few thrusts, Jeff climaxed with the haunted cries of a wounded animal. Olivia held his head in her arms, but he couldn't bear to look at her. Jeff knew he had committed a pointless revenge. He had wanted to know what it felt like. He had wanted to hurt Nora the way she had hurt him. Each kiss, each time he touched Olivia, he silently punished Nora.

Now Jeff had to disentangle himself from Olivia's bed. He felt clumsy. He had known Olivia for months, but she was still a stranger.

"Are you all right?" she finally asked.

He nodded.

"I think—" she started to say, but was interrupted when Kiara barged through the closed bedroom door.

"Mommy, I'm back," Kiara called, but her eyes opened wide when she saw Olivia's half-naked form on the bed. She also stared at the man next to her mother and caught her breath when she recognized Jeff.

Olivia rushed to cover herself with the comforter. "Kiara, you must always knock before entering! Go back to your room until I come for you."

Kiara stood clutching the doorknob, feet cemented to the floor. She gawked at them with curiosity and incomprehension.

"Kiara!" Olivia repeated, and Kiara scurried away.

Jeff stood up and rearranged his clothes.

"Jeff, I'm sorry," Olivia said. "I'll talk to Kiara."

His back was to her and he held up one hand. He didn't want Olivia to continue.

"I'll explain this away to her—"

"Olivia, I don't want to talk about this," he said softly. "I have to go. I'm sorry, but—but that's just the way it is."

Nora entered her house and dropped her bags near the coat closet. She was completely done in. The half hour delay at Heathrow had turned into three hours. A couple of passengers had ranted and raved about getting a refund for their inconvenience, and the word "bloody" threatened to sneak its way into her vocabulary. She hoped Jeff was home, and raced upstairs to their bedroom. He was lying down and she threw herself on the bed, snuggling tightly against his body.

"Jeff, I'm so happy to be home!" she said. "London was a nightmare! My flight was delayed, I was missing you, and then I found the silver box in my bag. Do you know how much I love you, how much I want us to be together? That's the only thing that matters to me."

Darkness washed the room. Nora clung to his rigid back, her body curving perfectly around his. She didn't notice his tense muscles or the angry heat he emanated. Her torrent of emotions overwhelmed the atmosphere.

"I don't like the way we've been living. Our marriage is falling apart, right before our eyes! And I know you hate it as much as I do. We're both to blame, but I don't want to go over that now. Can we just promise to love each other, to communicate and be honest with each other again?" she asked.

Silence.

"Jeff, please. Answer me," she pleaded. "I love you so much."

He sat up abruptly and she slid down the bed. "How can you say those things to me after you've been sleeping with Hilton? Is it your bad conscience talking?"

Nora's face contorted from hope to hurt and confusion. She knit her brows and asked in a trembling voice, "What are you talking about?"

Jeff jumped from the bed and flicked on the light. "Nora, I know the two of you are having an affair. When did it start? How could you do that to me? My wife and my best friend? Why would you want to hurt me like that?"

"Is that what Hilton told you?" she asked, astounded.

"Yes, damn it! Don't make me repeat it one hundred times!"

"And you believed him?"

"Why would he lie about such a thing?"

"To hurt you. To break up our marriage. To make you as hateful as he is."

"Nora, you still haven't answered my question. Why would you sleep with Hilton?"

"I can't believe you're even asking me that!"

"Answer the question!"

"I am not sleeping with Hilton! I am not having an affair with him behind your back! Are you satisfied? Why are you humiliating me with these accusations? We've been together for six years. Don't you trust me?"

"I've known Hilton for twenty years and I realized today that I can't trust anyone. Do I really know you? Can I vouch for what you would or would not do?"

"Yes, you can! Our marriage is sacred to me. No matter what happens between us, I would never stain it by sleeping with someone else!"

"Nora, I need to know. Are you telling me that you've never slept with Hilton?"

She cringed with remorse. Old memories assaulted her and she swallowed hard. Jeff stood over the bed, pain and fury in his face. She always had a feeling her secret would come back to haunt her.

"It's not what you think. . . ."

Jeff screamed, "I knew it! When Hilton said it to me, I had a sinking feeling that it was true. He's such a calculating bastard. I guess he managed to corrupt you too." His voice faltered. "Nora, why? You were my angel. I can't even think about it. You and Hilton together . . ."

"Jeff . . ." Nora gripped his arm.

"Don't touch me!"

She used all her physical strength and forced him to look at her. He sat back down on the bed, but refused to meet her gaze. She squeezed her eyes shut and spoke. "It happened once, six years ago. You and I had only been dating a few months. I came up late one night from D.C., but you weren't there. You had gone to Boston to see your sick grandfather. Hilton told me to stay until the next morning and we went to a party. We both got pretty drunk and kissed and . . ." Nora remembered that night so vividly—the dancing, the laughter, Hilton's hands all over her. She shivered. ". . . and one thing led to another."

" 'One thing led to another,' " mocked Jeff. "The most fucked-up words in the English language!"

"I don't know how else to explain it! I couldn't believe what happened. We didn't do it on purpose. We should have had more self-control, but I was young and stupid. I didn't know what was happening until it was too late. I was also insecure about where our relationship was going—"

"I love the way people like to blame their mistakes on insecurity! That's no excuse! Why did you go through with it?"

She pressed a pillow to her stomach like a shield. "I thought about it a lot after it happened. I guess I was acting out an insane fantasy—the one where I bed two best friends and don't care about it the day after. It was adolescent."

Jeff's breathing was heavy and his forehead shone from perspiration. "You're admitting, then, that you were attracted to him?"

Nora didn't want to hide anything from him anymore. "On the most surface level, I suppose so. Yes. I was attracted to both of you. It was hard not to be."

"Hilton was my best friend. I'd known him for much longer than I'd known you. What if he had told me what happened?"

"If you would have found out about it and never wanted to see me again, I wouldn't have blamed you. When Hilton and I spoke about it later, and I told him how strongly I felt about you, we agreed that it was just a foolish mistake. Neither of us wanted to hurt you. He promised never to say anything. He wanted us to be together."

Jeff dug his fingers into the comforter and asked, "Are you still attracted to him?"

"No! Since that mistake, he has only been a friend to me, to us. I married you. You're my life. Please don't doubt my love for you. There has been no infidelity in our relationship since that one time with—" She didn't even want to say his name.

She wasn't sure if Jeff was listening to her. He had put his head in his hands and was rocking slowly back and forth.

"I remember that time," he said softly, and Nora strained to hear him. "You acted really strange for a while, quiet and distant. I talked to Hilton about it. I thought you weren't interested in me anymore. He told me not to give up, to open up to you and tell you how I felt. Such great advice from my best friend."

"But, Jeff, I do think that he meant well then. I can't believe that he fooled us all this time. He's not the same person anymore."

Jeff dropped his hands and faced her with wild eyes. "How can you still defend him?"

His reaction startled her. She wanted to calm him, to erase the inflamed emotions that altered his mood from one minute to the next. She wrapped her hands around his and brought them to her chest. "Because I want to believe that there's still some decency left in us."

Their hands remained intertwined for several minutes.

"I've been so stupid, such a fool. Can you forgive me? I love you so much. Please say you love me too," Jeff begged.

"I love you too." She smiled. "That's what I've been trying to tell you. We've both been stupid."

"What am I going to do? How can I make things right with us?"

She looked bewildered and caressed his hair. "What do you mean? We're doing that now. Everything will be fine. Let's put all of this behind us. We'll make it."

Jeff kissed her urgently. Nora responded in kind, but was startled by the fervor of his movements. He made love to her as though his life depended on it.

CHAPTER 17

The stress and fatigue of the previous months had finally caught up with Jeff and Nora and they played hooky for two days. Nora assumed his melancholy was caused by Hilton's betrayal and Jeff didn't correct her. How could he? Jeff realized that for Hilton, the power of the attack had been its ambiguity. Hilton had planted a kernel of doubt in Jeff's mind, knowing that it would tear him apart. And Jeff had stupidly contributed to his own undoing. Every time Nora smiled at him or nuzzled his neck, guilt shot through him. She would never suspect what truly tormented him. He tried not to think about his transgression with Olivia. Sometimes he would forget it happened and his life seemed normal again. Then the moment would pass and the memory became sharper, more dangerous.

On the third day, Nora had to go back to work.

"This is so cozy. I wish I could stay with you," she told Jeff sleepily.

"Me too."

"What are you going to do today?"

"I don't know."

She squeezed his hand sympathetically. "You're not going in?"

He shook his head. "I'm not in the mood. I don't want to deal with all that stuff."

"Have you spoken to Hilton?"

"He keeps leaving me messages and e-mails, but I'm ignoring them. All he wants is for me to sign that deal."

"Follow your gut feeling. I'll support you no matter what. You'll be all right by yourself?"

"Yes. I'll be fine. Now go and make some money for us. I may not have a job to go back to," he joked.

She smiled and reluctantly began her morning routine. Jeff watched her get ready. She emerged from the shower fresh and glistening clean. She threw off her towel and climbed back on the bed, giving him one long kiss. She asked his opinion about what she should wear and he fixed her breakfast while she put on her makeup. As she sat sipping her tea and commenting on the morning's news, Jeff wanted to freeze the frame. Although she did normal, everyday activities, there was a distinct luminescence about her. He knew somehow that the pure happiness she emanated would be ephemeral.

Nora stayed focused at work and left at five to return home to Jeff. She bought their dinner at a gourmet shop near her office and treated herself to a cab ride home. The driver misunderstood her directions—cabbies never seemed to get it right uptown—and dropped her off on the wrong side of the street, right in front of ornery Grace Wheeler's front gate. Nora fumbled with her bags, slamming the door shut with her hip. She glanced up and saw Kiara sitting on Mrs. Wheeler's steps, her elbows propped on her thighs.

"Hi, Kiara," Nora called. "What are you doing there? It's getting darker earlier now. You shouldn't be hanging around the block by yourself."

"Mrs. Wheeler's babysitting me."

"When is your mother coming back?"

"Soon." Kiara walked slowly down the steps.

Nora put down her packages and opened Mrs. Wheeler's gate a crack. "What's the matter, honey? You look a little blue."

"Nothing. It's boring at Mrs. Wheeler's. She doesn't want me to make any noise and I have to be quiet all the time."

"You know, she's much older. You have to understand that. But she's nice anyway, right?"

"Yeah." Kiara sighed. "Can I ask you something?"

"Sure."

"You and Jeff are married, right?"

Nora nodded.

"That means you're together. It's legal and you did it in a church."

"That's right, Kiara. Why do you want to know?"

She shrugged. "My mother's not married."

Nora had always wondered if Kiara thought about that. It was such a delicate issue, but Nora remembered what Olivia had told her on the beach. "Yes, but your mother wanted you so badly and she didn't know if she was ever going to get married. Think of it this way: She picked *you* over getting married."

"Can married people be together with other people?"

Nora couldn't believe the questions Kiara asked. Such thoughts for a little girl! And Nora felt unqualified to answer them. Shouldn't Olivia be taking this up with Kiara? She thought it over and said, "Married people *shouldn't* be with other people except the people they're married to."

Kiara kicked a pebble with the tip of her left sneaker. "Then why did I see my mother and Jeff in bed together?"

Nora felt like she'd been punched in the stomach. "Are you sure about that?" she asked finally.

"Yes. I saw my mother on her bed without her shirt and Jeff was next to her."

The horrific words coming from Kiara's mouth were completely at odds with her pixie, innocent face. Nora's speech wavered. "Wh-when?"

Kiara creased her forehead in thought. "A few days ago. I don't remember exactly."

Nora tried to remain cool and crouched down. Her face almost touched Kiara's. "Kiara, listen to what I'm going to say very carefully. And I want you to tell me the truth. I won't get mad at you, no matter what." She paused. "Did your mother put you up to this? Did she ask you to tell me these stories?"

Kiara stomped her foot on the pavement. "No!" she cried. "She told me not to tell, but I had to ask you. I didn't understand. I needed to know. . . ."

That was all the explanation Nora needed to hear. She stood up and straightened her jacket. "Go on now, Kiara. Go inside to Mrs. Wheeler's and wait for your mother to come and pick you up."

"I want to stay outside—"

Kiara's whining made her sound every inch her seven years. In light of the news she had delivered, Nora had no patience for her. *"Go. Back. Inside,"* she said, and Kiara finally obeyed. Nora clutched her bag of gourmet food, but really wanted to hurl it into the nearest trash can.

Why was this happening? She hobbled across the street to her house and held the doorknob with shaking hands. She had to know, yet didn't want to.

Nora found Jeff sitting in the study. Orange wedges and a can of Coke were pushed to the side of the desk. He was reading the sports section of the *Times,* but she could see documents underneath the newspaper, as if he'd said, "Fuck it," and given up on doing anything remotely serious. She perceived apathy and it enraged her, but she approached him steely, her voice a monotone. "Now I understand why you've locked yourself in the house. Did you think I wouldn't find out?"

He said nothing.

"Do you know who told me?" she inquired.

He met her eyes and shook his head sadly.

"Kiara. Kiara! A seven-year-old wanted to know why you and her mother were in bed together! She was always precocious, but I would have never guessed you were the reason for her curiosity." She leaned on a wing chair to steady herself. "I felt like I was going to be sick."

"Nora, it was a mistake. I wasn't myself when it happened." His tone was weak and she detested it.

"So you're not to blame?" she accused.

"It is my fault, but I was confused," he reasoned. "I was so mad at you. I thought you and Hilton were having an affair. The situation was ripe for confusion."

She moved forward, her steps slow and even. Her eyes were set and she adopted the tone of an impatient lawyer cross-examining an unsound witness. "Let me get this straight: You were confused, so you hopped into bed with Olivia. Maybe I'm being too logical, but if you were confused, you should have asked me about it. Instead you assumed the worst and did the unthinkable! What does that say about the level of trust in our relationship? The minute something doesn't feel right you turn to someone else?"

Jeff got up from his chair and sighed in anguish. "I didn't turn to someone else. I'm not looking for someone else." He hesitated. "If you want to know the truth, I wanted to get back at you."

"Oh, God. This doesn't sound like a marriage. It sounds like sport, a game. Are we even now? Is that what you wanted?" she demanded.

His voice cracked. "No. I wish, with everything I have, that I could take those moments back. I wanted to punish you, but I ended up punishing myself. This has been killing me. I didn't enjoy it."

"Please spare me the details," Nora snapped. "Why Olivia? Because she was convenient or because you know I don't like her? If it was so easy for you to sleep with her—"

"It wasn't easy. The whole thing happened so quickly—"

Nora's hardened facade crumbled. "Stop it! You wouldn't have done it if you weren't attracted to her." She held her head between her hands and groaned. "I have been the biggest idiot. Anna warned me about this one day and I just laughed at her. She said 'How can you allow Jeff to spend so much time with Olivia? I wouldn't trust that woman with my own father.' And I explained to Anna about how I wasn't the jealous type. I didn't feel threatened by Olivia. You and I had such a mature relationship. I trusted you! I guess all this time Olivia has been plotting to put the moves on you, in spite of my relationship with Kiara, in spite of the fact I welcomed them to our house this summer. But I don't blame her. She would have never succeeded if you hadn't let her. You allowed this to happen!"

Jeff spoke in barely a whisper. "I don't know. Maybe I did. But it would have never happened if Hilton hadn't screwed with my mind."

"Please! Hilton is to blame for a lot of things, but he sure didn't make you share Olivia's bed!"

"Nora, I know you're angry and you have every reason to be—"

"How can you be so fucking calm?"

"Because I know that I'm to blame. I'm sorry."

"Saying you're sorry isn't going to make it go away!" She hit his chest with her fists. "You betrayed me! That woman is in my marriage!" Jeff caught hold of her hands, but she untwisted from his grip. Locks of hair behind her ears had come loose and flew over her eyes, getting wet in her tears. "My God. That night—that night we made love after you had been with her. How could you do that? I feel dirty. You've made me feel dirty!"

Jeff tried to reach for her, but she jerked back.

"No! No! Don't say that!" he said. "She's not in our marriage. We won't let her. She means nothing to me! It was a lapse in judgment. Nothing more."

"How can you say that?"

"Because we love each other. We can overcome this. I know it seems like a huge barrier now, but we can get over it."

"*You* want to get over it," Nora choked out. "Do you think I'm going to so easily? How can I ever look at you again the same way?"

Jeff's voice rose. "How can I ever look at you and Hilton again the same way? That hasn't been easy for me either. But I'm trying. I'm not letting that come between us."

"Don't play that with me. You can't compare the two and I'm shocked that you'd try," Nora retorted.

"My wife and my best friend—"

"The difference is, I wasn't your wife at the time and we were far from a trip down the aisle. I did something wrong, but I didn't betray our vows!" she shouted, pointing her index finger at him. "*You* did. You can't play that down, no matter how hard you try."

She turned away from him and stared out the window, depleted of words and energy. He moved behind her and laid his hands on her shoulders. "Nora, I don't want to lose you," he pleaded. "This is a test in our relationship. We can make it."

Her eyes bored through the glass, but the images outside were blurry. The clarity she yearned for was eclipsed by the tears spilling from her eyes. Her nose ran and she dried it with her shirtsleeve.

"Jeff," she said in a hushed voice.

"Yes?"

"Please leave me alone."

He hesitated but did as she wished. She followed the sound of his footsteps and once he'd left the room, she couldn't halt her tears. Her sobs were abnormal: gulping, howling sounds that seemed inhuman. But they touched the very essence of her humanity—all that she loved, cared and trusted. The picture of Jeff and Olivia together burned her brain. She imagined them clothed, naked, damp, joined. She finally understood what gut-wrenching pain meant, stabbing deep inside her, stealing her will to go on. Maybe she could forget by making herself fall asleep. She used to do that when she was a child. It had been such a convenient escape from times of gloom and fights with her brother or parents. She sat in a corner of the study and hugged her knees to her chest. She closed her eyes, and thankfully, the sweet darkness came swiftly.

No matter which room he went to, Jeff couldn't hide from himself and returned to the study an hour later. If he could only explain and apologize, perhaps Nora would come to understand what had driven him to his *madness*. The study was eerily quiet and for a moment, he thought that Nora had gone. Then he saw her curled up in a nook between the printer and the bookcase. She looked limp and vulnerable. He gently lifted her from the floor and carried her up the stairs. "Nora, we can work through this," he whispered. "It'll take time, but we can do it. I love you. Please forgive me."

He placed her delicately on the bed and raised the comforter to her chin. He got in on his side and turned off the light. But before Jeff could even reach for her, the sheets ruffled and he could make out the shadow of her body moving to the very edge of the bed. A huge gap separated them. She tossed and turned the whole night. A few times Jeff thought he heard her whimpering. He wanted to hold her, but knew she would push him away. He was left powerless and distraught, for it was he who had inflicted so much hurt. The tortured rhythm of that night would plague him forever.

Nora rose from bed as soon as the alarm went off the next morning. She did everything as she usually did, fighting for her stability. But her eyes were puffy and her head ached from sobbing. She did her best to hide the damage with makeup, but her assistant noticed the red eyes. "Oh, I'm just fighting a bad cold," Nora responded. She visited a designer's showroom and admired his new collection behind dark sunglasses and no one even flinched. Her biggest challenge was fooling Candida, but the Englishwoman donned typical British reserve and said nothing.

Burying herself in work gave Nora no consolation, so she began leaving the office at six and hiding in the countless coffee bars around midtown. She'd stake out a spot on a stool that faced a window and sit for an hour or two, sometimes three, trying to let go of her identity as a wife, an editor, a woman wronged. She looked at people and wondered:

Does he cheat on his wife? Is she happily married? Arriving home with the bitter aftertaste of coffee in her mouth, she'd find a precooked meal on the kitchen table that Jeff had picked up from the supermarket, and ate because her body demanded it. He never asked her where she'd been and she certainly didn't feel as though she owed him an explanation. She remained in their bedroom, but Jeff moved into one of the guest rooms. Although she hadn't asked him to, she knew her coldness had pushed him away and felt foolish from the sense of triumph she derived from it. She discussed only administrative things with him—bills that had to be paid, a leaky toilet, did he have any dry cleaning that needed to go out?

A wooden crate containing their purchases from Marrakech arrived at Hamilton Terrace. It stood in the hallway for days before Jeff finally asked her if she wanted to unpack it with him. Going through the crate would be like reliving those magical moments in Marrakech and Nora knew the exercise would be futile, phony.

"Just throw the damn things out," she answered.

"Nora, please talk to me," he beseeched, clearly pained by her dismissal. "Tell me how you feel. Tell me that you hate me. Anything. I can't stand this manufactured normal life."

She turned to him, unblinking. "Isn't that what you wanted? Pretending nothing happened?"

"I know we can't pretend nothing happened. I feel paralyzed. We're in the same room, and I know you're hurting. I am too. We can help each other."

She screwed up her face scornfully. "Don't you dare try to tell me how I should deal with this! There's no book telling a wife how she should behave after her husband has slept with another woman! Maybe you want me to cry and ask you all the time, 'Why? Why? How could you do this to me?' Or maybe I should march over to Olivia's and pull her hair, call her a bitch! If I did all those things, would it be easier for you? Could you handle it? You're not going to tell me how I should feel or how I should act. You can't begin to know how I feel. You have pulled the rug out from under me! I don't know which way is up or down, whether I'm coming or going." She walked to the base of the stairs and looked back. "So don't tell me what I should be doing."

Nora tried to figure out how she had gotten to this point, this *failure*. She had escaped Westbury wanting more—bigger horizons, open minds, freedom. Her insecurities had motivated her, the need to prove herself. On the surface she had done it—the high-profile job, the made-to-order husband. Is this what she was struggling to preserve? For whom? Nora certainly didn't think it was for herself anymore.

She had built up a defense mechanism. She wasn't even sure anymore where she'd learned it, but it had saved her from many periods of sadness and uncertainty. *Don't show everything you feel,* she'd say to herself. *What you keep for yourself is your power. No one can hurt you if you develop that strength, that control.* But now she didn't want to be so dignified or controlled. She had allowed Jeff to see all her vulnerability, and he betrayed her. If she wanted to maintain some semblance of sanity, she needed to simplify her life. She had to think about herself first.

Jeff came down the stairs as soon as he heard Nora close the front door. He still hadn't gone into the office or spoken to Hilton, but spent his days doing bits and pieces of work. He couldn't concentrate and thought mostly about Nora, counting the hours until she came home. Although they had very limited contact, just knowing she was around gave him hope.

She took off her shoes and shook her hair loose from her barrette. She didn't say hello, but began talking, as though in midconversation. "I've lived here for almost a year and not once has Mrs. Wheeler ever said a word to me. She'd give me snooty or disapproving glances, but tonight she was on our block just as I was walking towards the house, like she'd been waiting for me. As we passed each other, she stopped me and said, with pity in her eyes, 'Honey, I hope it all works out.' Can you believe that? It doesn't take a genius to figure out what she meant. I just stood there, shocked, and then sped off.

"And then it dawned on me," she continued. "Does the whole neighborhood know that we're having problems?" She clapped her hands. "I think so! Hamilton Terrace is like a small town. They all know our business. *That* is too much to take."

"We can move," Jeff said.

"What?"

"We can move from here. Go someplace else. Get away from"—Jeff paused—"this."

They both knew what the unsaid word had been—*Olivia*.

Nora looked at Jeff with genuine sadness in her eyes. "Jeff, *I'm* moving."

"What are you talking about?" he asked in disbelief.

"Just what I said. I'm moving out."

"Why?"

Nora let out a hollow laugh. "Aside from the obvious?" she asked. "I need to come to terms with this—with us—in my own way. I can't do it with you and I can't do it in this house."

"But I thought we would try and work things out."

"I know that's what you would like, but it's not that easy. If I continue like this, it'll be for you, not for me. I would be putting your needs ahead of mine and I can't do that anymore. I don't feel strong enough to take care of us both."

"We can help each other."

"Jeff, don't you understand? Our relationship is tainted. How many more months are we going to live in the same house without having a decent conversation? Or eating dinner together? Or making love? That's not a marriage. That's not a life."

"You may not want me to say this, but I like to know that you're here with me. That you haven't given up. I need you near me. You're the only good part of my life," he said in a raspy voice.

"And I need my space because for a long time now, I don't think anybody has been looking out for Nora."

"But we have a life together," he said. "We've been through so much."

"We have. And I wouldn't change much of it. But this, what has happened between us now, with Olivia—"

"Don't say her name."

"Why not? She exists. We can't make her disappear."

"You talk about Olivia as though I had an affair with her! It happened once. One time! Nora, I love you. Olivia doesn't mean anything to me!"

"The fact that you turned to her is a sign that something is terribly wrong in our relationship. You may not want to admit it to yourself yet, but I can." She paused. "We all started out fairly normal—you, Hilton and I. Young, hungry, fun. It was a perfect combination. You brought out things in me. I hope that I brought out things in you. But what have we been reduced to? You and Hilton are both searching for something and I don't know if you'll ever be satisfied. I'm caught in the middle of this and I don't want to be a part of it anymore. I don't have the strength— No. I *finally* have the strength to come up for air before it's too late."

"So you're leaving me?"

"That sounds so harsh."

"I don't think there's a kinder way to say it," he replied. "Is this a trial separation?"

Nora braided her hands in her lap. "I don't know. I don't know what to call this!"

"So don't do it!" he begged. The pressure of held-back tears made his eyes bright.

"I have to. I have to," she said mournfully. "If I stay, I'll disappear. Things aren't right the way they are."

"God. I did this to you."

"Yes, you did," she answered. "Maybe you should face up to that. I think you have some issues to sort out too."

"Where did it all go wrong? The business, you. It's all upside-down." The words caught in his throat. "Please remember that I tried. That I didn't want things to end this way."

Nora bent her head forward. Her own tears were thin lines gliding slowly from her eyes to her lips.

"Will you come back?" he asked.

"I don't know."

"Where will you go?"

"I'm borrowing the company apartment downtown until I figure things out."

"When do you plan on leaving?"

"Tomorrow."

"I guess there's nothing left to say," he murmured.

"Jeff," Nora said softly, "maybe you could give me a few hours to my-self tomorrow afternoon so I can gather my things."

Jeff didn't sleep at all that night. Ever since she had discovered his mistake, he had hoped that she might open her arms in forgiveness. How unrealistic that had been. She was not ready to forgive or forget, and now she was in their bedroom preparing to leave.

He heard her footsteps stop by his door very early the next morning. He imagined that she held her hand close, preparing to knock. He took a deep breath and waited. Then she crept away.

He left the house at noon. Nora hadn't said when she would return to collect her things, but he intended to honor her request. He trudged to St. Nicholas Park. Gray skies punctuated his bleak mood. Mothers with baby strollers chatted in small groups and he sank down on a bench. It was one in a row of benches occupied by old men, vagrants and other lost souls who spent their days wondering how the hell they got this way. Jeff finally understood—mistakes, disappointments and loneliness. His life had abruptly become similarly aimless.

Nora came back around two. The house appeared dim and depress-ing and she wanted to get her task over with very quickly. She hurried up the stairs and combed through the closet for her bags. She packed her belongings, only basic clothes and personal items, in two suitcases. She carried them outside, one by one, and the driver of the car service she had hired placed them in the trunk. She stared at the town house one more time. The limestone facade was still commanding, but they had made it a home, even for just a little while. She had held so many hopes for 35 Hamilton Terrace. It had embodied her and Jeff's dreams, their future.

"Nora, are you all right?"

Nora looked in the direction of the voice. "Anna? Is that you?"

Nora's next-door neighbor peeped out from behind an overgrown shrub. "Yes. I just happened to be planting." She hesitated. "Are you leaving?"

Nora nodded. She didn't ask how, but she could tell Anna knew why.

"Is that what you feel you have to do?" Her voice was filled with empathy.

"Yes."

Anna removed her gardening gloves and came around to face Nora. "I'll miss you."

Nora hugged her. "Me too, Anna. Thank you for always being a friend."

She pulled away and hoped Anna couldn't see her misty eyes. She signaled to the driver and he held the back door open for her. She stepped in and he shut the heavy door ceremoniously. Seconds later, Nora sat alone, on her way to the most uncertain time of her life.

Jeff had lingered in the park, and when he went back home, he felt that Nora had come and gone. She hadn't taken much with her. He fingered the clothes in her wardrobe, the fabrics rippling and exhaling her perfume. He opened her jewelry box. She had left her engagement ring and a first-anniversary eternity band. Her Love Bracelet from last Christmas rested neatly on the box's red velvet interior. He gathered these pieces and put them in the safe, praying she would want them— and all they symbolized—back one day. He spent hours searching through her possessions—clothes, books, drawers, notes. Some things he had given her, others he recognized, and still others were completely unfamiliar. He discovered an antique hairbrush, seashells marked with dates and places, satchels of potpourri between her lingerie. These items he examined with particular fascination, searching for pieces of his wife, glimpses of the Nora that was now lost to him.

CHAPTER 18

Hilton had a dilemma. Rum Records was scheduled to sign the NRG deal tomorrow, but he still hadn't heard from Jeff. Since that unfortunate scene, his partner had vanished. There was no sign of him at the office, and he didn't answer his phone at home or the numerous messages Hilton had left for him. The lines of communication had been cut off. Hilton wasn't completely convinced that Jeff intended to back out of the alliance. There was simply too much at stake and Jeff had been talking rashly. Jeff's self-imposed exile left Hilton with no choice but to delay the signing. He'd push it back by one week and try to mend the situation with Jeff in the meantime. *Mend the situation with Jeff.* They had almost come to blows and had hurled invectives at each other for the first time in all their years of friendship. It wasn't something Hilton was proud of.

He called Butler's office and told him that due to a family emergency, he had to leave for California right away. Could they reschedule for next week? Butler grumbled his assent and Hilton heard a hint of impatience in his tone. Hilton hung up in total frustration. One thing was for certain: Everything had stopped being fun months ago.

On impulse, he buzzed his assistant. "Please book me on the eleven a.m. flight to LA." He reached for his jacket and leather briefcase and went outside to catch a cab to LaGuardia Airport.

Six hours later, he veered a rental car into a parking spot at the Santa Monica Pier. He strolled on the beach, flinging sand in his shoes, but he had never been the "walking barefoot in the sand" type. He got as close to the coastline as possible without wetting his shoes. *Welcome to the edge of the country,* he thought. Although with the drama of Los Angeles life, it usually felt like the edge of the world. On the freeway, the thick smog had enveloped entire sections of downtown. Perhaps LA was a city that could be seen only through a seemingly endless, hazy cloud that veiled reality. Hilton had spent so much of his life on the East Coast, but California would always be in his heart. Ironically, his mother had sent him east to protect him, but his years growing up in Long Beach had been the most innocent of his life. He had grabbed a dose of the LA magic and taken it with him to Boston and then New York. Now when he visited LA, he was received like a player, an impresario, someone to be taken seriously. These days, he couldn't even tell the difference between LA and New York anymore. Both cities played the same entertainment game; people wheeled and dealed, mutually exploited each other and spent money like it was candy. All his childhood fantasies had come true. But at what cost?

Hilton could bear a lot. He had attended boarding school without the security of having relatives nearby. Financially, his mother had struggled to give him the best she could. Scholarships had paid for his education. Anything extra, Hilton had to work for or his mother had denied herself to give him. He had put up with spoiled, ungrateful executives during his first years in the music business. He had started Rum Records with everything he owned and still worried that one day it could all blow up in his face. If he sometimes appeared opportunistic and ruthless, it was because he had learned long ago that you either hustle or get hustled. But you don't hustle your best friend. His mother had raised him better than that.

Hilton wondered if he had always been jealous of Jeff. Was Jeff his silent adversary? Jeff had accepted him, never cared that Hilton's family wasn't wealthy or important. But all along, Hilton had tried to keep up with Jeff, to compete. At Andover, Hilton had been the better basketball player, even though Jeff was several inches taller. It had filled Hilton with silent satisfaction. In college, Hilton financed his spring breaks and nights out through part-time jobs and moonlighting at clubs. Jeff merely withdrew funds from a constantly replenished bank account. Even the money they earned at the Rum hip-hop parties had been a welcome infusion of cash for Hilton. Jeff never knew the extent of Hilton's financial strain. On Hilton's first Thanksgiving at Andover, when he couldn't afford to go home to Long Beach, Jeff invited him to dinner in New Rochelle. Hilton had been shocked to discover that only

Taylor and Angela Montgomery lived in that spacious house. Room after room of tasteful art and furniture sat unused. With the formation and success of Rum Records, Hilton felt that he and Jeff were finally on equal footing. If they sealed the NRG deal, Hilton would be assured financial peace of mind. If they didn't, Jeff would still have his family's wealth and connections to fall back on, but Hilton would still feel insecure.

But a little healthy competition was good. Hilton had produced some of his best work that way. All the events in his life had placed him on a course leading him to his present reality. Andover, Harvard, the glossy New York lifestyle. How else could a scrawny boy from Long Beach get this far? Much of it had been chance, but more of it had been a fight.

He had probably seduced Nora that night six years ago. It hadn't been premeditated, but he had subtly encouraged the flirtatious vibes—just to see if he could succeed. And when he did, his male vanity surpassed his consideration for his best friend.

Hilton drove to the ranch-style house he had bought his mother a few years ago. It was located in Hancock Park, one of LA's finer communities, but was deliberately modest. "What do I need a big house for, Hilton?" she had protested. Sally Frears was touched that her son wanted to buy her a new home, and in her eyes, the gesture surpassed the house itself. Hilton had also told her that she no longer needed to work, since he could afford to support her financially. "And what would I do with myself all day?" she had exclaimed. Grandma Henrietta had passed away several years before and Sally had never married. She had a gentleman friend whom she saw regularly. He professed to love her, but Sally had written off marriage long ago.

Hilton let himself in with his key and surprised her in the kitchen.

Sally shrieked, "Is this why you called me so early this morning and made me stay home from work, just so you could scare me half to death?"

"No," Hilton said, and almost crushed her in a great big hug. "I did it because I wanted to spend some time with my beautiful mother."

She beamed. "Make yourself at home on the porch. I have a surprise for you."

Hilton rested on a deck chair and surveyed the neighborhood of attractive homes and trim lawns. He was happy that his mother lived comfortably here, but he wouldn't have traded his childhood home for it. *I might have been even more screwed up if I grew up here,* he thought ruefully. Sally placed a tray with peach cobbler on the table.

Hilton inhaled the sweet aroma and said, "Mom, you didn't have to do all this."

"I wanted to."

He kissed her cheek. "You've always been so good to me."

"I wouldn't have it any other way. Now dig in."

They caught up on some news. He asked about her health.

"I know you didn't fly across the country just to ask me how I'm feeling," Sally teased. Her smiling face was animated, as it had always been. She exercised and paid close attention to her diet, but she wasn't interested in hiding her age. She said that the lines in the space between her eyebrows originated from constantly pursing them together, trying to see how two and two could make five.

"I wanted to see how you were doing. It's been a couple of months."

"I know. After all these years, I still haven't completely gotten used to you living so far away. I handle it, but still . . . you are my only child," she said.

Hilton spooned out a second helping of the peach cobbler. "Mom, are you proud of me?" he asked in a deliberately casual manner.

"What a thing to ask!" Sally exclaimed. "Of course I'm proud of you, what you've done with the talents you've been given. I'm so proud of you I could burst. But always remember that I was proud of you before"—she swept her hands in the air, indicating the house and the neighborhood—"any of this."

"Do you think I've been too greedy? Always wanting more?"

Sally was pensive. "If you have to ask me—or yourself—that question, then maybe you have been."

Hilton didn't answer. A blue convertible packed with teenagers sped by. The music was turned up high; hair flew in the wind. He envied their freedom, that untroubled spirit of youth.

Sally touched his hand. "Maybe some of it is my fault. It was always the two of us—three when Grandma Henrietta was alive. I think you always believed that you had to take care of us. That you had to be the 'big man of the house.' " She sighed. "Maybe it was only natural, not having a father in the family."

"I never needed a father," said Hilton defensively.

"Sometimes we don't even know what we need until it's too late." She paused. "I saw him again, you know."

"My father?"

She nodded. "I was at the bank. Many, many years had passed, but I still recognized him. He recognized me too. His hair was pretty gray and he had put on weight. He came up to me shyly—the cocky man from the plant was gone—and asked me how his son was. Just like that: 'How's my son?' My knees were shaking. I had imagined for so long how it would be to see him face-to-face again, but I still wasn't prepared when it happened. Finally, I said, 'You don't have a son,' and turned around. I left him standing there, looking pitiful. I couldn't believe I had done it. You were in college at the time and I really wanted to scream, 'He's in college. At Harvard. *Harvard*. Do you hear me? And we did it all without you.' "

Hilton forced a chuckle, masking his emotions. "I didn't know you could be so sassy."

"Did I do the right thing?" Sally asked seriously.

"Sometimes I've wondered about him. But . . . he didn't deserve us. You were right. We were fine without him."

"But are you fine now?"

Hilton lifted his shoulders. "I don't know. I may have hurt some people. Friends."

"We don't have a big family, Hilton. Friends are important."

He nodded.

"What will you do?" she asked.

"I haven't decided yet."

"Why?"

"Because so many things are involved. It's not only about friendship, but business too." He paused. "And money. A lot of money."

"I'd say that between friendship and money, the right choice is pretty obvious."

Her logical and uncomplicated line of reasoning sharply contrasted with the relativism he lived by. He didn't want to lie to her. "I'll have to think about it."

"Never forget that no matter what you decide, it's not worth it if you don't respect yourself." She picked up the tray. "I'll wrap up the rest of this peach cobbler. You can take it back to New York with you."

Two days later, Hilton paid Jeff a house call at Hamilton Terrace. He banged the door repeatedly and pressed his finger on the doorbell, hoping the annoying sound would provoke a response.

"Jeff, I know you're in there," Hilton shouted. "Let me in. I'm not leaving until you open the door."

He persisted until Jeff opened the door, but only by a few inches.

"Hi," said Hilton through the crevice, "are you going to let me in?"

"I really don't want to, but do I have a choice?" snarled Jeff.

Hilton shook his head, pushed the door open and marched ahead, disappearing into the kitchen.

"Damn! You look like shit. What happened to you?" Hilton asked. Unshaven and uncombed, Jeff wore a raggedy blue sweater with rumpled Adidas sweatpants.

Jeff scowled at him. "What do you want?"

Hilton lifted a plate from a pile of dirty dishes in the sink. "Maybe you should call your housekeeper. Nora won't like this."

"Nora's gone," Jeff announced.

"What?"

"She moved out."

"You can't be serious!" Hilton hesitated. "It's because of our fight? What I said? I came over here to apologize for that. Things got way out of line and I'm so sorry. Let me talk to her. She probably hates me now, but I never meant for it to come out. It never happened the way I led you to believe—"

"I know that. She explained it to me." Jeff jabbed a finger at him. "But why the hell would you want me to believe that the two of you were having an affair? That day was the worst day of my life. You can't imagine how confused I was. What kind of friend are you?"

Hilton sat down. "That's what I've been asking myself and I've realized, not a very good one. I've been so fucked-up. Not just now, but for a long time. Insecurity, jealousy, greed." He let out a fake laugh. "It's not a pretty picture. So many hang-ups and I've been dealing with them the wrong way."

"But what have I ever done to you, Hilton?"

"Nothing. Nothing at all. If anything, I'm probably the one who's gained more from our friendship."

Jeff ran his hands through his wild hair and said with great effort, "No. I'd say we were about even until this."

"You were threatening to take away the one thing that I really wanted: the NRG alliance and all that money. That beautiful green mountain of cash. You know how I sometimes have trouble sleeping?"

Jeff nodded.

"Well, I'd think about what I'd do with all that money, the things I would buy—an Aston Martin, a house in St. Barth, a G-IV to take me there—and fall asleep like a baby every time." He snapped his fingers. "The insomnia vanished."

"You would've been no better than Butler's lackey to get those things," said Jeff distastefully.

"Well, I called Butler to postpone the deal until next week. Figured I could persuade you to go for it again."

"Hilton, I don't—"

"Wait, Jeff. Let me finish. I've really thought about this a lot in the last two days. I'm sorry for the way I've behaved, now and six years ago. Friendship, your friendship, is more important to me than joining up with NRG. I think I lost some of my self-confidence and thought that I could only reach the big time with them. But I already have more than I know what to do with. In many ways, I've already made it. I don't need NRG to define me."

"So what did you do?"

"I called Butler back and told him, in no uncertain terms, that the deal was off. We were walking away."

"And how did he react?"

Hilton chuckled. "Like . . . like a pit bull."

Jeff couldn't help smiling.

Hilton elaborated, "Butler got all agitated, talking about breach of contract, asking in that condescending tone of his if we knew what we were giving up, threatening to bad-mouth us around the industry. But I kept it professional and let him make a fool of himself. His ass might be on the block anyway, so he better watch it."

"How do you feel?"

"Actually, pretty relieved. Like a huge burden has been lifted."

Jeff went to the fridge and took out a bottle of Snapple. "Hilton, I was ready to have it out with you, you know. I said to myself, the next time I see that bastard, I'm going to *punch the shit out of him*." He drank the iced tea in great gulps as Hilton waited nervously. Jeff chucked the empty bottle in the garbage bin and said, "But you're showing some self-awareness that I didn't think you were capable of."

"Well, it's been there. I just ignored it. It didn't fit in with my plans."

"I never wanted to sell us out."

"You were right. That's what we would have been doing." Hilton paused. "I've been doing a little research. We can still branch out into other areas."

"How?"

"We can get ourselves an agent to shop our ideas around. I've got some contacts at CAA. We can set up a production deal with a studio. We can find financial backers. There are lots of options. And we'd still be in full charge. I'm not worried about the future of Rum anymore. We'll be fine."

"A new beginning," Jeff muttered.

"That's why I need you to get your act together so we can go to the office and tell the staff they have nothing to worry about anymore."

"I'm not up to it today."

"Jeff, you can't hide in here forever. People are depending on you."

"I said I'm not up to it," he repeated roughly.

Hilton said nothing and finally, "OK. Wrong set of priorities. Go clean yourself up and bring your wife back home."

"It's not that simple," said Jeff evasively.

"Don't let your stupid pride get in the way. Just go to her."

"I can't," he whispered. "I did something to her."

"Jeff, stop stalling. What the hell happened?" Hilton demanded.

Jeff sighed. "She found out I slept with Olivia."

Hilton's mouth widened. "Olivia? That woman with the kid from the summer?"

Jeff's head moved down slightly and Hilton interpreted that as a yes. "Are you crazy? Were you trippin'? Why?"

"In a way, I was!" Jeff cried. "I did it after you threw that little tidbit about you and Nora in my face! I don't know. . . . It just happened. I don't know what I was thinking. I was just so fucking mad at you both."

Hilton backed off. "I admit that I wanted to get back at you, mess up your life for a while, but I never wanted your marriage to break up."

"Well, it did."

"What are you going to do now?"

"What can I do? She left me no address, no phone number. I only know she's downtown. All I can do is wait."

"You know where she works. Ambush her there."

"Hilton, you weren't there. You don't know how she looked. She told me that she needed her space. I have to respect that. I'll wait—as long as it takes."

"So she told you she's coming back?"

"No," Jeff answered.

"This can't be possible." Hilton placed his hand on Jeff's shoulder. "You'll get her back, Jeff. You'll get her back."

"Don't you see, Hilton?" Jeff asked. "I don't know if she wants me back."

CHAPTER 19

Nora's bravado had evaporated as soon as she set foot into her new living quarters. The apartment was decent: 350 square feet with a tiny kitchenette. The main room was divided by a Chinese silk screen that separated the bed from a small couch and table. The apartment was owned by *Muse*'s parent company and was normally lent out to visiting staff or the magazine's contributors. Nora planned to sublet it on a month-to-month basis. She needed the freedom to go through her range of emotions and make some sense out of her life. However, the clamor of Twelfth Street and Seventh Avenue South made her miss the picturesque charm of Hamilton Heights. And of course, she missed Jeff. But it was an unusual void. She longed for what they had once been. She didn't miss the reality that had compelled her to leave. When she had opened the door and carried in her two bags, she almost didn't want to go through with it. *I'm not strong enough to do this,* she had thought. Then she remembered that she couldn't return to Jeff out of her own weakness.

She had scrubbed, mopped and vacuumed that first night in the apartment. That had kept her busy for several hours, focusing on dust and clutter. The place was so small, she could already tell that the slightest bit of mess had the tendency to mushroom. She unpacked, stacking clothes in the medium-sized bureau and closet. She changed the sheets and drew down the bed. Her eyes stayed wide open in the darkness. She wished for sleep, a far-reaching slumber that could erase her pain. Twice she blacked out and thought that several hours must have gone by, but each time only a few minutes had passed. The realization struck her that if she grew bored or restless, she didn't have a town house to wander around in or a husband to wake up for company. Could the small confines already be closing in on her? She was alone, lonely and scared. Her eyes smarted and she knew that the tears would soon cascade, but she was determined not to cry anymore. Moving out had been her choice, her therapy. Deep down, Nora knew that it had been the right decision. Her mind replayed her last conversation with Jeff. She had uttered the dreaded words, "I'm moving." They had rolled out of her mouth numbly, detached. She had almost been outside of herself, watching a woman she didn't know.

An onslaught of memories flooded her mind. Too many of her sweeter moments included Jeff. It seemed like he had always filled her existence. Even before she had met him, he had been an invisible figure in her subconscious, her other half floating in anticipation until chance or design brought them together. With him, she had finally thrown her customary caution out the window and given in, slowly at first, but eventually surrendering to their connection.

After graduate school, Nora had accepted a position as a cub reporter for a daily newspaper in Washington, D.C. She began by writing obituaries (sometimes when her subjects were still alive!) and quickly moved up to cover the city beat. But after six months, she reluctantly admitted to herself that she didn't have the stomach to write about murders, rapes and other tales of desperation and despair in the big city. D.C. was an engaging place with its politics and culture, but the town turned out to be more conservative than she had expected and its political obsession could be claustrophobic. She longed for New York.

She visited New York as often as her schedule allowed, but sensed that something was different. Her beloved city was in continuous flux and the scene and styles changed every six months. She was between worlds, not quite making it in D.C. and feeling like an outsider in New York. She felt generally dissatisfied with everything and had been reluctant to go to a cocktail party that Erica and Dahlia dragged her to. The sequence of events—introductions, small talk and then that inevitable moment, *Should I even be chatting to this person, or is there someone more interesting in the room?*—bored her.

But her eyes connected with someone else's across the crowded floor and Jeff's gaze had been so powerful that Nora instinctively looked away, reverting to the awkward shyness of her youth. Nevertheless, from that moment on, she still felt his presence and found it difficult to concentrate on what her friends were saying. She was completely unprepared when he later introduced himself. Nora immediately liked his deep voice and openness. He was handsome and, just as important, at least four inches taller. Something in the room had reminded Jeff of a scene from a movie and they began discussing films. His favorite actor was Al Pacino. Nora had wrinkled her nose and said, "Al overacts. He's always shouting in his movies." Once the words were out of her mouth, she wondered if she sounded pretentious, opinionated. But Jeff seemed delighted that she disagreed and tried to explain the merits of Pacino's technique. She had wondered if he was a filmmaker or a struggling actor. He said no, just a movie buff in a lawyer's body. He really listened to her, absorbing her words in a thoughtful manner when she spoke. He waited for her to finish her point, never cut her off, rushing in to add his own views. She was accustomed to always being the interviewer at her job, so it was appealing to have someone really interested in what she had to say.

But Nora had the habit of often doing the exact opposite of what she wanted. She came up with a litany of mental excuses to avoid seeing him again. They lived in two different cities. What was the point? He also made her nervous—too nice, too attractive—there had to be something wrong. Her lot tended to be pleasant, bland men who failed to fuel a spark in her. But they were harmless, and she knew they wouldn't disappoint her. The party died down and she told Jeff that she had enjoyed meeting him. When he reached into his pocket and she saw the cap of a pen edging out, she said good-bye to him before he could ever say it to her.

Back in Washington, the grind of chasing stories became considerably more draining. She took a few personal days off and interviewed for one magazine job after another in New York. She brandished her clippings and writing samples, but was met by harsh critiques and a string of rejections. Nora had covered murders and serious inner-city problems—surely she could tackle a piece about a new restaurant or an up-and-coming actor? She emerged completely drained and distracted from yet another interview and crashed into someone as she turned a street corner. Her nose soon found itself pressed up against a broad shoulder and she could smell the pleasant, sweet scent of laundry detergent through cotton twill. A pair of strong hands clutched her arms in an oddly familiar way.

"Hey, there, pretty lady. You better watch where you're going."

She glanced upward, eyes wide.

"It's Jeff Montgomery," he said. "We met at Brad's party a couple of months ago."

"Oh, yes. That's right," she answered slowly. "Sorry for bumping into you like that. I can be so clumsy sometimes." She started walking and he fell into step with her.

"What are you doing? Are you back in the city?"

Nora smiled at him in spite of herself. It was nice to see a friendly face, especially after that wrenching interview she'd just had.

"I'm trying to get back. I've been going to a bunch of interviews these last few days."

He looked disappointed. "Oh. How are they going?"

She shrugged. "It's so hard to tell what they're thinking."

"Tell them what you're about. Your credentials will speak for themselves."

"You'd think so, but these people are more interested in finding out whether I'd be willing to traipse around the city hunting down colored cotton balls for a photo shoot, or retyping their Rolodexes, or picking up their dry cleaning. Fashion magazines are usually staffed by trust fund babes or girls with mile-high connections." She grinned. "I have neither."

Jeff checked his watch. "Do you have the time to stop somewhere for lunch?"

He was trying so hard, making an effort to talk to her, and truthfully, Nora didn't need much prodding. She already knew that she liked him and had thought of him many times since their first meeting. Once when she had trouble sleeping, she imagined his face and felt the sweetest shivers. She had been testing herself, asking herself what would have happened if she had been open to the next step and given him her number.

"That would be nice," she answered.

The peak lunchtime hours had passed and the blocks were relatively clear. Jeff's natural gait was quick and Nora had to increase her pace to keep up. She stepped on a subway grate and felt the vibrations of a moving train beneath her feet. They passed Rockefeller Center and she suggested Dean & Deluca. They ordered sandwiches and filled their plates at the salad bar. A table for two overlooking the famed ice-skating rink, which had been dismantled for spring, was free and they sat down.

"Whatever happened to good ol' ham and cheese? Or peanut butter and jelly?" asked Jeff.

Nora laughed. "I know. Everything has become so upmarket. Everyone on the street seems to know the difference between focaccia or ciabatta, a latte or a double espresso."

He picked at his pasta salad. "Why are you looking for a new job?"

"The newspaper world is getting to me. I want a change of scenery and the chance to do some longer pieces. I'd love to do some fashion journalism, but it's so flighty and competitive." She paused. "If I leave, my editor in D.C. will be really disappointed. I'd be leaving the beat to work on soft news—fluff pieces, he calls them—and he doesn't have much respect for that kind of journalism."

"But you should work on what you want. Don't even worry about what he'll say."

"I know, but a little voice inside my head wonders if I'm turning out to be a big disappointment. Most journalists would kill for a big-city byline and I want to work for *Vogue* instead."

"You shouldn't apologize for what turns you on. And I have a hard time believing you'd be a disappointment in anything. You've probably planned your life to the letter so far. I doubt you'll start stumbling now. But if you do, just laugh about it. At least you tried."

"Easier said than done." She smiled and popped a cherry tomato in her mouth. "Am I keeping you from something?"

"Yes, I'm very busy. A very important meeting is awaiting me in my jeans and wrinkled white shirt."

Nora liked him better slightly mussed up. He seemed infinitely more approachable and made her feel very comfortable. She doubted he was the type who sought security in conspicuous labels. His aura was confident, discreet—the word "quality" came to mind. He had nice hands, strong and smooth with neat fingernails. A stainless steel diving watch was on his left wrist. A bit scratched up from wear, it looked like the kind of graduation gift his parents would have given him.

"I thought you were a lawyer," she said.

"I was—still am—but I quit my job a few weeks ago. Disappointed?"

"No. In fact, I'm glad. This city can use one less practicing attorney," she joked. "Isn't law one of those professions you can always fall back on? It'll always be there for you. So what are you doing these days, besides taking long, lazy lunches?"

He leaned forward. "Can I share a secret with you?"

She hunched down and moved in closer. The tips of their fingers were almost touching. "Sure. I don't even know who I would tell."

"I've started a record company with my best friend from school."

"Really?" she gushed. "How exciting! What made you do it?"

"Timing. Like you, feeling that it was time for a change. It's basically now or never. My partner, Hilton Frears, was also a pretty convincing salesman. It's like what I tried to tell you earlier. Sometimes you just have to act on instinct, not common sense."

"But you guys are taking a huge risk. Do you think it's going to work?"

"I hope you don't think I sound cocky, Nora, but I know it's going to work. I feel it in my bones. And I'm having a great time doing it; even the hassles are exciting. It's an uphill battle at times—things can be a pain in the ass and take longer than they should—but I can't beat the adrenaline that I feel every day as Hilton and I are putting this company together. I wake up every morning and I don't know what the rest of my day will bring. When I worked at the firm, I had to account for how I was going to spend every minute of my twelve-hour day. Now I could be having lunch with a program manager at a radio station or with a beautiful, displaced New Yorker who should definitely be working in fashion," he said, and grinned.

Nora looked into his eyes and saw it then. This, his dream, was what moved him, what made his heart beat faster. She suddenly longed to be at that spot too.

"How long do you think it will take?" she asked.

"If I had to give you a number, I'd say two, three years."

"What if you fail?"

"If you want it badly enough, it can happen. You have to believe in yourself."

As he spoke, she watched him intently, admiring his confidence. She wanted to know more, wanted to wish him the best of luck, but he asked her a question before she had the chance.

"Nora, what made you want to become a journalist?"

She was taken aback. It had been so long since someone had asked her that. It had never even come up in her recent interviews.

"Well, I love words, ideas, stories," she explained, choosing her words carefully. "Observing people and society and putting it all down on paper. I like touching people, informing them, entertaining them. I guess I just want to make some sense of the things that go on around us."

"Sort of like you're doing with me," he remarked.

"I am not!" she protested, but her cheeks felt hot.

"You probably don't realize it because it's so inbred, but you're sizing me up, drawing your own conclusions from a distance, and I'm sure I'll never find out what you've come up with. You did it that first night we met. You're very careful. You don't jump into things."

She looked down. His words rang true. "I can be spontaneous."

"Really?"

"Yes. Really."

"So have dinner with me Saturday night."

"I can't. I'm going back to Washington really early Sunday morning."

Jeff gave a small laugh. She was getting back at him, giving him a little tap on the hand for having hit so close to home.

"OK. What about brunch, then?"

She took a final sip of her mineral water and said, "I think I can manage that."

She met him in SoHo at noon on Saturday and brunch lasted four hours. They were the last ones left in the restaurant, but the maître d' was kind and apparently didn't want to interrupt what was obviously a new romance. When the waitstaff tactfully began resetting the tables for dinner, Jeff and Nora finally peeled themselves away from their corner spot. A movie followed, then dinner. If she counted the total hours she had known him, it would be less than a day, but she had already told him about the dichotomy of growing up with parents from another country, how college had been the defining moment in her life, that her favorite word was "epiphany."

By eleven that night, she knew that she had to make it back to her parents' house on Long Island. She was booked on the eight a.m. shuttle to Washington the next day and still had a couple of things to organize before she left.

"I'll drive you back to Long Island," Jeff offered when she told him she had to leave.

Back to Westbury and possibly running into her mother and father! No! She had wanted to keep Jeff to herself for a while, away from her parents' well-intentioned but prying eyes.

"You don't have to do that," she answered quickly. "I've taken the train late at night since I was in high school."

"But I want to," he insisted, "and it'll give me an extra hour with you."

How could she say no to that?

They picked up his car, a worn-out blue Volvo, at a downtown garage.

"No point in having a nice car in Manhattan," he remarked.

"That car has Harvard written all over it," she teased.

He laughed. "I know. There were so many in Boston like it, I had trouble telling which one was mine. Then I hit a pole and dented the fender. It was the perfect identifying mark, so I never bothered fixing it."

They puttered along listening to a tape that Jeff had put together, a mix of soul classics and Blaxploitation movie tunes. *This guy is in a world of his own,* she thought, and felt as though she were being gracefully pulled into his orbit. He was curious, funny and charming. He defied classification, and yes, he had surprised her.

The lights were on in her parents' white Colonial. They had traded up from the starter home when Nora was thirteen. She wanted to say a quick good-bye, but saw Jeff unbuckling his seat belt and making for the handle on his door. He planned on coming inside with her! This was too much. She could have been back in high school, except in high school she never had dates. Her parents rarely met anyone she was seeing. Most of her relationships had been short romances with men in

Manhattan or Washington. She tried to think, but Jeff opened her door and she stepped out of the car.

"I guess my parents are still up watching the news," she said nonchalantly.

She unlocked the front door and found her parents in the den, sharing the comfortable amber couch where she had spent countless nights watching late movies. A teapot and a plate of cookies were on the table. Valérie and Pierre—the vision of suburbia incarnate.

"Hi. I'm back. I'm home," she called out.

Her parents looked at her warmly and Valérie said, "Did you have a nice time?" The words were still in the air when Jeff's tall figure crept up behind Nora.

Her mother swiftly patted her hair and stood up. "Oh," she chimed, "I didn't realize you had company."

Jeff walked smoothly towards her mother and held out his hand. "Hello. I'm Jeff Montgomery. It's so nice to meet you."

Valérie and Pierre returned his greeting and Nora knew that her mother could hardly contain her pleasure. She was at her utmost charming and Jeff indulged her, but not in a slick or disingenuous way. He was simply a nice guy completely at ease meeting strangers or a date's parents. The three of them chatted away like old friends.

"I guess I should be heading out now. I have to drive back into the city," Jeff said after about ten minutes.

Valérie beamed. Nora knew that Jeff had just gotten extra brownie points for bringing her home, even though he would have to make the tedious forty-five minute drive back to Manhattan by himself. Whoever said chivalry was dead?

Nora led him back to the front door.

"Thank you so much for a wonderful day. I had a great time," she said.

"Me too. When are you coming back to New York?"

"I don't know. Depends on the job."

"Promise you'll call me when you get back."

That could be months away! What was he talking about?

"I promise," she answered, trying to hide her confusion.

"No," he said firmly, as though something important had just come to mind. "I mean, promise me you'll call me when you get back to Washington."

Now it was her turn to beam. "I will."

Nora could hear her parents' low voices. They had turned off the television and would soon make their way up the stairs to bed.

She stood on her tiptoes and planted a peck on Jeff's cheek. "Good night," she whispered.

He pulled her closer to him and Nora almost died. She experienced the small quakes in her abdomen, the cravings that made her an awkward teenager all over again. *Please don't kiss me. Don't put those beautiful, warm lips on mine in the middle of my parents' hallway. Maybe I would have in the car . . . or, maybe not.*

He must have read her mind. He gently squeezed her hand and in an instant was gone. Nora closed the door behind her and leaned back against it. She could still smell him, that innocently sexy combination of cologne and fabric softener.

"Such a nice young man," Valérie said as she stood at the foot of the stairs.

Nora nodded.

"How long have you known him?"

"Not very long. This is the third time we've ever met, but I guess today was our first 'official date.' "

"Oh, so?" Valérie was setting up her interrogation.

"We met at a party. He's a couple of years older than I am, grew up in Westchester, did double duty at Harvard. Have I covered all your questions?"

"How interesting," Valérie reflected. "I could tell he was well brought up. What does he do for a living?"

"He's a lawyer," Nora revealed. Valérie's face nearly exploded with glee and then Nora decided to drop the bomb. "But he resigned from his firm a few weeks ago to start his own record company with a friend."

Valérie came crashing back to earth. "He left a legal career for the music business?" she cried, startled.

"Yes," Nora answered. "He has a dream and he's going for it. You can't fault anyone for that, can you, Mom?"

Valérie sighed. "No, honey. Of course not. We only want what's best for you."

She put an arm around her mother. "I know, but I'll figure it out. OK?"

She began to miss him as soon as she got back to her D.C. apartment. She spent all day Sunday debating whether or not she should call him. Tonight? Tomorrow? Or play it really coy—Wednesday? She decided to call him that night, nervously wondering if she would appear too eager.

"What took you so long?" he asked. "I thought you were going to call me the minute you got back."

"I didn't think you meant it literally," she laughed.

They continued like this for a couple of weeks—talking on the phone every day, sometimes twice a day, confiding intimacies, laughing. Both were busy with unpredictable schedules, but they had to speak to each other. The lack of face-to-face contact brought them closer together. Without the immediate pressure of the physical realm, they could be more honest with each other. They had to explore other things, strip down to their true selves and transcend the unspoken passion of their last meeting.

He finally drove down to see her three weeks after their brunch date in New York. She was practically waiting for him on her doorstep, she threw her arms around him the minute he got close to her, and they had their first kiss then and there. They dined at a fashionable Georgetown restaurant and Jeff ran into some old friends from college. In fact, he ended up saying hello to more people he knew that weekend than Nora ever had, even after almost two years in the city. He was a social star; he made people feel good and people felt good around him. She caught some of the afterglow as his date. People questioned her, couldn't believe that she lived in D.C. and they had never met. They offered her casual invitations and made tentative plans for the next time Jeff might be in town again. Nora could already see how it would be to have a relationship with someone like him. A woman could shrink in his presence and perhaps a lesser man would have made her feel small. Yet Jeff treated her beautifully, regarded her like he couldn't quite believe she had finally given him a chance. She loved how they didn't move from her couch on Sunday and watched videos of *Serpico* and *Dog Day Afternoon* that Jeff had brought with him. He joked that he would make an Al Pacino fan out of her yet.

Things also turned for Nora careerwise. She got the job as Jim Kay's editorial assistant and excitedly packed her bags for New York. She couldn't wait to begin her new job, but her relationship with Jeff filled her with trepidation. They had settled into the rhythm of a long-distance relationship. What would happen when she was in the city full-time? What would they expect from each other? Jeff helped her unpack her boxes in the studio apartment that would eat up half of her small monthly salary. They never talked about any new parameters for their relationship. They spoke all the time as before and made plans to get together every week, but Nora made a point of rekindling some old acquaintances in town. She went out with girlfriends at least once a week. She never wanted to be home alone on a Friday or Saturday night, even if the alternative was ordering in Chinese with Erica and Dahlia. She kept thinking that disappointment would eventually hurtle towards her like an express train and she would fall headlong, smashed into hundreds of emotional pieces. But it didn't. Jeff told her he loved her and she responded with all the love and tenderness that had consumed her for months.

She didn't think that things could get better, but they did. Jeff and Hilton had their first hit, and almost overnight, they became the darlings of the hip-hop music scene, earning lots of money and social cachet. They had crossed that bridge, ascended to that rare level, where larger apartments, spur-of-the-moment vacations and high-tech playthings were theirs for the asking. Jeff and Hilton had built their record company from scratch and Nora thought that they rightfully deserved the trappings of success. After all, the artists were happy, the company was growing, and New York City was the perfect place to be young, successful and wealthy. But Nora refused to let the money and glamour cloud her judgment or make her feel weak or dependent. She noticed the hangers-on, the people who wanted to get close to Jeff and Hilton because of what they personified. She would never be in that position. She was aware of the other women too, the way they dropped hints and tried to maneuver their way into Jeff's circle. She confronted him about it and he said that those women were interested only in the image, not the reality, of who he was. "You've been with me since the beginning," he replied. "I don't have to question why we're together."

Nora still didn't put two and two together when Jeff suggested a champagne picnic in Central Park. "What a lovely idea," she said, acting as though they did that sort of thing all the time. They sat on the grassy knoll near the Metropolitan Museum of Art, shielded from the midday sun underneath a hearty sycamore tree. Jeff had gone out of his way to outfit an authentic picnic carrier from Williams-Sonoma. Compartments were everywhere and thin leather straps held down the plates, utensils, smoked salmon, toast, crème fraîche, champagne and wonderful jar of beluga caviar. Everything was in its proper place for a jaunt out to the country, the races or the polo field. Except in New York City, Central Park was about as far as one got.

"Nora, why don't you open the caviar?" Jeff suggested.

"Mmmmm . . . yes . . . my favorite." She had tried caviar only once before and, to her dismay, had loved it. It was far too expensive a habit for her to develop.

Nora opened the lid and saw a small, carefully wrapped piece of tissue paper atop the bed of fish eggs. "What's this?" she asked, and picked it up. It felt hard and circular through her fingers. Her pulse skipped from normal to erratic. She glanced at Jeff and he motioned for her to continue. She unfolded the paper and inside found a perfect diamond ring. A bit of slate gray caviar had leaked onto the center stone, but nothing could eclipse the beauty of the cushion-cut diamond or the sparkling, dainty perfection of the supporting trilliants.

Nora slid the ring on and just stared at it, transfixed, tears running down her cheeks. She finally looked up at Jeff.

His eyes danced.

"Nora, will you marry me?"

That's when she let it all go. The dam broke and what had started out as soft sniffles crescendoed into all-out wails. She so desperately wanted to be beautiful, for Jeff to remember the glow in her face, her joy from his proposal. But she couldn't help bawling, couldn't help convulsing or having a runny nose and blurry vision because she was so damn happy!

"Is that a yes or no?" Jeff asked.

She opened her mouth, but nothing came, so she just kept nodding her head. They finally found each other and Nora cried into his chest. A well-coiffed elderly woman who had been out walking her precious Chihuahua stopped in front of them.

"Young man," she said in her Fifth Avenue lockjaw, "what have you done to that poor girl?"

They were married six months later. Nora had been euphoric and knew that being married felt absolutely different. Otherwise, why would one do it? They shouted to family and friends, *"Celebrate with us!"* Their promise to each other had been so solid. It had been the happiest day of her life, the supreme second when all of life's disparate elements finally fell into place. She had envisioned forever—never Hilton, Olivia or a solitary apartment on Twelfth Street.

By the third, homesick evening, Nora decided to call her mother.

"Hello," Valérie answered cautiously, as though bracing herself for a persistent telemarketer or wrong number.

"Mom, it's me."

Valérie's tone livened. "Hi, sweetheart. How are you?"

"Fine," Nora answered dully.

Naturally, Valérie picked up on it. "What's the matter? You sound strange."

"Do I? Tired, I guess."

"That job of yours. I keep telling you that you have to set limits."

"Hmmm . . ."

"What else is new?"

"Nothing."

"Nora," Valérie said, exasperated, "you must have called me for a reason."

Nora delayed her response.

"Honey, what is it?" Valérie pressed.

Nora cleared her throat. "Mom, I just wanted to give you a number in case you wanted to reach me. For an emergency or something. Do you have a pen? The number is—"

"Wait, wait, wait," Valérie interrupted. "What about your home number? Where are you now? On a business trip?"

"No. Just write this number down—"

"Nora!" Valérie shouted. "You're speaking in half sentences. Where are you now? Why aren't you home?"

"Oh, Mom," Nora sighed, "I won't be home for a while. I've . . . I've left Jeff."

"What?" Valérie cried. "Why?"

"I don't want to talk about it right now. My new number is 212–276–1580."

"Please tell me what's going on."

"Mom, please! I said I didn't want to talk about it! I didn't even have to call you and give you my new number. My problem is that I confide in you too much and you end up interfering in my life. I can never have any privacy. Do you want my new number or not?"

Valérie started to say something else, but held back. "Just a minute. Let me get a pen."

"My number is 212–276–1580."

Nora heard Valérie repeating the number to herself while she copied it.

"Why did you leave? What happened?" Valérie asked again.

Nora hated when her mother expressed selfless concern. It always made Nora reveal more than she wanted to. "Let's just say that we were having some problems. I needed to get away."

"What could be so terrible that you felt you had to leave your husband? Move out of your house?" Nora thought it was naive for Valérie not to have guessed the base truth. Valérie's affection for Jeff and faith in their marriage didn't allow her to conceive of infidelity.

"It didn't feel right. I wasn't happy."

"Why didn't you feel happy? Give me your address. I'll be over within an hour."

"Mom, I'm not in the mood to discuss this! You have my number. Call in case of an emergency. Otherwise, I'll call you." Nora hung up amid cries of protest from Valérie.

The phone kept ringing, but Nora didn't pick up. She thought her head would explode and finally took it off the hook. She got into bed and prayed it wouldn't take her all night to fall asleep.

CHAPTER 20

Work was hell. After two weeks on her own, Nora had come to the conclusion that what she did for a living was completely frivolous. It had no basis in a woman's daily reality. How could *Muse* expect women to embrace the color pink for spring or spray their laundry with rose water when their personal lives might be falling apart? Each morning was a struggle for her to get out of bed. *Muse* was the latest victim, but reading, writing and exercising had fallen long before. If she made it through the day without crying, *without tearing up,* she considered it a major accomplishment. Her own emotional vulnerability shocked her. *Who am I without Jeff? Who was I before Jeff?* She asked herself these questions again and again, but coherent answers escaped her.

She was always tired and sleep was supposed to give her solace, but she grew restless lying in bed. Nora would throw off the sheets and roam around the apartment, longing for something to do. She craved human contact, but also felt antisocial. She was extremely short with Erica and Dahlia when she met with them a few days after moving out. As with her mother, she had felt compelled to tell them about her separation from Jeff.

"He did WHAT?" screeched Erica. "I expected better from him! They're all the same! Their brains are in their pants! He doesn't deserve you!"

"Please don't go off on him," replied Nora. She couldn't bear the barrage of insults from Erica's hefty arsenal.

"Why not?"

"I'm not in the mood and it doesn't help."

She also told them about her long-ago tryst with Hilton.

"Humph, I can't believe you and Hilton slept together," remarked Dahlia, shaking her head. "I would have never guessed."

"That was the point."

"What other secrets have you been hiding from us?" asked Erica.

"Yeah—we tell you everything," added Dahlia.

"I was too ashamed to tell anyone," Nora admitted. "This wasn't like some college conquest where we sat around and gave details."

"It happened a long time ago. I think the statute of limitations ran out," said Erica.

"What are you going to do?" asked Dahlia.

They expected an answer, a plan of action, and she had none. She avoided their phone calls and efforts to see her. Erica and Dahlia's "heart-to-heart" conversations made her feel like a pathetic talk show guest. She was alienated from herself and everybody else.

Nora wasn't oblivious to her condition, but she didn't have the energy or motivation to pull herself together. This ordeal was also beginning to take a physical toll. Her cheeks were sunken and dark circles seemed to have found a permanent home under her eyes. She had never been so sluggish in her life and knots of anxiety turned in her stomach.

On an appropriately gray day at the office, Nora scanned her computer disks, searching for archived articles and features she had written. She always had too many ideas, and Candida told her to save them for future issues. Nora was grateful for this file. Her inspiration for new, original thought had evaporated. IS FASHION LOSING ITS EDGE? blazed a headline, full of self-importance. *Did I actually write that?* Nora thought. Pondering about the state of fashion and style was a luxury. If one had to deal with a broken marriage and an uncertain future, what place did all of this have? But she had devoted years of her life to this. Was she as superficial and flighty as those in her professional community whom she criticized? Is that why Jeff had been attracted to dedicated, unselfish Olivia?

The headache was coming on again. It never spread to her whole head, but her right temple would pulsate feverishly. She had to rechannel her thoughts. Taking deep breaths, she clicked on her e-mail icon. E-mail, the perfect distraction, had saved her day so many times. Four new messages were in the in-box. Two e-mails advertised upcoming sample sales: *Fifty to eighty percent off! If you miss them, you'll regret it!* Delete. There was no way she'd be joining other crazed women fishing for bargains. The third e-mail was a political joke. Delete. She had had enough of those. The final message was from jeff.montgomery@rum.com. Nora hesitated before opening it. Hands shaking, she clicked on the message and a letter appeared before her on the screen.

Dearest Nora,

It seems so trite to be sending you this letter via e-mail, but since I don't know where you're staying, I thought this would be the best way to communicate. I want you to know that I respect your need for space and privacy. After all that has happened, I don't blame you. You warned me, hinted that things were spiraling out of control, but I chose not to listen. Unfortunately, you're the one who got hurt the most and I'll never forgive myself for doubting you. I suppose, then, it is unfair of me to expect your forgiveness.

With this new loneliness, I've been thinking about LIFE. Arguably, I should have been doing this all along, but things just seemed to flow so naturally for us. Maybe I always assumed that we were entitled to our unique magic. Now I see how truly special it was. The loss of our emotional connection, the total understanding I felt with you from the first moment we met, is one of my biggest regrets.

If I'm not begging you to come back, it's because I want you to feel that you can live with me again, love me again. I will always love you.

Jeff

Nora printed out the letter and read it over and over again, until she could practically recite it by heart. Jeff had finally reached out to her. She had wondered if he would. Their parting had been so incomplete. His words moved her; she couldn't help that. She imagined him writing it, struggling for the words to convey his guilt and sadness. The misery in his voice mirrored hers. How ironic that they should share the same feelings, the hurtful husband and his wronged wife. Nora had never heard Jeff display such raw emotion. Maybe he had written directly from his heart, unconcerned about revealing too much.

On the one hand, she was happy that Jeff had written this heartfelt confessional. This piece of him, his words on paper, responded to so many unanswered questions since she'd moved out. How did he feel? How often did he think of her? Did he understand the consequences of his actions? But Nora was torn, caught between the strength of two competing emotions. Her anger intensified whenever she thought of Jeff with Olivia. No matter what she did, she couldn't banish the feelings of rage, jealousy and betrayal. The foundation of her life had come to pieces. She couldn't have stayed with Jeff, but had no precise plans for how to go on. And beneath the anger—perhaps it was buried deeply—the love lingered. One simply didn't stop loving someone else from one day to the next. Whoever said that was possible was lying. What did Jeff expect from her? How did he expect her to reply? Did he know her so well that he just assumed that she would submit to his declaration of love?

Nora considered Jeff's letter for a long time, but she still didn't know if or how she would respond.

Julian Cortès knocked on her door.

"Come in," Nora answered. She hastily put a stack of files on top of Jeff's letter.

Julian came around to her chair and commented on her funky black shoes. "Interesting design. Are those Prada or Frauda?"

Nora was dumbfounded. "You mean are they real Pradas or fakes? I've never heard that one before. Is it new?"

"Nooo, darling. That one's been going around the fashion world for a long time now."

"I guess I'm not sufficiently hip anymore."

"Question is, do you still want to be hip?" he asked.

"Hmmm . . . I'll let you know when I've figured that out."

Julian looked thoughtful. "How's the place on Twelfth Street?"

"Small, depressing." She pretended to examine her fingernails. "Does everyone know that I've moved into that apartment?"

Julian shrugged apologetically. "Pretty much. Can't keep a secret for long around here."

"Does Candida know?"

"I'm sure she does, but she would never say anything to you about it."

"God. My life has become mail room gossip. Everyone here pretends they're your friend, but I think they secretly love it when your life turns shitty."

"If anybody thinks that about you, it's because your life has always been so together. Why should your life be good when theirs stinks?" Julian hesitated. His green eyes were sympathetic. "And, Nora, you look like a completely different person. It's pretty obvious something is wrong with you."

"Listen, I'm trying to hold it together, trying to spare people the drama of my private life," she said defensively, waving her hands in frustration. "Should I march into Candida's office and tell her that I've left my husband, can't sleep at night and can't stand being here every day? Will I get extra consideration for my misery?"

"You might," he said lightly. "People love to express sympathy."

"I'm too much of a private person. I won't do it."

"Of course not," Julian remarked. "And I wouldn't let you, but focus on your work." He paused. "It's beginning to suffer. In spite of everything, you love the magazine. We've got to finish creating your debut issue. You don't want all your work to be for nothing. I know you, Nora. You're a perfectionist. *Muse* is so close to having your signature on it. You don't want to jeopardize that, do you?"

"No, but I'm just . . . just not"—she struggled for the right word—"*feeling* it right now."

Julian sat up in his chair. "Nora, honey, I'm saying this as your friend: You better start feeling it soon." His voice was firm but magnanimous. "More people are watching you than you think."

Nora bristled from Julian's words. "Who's watching me?"

"The higher-ups. Candida. The magazine establishment. They all want to see if a Black woman can successfully edit a broad-based magazine."

"I can do it. I know I can do it. They know I can do it," she insisted.

"Yes, but they have to be absolutely sure."

"So I have to deal with that pressure on top of everything else!"

"Nora, I'm only trying to give you the heads-up. You know I'll do everything I can to help you. Please just think about what I've told you."

After Julian left, Nora realized that he had probably been Candida's mouthpiece. Her boss was discreetly giving her the chance to reevaluate her commitment to the magazine. Nora was perplexed to find that her ambivalent feelings about her job had been so transparent. But if her career imploded, what would she be left with? Shouldn't she be grateful she had a place to go every morning?

She couldn't expect *Muse* to cater to her personal crisis. They had a business to run, a magazine to put out. She had to work. The topic wasn't even open for debate. She had already shown her weakness and a demotion would be the final insult. She moved the file folders from the center of her desk and picked up Jeff's letter. If she didn't answer it, she wouldn't be able to get through the rest of the day.

Jeff knew Olivia would be there tonight. It was only a matter of time before their paths crossed again. He had been avoiding her and she had also been lying low. He managed his basketball evenings with a new crop of student volunteers and Webster Parekh. Webster's wife, Anna, however, was visibly absent.

The gym vacated and only Jeff and Olivia remained. She picked up loose papers and candy wrappers from the floor, her movements slow and distracted. Jeff watched her from the corner of his eye. Tension was thick between them, the expansive force of two people who didn't quite know how to bring up the obvious. Jeff held off a bit longer, rehearsing words in his mind.

Olivia met him by the folding tables and broke the ice first.

"Jeff, I know Nora left. Please believe that I never wanted to come between you," she explained.

"What happened that day—"

"You just looked so lost," Olivia continued. "I guess I wanted to comfort you." She placed her hand on his waist.

Jeff gently brushed her hand away. "Olivia, I'm sorry about what happened that day. It should have never gotten that far. I never wanted to take advantage of you, never wanted you to believe in something that doesn't exist."

She nodded, as though she had anticipated his answer. "I understand this is hard for you, but be honest with yourself. We've spent a lot of time working together and I sensed that something was developing beyond friendship."

He hadn't expected her to be so blunt, but then again he had always liked her directness, her strong convictions. They were good qualities in a *friend*. "What you 'sensed' was my respect for your ideas," he said. "An appreciation that we shared similar goals."

"Which you obviously weren't getting at home from Nora," she remarked.

"We were going through a rough time," he admitted, and felt doubly disloyal for revealing this to Olivia.

"Jeff, you can't tell me that you're not attracted to me! I know you are. Or you would have never come to me the way you did! If you're fighting this, you don't have to anymore."

The situation was so tawdry, so unlike what he expected of himself. "I wasn't myself. I wasn't acting with a clear mind. I shouldn't have let things go as far as they did."

"Jeff, people change, grow apart," said Olivia. Her manner was soothing, in the way she might comfort Kiara after a small accident. "Maybe Nora doesn't understand everything about you anymore. I think I do. I see what you're trying to do with the center, your commitment. I can help you."

"Olivia, you have been a friend, a great source of support. But if . . . if I was ever attracted to you," said Jeff, "I'm not anymore. I love Nora. My bad judgment has cost me my marriage. The only thing I want to do is get her back."

"Jeff, can't you see the writing on the wall?" Olivia objected. "She's gone. Let her go. Start rebuilding your life."

"Olivia, you and I had one confusing moment that should never have happened!" he said, trying desperately to repudiate any deeper significance to their relationship. "Nora and I have had six years. I'm not prepared to give up. Please, as a friend, understand that," he begged.

Her ruddy cheeks turned white. "I thought you were different, Jeff, but maybe you come as advertised. The spoiled, successful man who uses another woman when it suits him—"

"Olivia, that was never my intention. You know that—"

"I was good enough for you then, when you needed someone other than Nora, but not right now? What's the matter? Am I not tall enough? Beautiful enough? Glamorous enough?" she riled.

"Olivia"—he hadn't wanted to say this, but a strange compulsion seized him—"*you* came on to me."

Her hand swung violently across his face. "What do you take me for?"

Jeff grimaced and bit down on his lower lip, fighting back the tingling in his cheek.

Olivia seemed startled by her own outburst and grappled to regain her composure. She tied a scarf around her neck and zipped up her satchel. "I'm sorry that I read more into this than I should have," she said coldly, scrupulously controlling all traces of emotion. "I usually don't get involved like this. I should have kept my distance. It won't happen again." She turned her back on him and walked to the exit. But halfway there, she addressed him again. "Jeff, one more thing: You're really on your own now."

His confrontation with Olivia left him numb. He had predicted the outcome; no good would ever have arisen from such a conversation. He would look like a bastard and she would hate him. But they both were adults and had to live with it.

Jeff went home and ate undercooked frozen pizza in front of his computer for dinner. He had consciously put off checking his e-mails all day because he knew once he started, he would look every ten minutes, praying that Nora's address would pop up. He had thought constantly about her reaction to his letter. SIX NEW MESSAGES, flashed the screen; "noradm@muse.com" occupied the third line. He swiftly double clicked.

Dear Jeff,

Thank you for your letter. Your honesty affected me and I know that it must have been difficult for you to write. But please don't write me anymore. Any kind of contact with you right now is too confusing. I'm finding it difficult to function as it is and I can't handle too much turbulence.

Nora

It took a while for the full impact of her words to sink in. Jeff had been unsure of what to expect, but Nora's fragile plea that he leave her alone confounded him. What had he been hoping for? A meeting in a restaurant to "talk things over"? An acknowledgment that she still loved him? *I had nothing to lose by writing her. I had to make sure she knew I loved her, that I wanted to try again.* He wanted to run to her, to her office if necessary. But she wouldn't just drop everything and take him back with open arms. Her letter told him carefully to stay away. If he went against her wishes, all hopes of reconciliation might be destroyed. He wasn't used to this new sense of powerlessness. He had been slapped in the face twice tonight—by Olivia's hand and Nora's words.

CHAPTER 21

"For a Black person, you sure look pale!" exclaimed Erica as she entered Nora's office. Dahlia, following behind her, nodded in agreement.

Nora looked from one to the other, puzzled. "What are you guys doing here? How'd you get past the reception area without my knowing?"

"That was so easy. *Muse* better beef up its security," Erica said. "Seriously, we just told your assistant that we, your dearest and favorite friends, wanted to surprise you for your birthday. She practically threw the doors open for us, thinks you need a little cheering up."

"So here we are!" screamed Dahlia. "Happy birthday! Happy birthday!"

Both women threw their arms around Nora and hugged her. Nora's initial pique faded as soon as her friends encircled her.

"How does it feel to be thirty-three?" asked Erica.

"Like nothing," replied Nora. "It's nothing special."

"Yes, it is," said Dahlia. "It's always special when you have a double-digit birthday like when you turn eleven, twenty-two or . . . thirty-three!"

"I've never heard that before," said Nora.

Erica shrugged. "Who cares if we made it up? We need to celebrate!"

"What's there to celebrate? My life has gone downhill. I was married, had a house, was working on a child. My thirties were going to be great. But now . . . it's starting to hit me that maybe things aren't going to be exactly as I planned."

Dahlia scowled. "Nora, you need to lighten up! At least for today. That's what we're here for."

"That's right," Erica echoed. "What'd you get as gifts? I see you have some beautiful flowers around the office."

"Those are from some people at work, my parents and Albert," Nora answered. "And I got a cake from the staff."

"Was it good?" Erica asked.

"Not really," Nora said. "It was one of those spongy-sweet ones. Kind of gross, actually."

Dahlia pretended to be shocked. "I would have expected better from *Muse*! Designer cakes from Gucci or Chanel."

They all giggled.

Erica snooped around Nora's office, poking her head in the closet and going through clothes on a metal rack. "Gosh! I love coming here! It's like a candy store: shoes, clothes, makeup. Do you have any freebies from fashion designers? Any rejects the magazine doesn't want anymore?"

Nora searched through a box behind her desk. "Let's see. I have a graffiti-print monogram pouch from Louis Vuitton."

"I'll take it!" Erica shrieked.

"Ooooh, that sounds a bit tacky, Erica."

"Who cares? It's a Louis and it's free," Erica answered, stashing the pouch in her tote bag.

"It's Nora's birthday. She's the one who's supposed to be getting presents," Dahlia chided.

"Who gave you those mini calla lilies? They're gorgeous. I love the burgundy color," said Erica.

"Those are from Jeff," Nora mumbled.

Erica's and Dahlia's mouths dropped.

"There must be two dozen of them! Where's the card?" Dahlia asked. "I want to see what he wrote."

"There's no card," Nora responded.

"What? Then how do you know he sent them?" Dahlia asked.

"He knows I love calla lilies. He always sends them on my birthday."

"So what are you going to do?" Dahlia pressed.

"Nothing," Nora stated.

"Aren't you even going to thank him for them?" Dahlia urged.

Nora shook her head.

Erica passed Dahlia a warning look and she shut up.

"Listen, sweetie, we know that you've been going through a hard time. We feel horrible about everything that's happened," Erica consoled. "But today is your birthday and we want to give you a little celebration."

"No, no, no. You don't have to do that. I won't be good company," said Nora.

"That's exactly why you need to go out tonight!" Dahlia insisted. "We won't take no for an answer."

Nora took in their earnest expressions. The dynamics of their friendship had scarcely changed in over ten years. One or the other, Dahlia or Erica, would propose something—a party, a trip, a dare—and Nora would always be the hardest one to convince. But each time she gave in, she never regretted it. The three women had singled out why they had remained such close friends over the years: They never competed with each other. They never pursued the same men, the same goals or even the same clothes. They never got caught up in the petty nonsense that broke apart other female friendships. Theirs was a true sisterhood that freely bestowed laughter when life was beautiful and support when it got tough.

And today was one of those times. Erica and Dahlia had come to Nora's aid, on a day they knew she would probably be wallowing in self-pity. A couple of hours of birthday fun would do her some good.

Nora hugged Erica and Dahlia again. "Yes," she answered. "Let's go out. Thank you."

They freshened up and breezed downstairs. Erica assumed responsibility for hailing a taxi and an overeager driver skidded to a halt. They filed in and Erica gave the directions.

"Ninth Street, Fourth Avenue, please. And please don't take Broadway. I just came from there and the traffic's not moving."

"Where are you guys taking me?" Nora asked.

"It's a surprise," Dahlia hinted.

"Please, no strippers," Nora pleaded, thinking of her twenty-first-birthday disaster.

"Nora!" Erica and Dahlia cried in unison.

"We're taking you to this fabulous restaurant that opened a few months ago. Good food, cool atmosphere and a kickin' happy hour on Thursday nights!" Dahlia said.

"I can't stand happy hours! I don't want to go there," Nora said.

"Don't be a party pooper! It'll be fun. This place is not at all cheesy, I swear. The vibe is really good. And so is the DJ, if you're in the mood for dancing," Dahlia said.

"Is it young? Are we going to be the oldest people there?" Nora asked.

"Well, you might be!" Erica crowed.

"The crowd is mixed, mid-twenties to early thirties. And it's not up-tight either. Nora, just come with us. If you can't stand it, we can leave," Dahlia promised.

"Why am I having flashbacks to college? Why do I feel like this is déjà vu?" Nora asked.

"Because you loved it then and you'll love it now," Erica said.

The cab deposited them on a corner, about ten yards from the restaurant.

Nora noticed the crowd of people milling in front of two red velvet ropes.

"There's no way I'm going to wait in line to get into that place," she informed Erica and Dahlia. "I don't have the patience for it. I'm not standing in line for clubs or restaurants in my thirties like I did in my twenties."

Dahlia rolled her eyes. "When was the last time you stood in line to get in somewhere—1988? You were always on the guest list. Especially with Jeff and his entourage."

"Don't worry. The guy at the door has a thing for me," Erica assured them, and then reconsidered her statement. "Or at least I think so. He better remember me."

Erica lightly pushed her way to the front of the velvet ropes, ignoring the rude comments and clacking tongues. The three friends held hands so they wouldn't get separated. Erica stood for about five seconds before the brawny, black-clad doorman equipped with a headset and walkie-talkie made eye contact with her.

"Hey, baby. Nice to see you." He gave her a peck on the cheek and unfastened one velvet rope. Erica still didn't know his name, nor he hers, but somehow they were already on a kissy-kissy basis. "How many are you tonight?"

"Three," Erica purred. "And it's our friend's birthday."

"Is that right?" said the doorman. "I think you ladies need some drink tickets."

Erica smiled innocently and pocketed the tickets.

"Erica, I think you have an admirer," Dahlia laughed.

"No wonder she likes coming here," Nora teased.

The restaurant was in one of those nondescript New York buildings that looked like nothing from the outside but housed an interior of trendy distinction. The space was huge, a hybrid of white walls, chrome fixtures and pillar candles. The dining room was downstairs and the bar and dance floor were upstairs.

"I can't believe they're making people wait outside. This place isn't even filled up yet," Nora commented.

"Yes, but it will be soon. By eight o'clock, it'll be jumping," Erica answered.

Erica approached the hostess and they were led to a center table perfect for people watching.

"What will you ladies be drinking?" asked the waiter.

"A Mojito, please," answered Dahlia.

"A ginger ale for me, please," said Nora quietly.

Erica tapped her hand on her temple. "Hello? It's your birthday!" She looked up at the waiter. "Forget their orders. We'll have a bottle of champagne instead."

The waiter returned with a bottle of champagne, uncorked it and filled their glasses.

Erica raised her flute in a toast. "Let me say this now, just in case I may get too fucked-up by the end of the evening." She smiled and looked at Nora affectionately. "Dahlia and I want to wish you a very, very happy thirty-third birthday. You're our best friend because you're a giving, funny, caring person. We want tonight to be a small token of how much we love you."

"And of how you can still find the laughter inside," added Dahlia.

Nora felt her eyes dampen. "Cheers," she said, and they clinked their glasses together.

Dinner was Nuevo Latino/Asian fusion cuisine, delicious and filling. A small cake with one candle was served for dessert and the women shared it with three spoons. Erica had been right. The place filled up to capacity. Some ate, others danced, and still more merely watched. Nora was surprised to see how many people were out on a Thursday night. She had stopped going out for the sole purpose of checking out the scene years ago. She and Jeff had rarely had time to do things like this anymore. Every one of their social engagements seemed to have an ulterior business angle. Had she been missing anything? Erica and Dahlia gossiped and joked, deliberately keeping the conversation cheerful. Nora was reminded that another happier world still existed and she could be a part of it again, if she wanted.

They left their table after dessert and ascended the stairs. Erica gave their drink tickets to the bartender and got three more glasses of champagne. Nora didn't feel drunk, but liked the floating sensation she was slowly reaching. The DJ played Diana Ross's "Love Hangover"—a classic favorite. She mouthed along to Diana's bedroom voice.

The song faded out and Nora's eyes darted to her friends. Someone patted Dahlia's back and she began talking animatedly. As Erica grooved to the music, two men circled her, ready to pounce if she looked their way. Everyone seemed to be talking to each other—smiling, flirting, laughing. It was an evening of promise. The unexpected might happen and they all were ready for it. Nora tapped her foot on the floor and disguised her unease with a strained smile. *I'm having fun. Of course I'm having fun. It's my birthday!* She put the glass to her lips again, but it was empty. She frowned. She had nothing to do with her hands anymore. *What am I doing here?*

"Can I refill that glass for you?" The voice belonged to a man on her right.

Nora turned and squinted at him. He was fuzzy in the dim light. "No, thank you," she answered dryly. "I've had enough."

He tilted his head and appraised her. "You don't look like you're having much fun."

"I'm having a perfectly good time," she retorted. She wasn't in the mood for making small talk with strangers.

"Do you like this place?" he asked.

Nora gave him her are-you-for-real-don't-you-get-the-hint look.

"Yes. It's nice. It's my first time here, but it looks like they've got a good thing going."

He smiled. "Yeah. I like it too. It's good to see people out having a good time. Happy birthday, by the way."

"How do you know it's my birthday?" she asked.

"I saw them bring you the cake after dinner," he answered, and caught Nora's startled expression. He laughed. "I guess you could say I've had my eye on you."

"I don't know whether to be flattered or just run away," Nora snapped.

"Hopefully you'll just take it as a compliment."

Nora sighed. "I'm sorry I'm being such a bitch," she apologized. "You're trying to be nice and I'm being difficult. But thanks anyway." Where was this boldness coming from? The alcohol was giving her an edge and she had said exactly what was on her mind.

"That's OK. I can't expect a woman to talk to me just because I offered her a glass of champagne."

"That's right," Nora said suggestively. She was enjoying this banter. It passed the time and she felt like someone else.

He held out his hand. "Do you want to dance?"

Nora smiled. What the hell? "Sure."

Nora followed him to the dance floor and hesitated for a split second. She had almost forgotten how to move, but the space was crowded and she got by with simple twists and shakes of her body. She deliberately avoided making eye contact with him. But she had sneaked a glance at him before and he *was* attractive—thick eyebrows, high cheekbones, close-cropped dark hair and slim black trousers. Very downtown. Very cute. Very dangerous.

The song ended and he led her off the dance floor.

"Can I offer you that champagne again?" he asked.

"I'll just stick to some bottled water."

He ordered one for himself as well and they sipped in silence. The bar was noisy. Nora was keenly attuned to the lack of words between them, but he didn't seem to mind.

"Are you a model?" he asked after a few minutes.

Nora laughed. This guy was killing her with his lines. "No. But I just turned thirty-three and that question made my day."

"Were you one before?" he continued.

"Never, but I do work for a fashion magazine. You're seeing my feeble attempts to be stylish."

"They're not so feeble. Which magazine?"

"I don't know if you're familiar with it. . . . *Muse.*"

He nodded. "I've heard of it. Seen it on the newsstands. I can't say that I've read it, though."

"That's all right. It's a women's magazine."

"What do you do there? Are you a writer? Photographer? Stylist?"

Nora was intrigued by his curiosity. Only in New York could a man ask equally intelligent questions about finance as well as fashion.

"I'm the associate editor in chief."

He smiled. "Sounds like a great job. I guess I should be glad that someone from such a trendy magazine is here tonight."

"Why?"

"I've been open only two months, but things are picking up. Maybe this is a turning point. You're a good omen."

"Is this your restaurant?"

He nodded.

Nora raised an eyebrow. "Congratulations. I think you'll do very well."

He gazed at her again and Nora fiddled nervously with her necklace.

"I see you're married," he said casually.

Nora took her left hand away from her neck and stared at the simple gold band gleaming on her ring finger. She had never taken it off. It was the only piece of jewelry symbolic of Jeff that she had taken with her when she moved out.

Reality check. "Yes, I am," she answered softly.

"Happily?"

She ignored that question.

"Who's your husband? Maybe it's someone I know."

With my luck, you probably do.

"Listen, I really have to go. Thanks for the dance and the drink. Good luck with this place," Nora said.

"You don't have to leave."

"I really should. I have to find my friends."

"I have a table downstairs. We can go down there. Bring your friends."

Nora found it difficult to turn him down because part of her didn't want to leave. "OK."

She searched for Erica and Dahlia. Both women were sitting on a couch with another group of people.

"Erica, Dahlia, please come downstairs with me," Nora whispered.

"Why? We're having a good time up here," Erica answered.

"I'll explain later. Please just come. I don't want to go by myself," Nora said, and then added, "The owner of this place invited us to his table."

"Us? Or you?" Dahlia grilled.

"Me plus you," Nora answered.

Erica rose. "Ah, maybe it's getting a little boring over here. We'll come."

Dahlia fluffed out her hair and asked, "Nora, are you sure you know what you're doing?"

"No, not really," she confessed.

Nora started to introduce Erica and Dahlia to the stranger, but realized she didn't even know his name.

"I'm Paul Nelson," he finished for her.

"And I'm Nora," she said, rather dumbly, in her opinion.

The crowd parted as Paul made his way down the stairs with Nora, Erica and Dahlia in tow. His table was in the corner, positioned unobtrusively, but with a good view. Nora was surprised to see two women and three men already seated. Paul pushed another table together and introduced them to the group. The women were slender, wore the nighttime uniform of Seven jeans and sparkly tops and offered the limpest of handshakes. They may have been models, but Nora guessed catalog rather than runway. The men had kept their leather jackets on inside and barely nodded in acknowledgment. The five of them resumed their conversation as though Nora and her friends had disappeared. Paul asked Nora, Erica and Dahlia what they wanted to drink. Nora thought that Paul seemed like a nice guy and couldn't understand how he kept company with such boorish people. Sobriety hit her like a brick wall and she suddenly felt old.

"Paul, we've really got to be going," she announced.

"But I thought you were staying for a little while," he said.

"I'm sorry, but we can't," she said, and motioned to Erica and Dahlia.

Her friends stood without any hesitation.

"We'll get the coats," Erica said.

Nora pushed back her chair and held out her hand. "Well, it was nice meeting you, Paul."

He took her elbow and pulled her aside. "Nora, why are you really leaving?" he asked. "You were having a good time before."

His spicy cologne was faint but nice. It was definitely time to go. "Honestly? The vibe went south as soon as we sat down. Your friends aren't as nice as you are."

"Those aren't really my friends. They're just people I know."

"Yeah, but . . ."

"But what?"

"I can't . . . ," she stalled.

"Can't what?"

". . . hang out like this. It's not a good idea."

"Because you're—"

"Exactly," she cut in. "Take care."

Paul grabbed her arm and pulled her aside. "I'd like to see you again." He fished in his pocket. "Here's my card. Call me—if you want."

She examined it: PAUL NELSON, RESTAURATEUR. She put the card in her handbag. "Bye."

Outside, Erica howled, "What was up with that table you dragged us to?"

"I'm sorry," Nora apologized. "Paul seemed nice. How could I have known?"

"Hey, hey. There's a cab on the corner. Let's get in," Erica suggested.

"Where to?" the cabbie asked.

"Let's all go back to my place. I don't want to be alone tonight. Twelfth Street and Seventh Avenue South, please."

At Nora's place, they made themselves comfortable on the oversized pillows scattered throughout the small living room. Nora served microwave popcorn and Coca-Cola.

"I'm always so hungry when I come home from going out," Erica said, stuffing popcorn in her mouth.

"Tonight was a real eye-opener," remarked Nora.

"In what way?" Dahlia asked.

"I see how tough it is out there. I haven't been in the dating scene for six years. I forgot what it was like. Women are so territorial and the guys know it. That's why they can't commit. They have five different girls after them," Nora said.

"And they're always wondering if something better is going to come along," Dahlia observed.

"For a minute tonight, I thought that maybe I had been missing something after all these years. Like maybe there's been this great party going on that I just didn't know about," Nora remarked.

"And what do you think now?" Erica asked.

Nora shook her head. "I don't think I've been missing much. Tonight was fun, but the whole ritual also felt kind of empty."

"Welcome to the club," Erica muttered.

"But didn't it make you feel kind of good to know that Paul was interested in you? That if you were single again, you could meet somebody else? That you still had it going on enough to meet an attractive guy?" Dahlia asked.

Nora considered that. "Yeah. I guess so. But a guy like Paul is probably turned on by what he can't have. I told him I was married and he didn't seem to care. Getting involved with a married woman means you can have all the sex and all the fun without the commitment. I bet he just wanted to see if I'd give in and he'd get me in bed."

"Tsst, tsst. You're getting cynical in your old age. Maybe he couldn't help himself from being attracted to you and doesn't care if you're married," Dahlia suggested.

"Or maybe Nora's scared because she was attracted to him too. Look at her face! Don't try to hide it!" Erica squealed.

"Fine. But it was only a fleeting attraction. It was over in five minutes. I never would have done anything."

"Why not? A revenge fuck might be exactly what you need," Erica said. The bowl of popcorn was empty and she set it on the floor near the couch.

"I've had no sexual desire whatsoever since I left Jeff," Nora said.

"Are you serious?" Dahlia asked.

"I'm serious. Sex has been the furthest thing from my mind." She could tell by their knitted brows that Erica and Dahlia were skeptical. "Tonight I did feel a little bit of something, but I never could have taken it to the next level."

"Nora, you keep saying you're married, but you've moved out of your house. You refuse to talk with Jeff. What are you doing? What do you want?" asked Dahlia.

She sighed. "I don't know. In my heart, I still feel married. Yes, I've left Jeff, but there's still some kind of bond that connects us. I can't sever it completely."

"You've been gone for practically a month now. How much longer can you expect to go on like this?" Dahlia asked.

"I don't know. One way or the other I have to figure it out," Nora said.

"What hurts the most? Knowing that he was with someone else?" Erica asked.

"Of course. But I've also lost my innocence and that bothers me," Nora admitted.

"Damn," Dahlia said, "I lost that a long time ago."

"Nora, I think I know what you mean," said Erica. "To the rest of the world, you're this pretty, confident woman, but you've always had this bit of innocence—which Dahlia and I have tried unsuccessfully to corrupt! You still believe in fairy tales. You met the man of your dreams and married him. But when he hurts you, you're completely traumatized. I've been there many times, and the first time is always the worst. You'll learn to cope. You'll have to."

"Now that sounds cynical," Nora said. "Are you still optimistic?"

"Yes. Everyone craves an intimate connection with another human being—beyond family or a best friend. I still have a romantic philosophy of love. I still believe in people and so should you."

"Maybe there's more than one person for us in this world. Maybe a Paul Nelson could be your next big thing," Dahlia said.

Nora laughed. "I doubt that. Paul reminded me of some other men I've known. They're a little too sure of themselves for their own good."

Nora was two hours late for work the next day. Dahlia and Erica had left around three in the morning and Nora had forgotten to set her alarm. She managed to save face with Candida—for the time being—and didn't want to jeopardize her situation further. Strangely enough, she had felt fine talking with Erica and Dahlia through the night, but still woke up with a dizzying hangover.

Around four thirty in the afternoon, as Nora counted the minutes until five o'clock, her assistant, Lisa, called her on the intercom.

"Nora, you have a Mrs. Montgomery here to see you."

Nora's mind was elsewhere. She had no appointments scheduled and didn't like drop-in visitors. "I'm not expecting anyone right now. Tell this person to call me next week," she answered absently.

"She says she's your mother-in-law," Lisa added.

The letters in the copy Nora was reading merged into a black blob. "Do you mean Angela Montgomery?"

"That's what she said."

Nora moistened her lips and paused. "Give me a few minutes and then send her in."

What was Angela doing here? She had never visited Nora at the office. They had never even met for lunch. Nora was surprised Angela even knew where *Muse* was located. She frantically threw the loose samples of clothes draped on her couch in the closet. The Polaroid pictures she had been examining were fanned out on her desk like a deck of cards. She stacked them together and hid them in a drawer. Nora heard Lisa's voice approaching and wiped her clammy hands on her trousers.

"Are you sure you wouldn't like an espresso or some mineral water, Mrs. Montgomery?" Lisa asked, her voice polite and professional. Angela had that effect on people. In her presence, one stood up straighter and enunciated words *clearly.*

"No, thank you," Angela replied.

Lisa put the CONFERENCE sign on Nora's door and closed it.

"Angela, what a surprise," Nora said. She tried to make her voice natural, but it sounded too high, too forced. "What brings you to the city today?"

"I attended a lecture at the New York Public Library. It's only a few blocks from here, you know."

"Oh, how nice. I often have lunch in Bryant Park in the summertime," Nora babbled. "When are you going back to New Rochelle?"

"I'm taking the five twenty train."

"Well, you're looking quite smart today," Nora complimented. Angela had on her suburban-dame-in-the-city ensemble: pink twinset, navy trousers, Burberry trench and a pair of Tod's loafers.

"Thank you. Do you mind if I sit down?"

"Oh, please do."

They faced each other expectantly. This was the disconcerting quality with Angela: She never filled in dead noise. Nora grew anxious and began twisting her ponytail with her thumb and index finger.

"Jeff told us that you and he have separated," blurted Angela.

Nora gasped. "Well . . . uh . . . hmm . . ." She was at a loss for words. This was not the sort of conversation she had ever planned on having with Angela.

"He also told us that it wasn't your fault," Angela went on.

Angela spoke kindly, but her eyes betrayed nothing. Had she come as a friend or a foe?

"Angela, this is a difficult conversation for me to have with you. I don't really feel comfortable. . . . I mean, after all, I'm married to your son. We're having some problems . . . ," Nora explained.

Angela crossed one elegant leg over the other. "Nora, this is a conversation just between you and me. Jeff doesn't know I'm here. Neither does Taylor. I came here on my own. Whatever is said will stay in this room. We can be frank with each other."

"OK," Nora answered. "What do you want to talk to me about?"

"From what Jeff said, I gather you left because of an—um, how shall I say it—indiscretion?"

Angela described the situation euphemistically, but it boiled down to the same thing.

"Yes," Nora answered sadly.

"Is this going to be a permanent arrangement?"

"I don't have an answer to that right now."

"Nora, if every marriage broke up because of a meaningless indiscretion, there'd be none left," she stated simply.

"I'm not quite following you."

"One party can make a mistake in a relationship! It's usually the man and usually involves another woman, and yes, it hurts, but it's not the end of the world! You're still his wife. You're still legally tied to him and you're the one he loves. Surely, you know that!" Angela exclaimed.

"I can't just forget that he was with another woman!" Nora protested.

"Nora, why do you think Taylor and I had only one child?" asked Angela.

"Jeff and I always assumed it was because you tried but couldn't have any more."

Angela tittered. "Really? Well, we never had another child because I barely let Taylor in my bed for five years."

The statement staggered Nora. *"What?"*

"Oh, he was unfaithful to me, soon after I had Jeff. Or maybe it was even before then, but I just didn't know about it. And it wasn't just a little something on the side either. He thought he loved this woman and wasn't sure if he wanted something more permanent with her or not. But, at the same time, he didn't want to lose me or Jeff. So I closed my eyes while he figured out what he wanted to do," Angela revealed.

"But for five years? How could you take that? Why didn't you take Jeff and leave him?"

"You just didn't leave people back then. At least not in my or Taylor's families. There's never been a divorce among us. That was never even an option. What would people say? What would my parents say?"

"But it must have been horrible for you!"

"Oh, it was. Make no mistake about that. But I had Jeff, I had a nice life, and I knew that Taylor loved me, in his own way. Maybe I just couldn't give him everything he needed. But I punished him by forcing him to sleep in a separate bedroom. That's the only weapon I had." She paused. "Nora, Jeff made one mistake, a silly fling with someone else. It was nothing in the larger scheme of things. I had to put up with five years of an unfaithful husband."

Nora was completely disillusioned. People were not what they seemed to be. Taylor had almost ruined his family and Angela had endured years of suffering. No wonder her behavior was inconsistent. She still carried the scars with her.

"Does Jeff know about this?" Nora asked.

"No. I never told him. He was too young to remember the separate bedrooms. I didn't want to shatter his image of his father. And Taylor was a good father. I couldn't have raised Jeff without him. Why do you think Jeff turned out as well as he did? Because I was determined to provide as loving and well-ordered a family life as possible. I made the sacrifices for him. You do that when children are involved."

"But, Angela, Jeff and I don't have any children," Nora pointed out. "There's no reason for me to suffer if I'm unhappy."

"Nora, happiness is overrated." She said it with the authority of someone who had discovered that long ago. "Who's happy one hundred percent of the time? You have to make choices. Think of security, companionship, moral support. Those things are just as important. You and Jeff should get back together and have a child. That would renew your relationship and bring you closer."

"No. It wouldn't be fair to bring a child into the world under these circumstances. I still don't know what I want to do."

Angela shook her head and gathered her bag and coat. "I see I haven't changed your mind."

"Angela, wait." Nora knew it must have been a big step for Angela to come here today. Maybe her mother-in-law hadn't disliked her as much as she'd thought. "Thank you for telling me your story. I know you're trying to help, but we all deal with similar situations in our own way. We're living in different times. I'm not you, and Jeff isn't Taylor."

"Nora, have you seriously considered all the advantages you have by being married to Jeff?" she asked icily.

"What is that supposed to mean?" Nora asked. The Angela that Nora knew was now rearing her unpleasant head.

"Your life. The life you lead. Do you really think you could just walk away from that? Take your job, for example. Journalists don't earn that much money. Being Jeff's wife has allowed you to pursue what you want, without having to worry about who's going to pay the rent."

"Why is it that all you people think about is money?" she cried. "In case you didn't know, Angela, I'm perfectly capable of supporting my-self. I haven't asked Jeff for anything." Nora paused. "Maybe we should wrap this up now, before we both say something we'll regret."

Angela stood up. "Good-bye, Nora. I hope to see you soon. And I really mean that."

Nora returned to her desk, but she couldn't concentrate. Too many secrets had unraveled. Angela had brought Nora into her confidence, but Nora did not want to accept the implications of her tale. She had spent so long thinking that these people were emotionally superior to her, that they were more in control of their lives. They obviously were not. All were the victims of deception, selfishness and immaturity. Could she look at anyone the same way again? Taylor, Angela, Jeff, Hilton, herself? Who was next? Her parents?

People weren't perfect.

Lives weren't perfect.

Some people just hid it better than others.

CHAPTER 22

BOB BUTLER LATEST CASUALTY IN ENTERTAINMENT WARS

ROBERT K. BUTLER, THE CHAIRMAN and chief executive officer of NRG Music Group, has been given his walking papers. Ironically, he was served them by his mentor and former boss, Lawrence Stark, chairman of NRG, Inc., the parent company. It has been a tough year for the record industry as a result of flatter sales and the threat of music piracy on the Internet. Butler had been mandated to revamp NRG Music's roster and image. However, sources say that his high-handed tactics alienated many people within his own company. "Bob is an operations guy. He's a perfect number two, but doesn't have the charisma or credibility to lead a music division," said one source, who insisted on anonymity.

Butler had been in charge for less than a year, but he encountered his share of headaches. NRG Music faced considerable controversy over one of its former artists, the rapper Loverdose. His offensive lyrics were cited as a factor in a high-profile rape trial. NRG Music was eventually absolved of any responsibility, but Butler was widely derided in the press. "Butler got a raw deal on that one," said Kevin Dannon, the lead counsel for NRG who successfully argued the case.

Most critical of Butler's missteps was his inability

to forge successful alliances or joint ventures with smaller, independent record labels. These upstart labels have increasingly become the fertile ground for musical innovation. They also possess the high "street quotient" that the major labels too often lack. Specifically, talks to acquire a fifty percent stake in ultrahip Rum Records broke down last month. "We have a lot of respect for Bob Butler and NRG Music, but we had some creative differences which couldn't be worked out. We wish Bob well," said Jeff Montgomery, cofounder of Rum Records.

Sources say that Butler should have no problem landing on his feet. Turnover among the entertainment industry's top brass has become more common and getting fired no longer leads to corporate exile. In addition, the twenty million dollars NRG, Inc., paid out to settle Butler's contract should go a long way towards soothing his bruised ego.

So that's how the NRG drama played itself out, Nora thought, closing the *New York Post* and putting it on top of a pile of papers on the floor. She had chuckled when she read Jeff's quote. He could be so diplomatic. Everybody knew that he couldn't stand Bob Butler. It was strange for Nora to be reading about her husband in the *Post.* She was so used to being up-to-date about his business life and felt a bit cheated reading about it when everybody else did. She wondered what Jeff and Hilton were up to at Rum Records. She could as easily e-mail him and tell him she had seen the news piece. But what good would that do? It would assume a rapprochement that she wasn't ready to give.

Deadlines were closing in on Nora. Her debut issue of *Muse* would hit the newsstands on January 1. She consulted her calendar. There were only a few more weeks left before it had to go to press. She had several ideas planned for her debut issue, including a major celebrity interview, fashion spreads where you could actually see the clothes and a new "Personal Style" feature that peeked into the closets of movers and shakers. She also had to start thinking about her "Letter from the Editor." She really wanted to establish her own voice.

Nora glanced at her watch. It was only eleven thirty, but she was ready for lunch. Her appetite had come back with a vengeance. Her period was due and she was craving tomatoes—sauce, ketchup, juice! She took her bag and went down to the deli next door. She heaped Greek salad, penne Bolognese and two chunks of Italian bread on a plastic plate. She paid the cashier and found a table in the back close to the fruit stand. Curls of steam escaped from her plate and the sight of coarsely chopped onion, basil and garlic made her stomach growl in anticipation. She dunked her bread in the rich sauce. It was heavenly. She'd eaten the same lunch for three days in a row. But the food stuck to her ribs, giving her much-needed energy. She alternated between bites of pasta and salad and cleaned her plate with the last bits of bread. On her way out, she bought a bag of Terra chips, mints, butter cookies and orange soda to snack on. If only Candida could see her, she thought devilishly.

The next morning she wobbled when she tried to get out of bed; an intense queasiness consumed her. She struggled to make a slice of toast and stuffed it in her mouth without even bothering to butter it. She went back under the covers and rested for an extra half hour. She felt better and took some Tylenol. Maybe she was coming down with the flu. With all the work she had to do at *Muse,* she couldn't afford to be ill. That same feeling of seasickness hit her at different inconvenient times for the next few days. The worst episode occurred on the subway. The cars lurched and stopped on the tracks, bringing her lunch perilously close to the surface, and the collective stench of sweat, fast food and urine settled like a cloud near her seat. The passengers around her became doubles, the originals and their transparent copies floating in and out of each other. She felt dizzy and trapped. At the Fourteenth Street station, she hurried home, wrenched off her clothes and gorged on a leftover box of Szechuan noodles. Ashamed and upset, she hid her face in her hands and sobbed. What was happening to her? She was a glutton, abusing her body with food, and she couldn't bring herself to stop.

Desperate, she dumped her handbag and found her Filofax. August,

September, October. October 14. October 14 had a red asterisk above it, the date her period was due. She had marked the dates for the entire year, twenty-eight-day cycles, so conscientiously when she and Jeff had been trying to conceive. Today was October 17. Her period was three days late. But there was no need for panic. She wasn't having sex and barring immaculate conception, she couldn't be pregnant. Unless . . . unless she hadn't menstruated in September either. She turned back the pages of her calendar. September 16 was asterisked. She had moved out of Hamilton Terrace on September 14, noted by a scribble on her daily planner to pick up the Twelfth Street key from the superintendent. Everything had been so volatile and Nora honestly couldn't remember if she had had her period. Maybe there had been a little spotting, but she couldn't be sure. So many other issues had mixed her up. August 20 was also marked. Nora remembered clearly that she had menstruated since she had avoided going swimming that weekend in the Hamptons.

She tried to be logical. It had taken a few months for her cycle to reg-ulate once she stopped taking the Pill. God knew she was stressed and that was probably causing the delay. But her period still had not ap-peared two days later and Nora forced herself to reconsider how she felt about having children. Two months ago, she would have been ecstatic, but now she just didn't know how she felt about having a baby with Jeff. She still hadn't decided what she wanted to do about their marriage. Taking care of herself was proving to be a chore. How could she take care of a baby? She had always assumed that she would carry a child under circumstances of sheer joy and certainty. Nora couldn't imagine being pregnant during her present misery.

She didn't have anyone whom she could talk to either. She couldn't call Erica or Dahlia. They had been so supportive, but she didn't want to involve them further in her business. Nora definitely couldn't tell her mother. Valérie would think only about the unborn child. She would tell Nora to set aside her personal struggles and concentrate on the baby. Julian—well, Julian was a man and she didn't want to hear his point of view.

Another option was lurking in her mind, starkly unfitting for a Catholic girl like herself. She could have an abortion—do it in secret so no one would ever know about it. She wiggled her body violently and mumbled a short penance. She was going insane. She was technically still married, and unless she or the baby was in harm's way, married people didn't have abortions. And it would be a major betrayal of Jeff, far worse than what he had done to her.

Nora knew she was getting ahead of herself. She still had no confirmation. Yet she became convinced that she was pregnant. She touched her stomach and thought she felt the pitter-patter of tiny moving feet. And the thought terrified her. All her old misgivings about motherhood returned. She was too busy to take proper care of a baby. She was too vain and would hate gaining weight. She didn't know how to take care of a baby—changing diapers, breast-feeding, burping. She didn't want to love another human being so much. What if something ever happened to the baby? She was separated from its father. How would Jeff factor into everything?

When her period was seven days late, Nora bought a pregnancy test from the Duane Reade drugstore across the street from her apartment. She opened the package and read the directions. Pee on the indicator for fifteen seconds and then wait and see if the second panel turns blue. She tore open the plastic wrapper and became immobilized, her hands suspended in the air. She could not take the test unless she was prepared for the result, and she knew she wasn't. She wanted to vomit from anxiety. All her life she had believed in signs, little symbols that guided her and represented the decisions she had to make. If she was pregnant, then she had to go back to Jeff. She could not raise a child on her own. It wouldn't be fair to the baby or him. She'd have to patch things up with him as best she could and think about their child. It wasn't supposed to be like this.

Nora cried softly on her bed, devastated that she was going through this on her own. Everything around her seemed tainted—people, experiences. She could not see the good a baby could bring to her life now. She was being forced to accept a situation she didn't want. Nora cried harder when she reflected on the harshness of her thoughts. Maybe she was selfish. An innocent baby should not have to pay for her and Jeff's mistakes.

She awoke early Saturday morning to go the bathroom. She had fallen into a fitful sleep, the unused pregnancy test by her pillow. She sat on the toilet, her underwear drawn down her ankles, and noticed a dark red spot, shaped like a leaf, in the center. Her period. Thank God. It came. She had been saved. Her endless, stressful speculation had been for naught.

She felt the sharp pains in her abdomen. The cramps were kicking in, as they always did. Nora showered, inserted a tampon and changed her underwear. She took two Motrins with a glass of milk. She followed the same routine every month on the first day of her period. She would just have to ride the cramps out until the medicine took effect. She went back to bed and tried to lie in one position, which usually helped. About an hour later, after which she should have been feeling better, the cramps became more acute, as though her insides were being twisted. She pulled the comforter up to her chin. She had the chills, but was sweating profusely. She hated that her body went through this. A natural function shouldn't be this painful. The aches continued and Nora tried to get out of bed. She had to get a glass of water, a banana, anything. She sat on the edge, leaned on the mattress and tried to rise. But the room spun; she stumbled and landed on the floor. She couldn't walk. She knew she was better off lying down and crawled back to bed.

As Nora pulled herself up, she gasped. The area where her midsection had been was covered in blood. Deep wet splotches were splayed across the white sheet like an abstract painting. Nora had never seen such heavy blood. Despite the soiled sheets, she sat down, leaning her head between her legs. She felt the blood trickling down her thighs. Her cramps were now even more severe and she wanted to die. She couldn't take it. Something wasn't right. This wasn't normal. She touched her forehead and it was burning up. She felt faint, feverish and scared, and a morbid thought crossed her mind—her dying in the apartment and days passing before anyone found her.

Still clutching her stomach, she picked up the cordless phone and dialed 911.

"Nine one one," came the mechanical human voice.

"Please help me," Nora sputtered. "I'm in pain."

"Have you been hurt?"

"No, but my stomach. I can't—"

"OK. What's your address? We'll send an ambulance over."

"I live at two twenty-four West Twelfth Street." Each word was a struggle.

"What apartment number?"

"Six—six G."

"Sixty-six G?"

"No!" Nora cried. "Six G. Please hurry."

She dropped the phone on the floor. Her head felt like it weighed one hundred pounds. She crashed on the pillow and curled herself into a fetal position, then closed her eyes and waited. The last images she saw were two EMS technicians in her apartment. *How did they get in?* she wondered. The room was too small for all their bulky equipment.

Nora opened her eyes, but didn't recognize the dull, faded blue paint on the walls. She tried to move, but her right arm was stuck. Something was keeping it down. She turned her head and saw the needle pushed into her vein. She noticed the long clear tube leading from her hand to an intravenous bag, and the white curtains that separated her bed from the others in the room. She also smelled the sickly, antiseptic odor. It didn't take Nora very long to figure out that she was in a hospital. Yet far from being scared, she was relieved. She had made it.

It seemed like hours before anybody came to check up on her. Finally, the curtains were yanked and a middle-aged woman dressed in a white lab coat appeared. She checked the IV and wrote comments in Nora's chart.

Smiling, she said, "Hello, Ms. Montgomery. I'm Dr. Nicholas. How are you feeling?"

Dr. Nicholas's voice was warm and made Nora felt more at ease. "Fine," she answered hoarsely. Her throat was so dry. "I feel pretty weak, though. How did you know my name?"

"The EMS technicians checked your purse for ID. It saves a lot of time later on."

"What happened to me?" Nora asked feebly.

"You were hemorrhaging severely and lost a lot of blood. Thank goodness you called 911 or it might have been too late." Dr. Nicholas paused. "Ms. Montgomery, you suffered a miscarriage. You lost your baby. I'm sorry," she said gravely, full of sympathy.

Nora needed air. Dread and remorse were pressing down on her.

"You did know you were pregnant, right?" Dr. Nicholas questioned.

"I suspected it, but I still wasn't sure," she said as tears coursed down her cheeks. "How far along was I?"

"We did an ultrasound when you were rushed in, and from the size of the fetus, you were about nine weeks pregnant."

"How are you calculating this?"

"There are two different ways to count weeks of pregnancy: from the date of conception or from the date of your last menstrual period. Counting from the day of a woman's last menstrual cycle is more reliable. Then we count forty weeks from that day to find the due date. When was the first day of your last period?"

"I was a little confused before, but my last period started on August twentieth."

"That makes sense."

"But wait, Dr. Nicholas. When was my date of conception?"

"Ovulation takes place two weeks after your last period started." Dr. Nicholas checked the calendar in her file. "I would say you conceived on or around September third."

Nora's mind raced back. September third, that fateful night she came back from London and the same day Jeff slept with Olivia.

"When would the baby have been born?" asked Nora in a strangled voice.

Again, Dr. Nicholas consulted her calendar. "Sometime near May twenty-seventh."

"Why?" Nora moaned. "Why did this happen to me?"

Dr. Nicholas pulled the chair near the night table and set it next to Nora's bed. She sat down and folded her hands in her lap. "I'll tell you a little bit about miscarriages, so you understand exactly what happened to you. They're especially common during the first few weeks of pregnancy and can occur for a number of reasons: diabetes, hormonal imbalances, problems of the uterus or cervix, drug or alcohol abuse, prolonged stress, exposure to toxins, excessive weight loss. . . ."

As Dr. Nicholas droned on with her scientific explanations, Nora thought back to the last month and a half of her life. She had been suffering from an incredible amount of stress and anxiety. Except for the recent food cravings, her diet had been poor and she was below her normal weight. On top of that, she had guzzled champagne on her birthday and often took sleeping pills to combat her insomnia. She had unwittingly endangered the life of her baby and now it was gone. It was all too much for her to take.

"I could have done things differently. It's my fault. . . ."

"Don't blame yourself, Nora. Is it all right if I call you Nora?" Dr. Nicholas asked.

Nora nodded.

"Miscarriages occur in one in six pregnancies. More women have experienced this than you think," Dr. Nicholas explained. "The fetus didn't have a heartbeat and from its size, it probably died a week ago, but you actually began to miscarry this morning. That's why you were bleeding so heavily."

Nora shuddered. The baby she had agonized for days over had already been dead. "But I haven't been taking good care of myself."

"You're a bit underweight for your height, but otherwise you're a healthy woman. No evidence of drug or alcohol abuse. There's another factor that I haven't mentioned in this—plain old bad luck."

"What do you mean?"

Dr. Nicholas leaned forward. "Certain conceived babies just aren't meant to be. It's nature's way of protecting the mother and the child from abnormalities. Not because you worked too hard, or had a glass of wine, or exercised too much. If you had done everything differently, you probably would have ended up with the same result."

"What was the cause of my miscarriage?"

"While you were unconscious, we did an endometrial biopsy, where we scraped the lining of your uterus, and it showed that you have a hormone deficiency."

Nora thought of the procedure and wanted to gag. "That sounds serious."

"It's not really. It's very treatable. I'll just prescribe some extra progesterone and the problem should correct itself. The odds are quite good that you could carry a baby to term next time."

"But I've been trying to get pregnant for almost a year and nothing happened. And when I finally become pregnant, I miscarry. I'd say that the odds are pretty bad."

"A hormone imbalance is often a onetime problem. Miscarriage doesn't mean that you won't be able to get pregnant again. Some women miscarry twice in their lifetime. If it were to happen more than twice, then I'd suggest more tests, but I don't think you have anything to worry about now. You and your partner can try again," said Dr. Nicholas. "However, I suggest you wait until after two more menstrual cycles."

Nora stared blankly at the ceiling. Dr. Nicholas touched her arm.

"I know this is a difficult loss for you to take. Most women feel empty and depressed afterward. It's normal. Plus, your body will go through some hormonal adjustments and you may feel very emotional."

"When can I leave the hospital?"

"You should be feeling better by tomorrow afternoon. We can release you then. It'd be better if someone came to pick you up. Is there anyone you would like us to call? Your partner? A friend? Your parents?"

She didn't want to see anyone; she didn't want anyone to know what happened to her. "My husband is away on a business trip and won't be back for a couple of more days. I just moved to the city and don't have any friends or family nearby," she lied. "I'll have to manage by myself tomorrow."

"OK. Get some more rest and please eat the food they bring you. You need to get your strength back up. Buzz the nurses' station if you need anything. I'll be back tomorrow."

Dr. Nicholas pulled the curtains together and Nora felt like she was in solitary confinement. Their child—hers and Jeff's—was sadly not meant to be. Dr. Nicholas had said it herself. Nothing could grow inside her because she was a tangled mess. She wondered what the sex of the baby would have been and whether it would have resembled her or Jeff. The fluttering in her stomach had not been a sign of life. It had been death, her creation slipping away, just like everything else.

Nora checked herself out of St. Vincent's on Sunday. She took a cab home and had difficulty going up the stairs to her apartment. She was still weak, as though all the vitamins and minerals in her body had been drained out. Yellow police tape was fastened across her door. Nora became wary, then remembered that the EMS technicians had had to break the lock to get to her. It must have all been quite a spectacle for her new neighbors. She called a locksmith and had a new bolt installed by dinnertime.

Nora knew she had to eat. She had no appetite, but was worried about her health and whipped up a quick omelet. She forced herself to swallow and read the pamphlets that Dr. Nicholas had given her. Most of them provided standard information on miscarriages, but one dealt with the emotional effects of the loss. Bereaved couples described their grief and sense of emptiness in detail. The pamphlet recommended that couples be patient, share their emotions over the miscarriage and not let their own feelings of helplessness prevent them from reaching out to each other. Nora presumed all the couples in the pamphlet had knowingly been expecting a baby and probably had stable marriages. She didn't have the comfort of either.

She was still bleeding on Monday morning. Dr. Nicholas said it would last for six to ten days so Nora packed extra feminine pads in her tote bag. She went to work looking haggard and physically ill. Candida ordered Nora to go home.

"But I can't," Nora protested. "I have so much to do. There are only a few more weeks left before we go to print."

"The magazine will survive," Candida responded firmly, "but I'm not so sure you will. Sign yourself sick and don't come back until you're feeling better."

"Will I still have a job to come back to?" Nora asked apprehensively.

Candida sighed. "Yes, you will. I know things have been wretched for you and you've been fighting all of it for the sake of the magazine and your position. I went through my second divorce while I was editing that interior-design magazine in London. Work was the only thing that kept me sane. I know how tough it is. And except for an early scare, you've gotten back on track. But you're not looking well. You must have the flu. Take antibiotics and sleep it off. I don't want to see you for the rest of the week."

Nora thought about Candida's words. Her boss had experienced two difficult divorces, but at least she was a hot magazine editor and got free designer clothes. Is that what Nora had to look forward to?

She took Candida's advice. On her way home, she stopped off at the supermarket and bought loads of canned soup, tea and bread. She slept for the entire afternoon, awoke only for a bowl of chicken soup and slept right through the night. On Tuesday, she slept less, ate more and watched television. She felt that her strength was slowly returning, but the hormone changes had made her more sensitive. She could not stop thinking about the lost baby. Guilt and sadness overwhelmed her. Her attitude had been so negative and now the baby was gone. A child was always a blessing, a gift. But she had been so torn and unable to understand that. She felt like she was being punished for her sacrilege.

If only she could turn the clock back. She would never have harbored such selfish thoughts. That way, she would at least have given the baby a chance. If only she could turn the clock back to her former life, to that time when she was so sure of who she was and what mattered to her. She had no guidebook and was going further adrift. Could she reclaim the old Nora? Or had she been through too much and it was already too late?

She kept having the same dream. She and Jeff were on a beach, the waves were breaking on the sand, and they threw something back and forth to each other. Their faces were animated, smiling and laughing. She saw that they were throwing a baby, a precious butterscotch cherub with curly dark hair and sparkling eyes. She and Jeff never missed and the baby loved it. But one time Nora threw the baby, and it kept flying farther and farther away until it disappeared into the clouds. She panicked and called out to Jeff, but he was somewhere out in the distance, a small speck on the beach.

Nora's eyes always flew open at this point. Her hormones were being cruel. The baby was so alive in her dream. It had become a real person. But at the end of the dream she had nothing. No baby and no husband.

The week off was restorative. Nora checked in with the office a few times but hardly did any work. Not since grade school had she spent so many days home sick. But she had been worn-out for weeks and it was liberating to finally accept that she needed to get better. She had been fighting it for too long.

Her mother called on Saturday morning, a week after the miscarriage. It must have been the crack of dawn and Nora was completely disoriented, but Valérie sounded wide-awake.

"Honey, I just wanted to make sure that you were meeting me at Joseph's this morning at ten o'clock," Valérie said. Joseph's was the hair salon where Nora and Valérie went every two months to relax, trim and style their hair.

"Mom, I'm not going to Joseph's today," Nora groaned.

"Why not? The time has come for a retouch. I can hardly run a comb through my hair and I bet you can't either. You know we have a standing appointment."

"I've been wearing my hair pulled back in a bun. I think it'll hold out a little longer," Nora answered.

"Your hair will break if you keep doing that," Valérie reproached. "I haven't seen you in weeks. I've been concerned. Daddy will be driving me into the city. Please come."

Nora glanced at the clock. She would have a little over three hours to herself before she had to meet her mother. "All right. I'll meet you outside the salon."

Nora arrived before her mother. Her parents were seldom punctual. She stood on Sixtieth Street between Lexington and Park Avenues. Nora shivered in her short wool coat and jeans. Ten minutes later, her father double-parked his silver-beige sedan next to a delivery truck. Nora went to greet him on the driver's side as Valérie stepped out of the car.

"Hi, Daddy," Nora said, and gave Pierre a kiss on the cheek.

"Hi, baby," Pierre answered. "How are you?"

She smiled for her father's benefit. She had finally confided in her mother about Jeff's betrayal, but had deliberately refrained from talking about it with her father, fearing her tears and anger would drive him to wring Jeff's neck. Whatever he knew, Valérie had told him. "I'm holding up."

He studied her appearance. "You look weak. Maybe you're anemic. You should check it out with a doctor."

"I've been to a doctor." At least that wasn't a lie. "I'm definitely not anemic."

"I'll bring you some vitamins from the pharmacy." A truck honked behind him. "I have to go." Nora pecked his cheek again. "Valérie, call me later if you don't want to take the train back home."

Nora and Valérie were buzzed into the salon and were greeted by a friendly receptionist with an elaborate upswept do.

"Hello, ladies. Nice to see you again," she chimed. "What are we doing today?"

They filled out client cards and exchanged their coats for short brown dressing gowns. Valérie was led to her stylist right away, but Nora had to wait until her hairdresser, Petra, finished with another client. She thumbed through dated magazines and hoped Petra wouldn't be in a chatty mood. When it was finally Nora's turn, she muttered something about being tired and purposely closed her eyes while Petra applied the relaxer. She evened out Nora's hair into its simple straight style and Valérie persuaded Nora to join her for a manicure and pedicure. They were out of the salon by four, looking pampered and refreshed.

"Let's go to Bloomingdale's," Valérie suggested. "They're having a sale and I want to buy a few nightgowns."

"You never buy nightgowns at Bloomingdale's," Nora commented. Valérie had always preferred the discount stores in Westbury.

"There's always a first time."

Bloomingdale's was deluged with weekend shoppers and tourists. Valérie wanted to visit each floor and by the time they reached the lingerie department on the fourth floor, Nora wanted to faint. Her mother normally disliked the city, but today Valérie was very enthusiastic, pointing at beautiful silks and laces. She ended up buying a long-sleeved cotton nightgown and a black girdle.

After Valérie paid for her items, Nora said, "Mom, I have to go home. I'm not feeling well."

"What's the matter? I thought we could spend the day together, walking around the city."

"I'm going to be sick, *really sick*, if we don't go now," Nora warned, sweat building up on her forehead. Valérie felt her forehead and rushed her into an elevator. Outside, Nora threw up on the sidewalk, right in front of a group of Japanese tourists. Valérie was aghast and muttered an awkward apology. She dried Nora's face with a tissue and steadied her into a cab.

"Put your head in my lap," said Valérie. The cab drove for several blocks. "Are you feeling better?"

Nora's eyes were closed on Valérie's lap. "A little. I just had to get out of there. It was too warm and all the people . . ."

"Did you eat breakfast?"

"I had some tea."

"That's not enough. I was going to suggest we stop and eat somewhere, but I'll make you something when we get to your place."

In Nora's apartment, Valérie opened a kitchen cabinet and found the red-and-white labels of ten Campbell's soup cans aligned neatly in a row.

"Do you want some soup?"

"No!" Nora answered, a bit sharply. "I'm so sick of soup."

Valérie put her coat back on. "I'll go to the supermarket and buy some real food."

She returned with two bags of groceries. It took only a half an hour for her to prepare meatballs, white rice and black-bean sauce. She called Nora to a hard stool next to the narrow counter and placed the food in front of her. Nora ate in silence, but she appreciated every bite. Her taste buds came alive again.

"Thank you," Nora said. "That was exactly what I needed."

She saw her reflection in the mirrored clock on the kitchen wall. Her hair looked beautiful, clean and shiny, with small wisps falling on her forehead. But all her other features—her eyes, smile—had dulled.

Valérie took the pot of rice from the stove and slammed it down in the sink. Nora jumped in her seat.

"Is this what a man does to you?" Valérie exploded. "Is this what you've become because of Jeff? Don't you see what's happening to you? You're falling apart and you need to get some help before it's too late, because I just don't know what to do with you anymore!"

Nora was astonished by her mother's outburst. Valérie's position had seemed so understanding and nonjudgmental before. Nora didn't know where this was coming from.

"When are you going to realize that you have so much going for you, so much to live for—with or without Jeff? I've tried to be sympathetic, but the time has come for you to get ahold of yourself. You've been through a lot, but millions of people have been through worse experiences. You can get through this. It's not the end of the world!" Valérie paused from her tirade to catch her breath. "And you have to decide what you want to do. You either go back to Jeff or leave him for good, because this limbo you're living in is killing you!"

Nora turned on her mother with fury. "I had a miscarriage last Saturday! Is that enough of a tragedy for you? Is it all right for me to be just a tiny bit upset and depressed?"

Valérie was speechless and rushed to put her arms around her sobbing daughter. "Honey, I'm sorry," she whispered. "So sorry. Why didn't you tell me this before? I could have helped."

"I didn't want to tell anybody," Nora wailed. "I didn't know I was pregnant. Everything happened so fast."

"Have you told Jeff?"

"No. I can't. I don't know how."

"Just tell him. It was his baby too. He has a right to know."

"But I don't know how he'll react. I don't want him putting pressure on me."

"Pressure on you for what? To get back together?"

Nora nodded.

"But, Nora, what do you expect? You left him two months ago. I'm sure he wants to know where things stand with the two of you. You can't go on like this, with your life and his life up in the air."

"Why should everything always be so smooth for him? Jeff ruined our marriage, not me! I want him to suffer a little!" Nora cried.

"But do you want him to suffer for suffering's sake or are you really confused about what you want to do? Because if you're playing a game with him now, when you finally decide you do want him back, he might not be there anymore," said Valérie.

"I'm not playing a game! I don't like this! But I can't help it. . . . I just can't help it."

Valérie released Nora and resumed cleaning up the kitchen. "I've never been in your situation. I have no right to impose my opinions. But I do know about survival, about being strong in the face of obstacles. Your father and I moved to America with nothing—no jobs, no home of our own—nothing. But we got up every day, fought to make better lives for ourselves, for you and your brother."

Nora had heard this story before. According to Valérie, Nora and Albert were sheltered and didn't know true suffering.

"Would you be upset if I went back to Jeff?" Nora asked tentatively. "Would you think less of me? Or him because he hurt me?"

Valérie sponged the stove. "It's your life, Nora, nobody else's."

"What does Daddy say?"

"He hasn't said anything bad about Jeff. Like me, he's devastated that you're so upset. But we're waiting to see what you decide to do. If you divorce Jeff, it won't be easy starting a new life, but we'll help you. We would never tell you to stay in a situation that's too painful. But if you get back together, we'll support you too. Jeff will still be our son-in-law, we'll treat him with respect, and we'll never mention what happened between the two of you to him. It would take some time for things to be like before, but the mind doesn't like to have a memory for pain. If you and Jeff decide that you want to work things out, it's nobody else's business. Don't pay attention to what others say. It's your future, your happiness."

Valérie had a unique gift for weaving order out of chaos and Nora wished she hadn't shut her mother out. "You're right. Everything you've said is true. The more I live like a wounded bird, the more I become one. I have to take back my life," said Nora, determination creeping back into her voice.

Valérie hugged her. "You've always been my introspective child, the one who would only do things at her own pace. And you can. I know you will."

CHAPTER 23

Nora returned to work on Monday pledging inwardly to rise above the rubble of her life. She knew that she still had many issues to sort out, but a new sense of purpose had replaced her despair.

She called a release meeting to finalize her debut issue. A mock-up of the magazine, all the editorial pages minus the ads, was propped up against a long narrow shelf in the creative department. She walked slowly, a pencil to her lips, examining each page. Julian, Paola Vizzi, the fashion editor, and Trevor Smythe, the sittings editor, were with her.

Nora paused at the cover. "This model looks completely bored and I don't like this blouse she's wearing. It's too see-through." She peered closer. "You can practically see her nipple."

Trevor squinted at the image. "No . . . I don't think so. . . . Well, it's not that obvious. Only when you really look at it."

"Well, I want people to 'really look' at the cover and I don't want them seeing a nipple. We have to change it," said Nora.

Trevor shook his head. "We don't have time to shoot a new cover. It took weeks to get the photographer and model lined up."

Nora didn't answer him. People always said no. They never said, "Sure, boss, whatever you want." She'd been out for a week and the sharks were already circling. She moved to the main fashion spread. Four models, all singularly beautiful, representing women from blond to brunet, ivory to mocha, were styled in the coming season's designer clothes and accessories. They laughed, pouted and jumped in shots taken at the Brooklyn Promenade.

"Paola, these pictures are fantastic. They're *alive* and hitting all the right notes—young, fresh, hip." Nora pointed towards the page. "This is what I want. Look through the contact sheets and find me one with all four girls that I can use as a cover."

Paola nodded her head vigorously, the pink tourmaline stones of her chandelier earrings hitting her cheeks. Trevor opened his mouth to object.

"And I want this by tomorrow at the latest," preempted Nora. "A new mock-up of the cover."

"I don't see how that would be a problem," added Julian, staring straight at Trevor.

Trevor, knowing he had been outranked and outvoted, shoved his hands into the pockets of his trousers and muttered yes in agreement. He and Paola gathered the images on the wall and left. Nora could only imagine what vitriol would spill from his lips once she was out of earshot.

She sighed and said to Julian, "Was I too hard on them?"

Julian looked at her approvingly. "No, it's good you're taking charge. People respond to that."

She ended her day at eight in the evening and decided to walk home to unwind. The streets were well lit and sprinkled with other pedestrians. The autumn air had turned chilly, hinting that a cold winter was on its way, and Nora tightened her scarf around her neck. She was mentally exhausted. Revamping *Muse,* brainstorming and tweaking other people's ideas consumed every bit of her energy. She would be so glad when her debut issue came out. The public would see what she had to offer and then render their verdict. She did not want to fall flat, but meaning and personal validation had to come from within too. On Fourteenth Street, she turned west in the direction of Fifth Avenue. She loved lower Fifth, with the arch of Washington Square Park in the distance and the cozy mews houses nestled in narrow cobblestone streets. Walking always made her feel good and she couldn't remember the last time she had taken pleasure from it.

Nora and her staff submitted the final drafts of the January *Muse* the day before Thanksgiving and celebrated with champagne in plastic cups. They could all relax over the holiday—for about five minutes—before they had to worry about the next issue. She took the train to

Westbury, where she was spending the long weekend with her family. As the cars rocked forward, Nora thought about last Thanksgiving with Jeff. His mother's side had organized a family reunion and an assortment of sisters, brothers, cousins, aunts and uncles converged on Angela's family house in Oak Bluffs. The weather had been gray and windy, but the salty air, the coziness of piling on thick clothes, and going to the beach had been invigorating. Everyone pitched in to make Thanksgiving dinner and Nora and Jeff were put in charge of the corn bread stuffing. They followed an old recipe that had been handed down for generations and joked about why they had been entrusted with such a major part of the meal. Didn't everyone remember that Jeff was hopeless in the kitchen? He diced the vegetables and Nora did most of the actual cooking, but they joined in the bonhomie as his relatives dressed two large turkeys, prepared sweet potato pie and slapped greedy hands away from steaming pots. Since the dining room couldn't fit them all, people ate sitting on couches and chairs or squatting on the floor in front of the wide coffee table. There was a wonderful lack of formality and as Nora watched Jeff's clan, she wished she had stronger ties to her own extended family. It was the first time Nora hadn't felt like an outsider among his relations.

Now Nora's father picked her up at the station and gave her a bag of vitamin supplements. "In case I forget over the weekend," he said. She accepted them appreciatively, a small smile on her face. If only vitamins could really heal the soul.

She deposited her weekend bag in her childhood bedroom and tried to settle in. Valérie had changed the decor when Nora left for college and Nora's canopied bed and ruffled pink coverlet had long since disappeared. Two oak night tables flanked a queen-sized brass bed, and the walls were painted soft blue. But when Nora opened the closet doors, she saw that her mother had saved boxes filled with certificates, stuffed animals, a dried corsage, paperbacks and forgotten clothes. She couldn't resist going through her old stuff. She took out her collection of Judy Blume books (*Forever* was particularly dog-eared) and discovered a diary. On the laminated shocking pink cover, MY DIARY was written in swirly gold script. Nora opened it to a random page and read:

MARCH 16, 1985

Dear Diary,

Christopher picked me to be on his team for kickball at lunch today. He is so fine!! I got a home run and our team won 10–8. Christopher hugged me. I wonder if he likes me. . . .

MARCH 18, 1985

Dear Diary,

Christopher asked Marie to go out. He even bought her a gold bracelet. It's because she has bigger boobs than all the other girls in our class. I can't believe it. When will the guy I like like me back???

Yes, Christopher had consumed much of her adolescent thoughts. He had been adorable, a little more developed than the other boys, with small tight muscles and long legs. He had teased her a lot in school, calling her Chicken Neck and hiding her pencils. Could it be that he had liked her and all that taunting had really been flirting? She closed the diary and put it back in the box. Delving into the past was too complicated. Confronting the shy insecure girl she'd been made her question how far she'd actually come as a woman. Deep down, wasn't she still the same person? She wished she could zoom into the future and see her life a year or two from now. She wanted the benefit of foreknowledge and to look back on these rough months as a person unburdened by sorrow or bitterness.

Her brother, Albert, arrived on Thanksgiving Day with a surprise visitor, his new fiancée. Valérie and Pierre had met her twice before in Chicago, but Nora never had. Her name was Michelle and she was completing the last year of her M.B.A. at Kellogg. Nora doubted Albert had ever suffered from an identity crisis or bouts of insecurity. As a kid, he had loved science and sports and his current universe revolved around his residency, grabbing a beer and catching whatever game was on television. He made no apologies for his unabashedly conventional lifestyle. But it was evident by the tender way he held Michelle's hand that he had met his match. She also shared Albert's passion for basketball and the outdoors and Nora imagined them mountain climbing on their honeymoon.

Valérie always prepared Thanksgiving dinner with a Haitian twist, adding macaroni pie, mushroom rice and corn soufflé to the traditional fare. "Do you remember how much Jeff ate the first time he had Thanksgiving dinner here with us?" she asked, carving a portion of turkey breast.

An awkward silence settled on the table. Pierre stared into his wineglass, Albert drummed his fingers on the table, and Michelle—the poor girl had never even met Jeff—covered her mouth with her hand. But Nora knew what her mother was doing. *She wants me to stop pretending he doesn't exist, that he was never a part of our lives.*

Nora took the plate Valérie offered her and said, "He was so stuffed he couldn't even drive home. He blamed it on you—the food was so good he couldn't say no to seconds."

"Or thirds," quipped Albert.

Relieved laughter replaced the tension, and the subject turned to Albert and Michelle's wedding plans. Nora realized that mentioning Jeff without breaking down or fuming was a big step for her. Would he become part of her history, someone she referred to in the past tense, her marriage a parenthesis in the trajectory of her life?

After dinner, Valérie, Pierre and Michelle shared coffee in the living room. Albert cleared the table while Nora rinsed dishes for the dishwasher.

"Did you mind?" he asked as he passed her a serving bowl and spoon. "All that talk about food and guests and churches?"

Nora shut the faucet and took off her gloves. She put an arm around Albert's broad shoulders. He was a shade lighter than Nora, but they were both tall and possessed the same full heart-shaped lips. Albert could look imposing in his hospital scrubs or very boyish, as he did now, in jeans and a long-sleeved polo shirt. "No. Not at all. This is your moment. Michelle seems like a great girl. I want the two of you to be happy."

"It seems unfair that we should be celebrating when—"

Nora smiled. "When my life's a mess? I think that it just proves how life goes on. Don't feel guilty on my account." She poked him in the stomach. "Just don't screw her over."

CHAPTER 24

Jeff celebrated Thanksgiving dinner with his parents and ten other people, mostly relatives from his father's side, in New Rochelle. Taylor and Angela had not told anyone that Jeff and Nora were separated and had a rehearsed response to account for her absence. Nora and her parents were entertaining family from Haiti, they explained. The story was actually Angela's invention. Taylor didn't think it was anyone's business one way or the other and had wanted to stay mum on the subject. But Jeff knew that Nora's absence would be obvious, and for the first time in years, he went along with his mother. In order to maintain the illusion of Angela's story, he spoke of Nora as though they were still together, telling the others about her promotion at work and how their town house was coming along. But Jeff had a hard time listening to his own voice. He could hardly reconcile himself to the fact that she was no longer in his life.

In a weird twist of fate, Bob Butler's ousting and the leak that Rum Records had been close to cementing a deal with him at NRG opened several new doors for the company. Jeff and Hilton had received feelers from a few other big labels, but this time they were unflinching. They would remain independent. However, they had made several new high-level contacts and were working on a development deal with one of the major Hollywood studios. Hilton would end up with his life's ambition after all. Jeff could not get over the irony. Hilton lived his life only inches from the edge of going too far, but things had a way of working out for him. He always landed on his feet—probably because he never looked back.

Jeff tried to beat a hasty retreat from his parents' soon after the first guests left, but Angela called him into the study.

She straightened his shearling jacket. "It's freezing outside. You should button up."

"I'll be fine. I'm only going outside to the car." Jeff kissed her cheek. "Good night and thank you for dinner. It was delicious."

Angela crossed her arms over her chest. "I can't believe Nora abandoned you on Thanksgiving."

"She didn't 'abandon' me."

"She should have reached out to you. She's embarrassing the whole family with her stubbornness."

"Mom, we've gone over this before. She wants her space. I'm giving her time to figure things out."

Angela walked to the mantel and picked up a silver frame with Jeff and Nora's wedding picture. It was a candid shot of them leaving the church, and rose petals showered the bride and groom. After several moments, she said, "I think you should divorce her."

A shadow fell over Jeff's face. "I can't believe you said that."

Angela shrugged self-righteously. "Why not? Divorce doesn't have the same stigma as it did before. Do you want her to file the papers first? At least this way you can save face."

"I don't care about saving face," he said, tightening his grip on his car keys. "I'm surprised you'd want to admit that your thirty-six-year-old son couldn't make his marriage work."

She moved to where Jeff stood beside an illuminated painting by Jacob Lawrence. "Jeff, I'm only thinking about you. You have to pick up the pieces of your life. How much longer are you going to wait?" She touched his arm. "How much longer?"

Jeff's whole body stiffened. "Mom, stay out of this part of my life. And get this divorce idea out of your head," he said in a measured voice.

Angela studied him for several seconds. When Jeff was younger, he would have turned away and lowered his head, but tonight he wouldn't back down. His mother was still stunning, but the heavily concealed lines near her eyes had deepened in the last years. He sensed frustration and an inexplicable sadness beneath her cool facade. Unpredictably, a wide smile appeared on her face. "Well, just think about what I said," she remarked airily, as if they had been discussing vacation plans.

"Think about what *I* said," answered Jeff, and he stormed out of the room.

*   *   *

Hilton sat in his car behind a taxi as it dropped off a passenger. A young woman got out and ran up the steps of a walk-up. Although he had seen only her profile, he would know that face anywhere. It may have been a city of eight million people, but they were bound to run into each other eventually. Nora couldn't hide forever.

Traffic started moving again and Hilton arched his neck to make sure he got a good look at the walk-up. He had to talk to her, but first he had to park his car. He drove around for several blocks until he found a vacant spot on Ninth Street and Fifth Avenue. He was probably illegally parked, but didn't care. He walked briskly to Twelfth Street and followed it west. He saw only row after row of brownstones and got confused. Which one had Nora entered? He cursed to himself. He had been so close. He patrolled the block and ten minutes later saw Nora emerge from one of the buildings at the far end. She carried a bundle of newspapers and placed them in front of a recycling bin.

"Nora! Nora!" he shouted, and raced to catch up with her.

She seemed to reel upon hearing her name. He stopped directly in front of her, out of breath.

Nora viewed him quizzically. "What are you doing here?"

"I saw you getting out of a cab," he panted.

She pursed her lips up sardonically. The thought of him chasing her down seemed to amuse her.

"I suppose you want to come up," she said.

"At least for something to drink," Hilton responded.

Nora climbed the steps of the steep walk-up two at a time and Hilton trailed after her, breathing heavily. Inside the small studio apartment, he felt very inept and shuffled to a safe spot on the sofa.

She opened the fridge and asked, "Is water OK?"

"It's fine."

Nora threw a plastic bottle of Evian across the room and Hilton jerked up to catch it. He untwisted the cap and knocked back the ice-cold water. She sat in a chair and watched him with the same crooked expression on her face.

"I know you hate me," Hilton blurted out.

"I don't hate you," she said slowly.

He didn't know whether or not to believe her. Nora had an inbred sense of decorum. Good manners prevented her from demeaning her-self and giving him a verbal whipping—even though it would have been justified. Still, her stony gaze told him that she had no intention of putting up with his shit.

"How have you been?" he asked awkwardly.

She shrugged. "Surviving, I guess. Trying to get my life in order."

"I know this hasn't been easy for you. And I am so sorry for my part in all of it."

"We've all done things that we're not proud of," she replied.

"I've been doing some of my own soul-searching."

"Well, I'm glad to hear that. I think a little bit of that is good for everybody." She paused. "And I was worried about you, Hilton, from the very beginning. But you led me to believe that I could trust you."

"And you could. You still can! I want to earn your trust again. Yours and Jeff's," he asserted.

Nora avoided Hilton's gaze. "How is he?" she asked.

"Like you. He goes up and down. He's completely torn up by what happened."

"So, are you guys friends again?"

Hilton guffawed. "By default. After you left, Jeff was alone. It was ei-ther me or no one."

"You guys have always been as thick as thieves. I'm not surprised," Nora said, a bit scathingly.

"I haven't been taking Jeff around town and reintroducing him to the single life, if that's what you mean. Nora, Jeff has always been faithful to you. That one incident was a mistake, a freak occurrence. Even now, when Jeff's not at work, he's at home—by himself. He's not ready to let go."

"That's a sobering thought," she answered sarcastically. "Should I be jumping for joy?"

"Nora, I know Jeff and I have fucked up your life. But please tell me we haven't made you this hard and cold."

Nora ran her fingers through her hair and sighed. "No. But some-times I really wish I were that way. I feel stupid because I still care for the both of you. I think back to old times and want to cry. Everything was so easy."

Hilton nodded. He felt the same way. "Listen, you and Jeff are family to me. I desperately want the two of you to work things out. You guys belong together."

"That's what I always thought, but sometimes I just don't know anymore. I've learned a lot about myself these last few months. I'd forgotten that I could manage on my own. I had become so much a part of Jeff's world and frankly, he let me down."

"He knows that." Hilton paused. "I guess we both always felt like we were in his shadow. Like maybe he was more honest or decent than we were. He had certain standards and we always tried to measure up to him."

"Or to measure up to our image of him and what he thought of us."

"But he's just a man."

"A man who made a big mistake."

"Just like I did. Just like you did six years ago." He played with the Evian cap, rolling it between his fingers. "Nora, is a long-standing lie—our mistake—any better than a recent betrayal?"

She turned to him sharply, her features tense. "I . . . I don't know. I never thought of it that way."

"Well, I don't think it is," said Hilton. "I never meant for what happened to come out. I guess what I'm trying to say is that we're not perfect. I know that I've stepped off a lot more times than should be allowed, but I finally see what's important to me, what's going to give me back my self-respect. I can't change overnight, but I want to start with you and Jeff. We were all at a point in our lives when everything should have been perfect. We had—or were at least getting—everything we ever wanted, but there were so many unchecked emotions. I don't know—maybe we were supposed to crash. There are no more secrets between you, me and Jeff anymore." He scrutinized her. There was no artifice, no obligation to be other than what she was. "Being on your own has made you stronger. I can see it."

She rose and looked uncomfortable. "I can't believe I'm having this conversation with you."

"Why?"

"I've never heard you talk like this before and I'm a little suspicious of your new, sensitive side."

"Don't be," he assured her, and exclaimed, "Damn! Have I got a lot to work on!"

This triggered a faint smile from Nora. She leaned back ever so slightly, her right foot pointed outward. Hilton, still seated, craned his neck to meet her eyes.

"I suppose you'll tell Jeff where I am," she said.

Was she daring him? Did she want him to? "No," Hilton responded. "That's up to you." He dropped the Evian cap in an ashtray on the table. "You know Jeff's little project? The community center?"

"Of course. It was one of his passions."

"Well, it's done. He got the funding and the renovation is complete."

"Great," said Nora wistfully.

"He's having a cocktail reception on December twenty-first. It's just a little welcome event to get the word out."

"Why are you telling me this?"

"Just thought you might like to know." He got up and stretched his legs. "Thank you for not kicking my ass when I showed up on your doorstep."

"Ha-ha."

Hilton asked himself if he had reached her, if he had opened the door to future dialogue. He longed to give her a hug, but thought against it. Then he changed his mind. Life was too short to be so closed up inside. He drew her to him and locked her in an embrace. She didn't pull away, but her arms remained stiffly at her sides, like a wooden soldier. Then she softened and hugged him back.

"You really are a beautiful person," Hilton whispered. "Jeff will be the luckiest man in the world if he gets you back."

He let himself out, noticing the confusion on her face and wondering what she would do next.

CHAPTER 25

*M*_use_ decided to throw its annual Christmas party in conjunction with a preview of the January issue. The magazine rented a huge photography studio and converted it into a winter wonderland. As always, word got around and the guests multiplied by the dozens, far exceeding *Muse* personnel and their significant others. The mood was loud, food and drink were extravagant, and Nora wondered if there would be anything left in the magazine's coffers when she formally took over after the New Year.

Gigantic blowups of the January cover dotted the walls. The four models were poised on a bench at the Brooklyn Promenade. A pair of the girls sat down, while the other two leaned behind them. Styled in haute couture gowns, they smiled flirtatiously for the camera. Atop the black-and-white photograph, the *Muse* logo was rendered in fuchsia. The only text, also in matching fuchsia, heralded: HOW TO BE A MODERN MUSE. Nora had to stop herself from doing cartwheels of joy. Her instincts had been spot-on. Skimming through a sample copy of the magazine, she stopped at the "Letter from the Editor" page. A photo of Nora entering a taxi (it was meant to look unrehearsed, but the shot had been taken about twenty times) prefaced her words: As the new editor in chief, she promised to present the best of fashion and contemporary living for women "with minds and styles of their own." Nora had also experimented with the typeface and graphics and was delighted with the results. She remembered how she had been drowning in depression and asked herself how she had come through. Naturally, she couldn't have done it without her staff, but she had given them the vision.

"Nora! Darling! The magazine is genius! Just beyond! You've done a brilliant job!" trilled Candida when she saw Nora. "Come with me. I want you to meet some more people."

She escorted Nora through the glittering throng and Nora spent the next hour shaking hands and air-kissing people she probably wouldn't remember by tomorrow. It was difficult to tell where one person ended and another began, since they all meshed into a blur of sparkly dresses, kitten heels and tonal suits.

"Nora, well-done!" said Randall Baldwin, *Muse*'s publisher. He took Nora's hand. "Superb job!"

"Thank you," she said.

"Where did you find those models?" he drooled. "You'll have to introduce them to me."

Candida slapped Baldwin playfully. "Shame on you, Randall! You're going to get us all in trouble."

Candida and Baldwin giggled uproariously and shared a private joke. They seemed very familiar and Nora asked herself whether they spent time together after hours. She felt slightly uncomfortable and racked her brain for a smart getaway. Luckily, Julian came to her rescue.

"Let's go outside. It's starting to snow," he whispered conspiratorially.

"Please excuse me," Nora said brightly to Candida and Baldwin. She gave a small wave. "Nice talking to you!"

"Nora," Candida sang, "remember to come see me tomorrow morning."

"If she can find her way to work tomorrow," Julian muttered naughtily.

Nora and Julian grabbed their coats and left the party. Nora walked towards the elevator bank, but Julian headed for the stairwell.

"Julian, down is this way!"

"Didn't I tell you? I meant outside on the roof," he said innocently.

"I don't think so! If I don't freeze to death, I'll probably slip and fall off."

"It's almost Christmas, Nora. Nothing bad is going to happen."

Julian was so cute, and against her better judgment, she followed him through a rusty door and up a compact flight of steps. A thin layer of snow had already dusted the rooftop, and fog rose from the building's steam pipe. Everything looked murky and mysterious and Nora refused to look below. But straight ahead, glowing skyscrapers and the beautiful George Washington Bridge—with its vista of red and white lights streaking up and down—caused her to sigh contentedly. *This* was why she loved New York.

"I'm all partied out," she said, digging her hands deeper into her coat pockets. She would have preferred Gore-Tex to the kid leather clinging to her icy fingers.

Julian lit a cigarette and inhaled deeply. He blew out small spirals of smoke. "I hate office Christmas parties," he observed. "Everybody gets too drunk and too friendly. They say stupid things. That's why I never drink at these parties. I just work with these people. I don't want to get to *know* them."

Nora laughed. "I think it's always fun to see everyone's significant other. Couples that you would never expect are together. Who would have thought that weird girl in promotions had such a hot guy?"

"She probably borrowed him from one of the modeling agencies."

"Why didn't you come with anyone tonight?" Nora asked.

"It's been a slow year," he joked. "I should have borrowed a date. It would've made the perfect accessory."

"Yeah, but too high-maintenance."

They watched the snowflakes fall, land and then melt into nothingness.

"This city is too much. You can't even get the snow to stick properly," he remarked.

"So, Julian, what do you want for Christmas?"

"A Porsche Boxster, but I doubt I'll get it," he answered as he snuffed out his cigarette. "What I'd really like is to stop smoking. Nasty habit."

"You should start eating that nicotine gum." Where had she heard about that? Of course, she had been in stitches when Jeff described Bob Butler's addiction to Nicorette.

"I'd probably get hooked on them. What do you want?"

"That's easy. I just want to put all this drama behind me."

"You can—poof!—just erase it from your mind. Decide what will make you happy and go for it."

"I think that's the trick question. I'm not sure what will make me happy."

"Dwelling on the bad parts just holds you back," he continued. "Christmas is a time for forgiveness and reconciliation. But what do I know? I'm only Julio Cortez from the South Bronx." He pretended to look around and said under his breath, "But nobody else knows that except you."

Nora hugged him. "You're the kindest man I know."

"So will you get me that Porsche Boxster?" he asked.

Nora was elated she hadn't made a professional embarrassment of herself. In another world, Jeff would have been at her side and they would have celebrated her success. Instead, she came home alone and fell asleep watching the news. She received a nice invitation in the mail for Jeff's benefit reception. She assumed that Hilton had sent it to her, and put it with all of her other nonpressing correspondence. Nonetheless, she could not stop thinking about it or Hilton's words. *Longstanding lie. Recent betrayal.* Who among them was without guilt?

Nora did not get caught up in the whirl of Christmas, buying only simple presents for her family and sending out a few Christmas cards. At this time of year, she always thought of people with whom she had lost touch. Life thrust people in different directions and Christmas was a time to reconnect with those she really cared about. Maybe it was time to set aside old fears and resentments. Each day she woke up with a clearer head and life seemed less daunting. The sight of children running freely, lovers on the street, their foreheads touching as they whispered between themselves, no longer made her turn away. Maybe wisdom was a consequence of pain and Nora had to figure out what she wanted to do with this unexpected enlightenment.

Surely Jeff would feel alone at his own reception, just as she had felt at the Christmas party. Part of her wanted to be there for him. He invaded her thoughts relentlessly and she realized that only seeing him would give her peace. She hadn't felt this urgency for three months, yet she was afraid to follow her intuition. She reasoned that her presence at his reception would be supporting a good cause. She was feeling generous in the spirit of the holidays. Then she laughed at herself. Who was she kidding? Why was she constantly in denial?

Nora took a cab up Amsterdam Avenue on the evening of December 21. She had timed her arrival an hour late, so she could enter the reception inconspicuously. The address was a handsome brownstone, fresh from the stripping, resurfacing and painting of a much needed renovation. A simple brass plaque was affixed to the glossy black door: OUR HOUSE: HAMILTON HEIGHTS COMMUNITY IMPACT. Nora ran her hand across the letters. She almost cried.

The atmosphere changed for Jeff the precise moment Nora walked in the door. He had been making the rounds, greeting and thanking supporters, sipping wine, bobbing his head lightly to the strains of cocktail music. But a warm rush passed through his body and the high notes of the jazz bass seemed to echo the anticipation tickling his heart. He turned away from a small crowd and though he could not find the source, he felt her presence. Then he spotted her. She waited beside a large urn of red chrysanthemums and wore her strapless black dress with a matching coat. She was understated and elegant, but there was a nervous glint in her eyes. She was not far from the door and her feet were planted firmly in place. She seemed removed from everyone else in the room, uncertain about entering Jeff's circle or simply slipping away unnoticed. Their eyes connected, just as they had across another crowded room many years ago.

He walked over to her. "Hi," he said shyly, barely hiding his surprise.

She smiled that familiar wide grin he had been missing for months. "Hi," she answered softly.

He had to ask her. "What are you doing here?"

"Oh, I was just in the neighborhood." She laughed lightly and said, "I came to show my support—for you."

"Thank you." He paused. "You look good."

"So do you."

After a separation of three months, he was self-conscious. How must he really look to her? He felt as though he'd aged overnight. When he dressed earlier for the reception, he had noticed a definite loosening by his abdomen. He searched Nora's face for signs of change. The faint shadows beneath her eyes had not been there in happier times, but on her they expressed a survivor's dignity, giving strength to her beauty.

"Would you like something to drink?" Jeff asked.

"White wine would be nice."

He proffered a glass from a passing waiter. She took it from him but made no motion to drink. They faced each other, but said nothing. Their vocabulary seemed too meager, too awkward, to explain the moment.

"This is strange," Jeff muttered.

"I know," she agreed.

Someone tapped Jeff on the shoulder. "Excuse me for just a second," he told her, and turned around to exchange a few words with an acquaintance. When he finished—it couldn't have been more than thirty seconds—Nora was gone. He scanned the room, thinking she had blended in with the rest of the guests, but couldn't find her. Their brief encounter had been so abrupt. She had smiled at him. They had begun to talk. What had he done wrong?

Nora had wanted to come tonight, but was completely unprepared for the furor of her emotions. She had thought she could remain calm, but being so close to Jeff again put her in a state of confused excitement—almost as though on a first date. She took cover in a corner next to a tall potted plant.

Jeff had organized a low-key but very polished reception. Nora inwardly complimented him for having pulled it all off. He had managed to assemble a crowd of local decision makers, activists and philanthropists. A few celebrities were also thrown in for good measure. Yet it was not in the least bit self-serving and she knew that Jeff would never want to be the primary focus. He had aimed all his energy into this project and she felt very proud of him.

Nora saw Hilton in a tête-à-tête with a woman, which was not surprising since he seized every opportunity to flirt. She saw Jeff's parents engaged in conversation with a former singer turned human rights activist. Nora wanted to stay clear of Angela's radar vision. She surveyed the crowd twice and one person was distinctly not in attendance: Olivia. She relaxed, although she had braced herself for seeing, or rather ignoring, Olivia.

"Nora, why are you hiding from me?" Jeff murmured in her ear when he found her.

His voice startled her and she felt embarrassed. Her plan had been to regroup and then meet up with him again. "You must think I'm really crazy, but I sort of feel like I'm in the way tonight," she said.

"You could never be in the way."

"Maybe tonight was not a good time for us to see each other. You have your obligations here, with all these people. . . ."

"No! Please. I want you here tonight. I can get away for a little while. Let's go someplace else and talk."

She nodded. He led her into a small anteroom and shut the door. The hum of the crowd ceased, but the mellifluous sounds of the musicians Jeff had hired for the evening filtered through the door. The room was packed with cardboard boxes. She and Jeff stood in the small bare center and if only one of them took a few steps forward, they would be touching.

"I'm so happy you came tonight," he repeated.

"Thank you. Me too. You've done such a great job with everything. I'm really impressed."

"There's still a lot of work ahead. I have to worry about fund-raising and kiss up to those people out there for the rest of my life."

She laughed. "It'll be worth it."

"I know. But I can't believe it's done. I've been so preoccupied, I thought about giving up so many times."

"I'm glad you didn't," she said, and aware that her words had a double meaning, she added, "I mean, it's a good thing you focused on doing something really positive."

"You have such a way of talking in circles."

"I guess it's because I'm a little nervous."

"So am I. When I turned around and you weren't there anymore, I could have hit myself. I've waited for this for so long."

"I know," she whispered, "but I just couldn't before."

"And now?" he asked.

"I hope you understand that I had to be on my own. We were so fused and what happened was a terrible shock for me." She hesitated. "I owe you an apology too. I made a mistake and deceived you all those years ago. Neither of us is perfect."

"So where do we go from here?"

"I don't know, but I don't want any reminders of the ugly past."

"Neither do I," he replied. "I swear that you will never get hurt again. I promise you we'll be happy."

She began to weep silently.

"Why are you crying?" he asked.

"Because I'm already starting to feel happier and for so long, I wasn't sure I could. I wasn't sure I could ever forgive you."

He made the first move and embraced her.

"We're not the same people we were before, you know. Too much has happened. Too many hard truths," she said, welcoming his arms around her.

"But we still love each other. We lost each other, but we're getting a second chance. We can make it better and stronger."

"I want to," she said.

"There's so much I want to tell you."

"Me too, but we have time." There were so many things to talk about—life, their future, the baby they had lost.

They heard a knock outside the door.

"Come in," said Jeff, and they separated. Nora straightened her dress and dabbed her eyes.

It was Hilton.

"Jeff, it's time for you to say a few words. Everyone's looking for you." He saw Nora and grinned.

Hilton was also a part of their lives and Nora was again awed by the power of second chances.

"Do you want to go back in with me?" Jeff asked.

"Oh, I can't. I'm a mess."

"Please." He held out his hand.

In the end, she took his hand because she loved him. Her love was not naive or unprincipled or impervious to disappointment. It was a love born out of passion and pain. It came from having experienced sublime happiness and then seeing it all shattered. But she was ready to open herself to him again. They had both been through hell and she knew that neither of them wanted to go back. Reclaimed from those depths, they still wanted to be together. And that was enough.

UPTOWN AND DOWN

Jennifer Anglade Dahlberg

A CONVERSATION WITH
JENNIFER ANGLADE DAHLBERG

Q. What inspired you to write Uptown and Down *and what questions did you ask yourself while writing it?*

A. A 1993 article in *Vanity Fair* about the rise of hip-hop record labels and how they were becoming attractive to mainstream media companies inspired me to write *Uptown and Down.* The mass appeal of hip-hop and the social intermingling that seems so commonplace today was not evident ten years ago. I was also living in New York City at that time and it was a particularly exciting and fluid place. Everything seemed possible. There was a sense that groundbreaking things were happening with technology and music and a lot of new wealth was created. I was interested in exploring how these social and economic changes would affect a trio of on-the-rise Black Americans. What happens when you're finally given a seat at the table?

Q. What do you want to convey to readers with Uptown and Down? *What do you hope people will take away from the novel?*

A. With *Uptown and Down,* I waned to create a world where privileged and upwardly mobile Black Americans flowed in and out of the corporate offices and status-conscious gatherings that make New York City so enticing and dangerous. Within that context, I wanted to highlight the feelings of guilt associated with privilege and the pressure to be "down" and remain authentic. I see *Uptown and Down* as a multifaceted book that explores the complexities of marriage and friendship, observes a new social order, and describes a business drama that could be taken out of today's headlines. I hope that people will read *Uptown and Down* and feel that the characters have depth. I also hope that there is universality in the struggles and demons each character faced.

Q. *What was the toughest scene in the novel for you to write?*

A. The most difficult scene for me to write was Jeff's indiscretion with Olivia. I wanted to avoid clichés and get inside Jeff's head to explain the thought process that led him to carry out the act. I wanted the reader to sympathize with Jeff's anguish even while he ultimately betrays his wife and creates a complicated situation with Olivia. Also, Jeff had been such an upright character to that point, it was almost painful for me to lead him down that path!

Q. *Your characters seem so lifelike. Were any of them derived from real people?*

A. When I created some of the characters, I was inspired by various people who have meant a great deal to me. Nora was attracted to Jeff's lack of pretension, integrity, and social ease. Those are all qualities that drew me to my husband. Hilton is a collage and was a very interesting character to create because I kept asking myself how far I could go in making him sly and ambiguous. Nora's mother is based on my own mother, and many of the historical references to Haiti and being a first-generation American are from my own upbringing.

Q. *Which of the events in the novel were based on actual experiences, if any?*

A. Nora and Jeff's trip to Morocco is based on an actual vacation my husband and I took to Marrakech. The Montgomerys' shopping spree with Boss is basically a play-by-play of our own encounter! I included that scene because I wanted to break the tension and have Jeff and Nora reconnect. Vacations are the best way to rediscover why you fell in love with your partner.

Q. Thus far, what do readers tell you they like most about Uptown and Down?

A. Readers have appreciated that the characters are intelligent and sexy and that they interact with one another in a mature way. They've also enjoyed reading how I've portrayed New York City.

Q. Which books or authors have inspired you in your own writing?

A. Writers who have inspired me for the sheer beauty of their stories and the elegance of their writing include Toni Morrison, Edwidge Danticat, Ian McEwan, Ralph Ellison, and Ayn Rand. In addition, I've always been interested in books and authors who incorporate social commentary in their writing. In terms of classics, Jane Austen, Henry James, and Edith Wharton have brilliantly captured the privileged and striving set of their eras. Contemporary writers like Tom Wolfe and Jay McInerney have astutely depicted the allure and precariousness of modern-day New York.

Q. Where do you see yourself as a writer ten years from now?

A. I hope that I will grow as a writer, that I will "hone my craft," and that I will continue to be inspired to write stories of interest to me and my readers. I hope that I will be able to come from a different place each time.

QUESTIONS
FOR DISCUSSION

1. Which character was the most endearing to you, and why? Which was the least likable?

2. What valuable lessons will you take away from this novel?

3. Marriage is explored in great depth in this book. Does the novel leave you with a greater or lesser sense of optimism about marriage?

4. When Nora is devastated about her personal life, she throws herself into her work. Do you respond to stress in a similar way? What are the pros and cons of dealing with problems in this way?